NEVA LOMASON MEMORIAL LIBRARY

ALSO BY MARK LINDER

*There Came a Proud Beggar*

# LITTLE BOY BLUE

# MARK LINDER

# LITTLE BOY BLUE

RANDOM HOUSE

NEW YORK

Copyright © 1992 by Mark Linder

All rights reserved under International and Pan-American Copyright Conventions.
Published in the United States by Random House, Inc., New York and simultaneously
in Canada by Random House of Canada Limited, Toronto.

Library of Congress Cataloging-in-Publication Data

Linder, Mark.
Little Boy Blue / Mark Linder.—1st ed.
p.    cm.
ISBN 0-679-40981-5
I. Title.
PS3562.I51116L57 1992
813'.54—dc20   91-51027

*Manufactured in the United States of America*

FIRST EDITION

*Book design by Carole Lowenstein*

*in memory of*
*Paul Erez*

# PREFACE

*Little Boy Blue* required much research and many interviews, and I wish to thank those who gave their time and knowledge in my behalf.

Lee Richards and Richard Huffman, former assistant United States attorneys, answered my questions with patience and exactitude. They pointed the way, and provided an insider's view of the unique world of the federal prosecutor. Anne Driscoll, making time in her very busy day, walked me through Eastern District's headquarters at Cadman Plaza, where various men and women let me pick their brains for choice morsels.

Special thanks to Gordon Mehler. He made himself available, and illuminated many procedural and legal obscurities. We explored, too, that rather complex syndrome known as the human condition, and some of what we spoke about has been incorporated into the novel. Next time, Gordon, let me pay for lunch.

I spoke with a number of FBI agents, active and retired. To all of them, I express my appreciation for their willingness to trust a civilian with closely held Bureau lore. To the late, great Jim McShane, a very special agent, my thanks.

Men and women of the various intelligence services with whom I spoke insisted, without exception, that their names and affiliations not be cited. To them, here and abroad, I offer this brief, inclusive expression of gratitude.

To my wife and children, whose fortitude in dealing with a man in the prolonged throes of creative ferment was truly unflagging, my love.

My parents and brothers were always encouraging, as was the multitude of my extended family, whose diverse personalities and unique histories are a neverending source of interest and pleasure. Your support has made my work easier.

My brother, Chuck, a scientist with a literary bent, contributed more than he knew. A few of his scholarly adventures found their way, abridged and reduced to a layman's understanding, into *Little Boy Blue*. I hope that my attempts at rendering the intricacies of polymer chemistry have done no violence to the mystery and beauty of that discipline.

Miriam Stern, my agent, persevered and made it happen; we shall have to do it again.

*Little Boy Blue* is a work of the imagination. The men and women on the following pages do not exist, nor did any of this ever happen.

# PART I

To: United States Attorney General
From: James Newcombe, Asst. U.S. Atty.,
      Southern District
Re: Operation Keelhaul

On January 4, 1978, Martin Daniel Ellis, an American citizen 28 years of age and domiciled within the continental United States, and herein referred to as "suspect," was hired by the Field Operations Signal Intelligence Section of the Naval Security Group, herein referred to as NSG, of the United States Navy. From January of that year through July 1983, the suspect held the title Intelligence Research Specialist within various sections of NSG. In July 1983, suspect was offered employment as a desk officer in the Anti-Terrorist Alert Center, herein referred to as ATAC, in the Threat Analysis Section of the Naval Investigative Service, herein referred to as NIS, of the NSG. Suspect accepted such employment and began work at ATAC the following month, August 1983.

In or about December 1983, suspect was offered employment as an Intelligence Research Specialist at ATAC. In this capacity, in which suspect is currently employed, suspect's duties include, but are not limited to, research and analysis of SIGINT and HUMINT data pertinent to terrorist threats in the Middle East and Europe, research and analysis of intelligence pertinent to Soviet weapon technology as it impacts upon such threats, etc. In pursuance of his duties during his employ suspect applied for and was granted security clearances to request, obtain, and utilize materials designated Confidential, Secret, Top Secret, and Special Compartmentalized Information, herein referred to as CONF, SEC, TPSEC, and SCI.

Pursuant to Executive Order 12356 and antecedent ExO 12354 and their predecessors, material is classified CONF if improper disclosure can reasonably be expected to inflict *damage* to national security. Pursuant to the above ExOs and their predecessors, material is classified SEC if improper disclosure can reasonably be expected to inflict *serious damage* to national security. In similar vein, material is classified TPSEC if improper disclosure can reasonably be expected to inflict *serious and grave damage* to national security. The SCI designation is given to materials the disclosure and distribution of which is severely limited to those individuals who in their military and intelligence functions have an established and recognized need of such material. Improper disclosure and dissemination of SCI material can be reasonably expected to inflict *serious and grave and lasting damage* to national security.

In the autumn of 1984, a colleague of the suspect informed the suspect that the colleague had recently in the course of enrollment in graduate studies at Columbia University met an officer of the Israeli defense establishment. The suspect indicated to the colleague an interest in meeting this officer. Shortly after this interest was made known, the colleague introduced the suspect to the officer, Col. Shlomo Avrami. Col. Avrami was then an adjunct professor at Columbia University participating in a joint scholar exchange program under the auspices of the International Intelligence Research Foundation, herein referred to as IIRF.

At this meeting, suspect detailed for Col. Avrami the materials for which the suspect had clearance, his access thereto, documents he was able and willing to provide, including but not limited to those areas of specialty for which suspect was, and continues to be, employed, and including but not limited to Electronic Intelligence (ELINT), Radar Intelligence (RADINT), Signals Intelligence (SIGINT), and Telemetry Intelligence (TELINT). At present, suspect's access includes, but is not limited to, production specifications and maintenance manuals for the Worldwide Military Command and Control System (WWMCCS) and the Joint Tactical Information Distribution System (JTIDS). WWMCCS and JTIDS are integral parts of the Command-Control-Communications-Intelligence Network (C-cubed, IN), and a vital link in the communications linkage between the United States Defense Forces and their NATO supplements.

Soon after this meeting, suspect and Col. Avrami met in Washington and, pursuant to suspect's representations, suspect produced for Col. Avrami various classified materials. Further representations were made by suspect indicating his willingness and ability to produce on an ongoing basis other materials relating to suspect's area of employ. At this time Col. Avrami made clear his interest in obtaining such materials, and suggested that further communications between them be conducted under cryptographic security. Col. Avrami suggested a code system based upon various Old Testament passages, and a system of contact signals based upon the Hebrew alphabet. Col. Avrami gave the suspect a list of pay telephones in the Washington and New York areas through which they were to maintain contact using the agreed-upon codes.

Shortly thereafter a third meeting was held in a Brooklyn location in what has been identified as a "safe house" used by Israeli intelligence operatives. Present were the suspect, Col. Avrami, and another gentleman introduced as "Ari." Tentative identification of Ari indicates probable employment by the military intelligence arm, herein referred to as Aman, of the Israeli Intelligence Service. At this meeting the suspect produced for Col. Avrami and Ari a selection of materials drawn from various and different categories of classifications. These samples included, but were not limited to, Signal Security Intelligence utilized by the Rapid Deployment Force, Middle East, technical training manuals acquired by United States intelligence pertaining to the Soviet Sagger antitank missile, and other numerous documents as yet unidentified. Two unidentified individuals were observed entering the safe house during this meeting; subsequent trace requests have not yet provided positive identification of these individuals. Subsequent surveillance and analysis indicate Ari is suspect's handler, responsible for tasking, collection, and payment. Surveillance and analysis indicate a high probability that suspect's wife is accessorially involved. Suspect has been given the code name Boaz. Suspect's wife's code name is Ruth. Communications are effected through various telephone signals originating in suspect's residence and personal advertisements placed in *The New York Times* and/or *The Washington Post*, as well as other surreptitious means as yet undiscovered.

To date there have been no further meetings between the suspect and Col. Avrami, though suspect continues to meet at odd and infrequent intervals with Ari. The times and places of these meetings are set forth in the attached supplementaries, pages 2–5. A study of these supplementaries suggests a far reaching and ongoing intelligence operation conducted by and for the benefit of a foreign power. The Federal Bureau of Investigation and the Naval Investigative Service continue their monitoring of suspect and his movements in accord with proper legal procedures as set forth by the Justice Department, Internal Security Division, in accord with all internal procedural guidelines of the FBI and NIS, and in accord with all pertinent Executive Orders. At such times as are deemed appropriate, further memoranda shall be forwarded.

Respectfully submitted,

James Newcombe
Assistant United States Attorney

# CHAPTER 1

Long before the assessment results came in, Blake knew the operation had gone poorly. First, it had been scheduled for the worst possible time, a couple of weeks before Liberty Weekend, and Blake's head had been full of data pertaining to coverages and overtime and agent assignments.

Second, they had all been together too long and were getting on each other's nerves. Blake would have preferred to pair up with either the woman—Agent Robbins, very sharp, slender, pretty—or the younger man with the mustache, a hotshot kid ten years his junior and already at the same level, but it just worked out that he was partnered with the older, heavier gentleman from the Washington metropolitan field office, an agent by the name of Robert Glynn.

He and Agent Glynn were an incongruous pair. Watching the man sweat in the inefficient air-conditioning of the motel's conference room, Blake again cursed the luck of the draw. Perhaps it wasn't luck; you never knew what trials the higher powers had in store for you. They were like a Mutt and Jeff team and, using his hypersensitive sensory faculties, Blake could almost hear the silent snickers of the other agents.

Blake was a slender, somewhat smaller man, dapper in dress, hair close-cut and of a fine, middle-aged gray. Always watching his weight, he had a faint, subliminal contempt for fat people, and he feared it showed, especially during meals. Agent Glynn was overweight by a good thirty pounds, and towered over Blake by almost half a foot. When Hoover had been around there had been strict weight regulations, and though everyone bitched and moaned, they had all been better off for the old codger's despotism. Now most of the older agents had let themselves go; in the New York office, where Blake had been working for the last eight years, the ten o'clock coffee wagon was the highlight of the morning.

They had been given the case the night before, told that they would make the arrest in the morning. Immediately Blake's appetite had vanished. Not Glynn's: He ate everything in sight. Watching, Blake had experienced a fleeting revulsion. Not that Glynn was sloppy: He ate fastidiously, his plump fingers handling the silver deftly as he scooped the shrimp from the piquant sauce, buttered half a loaf of bread, then attacked the thick red slab of prime rib with a ravenous delicacy. He finished off with the quarter circle of nesselrode pie whose whipped topping was dotted with lumps of dark chocolate. The man was possessed by a gluttonous intensity and ate as if this was going to be his last meal, which, in a way, looking back on it now, it might easily have been.

It irritated Blake that they had given them the assignment on such short notice. They were supposed to have a free evening—it was on the agenda, Free Time—but he had been warned by Campbell, who had been through one of these, to expect the unexpected. Reality training, they called it.

It was a Banking & Fraud case, just up Blake's old alley. Glynn, too, had put in his early years in B & F and was familiar with the basic sting. They had reviewed the case file. Blake and Glynn were coming in on the tail end of the operation; theoretically, it was to be a simple arrest. The target was arriving with a suitcase full of cash. The night before, and early this morning, Blake and Glynn carefully went over the material, a thick packet of forms and surveillance reports, memorandums and airtels. In the room where they now waited, and where they were going to do the sting, were hidden microphones and a video camera. Again, Campbell had warned him about the bugs. Maybe he shouldn't have; Blake found himself tentative, acting and talking a little more assertively.

He checked his watch. A little after ten. The call was supposed to come before eleven. Glynn was at the window, pushing aside the curtain. The morning was bright, and sun pressed hard against the window, getting in around the edges. It would be hot out there, another muggy June day.

He and Glynn had talked about the arrest, argued really. It was an artificial situation. Normally, agents of their rank would be in a supervisory role, directing at least a dozen other agents with shotguns, radio hookup to a command post, an open line to a U.S. attorney.

The phone purred, and Glynn turned from the window and got it in his meaty paw on the second ring.

"Glynn here."

Blake stood in the middle of the room, in shirtsleeves, his shoulder holster on the night table.

"Roger." Glynn replaced the receiver. He nodded to Blake.

"The pigeon's landing."

Blake was already slipping into his harness. Glynn took his .38 from the night table and forced it between his waistband and his belly, where it disappeared. Blake turned away and shook his head. Ridiculous, he thought, a little gun like that on such a big man. Blake used a heavier Sigsauer.

They each took a walkie-talkie.

"Ready?" asked Glynn.

Blake had to say something, if only for the microphone.

"All the way," he said, and stepped out into the hall.

●

Outside, they hit the wall of humid heat. The parking lot was full and the glare coming off the glass and chrome was blinding. Glynn had sunglasses ready, but Blake had left his in the motel room where they wouldn't do a goddamn bit of good. Lose a few points right there.

"The Buick," said Glynn, referring to the vehicle about to turn into the motel's parking lot.

"Marked," replied Blake. He breathed a little easier. It was a two-door gray job, as expected.

"Let's go," said the fat man. He moved off to the left, with Blake heading, as per their plan, to the right around the pool.

There were a few bathers in the water, a mother and a young child splashing in the shallow end, a lone hairy man lying greased on a chaise. Blake followed the curving path, keeping an eye on the gray sedan that had pulled into a spot against the fence. Trees formed a barrier between the fence and the parkway just beyond, where eight lanes of traffic rushed ceaselessly. It was a good spot for a drop; you could be in and out and gone in a minute, and a tracking team wouldn't stand a chance. Blake ducked behind a van, pulled his walkie-talkie from beneath his jacket. His signal was short, a mere phrase.

"Pigeon landed."

Over the static, which sounded like food being fried, came Glynn's acknowledgment.

Their plan was that Blake would meet the driver and take him back to the hotel room, where a third agent, the Stinger, would meet them. They would establish their bona fides, parlay about money, and make the arrest. He and Glynn had reviewed the pitfalls. Entrapment was what they had to avoid. It was agreed that, as a master of nuance, familiar with the essential psychological aspects of human intercourse, Blake would handle most of the negotiations. This was a simple operation of the sort that Blake had participated in, in one capacity or another, at least a dozen times. When he had begun his Bureau career, Banking & Fraud had dealt mostly with white-collar people, men and women kiting checks or cooking their bank's books, a nice group really: well mannered, educated, wanting more money for a car, the kid's college, new furniture. These days, the money launderers were a nastier crowd, drug-related, considerably more violent. Dangling beneath his jacket and under his arm was his Sigsauer. He had bought it a year and a half ago, had fired it twice. The slide was still a bit tight, the heft much different from his old .38.

●

The Buick's ignition was cut, and Blake made a beeline across the hot, glaring pavement. Had he known he would be doing some outside work he would have packed his tropical suit, taken a short-sleeved shirt. The instructions were that the driver would remain in the car until one of the agents approached. This was a blind rendezvous, and he did not know what to expect, except a man with a blue shirt and a baseball cap. Blake came around the line of cars against the fence. His peripheral vision was on high, and he was aware of Glynn's shadow off to the side, was aware, too, of presences on the roof, watching. He wanted to do it right, the Bureau way, which meant by the book.

He approached the Buick, squinting, then stopped for the briefest of moments, went on again.

There's a mistake, he thought.

The driver wasn't a man with a blue shirt and a mustache, but a woman.

She was stepping out of the car, turning toward him.

He was about to smile and apologize, for clearly he and Glynn had got the wrong vehicle, when he looked down at her hand.

A terrible, terrible mistake.

The bastards, he thought.

Held just above her purse, concealed except for the hole in the muzzle, a semiautomatic was pointed directly at his heart.

The woman smiled.

The goddamn sadistic bastards.

# CHAPTER 2

F or Ellis, they wanted a helicopter.
Any operation worthy of the New York field office had at least a helicopter and, if you could get the right signature on the paperwork, often one
of those spotter planes that zip around in the sky chasing the target's
car, flying to the right and a little behind, precisely in the driver's blind
spot. The request was put in as a matter of course. The plane was to be
used for open-road tailing, the helicopter for the in-city phase of the
operation, most likely in the last stage immediately before the arrest, or
during it.

The arrest per se, as George Murphy put it, was going to be efficient,
clean, and quick, one of those captures that only the Bureau can pull off.
The operational area would be swarming with agents, naval security
contributing their quota—an administrative eye always on the overtime
sheets—cars ready and the helicopter or plane circling above. It would
take place downtown during lunch hour, at one of the drop sites that the
suspect had been using regularly for the last four years. At that point in
time the arrest was a mere formality, the final act of a dramatic exercise
conceived and staged by the collective mind of the counterintelligence
division of the New York office.

Frank Campbell was to be given the honor of the actual arrest; this
had been agreed upon by all parties, for Campbell, a squad supervisor
and the case agent, was retiring in about six months and was being
granted a last quota of glory. He, Campbell, would speak the words, the

time-honored words of the field agent: "Freeze! FBI! You're under arrest!"

Immediately after, the nervous lawyers from Justice would race up to be certain that all technicalities were observed. Campbell would decide who was going to read Ellis his rights, for this was one of the honors to be apportioned out, as was the selection of the cuffing agent—after an important arrest handcuffs often became part of the agent's personal memorabilia—and the driver of the car in which Ellis was to be shoved with just the right amount of force. Murphy would decide who was to stand on the steps of the Federal Courthouse in Foley Square when Donald Ricciardi held his inevitable press conference, lisping through his announcement of another felon apprehended, truth and justice prevailing yet again. As much planning goes into postarrest as into the arrest itself, perhaps more. Tom Donnelly, second in command of the New York field office, was to be there in pride of place, which was back and to the left of Ricciardi, but squarely within camera. Maybe, thought Murphy, they could squeeze Matthew Blake in, just for the high-level exposure. There would be, among the crowd of glory seekers, a couple of dozen U.S. attorneys, a chief or two, and their deputies, all from Southern District—Eastern frozen out on this one, but too bad, they've got to learn to move faster. The attorney general was going to send someone, and a grand time would be had by all.

Donnelly knew how important it was to get the political heavies in on this because, as always happens in these kinds of cases, more so when there are these particular ethnic considerations, there was going to be hell to pay. State would throw one of their dandified tantrums, and the CIA would be clamoring for interrogation rights, all the while claiming to have known everything all along. The administration would do its usual hand wringing and the Israelis would act surprised and cha-grined, disclaiming any involvement.

In the meantime, the Bureau and Navy and Justice had to worry about coordinating the arrest of that treasonous son of a bitch, Ellis, while covering their godforsaken posteriors all the way.

# CHAPTER 3

In the room where the woman had taken Blake was a man of about forty, muscular. He was at the window peering through the blinds when Blake was pushed in.

"Goddamn it," the man had said, looking at her.

"Mel, he's got a radio." She threw the black walkie-talkie on the bed. The man had looked at it, then at Blake.

"What are you, a fucking fed?"

Blake fought to bring his turmoil under control. In the space of a very few minutes he and Glynn had committed half a dozen fundamental errors, the worst being loss of visual contact followed by severance of their radio connection. At the thought that he might be disarmed, Blake had come dangerously close to panic. The loss of an agent's firearm to a felon under these circumstances was an automatic demotion.

"Because if you are, asshole, it's your fucking end."

"Hey," said Blake. "Hey, cool it!" He moved slowly into the room, putting out his hands in a palms-down motion, the suppression of anger. He had to get the right tone of exasperation and humor into his words. "Come on, man, just calm the fuck down."

The expletive, as unaccustomed as it sounded in his mouth, seemed to work, and Mel's expression changed from angry apprehension to one slightly more relaxed. There had even been a touch of genuine curiosity in his eye as he looked at Blake across the bed. The woman, standing to Blake's left, about six feet away and out of lunge range, had taken her gun out of her purse and was training it on Blake's chest.

"Would you call off your storm trooper, Mel?"

The man looked at the woman, then at Blake.

"Okay, Alice," he said, and after a moment's hesitation, during which Blake saw a frown cross her face, the woman moved backward to the chair, lowered the gun, and sat. Mel moved around past Blake, almost touching as he passed, thus establishing his greater height and bulk. He took up position at the side of the seated woman. Then he put his hand on her shoulder, a controlling gesture which elicited another frown from her.

"Talk, asshole," Mel commanded.

And Blake did, praying all the time that fat Glynn would, for the love of god, do something to get them both out of this goddamn mess. In a precise, almost deferential manner, Blake spoke. He took heart, as Mel nodded and the woman, the gun in her lap, continued frowning, from the little, black, round disk unobtrusively affixed to the underside of the lampshade. From it a thin black wire went around the rim of the shade, down the lamp's brass body, and across the table—secured with a piece of jagged masking tape—to disappear over its edge. There must be, too, Blake realized with a pang of hope, and despair, a hidden video trained on him, else why did Mel and Alice maneuver to position him so precisely?

Those sadistic bastards, thought Blake, think of everything.

●

The trick, Blake had seen very soon, was to play off Alice against Mel. He had had a fleeting thought: this was like that play *No Exit* he had read years ago. Here the three of them were trapped in this motel room, in a kind of hell, and it was Blake's job to turn the man and woman against each other so that he could make an arrest and come out of this with his professional pride and his career intact.

Because, make no mistake about it, he was in a fucking, as Mel would say, mess. They were arguing with him about his backup, wanting to know where the suitcase of money was, accusing him of trying a double-cross, and he had decided to take the line, repeating it over and over, that it was Mel and Alice who, from his point of view, were doing the double-goddamn-crossing. This was a good approach, and they argued it back and forth, but he couldn't exploit it. Like actors in an improvisation, the man and woman seemed to be waiting for his cue. He soon sensed their growing impatience. It had been too long since he had been in a field situation of this sort and his training had deserted him completely. The microphone and the video were picking everything up. He couldn't diddle around like this much longer. Where the hell was Glynn? Probably eating dessert in the motel's cafeteria.

He had to do something. There was a key here, something that would allow him to psyche out this couple. He sensed the animosity between them. Mel was a typical macho-type felon, Alice kind of a street-tough lady, but pretty and much too well-spoken for the role of killer woman—and his best bet was to work them against each other. But his fearful predicament, the confusion of the unexpected, had short-circuited his thinking. And he knew—looking back on it later—that he was doing it all wrong. Too much talk. He should have done something dramatic, fantastic, even if it was stupid, or even contrary to Bureau procedure. You get points for originality. A line of training came back to him, a voice from his rookie days at Quantico: Announce, Identify, Control. He had to get them out into the parking lot again, where maybe Glynn was hiding, or into the other room, where their secondary was waiting.

Then the woman, tired of playing around, spoke, tough and to the point.

"You're a cop."

Blake was silent.

"Mel, he's a cop."

"Alice, fuck off."

"Mel, goddamn it, he's got a gun."

The man looked at Blake for a long time.

"Mel, take his gun. He's got it under his arm."

Blake remained silent. Mel, still watching him, made a tentative move toward him, then stopped when Blake, putting both hands on his waist, allowed his jacket to fall open. Though younger and of obviously greater strength than Blake, it was clear the man did not want to make physical contact.

"Mel, goddamn it, take his gun!"

The man hesitated.

The woman was standing. She held the gun up again, pointing it at Blake's chest.

It was a Sigsauer, like his. He stared at it, knowing all the time that of course she would never shoot, that it was not really loaded. She had not primed the slide, so that if he made a grab for it there was no way she could get off a shot.

And then everything happened very quickly, and at once.

There was a banging on the door.

Mel and Alice shot quick glances at each other.

They too, Blake realized in a flash, were mere parts in a greater, inexplicable whole.

The banging continued.

"What the fuck," said the man.

Suddenly the door burst open.

Glynn, his jacket pulled down across his back, pinning his arms, was pushed in, followed by a man in blue shirt and cap.

"They're fucking agents!"

Glynn looked at Blake and shook his head.

But now Blake had his gun out.

"Fucking right we're agents!"

"Shit," said Mel.

But the woman kept her gun up.

"Drop it!" Blake growled. "Drop the fucking gun."

"Fuck you, asshole."

"Alice, they're feds!"

In Blake's other hand was his wallet, open to show his badge.

"FBI! You're under arrest!"

But it didn't go the way it was supposed to. Rather, it went too far.

The woman didn't lower her gun.

"Asshole," she said, smiling.

Okay, Blake had told himself, I'm supposed to believe she's on drugs.

"Dick head," she said.

The other men said nothing. It was between Blake and the woman.

"Alice." Blake spoke carefully, slowly. "Alice, lower the gun."

She did, but only to aim it at his crotch.

Okay, thought Blake, they want to play tough.

Blake slid back his slide, remembering that he hadn't checked the clip, and that maybe there were rounds still in it from his last target session.

The woman paled.

"Drop it!"

But she held the gun on him.

Glynn was shouting. "It's enough—God's sake, both of you, it's enough!"

"Drop it, Alice." Blake's voice, quiet now, trembled with fury.

"You'll have to kill me, asshole."

The room was absolutely still. Fat Glynn, his arms still pinioned by his jacket sleeves, was sweating. His eyes pleaded with Blake. Mel and

the other man watched him. The woman held the gun up. There seemed
to be the tiniest of smiles on her mouth.

"Drop the gun."

"Uh uh."

This was the classic standoff. The manual, the training, had instructions for this very situation: you never, ever, surrender your weapon, or
back down.

"Alice." Mel spoke. "Come on, put the gun down."

Instead, she pulled back the slide. Blake, amazed, thought he heard
a round lifting, with a soft click, into the chamber.

This was crazy.

The woman took a step toward him.

"Okay," said Mel, "I'm calling time."

But Alice shook her head.

He watched her finger bent around the trigger. It was a thin finger, the
nail polish a pale red. Her other hand had come up to wrap itself around
the grip, steadying the pistol. She was in the practiced stance of the
professional shooter, elbows only slightly bent. That little smile played
about her mouth and chin.

This is a test, Blake remembered telling himself, this is only a test.

His gun, too, was up, pointing muzzle to muzzle.

Glynn had lifted his jacket back onto his shoulders.

"Time for coffee," he said.

Blake was watching the woman's trigger finger—a fundamental
error, for that way he allowed the other man to come around behind
him. Sensing the moving figure as a disturbance in the light, he
flinched, started to duck, but was unable to evade the chopping blow
that struck with a sharp, stinging impact just below his wrist. The pain
went through to the bone, but he held on to his gun. He whirled toward
the man. He was cursing—"Bastards, you fucking bastards." Now Mel
and Glynn were on him. The fat agent had him in a headlock and Mel
was twisting his gun hand around to his back, pinning it.

"Matt," said Glynn, "drop it. Jesus, man, drop it."

The woman was watching dispassionately, her gun at her side.

His hand was twisted back, hard, and his fingers opened. He felt
another hand taking the gun from his. He was bent down, fat Glynn's
arm around his head, over his ear, squeezing. Blake asked to be let go
but his voice, constricted, was lost in the general commotion and the
soft absorbency of Glynn's fat. The pressure continued. He began to feel
light-headed. He heard someone, Mel, he thought, say it was okay to
let him go, but the pressure continued. Glynn's belly was like a wel-

coming pillow, and the darkness closed in on him. Just as Glynn released him, Blake lost consciousness and slipped, gently and without a murmur, to the floor.

# CHAPTER 4

A week later, three thousand miles away in London, another man stands at a hotel window, waiting.

He is a man who travels a great deal and has affections for different lands. He likes England. The English are a civilized people, enervated perhaps, but no longer driven by dreams of empire or visions of conquest. A sorry people, in a way. But they do certain things well. Their sense of public politeness has been cultivated to a high degree; their transportation system is reliable; the average British citizens, with their heritage of language and love of self-expression, are fairly articulate. Yes, quite a civilized realm.

The hotel room is well appointed and looks out on the Thames, with the sun casting its slanting light upon the rooftops. Behind him the telephone sits silent upon the desk. It will ring soon, and there shall be a voice on the other end, speaking quickly and in code.

For one of their agents is being hunted, and it is feared he will be caught. There is a woman involved, the agent's wife. They have asked the man to wait in England for the quick, low voice on the telephone, for the code words.

Outside, the soft English dusk holds a happy light, a gently deepening blue. Such a lovely time of day this is, the man thinks, unless you are being hunted.

# CHAPTER 5

F rom the twenty-eighth floor of the
FBI's New York field office headquarters, the southeastern tip of Manhattan is a sprawl of buildings that, to Blake, seem to have sprung
without rhyme or reason from the bedrock. At this hour, ragged and
beautiful, their towers and toothcut spires gleam in the afternoon sun.
Between the United States Custom House, with its more traditional
gothic architecture, and the austere, sterile telephone building, Blake
can make out the arc of the Brooklyn Bridge yearning toward the farther
shore.

Blake takes his binoculars from his desk drawer. These are naval
surplus glasses, of very high magnification and resolution, optically
corrected for water viewing, polarized, very long in the barrel, extremely heavy.

The bridge's walkway is dense with people, but the power of the
lenses is such that a few heads and shoulders fill the glasses. At this
distance and magnification the slightest twitch is multiplied many
times; Blake holds steady. He has learned the trick of keeping both eyes
open, the binoculars adjusted so that the separate images of each eye
overlap. He finds early evening light best for visual reconnaissance,
coming in low from the west in just the precise wavelengths to give
objects sharpness and contour.

After a minute of concentrated gazing Blake has had enough. He will
work late tonight, putting in the mandatory voluntary overtime that has

been his lot for the last twenty years. As always, his calendar is smudged with pencilings and erasures, his spike jammed with buck slips.

Everyone will be glad when the harbor celebration is over and the statue is lit and all the visiting dignitaries and politicians clear out. Blake and his people have been meeting for months with the Secret Service, State Department Security, and the NYPD Bomb and Terrorist Squad, and have interfaced, with mutual reluctance, with the CIA domestic liaison. The meetings have been endless, many of them neither pleasant nor productive nor even necessary, but that's the way the Bureau does it. He has not had a vacation in almost a year. At least he doesn't have to deal with the foreigners, except peripherally by maintaining a cordial liaison with the various embassy security attachés. The Italians are manageable, the French are not, but that's State's problem. He'll be working this weekend on phones and paper, begging, cajoling, and demanding agents from the Philadelphia and Baltimore field offices. He will then take a brief respite on Sunday when he and his wife host a barbecue for their friends and family and the immediate family of the man his older daughter will be marrying in October. The groom's parents are coming in from a little town in Wisconsin.

He looks at the family photograph on his desk, taken last year. Margaret, the bride to be, will be twenty-seven a week after the wedding. His younger daughter, Maureen, exceedingly pretty in the picture, is nineteen. He can remember the very nights they came into the world, a mere dozen light-years ago.

•

Blake began life as a special agent, moved rather quickly into a supervisory role as squad leader, and became an ASAC, assistant special agent in charge of a small office in the boondocks, which in Blake's case was Kansas City, Missouri, which really was a nice place and not that boony. Then he was brought to SOG, seat of government, in Washington, Bureau headquarters, where they put him at a desk receiving, abstracting, and filing field reports, which he did in precise and respectful Bureauese, suppressing his natural instincts for a more energetic prose. He thought of himself as a closet iconoclast. They sent him out as an inspector to conduct administrative audits of FOs, field offices. He did that well too, establishing himself as the very model of a moderate middle manager. Then he was moved again to be the SAC, special agent in charge, of a small office in Rochester. All this time he moved up through the General Schedule pay levels, got his merit and grade increases, letters of citations, an occasional bonus of a hundred dollars or so, the EMA, Extraordinary Merit Award. For what the Bureau—guided by the frugal hand of Hoover—gave, it gave grudgingly.

His wife and daughters followed, faithful and obedient camp women, from one suburban tract house to another someplace else. Family rooms, finished basements, the bedrooms upstairs, and the barbecue pit in the yard. And then at last they made it to New York, back home to the lawns of Long Island, where his wife had spent her childhood and where they had lived when they were first married. And where Blake desires to remain for the rest of his career, which he figures is another five or six years, and after that for the rest of his life, spending his days in the shade of the justly famous maples of Eastmere, his own little quarter-acre sanctuary.

Casual mention has been made of a possible transfer, but Blake has let Murphy know, equally casually, that he is not willing to move again. The New York FO is top of the line, the largest, the most sophisticated in terms of support and political pull, the place where the action is: bombings, terror, organized crime, drugs, financial and securities irregularities, a little espionage. The only field office with an assistant director—that's Tom Donnelly. George Murphy is his deputy.

Murphy is also Blake's mentor. He got Blake into the assessment center in Princeton, the Higher Management Potential Assessment Program, known as H'MP ASS. Blake had spent four goddamn grueling days with a dozen other managerial aspirants jumping through goddamn hoops of fire. The program was something new. Once Hoover left, the Bureau decided it was time to go scientific, and they hired a consulting firm to develop a program to identify and track those agents most likely to succeed in the higher realms of bureaucracy. A bunch of psychologists and other abstractionist types came up with a leadership profile and devised a test that they claimed would identify those most in possession of it. At the assessment they role-played with each other, were subject to hostile inquisitions by assessors, were given impossible field hypotheticals. It was torture all the way. Campbell had gone through it, and having failed miserably, had prepped Blake. Blake's been second-guessing his performance ever since. Thinking of it now, a week later, he still sweats. The fiasco in the parking lot! He really lost it there. A major embarrassment. No such displays are allowed in the Bureau. Still, I am good, he thinks. He has done very well for almost twenty years and, if he is careful, with Murphy pulling for him behind the scenes, he still has a good shot at promotion.

He wants to do it like Campbell is doing it, retire at fifty-five and set up his own security consulting firm, maybe even join the Irishman's. He wants to leave all this mind-numbing paperwork behind, all the ass-covering and defensive maneuvering. He wants to stay in Eastmere in their nice house with the bedrooms upstairs and the barbecue in the yard, at least until Maureen graduates from Oberlin. Margaret's about to be married, so she's safe. He never feared for her as he does for his younger daughter. She's more out there, more vulnerable, like himself—

"Matt."

Blake looks up.

It's Murphy.

They have a problem. One of Blake's agents, now on the terrorism squad, has an informant who it seems has been double-dipping now and then with the organized crime squad, selling the same information in slightly different form. One of the assistant U.S. attorneys, Southern, wants a tap. The kids always do. Taps carry status. The AUSA's got to show probable cause. There's a certain minimum of bio material he's got to display just to show that the source is not a figment of the attorney's prosecutorial imagination. The judges are serious about this, which always seems to surprise the AUSAs. Blake's agent is holding back; it's his source, cultivated over a long period of time, and he doesn't want to compromise the man. The attorney's chief has been harassing the agent. This is a no-no.

Normally, Blake wouldn't get involved. But the agent used to be one of his, and Blake has a reputation for mediatory skills. Also, in keeping with his career advancement plan, Murphy wants him to get more exposure on the political side. Walking slowly, they review their points. It's a question of how much they can reveal without blowing the informant's cover; men have been known to be killed as a result of court exposure. But these young, hungry AUSAs, what the hell do they care? They come in gung-ho on the trail of truth and justice, which at their age and level of maturity means facts and punishment. They want big cases, they want litigation experience, they want to prepare for the big time. Even if means walking over a body or two.

Blake and Murphy ride up two floors and proceed to the room with the hanging sign that reads Stock 101. The renovation has been going on for more than a year, with no end in sight. Having gone through a number of his own home renovations, Blake holds contractors in exceedingly low esteem. God, he thinks, created the world in six days; had it been subcontracted, it would have taken years. There are six people in the room. Spotting the prosecutor is easy: he's young, his suit is stylish and expensive, nice medium-spread collar and a red power tie. The agent is in polyester just a tiny fraction too bright a blue. Blake nods to Ralph Craigson, chief of special prosecutions. They've worked together before. He's got the usual bias against the Bureau, but then, hasn't everyone?

The young agent, very besieged, wants to stonewall. Blake, sympathetic, knows they must give something. Not only is a life at stake, but pride and power, too. There is a middle ground here. He takes the young man aside, explains how you win some and how you lose some, and that there is always another case. Assistant U.S. attorneys come and go, only the Bureau abides forever.

Half an hour later Blake's ready to leave, already feeling tense. He's got to talk very soon to Donnelly about his next assignment, but that will have to wait until he gets his assessment results—sometime within the next few weeks—and then he will know which way to jump. His phone is ringing. It might be his wife, but he lets it stop on its own.

●

It is after eight, traffic on the Long Island Expressway has been, as usual, horrendous. The road morons, gathering at the Elmhurst tanks, had cost him twenty minutes. Now, as he walks up the flagstones to his front door, Blake hears music through the open windows. It is loud organ music, unmistakably the Bridal March. As he steps inside, his ears are assaulted by its blast. His younger daughter had counseled them on audio equipment and the bass is overwhelming. Wincing, he strides across the pale, gray carpet and turns down the volume.

The Bridal March is over and a trumpet piece is beginning. His wife, who has played this often enough during the last weeks for him to recognize it even though he doesn't, must be upstairs. He takes ice water from the fridge and drinks leaning against the sink. The smell of a distant barbecue fire wafts in the window.

On the stove are two covered pots. Tomato sauce in one, water in the other. In the fridge lettuce and slices of red pepper sit in a wooden bowl. A book is on the kitchen table. Maureen's. *The Stranger*. For her summer school, so she can graduate from Oberlin a half year earlier, maybe even a year, and save them about twenty-two thousand dollars. He likes this music. In the living room he finds the album. *Musique pour un Mariage*. In the brief, dead silence between selections he hears his wife in their bedroom, and goes up to say hello.

●

"So you'll be home for the party?" His wife is sorting out sheets and towels on the bed, talking into their latest acquisition, a cordless telephone. With the receiver jammed between shoulder and cheek, she acknowledges Blake with a lift of her eyes. There is a long pause on her end. Blake tugs at his tie.

"How was traffic?"

He makes a face, shakes his head, and turns toward the bathroom.

Showering, he thinks how his daughter's marriage is going to be a convenient Rubicon of sorts, over which he shall cross into a permanent middle age. Except for the refinancing, however, he expects nothing traumatic or overly disconcerting. His daughters have been, all things considered, remarkably easy and very discreet; this attests to his wife's rather civilized demeanor and his own enlightened approach to family intercourse. Blake thinks of himself as tactically astute, and has managed to elicit from his younger child a finely wrought, argumentative affection.

Maureen has seized upon Margaret's marriage as an excuse to conduct all sorts of inquiries into modes and mores. At her prodding, he had admitted his belief that the affianced couple had been intimate. This led to a discussion of sex and chastity. She was quick and nimble, and displayed, toward her father, an amalgam of careful sarcasm and backhanded respect. He has heard from his colleagues tales of ferocious adolescent eruptions, and is pleased to have been spared those agonies. Timing, he thinks. Margaret and Maureen were too young for Vietnam, and everything since then has been mired in murky politics—Latin America is incomprehensible, the Middle East just too crazy—and not conducive to satisfying controversy. Sons might have been difficult; young men are so juiced up. Downstairs there is beautiful music playing, a gently undulating trumpet line.

"What is that?" he calls from the top of the steps.

The music is beautiful, beating the air into indescribable shapes. His wife's voice reaches him. He cannot make out the words, sounds like "Albino," and he returns to the bedroom to dress.

In a few minutes, Blake is at the table. His wife spoons sauce over the pasta. After a few forkfuls, he says, "I've got to be up very early tomorrow. Conference calls."

"How does it look?"

Meaning Liberty Weekend, he assumes. "Good. Just crazy."

"Any news on the assessment, Matt?"

"No. It's going to take some time. They have to analyze the results. What about Sunday?"

"Everyone's coming. We'll have six sleeping over."

He can't be bothered wondering where they'll sleep. "And everything is under control? The food, the drinks?"

"Yes, Matt. I want you to look at the mortgage commitment papers."

He will, after supper. There is a list of about a hundred items dealing with the wedding. Music, flowers, invitations, menu, seating, the ceremony; the minister. The refinancing. Just when he had hoped to see daylight at the end of each month, Margaret decided she wanted an old-fashioned wedding.

"Have you done anything about the camera?"

Right. A new camera. Next week, he tells her.

"Where is Maureen?"

At a friend's house, he is told. When is she due home? Late.

"Is she still dating Jonathan?"

The Goodman boy.

His wife hasn't heard the question. Most likely, she doesn't know. But he, her father, special agent, trained to read the clues, knows the secrets of his daughter's heart. He suspects, having pulled the knowledge out of the air, that there's trouble in paradise.

# CHAPTER 6

————●————

**H**ow they found out, he does not know, but he is being followed, morning, noon, and night. There is no escape. Even here, in this small, quiet place, in this still, soft darkness, he is not safe. A few minutes, perhaps, and then he will have to run again. Already, outside the confessional, he can hear the footsteps of the hunters and their hurried, hushed talk.

*Did you see him?*

*No.*

*Which way?*

*Are you sure?*

*Shit.*

He can hear, too, the music of the organ, the voices of men and women and children commenting on the beauty of the stained-glass windows, the magnificence of the cathedral.

He has never before been in one of these little boxes, a tiny room actually, and now its strangeness holds his attention. It is comforting, the muted light, the odor of polish, the softness of the wood worn smooth by countless hands. And a faint trace of perfume too, almost not there, left by a penitent, he assumes.

Outside, the voices have returned, accompanied by the harsh cackle of a walkie-talkie. He hears only bits and pieces, phrases like *Two team will cover Fifth, put Tom on Fifty-fourth.* They are picketing the exits, hunting him down.

He had made a mistake. Many, many mistakes. He had rushed into the cathedral, the hunters behind. He had never been in a church before. He had looked around, confused, slipped unseen into this little sanctuary. Now there is a soft tap on the door. He does not respond. Through the open carving on the door he can see the black of the priest's shirt.

The walkie-talkie is no longer cackling, the voices of the hunters have gone.

A woman's voice. *Yes, Father, I saw him go in.*

The priest.

*Hello, hello. Is there anyone inside?*

The woman speaks again.

The priest presses his mouth to the door.

*I'm sorry, but you will have to come out.*

The priest's voice is very gentle, firm.

The door opens. From the little seat in the confessional the man looks up into the face of the young priest, neck banded in a thin circle of white.

"I'm sorry, if you wish to confess—"

And then he is out, running down the aisle, behind him sudden shouts, radios spewing static, and then the angry footfalls of the hunters drumming in hard, inescapable pursuit.

# CHAPTER 7

I t is almost impossible to grasp the logistical nightmare, from the security point of view, of Liberty Weekend. The jealousies, petty and otherwise, created a minefield, and the first six months of planning were spent establishing turf parameters.

As always, the Secret Service considers itself king of the hill. Blake cedes this, for the president is indeed the sacred treasure. The Secret Service calls the shots, followed by the security arm of the State Department, responsible for the foreign equivalents of the president. Their people move in the more rarified atmosphere of high diplomacy. Part of their training had been in protocol, the niceties of international intercourse; they get to drink the champagne.

Then there are the beer boys. The local cops, transit police, fire and ambulance personnel, city SWAT teams. The street people who get their hands dirty handling the masses.

The Bureau has its place, as usual, in the middle. Special agents are not part of any military grouping, and have no spiffy uniforms or heavy firepower, nor do they belong to an elite cadre of plainclothes commando types. No glamor, thinks Blake, and no respect. We are the methodical plodders of middle America, not so much keepers of the flame as protectors of the hearth.

But now Blake feels the excitement. He sits in the command center in lower Manhattan, scanning the dozens of display terminals. He is part of a great and magnificent whole. He has organized the macro security teams for sectors A and B of the financial district. It's rooftop surveillance, a bunch of good guys with guns watching for bad guys with guns. There are thousands of his people prowling the streets, but Blake knows how precarious the security is.

In the early phase of Operation Hide-and-Seek—Blake had chosen the code name—a senior security analyst had been brought in; no presentation is complete without a computer model and graphics, and this was no exception. It was rather esoteric: the intersecting curves on the screen, horizontal axis being security in terms of number of agents, vertical axis the ascending scale of potential breaches. The program had sprung from the overheated brain of an MIT statistician on contract to the CIA. The lines crossed at the point of total coverage, an agent for every spectator. The lecturer had the benevolent, slightly condescending smile of the master addressing the novice. This is not, he smiled, gentlemen, another smile, a perfect world. Indeed. On the screen another display showed a bright parabola, crossed by an equally bright line in blue, the interplay of chance and probability.

All this brought them to what is called the Security Lattice. The SECLAT. More popularly known as the Sieve, a concept basic to all security work. The Theory of Holes: how big of an opening do you tolerate before the risks became unacceptable? How small of an opening can you afford?

Blake, ever nimble, kept pace as the lecturer displayed diagrams of the cerebral cortex, schematics of nerve pathways, sketches of synaptic exchanges. They were offered tantalizing if idiosyncratic speculations tying together psychology, physics, and philosophy, finishing with a wry observation that eternal vigilance is, from the neurological point of view, a contradiction in terms. His best advice, operationally: change the guard often.

But Blake has a budget; overtime kills you. Cost-effectiveness is the byword; everything, regardless of value, has a price.

Now, as he stands in the half-light of the control room watching the screens, he is thinking of tomorrow. Tomorrow, the sun will rise: that is guaranteed. His scholastic memory is excellent, and he recalls the British empiricists and how they assured themselves that one may take the sun's daily appearance as a certainty. The world proceeds on course though the individual remains subject to the vagaries of time and chance. He stands quietly. The computer monitors are glowing. The world is secure.

●

There is a distant ringing, much like a telephone, barely audible and not unpleasant.

He is a man of fifty years and is sleeping fitfully in a hotel in yet another city. The space around him is a matrix of pure silver, stars and filaments of tiny, bright dots filled with a light that is alive. These are the very molecules of existence. They are his life's work, these brilliant specks of light, atoms that bump and collide and bob and weave in a happy cosmic dance. The ringing continues, closer now. Silvery and beautiful, there is joyful music, lilting, a lovely ballet from Tchaikovsky, around him. He is in the midst of these dancing stars, and the beautiful music dances too; everything is in motion in this eternal and wonderful firmament.

And in the core of this happy cloud there appears a glow, a pinprick of angry color, yellow like a pale sun. And it grows as the ringing in the distance becomes louder and louder, coming closer, drowning out the gentle leaping music. It grows until his senses are filled with a roaring, rushing fury.

And there is no more silvery happy light, only red flames and a rising wailing shriek. Then there comes a terrible thud he feels throughout his body, a blow from out of the red chaos. He wakes to the screaming of sirens.

He had been in his laboratory, the phone ringing on his desk, much as it rings now, pulling him from sleep. The voice on the other end had told him there was bad news. There had been an accident in the Old City. He must come at once. Without taking off his white coat he dashed out. The streets were filled with screaming police vans, ambulances, army jeeps with green-clad men holding rifles. Through the streets he ran, toward the wailing that filled the sky. There was the twisted tangle of metal, still smoking, rubble of stone and wood. Bodies were lying around—he sees them now and forever—and the voice in his ear came from one of the armed green-clad men. He must stand away. There is nothing he can do.

It is in the nature of things, is it not? the very essence of life, is it not? that death's dominion knows no bounds? And he the scientist, he the synthesizer of all those dancing atoms, those specks of life. Had he not, in the pristine peace of his laboratory, held them together against all odds, binding them one to the other, holding them to his own flesh, never to let go, never, until death did everything part? And this death, alas, inevitable; he, the scientist, knew. For this world, this mortal world of hope and light and happy form was but a brief respite in another world of wailing sirens and green-clad men who shouted at him that he must back off, for there was nothing he could do. For this was the street of the Old City, not his laboratory.

And he can do nothing but mourn.

But now he is awake. The phone by the bed is ringing, impossibly loud, shattering the darkness.

And slowly, as if still in a dream, he reaches for it.

●

"What's that?"

Blake, holding a large plastic bag into which he has been dropping paper plates, napkins, and hot cups, has come upon his wife and daughter talking just outside the patio doors, and has heard the word *penis*.

"Our daughter has been indulging herself with comments on sex and morals."

"I wasn't indulging, Dad."

"Maybe," says his wife, "in Oberlin, God knows, all the girls discuss male anatomy in such frank terms—"

Maureen rolls her eyes.

"—but if it's one thing you are going to learn it is that there's a time and place for everything."

Blake looks at Maureen.

"Dad, all Mom heard was a sentence out of context."

"And you will also learn to curb—do you understand—curb your taste for shock value."

"You know, Mom, that's real stupid."

"Maureen."

"Dad."

"Matt."

Blake must be careful. In most things he is his daughter's natural ally, and often negotiates between her and his wife.

"Maureen," says his wife, "most people do not want to discuss those things you seem to be so interested in. They just want to have a good time."

Blake agrees.

"I know, Dad. A good time. That's what everyone wants to have, Dad."

"Yes, it's important to have *significant* conversations." He uses his voice to italicize; he had taken an in-service course not long ago in verbal communications skill, taught by an unemployed actor. "But your mother is right. You have to keep things light." He turns to his wife. "What did she say?"

"She was talking with Jerry's aunt and his brother."

Blake waits.

His daughter's silence is very calculating.

"She was talking about, I assume, birth control," suggests Blake.

"It was about sex in general, Dad."

Blake looks to his wife, expectant.

Maureen's mouth has just the ghost of a smile as she holds her breath.

"What I heard," says his wife, turning to Blake, "is that the rules for women are being made by a bunch of men who don't know how to use their penises."

There is a long silence, which Maureen breaks.

"Well, it's true, Dad."

"It probably is." Both women are watching him carefully, and he in turn, them. He has to decide if this is potentially a serious fight, which he can try to head off, or whether, with some skillful maneuvering, he can turn it into an amusing footnote.

He speaks. "But it wasn't the proper time or place for that particular truth."

"Dad, no one took it seriously."

"Maureen, please," says her mother. "People aren't accustomed to hearing the word *penis* from a young lady in ordinary conversation."

"Your mother's right."

"Dad, no one took it seriously!"

Blake's wife frowns.

"Well, Maureen, it's difficult making a point with you," says Blake, moving away from substance into process, intending to diffuse the tension. "First, you want to talk about things that matter, and you bring up sex and morality, a serious topic, and when you're accused of doing just that you turn around and say it isn't really serious." Recalling the actor's advice, he pauses for effect. "Two new families," he continues. "We have to feel each other out. Until you know people you don't want to run the risk of offending them."

"You mean wait until you know them and then offend them?"

Blake gives her three seconds of reproving silence.

"There *are* proper ways of giving offense."

Maureen does not react.

"I mean that you don't know how people are going to react."

"But Dad, isn't this one way of finding out?"

"Yes, Maureen," says Blake, removing all parental indulgence from his voice, "that is one of the ways." He puts in a touch of exasperation, a dash of weariness. "I and your mother would really like you to learn more circumspect and mature ones."

"You mean, like investigating them, Dad? Go through their files?"

Blake and his wife exchange a look. Surprised by the sudden turn of his daughter's anger, he is about to head this off, but Maureen strikes quickly.

"So, Dad, have you checked the files on Jerry and his family?"

"Let's not change the subject."

"No, Dad, let's. Besides, it's really the same. Have you checked their files?"

"Maureen, I know you don't care for the FBI these days, it's part of your late-adolescent rebellion."

"That's really offensive to me, Dad."

"I'm sorry it is, but there's some truth in my comment."

"And what about you, Dad? You like truth too. Your job is finding out the truth about people. You make files on them. I know, you call them serials. So how are the serials on Jerry and his family? Well?"

In spite of his growing anger, Blake almost smiles; it would be hilarious if it wasn't so nasty.

"Everything in those files," he says, "is on the public record, more or less."

"Yeah, more or less, Dad. Hah."

"I am not going to apologize for the extra measure of care I take regarding my family."

Of course, he is doing just that, and Maureen knows she has him on the run.

"Yeah, Dad, sure. What are you protecting me from? People who have the wrong ideas?"

Blake is silent.

"You know what I mean, Dad."

Silence.

"Jonathan," says Maureen.

Blake's wife lifts her eyebrows; the chickens, Matt, are coming home.

Indeed, in his weariness, he hears what sounds like the rushing of wings above the roof of the garage.

Says Maureen to her mother: "He doesn't like Jonathan's background. Right, Dad? You don't like him because some of his family were investigated in the fifties for being Communists.''

''Maureen, your father wasn't even working for the Bureau then.''

''Those were the McCarthy days,'' says Blake.

''A stupid time!''

''Yes,'' agrees Blake.

''But you don't like Jonathan.''

''I don't know him at all.''

''That's right, Dad, but you don't like him.''

''Maureen, you know I never pressure you about things like that.''

''Come off it, Dad. You always do. Ask Meg, Dad, just ask her. She never told you the correct last names of her boyfriends because she knew you'd check them out. How do you like that?''

Blake is stunned; that explains a lot.

Again, the sound of wings fills the air.

''So I bet you checked Jerry out. Come on, Dad, is his uncle a Communist? Or maybe they're hit men for the Mafia? You see, Dad, you're a real sneak. You talk about how everything has to be out in the open and then you sneak around looking at everyone's secrets. And if you don't like the things I say, next time don't go around snooping and you won't hear it.''

''Maureen!''

Blake and his wife watch their daughter disappear through the patio doors.

He shakes his head.

''Let's finish here,'' says his wife. ''Then we have to talk.''

●

They sit on their flagstone patio, each with a glass of wine.

''She doesn't want you checking up on her friends.''

Blake snorts in false laughter, agitating the wine, retorts that he's never hidden the fact that he occasionally runs a serial search.

''Your honesty is a constantly redeeming factor, Matt.''

Blake glances quickly at his wife; her face is in shadow, but the irony is showing around her mouth and eyes.

''It's an occupational hazard,'' he offers in wry defense.

''I told Maureen that. The Bureau is a gossip-gathering factory and the files are your scandal sheets.''

His wife's description is a revelation of how others see his activities. Blake stares at the shadows that just touch the grass beyond the stone.

His work has become the object of his women's mirth. He pictures them up in Maureen's room, his daughter lotused on the bed holding her toes, his wife standing near the dresser, both laughing. My dad's a gossip monger for the feds.

Suddenly there is more light in back of them. Blake glances toward the patio doors. Maureen is moving across the room, then is gone. The light remains, altering the quiet of the night into something more hard and brittle. His wife's brisk words now fit this new mood.

"Did you check on that Goodman boy?"

"Yes."

"What did you find?"

"His family were immigrants in the thirties. Suspected of Communist sympathies. Old Lefties, they call themselves now. Thought Stalin was the Second Coming."

"And the boy?"

Blake shakes his head, sips wine. Actually, he likes Jonathan a lot.

His wife says, "You never said anything about Jerry and his family so I assume they cleared."

His wife's voice holds none of the humorous, quick irony the words might carry, and he tells her, yes, they cleared.

"Suppose there had been some problem, Matt. What then?"

"Things might not have progressed this far."

He has left himself open to a flanking attack which his wife, turning in her chair and leaning into the light between them, begins: "So you're saying you don't want our daughters involved with anyone unless they're politically acceptable to you?"

"I'm not saying that at all. I'm apolitical and you know that."

"Matt, your politics are so much a part of you you don't even see them."

He is irritated; everyone is assessing him, and finding him lacking.

"I'm not so much concerned these days about people's politics," he retorts. "Half our congressmen were draft dodgers during Vietnam." He talks with the slightest edge to his voice. "I am concerned, however, about good old-fashioned criminal activity. Like fraud, embezzlement, drugs. I can't put myself or our family in a position where I might have to, to give you a real life example, put our daughter's father-in-law in jail. Damn it! That would be, goddamn it, intolerable."

Too loud, he hears the echo of his words bouncing off the hard curtain of darkness just beyond the fall of the light.

Blake stands. It's almost 2300 hours. The other yards are dark. From the backyard across the way floodlights carve cones of light from the darkness. They still have some cleaning up to do, paper cups and plates, beer cans in the flower beds.

He's tired, wants to lie down, soothe his mind with a little late-night news.

He turns in time to see his wife entering the house. He pauses for a few moments, raises his goblet, and then, knowing he doesn't want any more, throws the last of the wine into the night, where it catches the kitchen light for a moment, a pale gold sparkle of rain, before wetting the grass.

●

Once he picks up the phone, there is a long interval of silence. At last, he says *yes,* his voice deep with sleep. He listens to the voice coming from the phone and then, without a word, replaces it.

Rising now from his damp bed, he goes to the bathroom and wipes the sweat from his neck, his chest. He stands naked in the dark, toweling himself dry. It is not yet dawn, but the spires of the ancient city of Düsseldorf can be made out from the window of the Hotel Briedenbacher Hof against the graying, German sky. He will not go back to sleep and so he dresses, still in the dark, then goes to the desk in the antechamber of his hotel suite. He works until breakfast, which he has in the outdoor café area of the hotel, in the happy sunshine. He has business to conduct in Düsseldorf, patents he wishes to sell, contracts to negotiate. Later he will go to Cologne and conduct more business there. Cologne is a beautiful place, what remains of it. The double towers of the cathedral are the focal point of the city, and he will take a hotel room with a view of those architectural wonders.

Then, later, tomorrow or the next day, he must change his plans and go to Frankfurt. It is an ugly, depressing, modern city, rebuilt completely after the war. It is a city where grown men trade money, secrets, and sometimes lives. That's the sort of men he needs. And after Frankfurt he will go to Rome to look for still other men.

●

"Matt, come here!"

Blake is finishing in the bathroom, and he puts down the toothbrush with the paste still on it and crosses the bedroom carpeting. Maureen's door is closed, so he doesn't bother to wrap himself in a towel.

His wife is in bed, the television on.

"Frank Campbell," she says.

So it is!

She says, "They caught a spy."

So they have.

There is Campbell as big and burly and red-faced as in life. He is standing to the left of and just very slightly behind the man talking into the microphones. This is Donald Ricciardi himself, the United States attorney, Southern District. Ricciardi has his rug on, and one of his red ties. Ellis. They've caught a man named Ellis. Other men are standing around them, filling the screen.

"There's Ed Spanakos," says Blake, making out one of his agents on the edge of the screen. They are all on the steps of the Federal Courthouse on Foley Square. Suspect Ellis was caught while attempting to drop his handler, says Ricciardi, his terminology not quite idiomatic but sounding street smart. Yes, he says in response to a question, there are indications that Ellis was connected with Israeli intelligence, but more than that he is unwilling to say at this point in time.

That's the Don's thirty seconds.

"When did it happen?" asks Blake.

"This afternoon, they said."

He stands there naked, staring at the screen. He wants more. The meteorologist has his weather map out. Blake crouches, his testicles dangling, and turns the channels. Campbell caught a spy. All the other news shows are on the weather.

He's tempted to go downstairs and work the phones, but it's too late. It will be in the morning papers.

"Good for Frank," says his wife.

Blake is suddenly aware of his nakedness. Yes, good for Frank. The man'll go out in a blaze of glory, the goddamn son of a gun.

# CHAPTER 8

The next day, Campbell is entertaining a full audience of agents with an account of Ellis's arrest, Blake among them.

Campbell talks technical, giving out details of the surveillance, citing times and places, movements of Ellis, the countermovements of his team. What you get if you listen carefully is a sense of how the operation, as most of them are, was held together with chewing gum and baling wire.

From the beginning, Campbell explains, glaring in satisfaction, we had agents over Ellis like flies on shit. They were waiting for the right moment. It's a judgment call. The agents know what he means. You want to keep the thing going, you want names, connections, maximum embarrassment, but then on the other hand you don't want to play it out too long and lose the fish. And there is where Navy fucked up. The agents murmur, bask in Campbell's approving scowl. The prey had spooked.

Campbell, running the field operation, knew something was wrong. And not just with Ellis. There was pressure from Justice to close the operation down because Justice was getting pressure from any number of other sources, primarily the State Department and a couple of congressmen and a particular senator, who he will not name, but who is known for his sympathies in a certain direction. Let's call him a Semitophile, which sounds better than Jew lover. And Campbell had this feel, you see, this field man's gut reaction, that Ellis was on to them. Don't ask him how it happened. A mistake in surveillance—the Navy field people don't know their fucking asses—or a warning to the Israelis which might have come from any number of sources, perhaps even from within the New York field office, or from one of Ricciardi's assistant U.S. attorneys, or from Justice; or, most likely, from State.

Okay, says Campbell, we double our surveillance. We know when the son of a bitch farts. Later that night at approximately 2230 hours Ellis leaves his home and walks to Wyoming Street, turning left at the corner and proceeding at a somewhat fast pace toward Sunrise Boulevard. Ellis has got to know at this point that the young couple necking in the front seat of the car parked at the end of Cedar Road beneath the lamppost are a surveillance team, as are the three men with construction gear making a show of working in the street outside his house. At 2305 Ellis stops at a Pizza Hut and is observed making a phone call. There's no pretense any longer on the part of the surveillance teams; the couple in the car follow him to the Pizza Hut, wait outside, nod when he comes out, and later park outside his house. His wife is observed peeking out from behind an upstairs curtain.

Later analysis of telephone records will show the phone call was made to an untraceable number in lower Manhattan. Subsequent events reveal, says Campbell, the possible content of those conversations. Ellis has been instructed to go into Manhattan on Sunday, at eleven o'clock; there he is to stand on the steps of St. Patrick's Cathedral, a copy of *Scientific American*, June 1975—which was part of the materials kit Ellis had been provided with at the time of his recruitment years prior—in his right hand. His field contact is to be someone he has not met. Future interrogation will show he understands that this person, or persons, is being called in on an emergency basis and was at this point still in transit. No description of the contact is given to Ellis. Ellis is told to keep the cover of the magazine prominently displayed and that the man or woman's recognition signal will be clear and unequivocal.

Further, it is emphasized that Ellis is to arrive at the rendezvous point clean as a fucking whistle. He must shake his surveillance. To this end he is given instructions as to his travel route. There is a prearranged fallback sequence. The usual call signals and telephone format to be employed. The unidentified person or persons has been instructed to arrange for Ellis's removal. He is advised to be ready for immediate and long-term travel.

Okay, says Campbell, so far so good. We know everything. We want to move, because the pressure from there, and he jerks his head and indicates with his thumb a higher region of authority, was beginning to build. But now Washington's playing cute. The Irishman's cheeks are aflame. Blake understands. Campbell, taking orders from Donnelly, who's got to sail with the wind, always capricious, blowing from headquarters, has no choice. It's no longer just Navy's fish, and someone wants to play it out a little longer.

All parties agree to move back into discreet surveillance to give Ellis the impression he's managed to evade the watcher teams. We back off a little, Navy trims their sails. We want the man to have some running room.

On Sunday morning Ellis takes the Long Island Rail Road into Manhattan, to Penn Station. Midtown is filled with tourists. Ellis proceeds to the designated rendezvous. The *Scientific American* is pressed to his chest, Ellis holding it like a shield over his heart. He remains on the steps of the cathedral from ten-thirty until eleven forty-five. Agents are disguised as tourists, utility workers, cab drivers. Ellis must have known, any asshole would, that whoever it was they were sending in wasn't going to show. The poor bastard was being set up. Try to explain it to Navy. Okay, Ellis ducks into the church. We had no one goddamn inside! Campbell glares as he tells this. There's always something you completely screw up and the church was it. No one inside, if you can believe that. We send someone in and there's a ten-minute wait and they come out. Ellis's disappeared. Everyone goes crazy. A few minutes later, it feels like a month, we spot him on Fifth.

Get this, he had actually gone into a confessional to hide and was asked to leave by a priest. Campbell shakes his head.

So he's proceeding down Fifth Avenue. He's carrying the *Scientific American* rolled in his right hand. We know where he's going. The Israelis have a consular office a few streets away. He runs from Fifty-first Street to Forty-ninth Street, just a crazy son of a bitch. Blake and the other agents imagine the scene: the watchers, a posse in pursuit, are running along, their jackets open and flapping, guns showing. One agent is pushing his hot dog cart as fast as he can, buns and napkins falling off, two women supposed to be tourists are dodging through traffic holding their badges above their heads. This would be great for a recruitment video, better than showing bored agents looking at files or sitting in a classroom at Quantico.

But the best is yet to come. About three doors from the Israeli office, as Ellis is sprinting down the street, a Navy officer comes in from the left—Campbell uses his hands and a lot of unconscious body language, giving angles and heights—makes a flying goddamn knee tackle, and takes the bastard down rolling.

People are running away, screaming for cops. It's a pileup. Guns all over the place. From the consular windows someone's taking pictures. We take pictures back.

Campbell is quick enough to maneuver Ellis into a bureau car for the ride downtown. Campbell sits in front, a bureau man drives; Newcombe, an assistant U.S. attorney, arriving on the scene not a minute too soon, pulls rank over another agent and sits to Ellis's right, a Navy security man to his left.

It's interesting, Blake thinks, remembering the brief television bits, the way men go into shock as Ellis did, complete and quiet shock. Blake had seen that palpable catatonia in the man's face. The muscles do something funny, he doesn't know what it is, they go spastic and liquid when you put the cuffs on. You see it in the eyes, and the captive becomes a submissive animal.

Campbell is talking. So Ellis is placed in custody pursuant to warrant and taken in a three-car motorcade, running the lights, to the U.S. attorney's office in lower Manhattan.

●

On the steps leading up to the Federal Courthouse the shit hit the fan.

Two assistant U.S. attorneys, Eastern District, with the support of U.S. customs agents, confront U.S. attorneys, Southern District, Naval Investigative Service agents, and special agents of the FBI, and demand that Ellis be released into their custody.

As Campbell puts it, it's an absolute holy fucking free-for-all. One of the Eastern assistant U.S. attorneys—a guy named Halpern—has his sleeve ripped halfway off. He's wrestling with one of the attorneys from Southern, who falls and fractures his wrist, accounting for the only casualty—other than Ellis's knees—sustained in the operation. Over the shouted protests and curses of Eastern attorneys naval agents hustle Ellis inside. In hot pursuit Halpern and his buddies bust in and are stopped by Ricciardi's deputy administrative officer, who threatens to have them arrested by U.S. marshals if they trespass on the fourth floor, where Ellis is being held.

There's an ancient history here, which the Bureau agents know. Eastern and Southern have always been, and shall always be, locked in mutual antagonism. It does not escape anyone's notice that the usurpation of jurisdiction by Ricciardi had to be carried out with the de facto

approval, direction, encouragement, and connivance of the Bureau
headquarters, Justice Department factions, Naval Intelligence, and
members of both Senate and House Intelligence Committees.

Campbell gives out the latest scuttlebutt, which is that Halpern's filed
a complaint with Justice's Office of Professional Ethics. And sometime
this afternoon Eastern and Southern are supposed to have a peace
conference where they're going to kiss and make up.

Yeah.

Blake is thoughtful as he goes back to his desk. As an inside observer
of interagency politics, the real question, he believes, is how long Navy
will get to keep its candy before a bigger, tougher kid, like the bully
CIA, swipes Ellis for itself.

●

The young woman has very specific instructions. She is to pick up her
first passport in Haifa and pass through Athens on her way to Iceland,
where, in Reykjavik, she is to make contact with another party, who
will deliver a second passport, along with supporting documents. From
there she is to fly to Canada and await instructions in Montreal.

It is a very simple set of instructions. Codes are also very simple. All
she needs is a book of nursery rhymes. Contact will be made once she
crosses over into the United States. She has been named Monday's
Child. At this point she needs to know nothing more. She is apprehen-
sive, however, for she had just barely made it out a week earlier, just
as the net around Ellis had started to close, and fears that too soon a
reappearance will compromise her security.

Nevertheless, she picks up her first set of papers in Haifa and begins
her journey in high spirits, as she has begun all her missions.

●

"Matt, m'boy."

It is Frank Campbell, basking in the sunshine of the twenty-eighth
floor, who catches Blake in transit between floors. Campbell's taking a
smoking break outside room 2802, where Justice is hearing Eastern's
complaint. Campbell indicates the door with a twist of his head. Blake
stops, lifts his eyebrows.

The door is cracked and one can hear voices. Halpern—Blake remembers his distinctive voice, smooth and quick—is talking, citing improper case management on the part of Campbell's squad, violations of
professional courtesies and abuse of substantive jurisdictional guidelines by Southern.

"I'm needed," says Campbell. "Come in, Matt."

Blake follows the Irishman in. Campbell moves around the table to take a seat between his two agents, who are looking very sullen. Donnelly, his usual dapper self in a very fine gray suit and a tie that is the newest power tint of deep mauve, nods at Blake.

"Tom," John Guthrie, the ethics man from Justice, is saying to him, "I want to get to the bottom of this. What happened, Frank?"

"Ellis spooked," says Campbell. His blustery delivery fits his complexion and pale, quick eyes. "He was about to be lifted. We moved in."

From Naval Intelligence, with a soft, Southern drawl, comes, "Internal Security approved the arrest."

Halpern's chief, Walsh, is quick on the draw. "Bullshit. You guys forced the man. You stole him. We want the case."

"Glen, that's not going to happen."

Walsh turns to Craigson; they're equals, chiefs, and are allowed a certain tone. "Ralph," he says, "Mullady is ready to go all the way on this, he's had it up to here with Don, and we can make it goddamn unpleasant for you guys."

"Hey, Glen, we're not required to hand you cases."

"Look, if you want it to be war, we'll give you goddamn war."

"Frank, what happened?" asks Guthrie again.

"I don't know." Campbell's being coy, very obviously coy. "Newcombe," he says, "had warrants. Signed off by Wright." Pendleton Wright is head of the Internal Security division. He's known as Penny Weight. "We executed the warrants. In case you don't know, that's our job."

Guthrie turns to Newcombe, who's looking very smug and trying not to show it. He's about twenty-six or -seven, the youngest an assistant U.S. attorney can be, and this is his first major case. He speaks a fine legalese.

Spy cases are confused, the guidelines Byzantine in their purposeful ambiguity, and Newcombe's references are only partially intelligible. Even Walsh, the Eastern supervisor, loses patience.

"Cut the crap, Newcombe."

Craigson's eyes narrow; Walsh is overstepping. James Newcombe is his kid; you don't insult down, only across.

"You fucked us up," says Halpern.

"Next time," interjects Campbell, "move your asses."

"Fuck it, Frank," says Walsh. "You were at the conference, the way your boy Donald talked about how fitting it was that on July fourth it was so gratifying to be able to arrest an American citizen intent upon harming our great country. Come on, Frank, he's milking the case.''

"Gentlemen, gentlemen," says Guthrie. "It behooves us all—''

"It behooves them to take a flying fuck," says Halpern. "It was a goddamn cheap arrest.''

Everyone's quiet; Blake thinks, he's right.

"You shut down the operation." Halpern is speaking to Campbell. He is an elegant young man, dark and passionate, his voice pained, disbelieving. "I can't believe you did it. Why did you agree to the arrest?'' He's looking now at Guthrie.

Donnelly steps in. "This isn't getting us anywhere. Frank, what happened?''

"We were given the warrants," Campbell says, glaring at everyone, "and we executed.''

He's stonewalling in the finest tradition.

Donnelly leans forward in his chair. "Unless we work something out I'm going public on this. I don't want my agents in the middle of a jurisdictional dispute." Blake feels the tension rise. Donnelly's applications of power are always deft, and ruthless. "And I'll work it so you guys"—meaning Justice, and both sets of U.S. attorneys—"come out smelling like shit.''

●

An hour later Blake gets a call. Murphy wants to talk.

●

"Assholes," is what Blake hears when he opens Murphy's door.

"Frank.''

Campbell is standing by the window, red in the face, smoking.

"I'm leaving in four months," Campbell is saying, "and I'm not going to spend my life in court because some shithead assistant decides I violated some asshole's rights.''

On the wall to the left, in vaguely Hebraic lettering, is a Murphy admonition: THOU SHALT NOT COVET THY NEIGHBOR'S ASS.

But the *t* in *covet* is really an *r*.

On the wall opposite, which you don't get to read unless you make the effort, is another commandment: THOU SHALT HAVE ONLY ONE DIRECTOR BEFORE THEE.

Murphy, who likes Campbell because among other virtues he had never wanted to be more than a squad supervisor, leaving the higher rungs for men like himself, and possibly Blake, is mollifying. "These are political times, Frank."

"That's what I liked about Hoover. He kept us out of politics."

"Which is politics of another sort," offers Blake.

Campbell glares. "Let's not go intellectual on us, Matt. He stayed away from this stuff. They're going to jerk us all over on Ellis."

Campbell has a point; with Hoover gone the Bureau was always taking the political hit, from Wounded Knee to the Walker spy ring.

"Frank, can I tell you something?" Murphy pauses for attention. "In case you haven't heard: Hoover was an asshole."

Says Blake in an even tone, "But he was a smart asshole, George."

"Yeah."

"And he protected us lesser ones."

Both Campbell and Murphy appreciate this. Blake is known for his temperate, ironically telling humor.

Now Murphy interrupts himself to get personal, asks Blake about the assessment: brutal, wasn't it? Indeed, a H'MP ASS if ever there was one. And the family, his daughter's marriage? September, isn't it? Early October. A small fortune, weddings, aren't they? More than small, Blake replies. Murphy's glad he has boys.

Murphy raises himself in his chair; back to business. "We're trying to work something out with Eastern."

Blake puts forth a careful silence.

Campbell turns away to look out the window.

"Halpern's going to be calling you. You've worked with him before."

"I have."

"He's a sharp kid."

Blake contributes more silence. His political instincts had put him on alert, and he's already done some background work. Halpern won a few, then lost a big case, with a reprimand from the bench for sloppy preparation.

"It's been cleared with headquarters, and Justice. Eastern's coming back in."

Blake computes rapidly. He feared precisely this. He's going to be caught in the middle, ground he usually occupies quite skillfully, but not under these circumstances.

He keeps his tone even. "I've never seen a shared jurisdiction that works, George."

"I know."

Campbell, still turned to the window, offers an angry back.

Blake speaks to various points, political and administrative. They're going to have to beg Southern for access; Navy's going to drag its anchor; he's going to have to run and dodge between Mullady and Ricciardi, the paranoid don. Blake keeps it moderate and reasonable, but lets an edge appear in his voice. It's clear to him there's been some political back-maneuvering and he's being put on the receiving end of someone else's bad bargain. Assigning him to this Halpern kid is a de facto demotion. He feels his anger rising, and his sweat.

"It's not Ellis, per se, Matt." Murphy likes the *per se* expression, its definitive mode. "You and Halpern are going to be working with Navy on the Ellis spinover." He means spillover. He has a penchant for mangling his idioms.

"Who do I attach to?"

Murphy and Campbell look quickly at each other.

"Frank is going to work *with* you."

Blake and Murphy hold a long look; Murphy nods. Campbell winks.

"I want you and Frank to turn the stones. I don't know what Halpern has but let's find out and we'll take it from there. And whatever the hell it is, for the time being you run this as a Bureau special."

Meaning, off the books. Meaning, thinks Blake, everyone's running scared.

Murphy has to dish off now, he says, he's due in Philadelphia. He wants to know when Blake's assessment results are coming in. Blake doesn't know. They'll talk then.

"Frank," says Murphy, and the big agent and Blake leave.

"Lunch," says Campbell in the corridor, and Blake agrees.

●

They're at O'Callahan's with their trays of sandwiches, their sides of slaw and fries. Campbell has his beer, Blake a seltzer with lime. Campbell leads Blake to a table in the rear.

"Four months, I'm out." Campbell's opened his bread, has the mustard on the spoon. "You're at the goddamn beck and call of every hotshot assistant who wants his name on a case."

Blake stares at his turkey. It looks dry.

"Have you ever been cross-x'd by one of those bastards?"

Blake has, and agrees it is not pleasant. They know the ropes too well, know too many of the Bureau's tactics, know how to make you look like a fool.

Campbell applies a thick Van Gogh smear of mustard.

"I was talking," he says, "with my accountant, and with all the tax changes, he wants me to incorporate before the end of the year, but there's a new regulation out about conflict of interest, and we don't know if it applies."

"I heard."

Campbell starts his sandwich with a big bite.

Blake asks: "What did Donnelly work out on Ellis?"

"We're off Ellis. Except for a little cleanup."

"How the hell did that happen?"

"Are you innocent, Matt, or milking me?"

"A little of both."

Campbell looks around, checking for eavesdroppers in a reflexive habit. From his sandwich a string of fat is dangling, which he pulls off and lays carefully on the exposed meat, to be taken with the next bite. "State," he says. Blake nods. The State Department is susceptible to pressure, especially from a country which has a high-profile domestic constituency, Israel being one such country. The State Department is always screaming at Justice, accusing them of poisoning the diplomatic atmosphere. "And Justice is getting it from the AG's office." That too is expected. The attorney general, theoretically above the fray, is really the president's point man on domestic politics, and reins in the mid-level Bureau functionaries on sensitive issues.

And Blake knows all this is just for starters. The National Security Agency has objections—they've got listening posts in sensitive areas they don't want jeopardized. And then there's the Air Force—they love the Israelis, so they're upset.

Everyone assumes, too, a CIA connection somewhere in there with Ellis, but no one knows exactly where.

"We haven't even heard from AIPAC yet," Campbell says.

Blake runs the acronym through his vast collection, comes out with American Israel Public Affairs Committee.

"Give them a day," he replies.

Understood, then: Ellis is a battleground.

Blake sips thoughtfully from his seltzer. Campbell is playing a careful game in making Ellis so problematical. Is this a genuine and sincere warning, or professional jealousy? And if Ellis is going to be so perilous, why does everyone want a piece of the man, their pound of flesh?

"And this burns me, Matt. I'm only the shitass squad leader who arrested the SOB." Campbell drinks his beer.

"And Navy?" Blake's fingers touch the mustard crock lightly.

"They're not dumb, Matt. They put Ellis in quarantine."

Campbell's face, so fair with a flush of color on the cheek, is reddening.

"So what kind of access do I have?"

"Get it from your boy at Eastern."

Blake's fingers are still on the mustard crock. Blake understands the Irishman's anger: He thinks I did an end run around him, pulled a few strings to get in on Ellis. Blake remains very contained, bites into his sandwich discreetly, sips his seltzer. Let him think that, spread the word in the lower echelons of the New York field office; the perception of power is very often power itself.

Yet there are dangers here; espionage is very, very problematical. And he doesn't care to be linked so intimately with this Halpern kid.

Campbell has pushed back his chair and stands abruptly, his sandwich half finished, his glass dreg-dirty. He's a big fleshy man with red cheeks and an angry heart from a lifetime of too many beers and half-won battles.

"Navy wants to stick it to the Israelis on this," he tells Blake, who follows him through the maze of tables past the long, crowded steam table toward the door.

"And I'll tell you something, Matt. It's about time."

●

Formally, in a standard work arrangement, the assistant U.S. attorney calls the legal shots, shaping the investigation, while the agent works the field. The agent executes warrants, serves subpoenas, chases down witnesses, conducts interviews, and can easily become the AUSA's gofer. Not that Blake is overly sensitive, but he is sensitive enough: he has his professional standing to consider.

In practice, however, it's the agent who usually guides the attorney. Blake has a number of times taken an AUSA under his fatherly wings. There are many procedural pitfalls and personality traps out there, and the young men and women of the U.S. attorney's office have been known to stumble into them with alarming regularity. Especially common are the turf disputes of which Halpern's was but the latest.

A consideration is the case itself. Ellis is a genuine, few-and-far-between spy case. Everyone wants a piece of the action. The man's hot. Perhaps too hot.

Taking that into account, Blake doesn't like the neatness of the arrangement. Campbell rolled over and played dead, and that is not good, because Campbell's political instincts are the best, and if he wants out, or, rather, if he's not fighting to stay in, there's a reason.

Clearly, Ellis is more political than operational, and the case, should Blake come in on it, is going to put him on point.

He bends a paper clip into a triangle, and jabs the end of the wire into a small pine block. Then he reaches for the phone and dials Eastern District.

●

This very night a man passes through customs at Kennedy International without incident. He is an older man of retirement age, benign of expression, and his luggage is given the sort of cursory search that is allotted to those in the lowest category of risk.

Though his passport does not show it, his route has taken him through Frankfurt, where he has made contact with the operation manager's representative. His journey to the States has taken almost a week, and by the time he deplanes in New York he has become Albert Deere, age sixty-seven, a citizen of the United States, born in Poland, and a carpenter by trade—his age and nationality are true as stated. He is a master craftsman, having acquired his skills when, arriving in Palestine as a postwar refugee, he was assigned to work on the construction crew of a kibbutz in the shadow of the Golan. A large portion of his income is still derived from carpentry. He is here now on special assignment. Also, there is a renovation in a Brooklyn brownstone that will occupy him for the next two months, and he is looking forward to the work.

Deere is a pleasant-looking gentleman, very fair, his hair almost colorless. And there is a line to his mouth that makes him appear to be always smiling—a kind of pull to one side, perhaps due to a lazy set of nerves, perhaps merely the outward manifestation of a philosophical amusement.

In height he is average, though his slightly rounded back has the effect of compressing his physique. He possesses great strength, most of which resides in his shoulders and arms. His hands are especially strong, broad in the palm, rather short in the fingers, and covered with many brown liver spots. Passing through the crowded airport, he carries his two pieces of heavy luggage easily.

Outside the arrivals building Deere is approached by a young man who asks if he needs a taxi. No, thank you, replies Deere. He has his own transportation. In that case, responds the young man, whose name is David, perhaps they might share it.

Indeed, they might.

They cross over into the parking lot together, David leading them to a blue van. Deere gets into the passenger's side, and once David gets in and locks the doors, they are able to speak freely, in Hebrew. In a few minutes they are on the parkway, speeding west to Brooklyn.

# CHAPTER 9

H alpern, like a great many of the AUSAs, is a zealot, a quality Blake appreciates. Such pointed passion, and its aggressive expression, can be put to use. The question Blake now ponders, as he sits in the lawyer's office at 225 Cadman Plaza East in Downtown Brooklyn, is just how to do it.

The protocols of the interface are well established. The AUSAs deal with the line agents, the field people; deputy unit chiefs deal with their counterparts in the Bureau, the squad supervisors; full chiefs deal with ASACs—that's assistant special agent in charge—and so forth up the ladder. There is a discrepancy in rank here of which both Blake and the young lawyer are aware. If Halpern is on rung one, Blake's on four.

This morning Halpern is jacketless, his tight-knotted tie pulled down, shirtsleeves rolled to mid-forearm. His style is scholarly but casual, and he briefs Blake quickly and efficiently on the turf dispute. It's more or less in keeping with what Blake has heard from Murphy, which is that Eastern and Customs were outfoxed by Ricciardi and Navy. Campbell went with the winners. The wounds are still too fresh for the young lawyer not to express rancor and irritation, and Halpern throws out a few epithets casting aspersions on various agencies and personalities.

Blake, sympathetic, offers a few comments as to how these problems are not uncommon. Indeed, he is surprised they don't occur more often, given the vast areas of potential conflict. He has some fatherly, professional advice.

"You have to put it behind you." You'd be surprised how well that works out. "There's always another case."

Halpern appreciates this. Which brings them to Ellis.

Has Blake read this morning's *Times*?

No, he picks at it during the day.

Halpern unfolds the newspaper and passes it across the desk.

On the bottom left, an article, two columns wide, is boxed in black marker. A photograph of Ellis, three quarters profile, a couple of days growth of beard. The alleged spy. Ellis's wife arrested too. Blake comments that he was unaware the wife is pregnant. Yes, replies Halpern. Justice expects a negotiated plea. Blake reads between the lines. They caught the man red-handed and now he's going to spill his guts to save his hide. The wife as leverage. He turns to page eight, speed-reading. Various categories of top secret documents pertaining to electronic weaponry, etc. It's technical stuff, and Blake will save it for later.

"There's an interesting piece on the op-ed page," says Halpern.

Blake manipulates the pages over and back, halves it, skims. Written by one of the regulars, a conservative type, the article purports to give the inside scoop on the dealings and positionings and countermoves and recriminations the Ellis case has set off. Pressure on all fronts, just as Campbell has foretold. The writer gives only the barest outlines; his sources have sworn him to secrecy. Watch for further news or, if things go as they usually do in the world of espionage, chuckles the writer, watch for nothing more, the sign that a deal has been cut.

"This can be big," say Halpern.

Blake reworks the paper and passes it back to Halpern.

Okay, says Blake, uncrossing his legs, what he wants to talk about first is what Halpern has.

The attorney nods.

And second, what, if anything, they can do with it.

●

It very quickly becomes clear that Halpern has very little.

The deal, if you can call it that, excludes from Halpern's purview Ellis, Ellis's wife, and the half dozen men and women tentatively identified as Ellis's handlers and couriers and cutouts; it excludes, too, active participation in Ellis's interrogation.

"Do you have observer status?"

Halpern does not.

Blake pursues this, the lawyer answering in the negative to every question: he has no formal liaison, no jurisdictional prerogatives, no mechanism whereby he will be able to enjoy any of the fruits of the Ellis harvest, which promise to be bountiful in the extreme.

Blake produces a long silence, finishing it with the slightest shake of his head. It's apparent that Halpern, once again, has been outmaneuvered. He had thought himself clever and intelligent and knowing, but others less clever, less knowledgeable, are using him. They're going to run him around a little, let him think he's actually casing a lead, then shove him, gently or not, out the door.

Blake's heart sinks a little; he had hoped for something big.

"Have you ever taken an espionage case through?"

Halpern has not.

Blake, from his brief but bitter experience, speaks. "They're rare, very rare, and every one is sui generis. They're quagmires. A lot of jealousies, as you know." Halpern does indeed know, as his unblinking gaze indicates. "And in CI—counterintelligence—you've got a group of people who distrust everyone. Not just outsiders. Their own people. It's their mind-set. They are some of the most difficult, obnoxious, and uncooperative bastards you will ever meet." Blake's tone, his expression, effectively convey the frustrations and complexities he speaks of, and Halpern purses his lips. His eyes are narrowed, and he's watching Blake with a steady look. Blake suddenly feels ill at ease. Halpern has also made his inquiries—United States prosecutors have many powers—and knows Blake's professional past. He has been looked at like this before by his younger daughter, knows the thought behind the eyes: This older man has a dozen cautions, all reasons for doing nothing.

Undaunted by this silent criticism, Blake questions further: who has Halpern been working with at Immigration? What sources does he have into Navy? Who are his contacts at Justice? Blake writes down names, recognizes a few. The deal is that Halpern is supposed to go down to Washington and be briefed by Navy Intelligence on the Ellis interrogation, be given a few leads, set up an interface with NIS, the Naval Investigative Service.

That's a start, agrees Blake. When is this going to happen?

Halpern is waiting for the call. He has a couple of contacts that he is certain will produce.

They talk a little more, then Blake goes through some body language—sitting up on the edge of his seat, buttoning the middle button of his jacket preparatory to standing—indicating he is about to conclude their meeting.

"See what they have for you in Washington, and we'll take it from there."

Blake stands, as does Halpern. The lawyer is taller by half a head, the broadness of his shoulders contained by the compressive effect of the dark blue and green vertical pinstripes of his shirt. They shake hands. In the grasp of the young man's hand Blake feels a supplicating pressure, a touch of uncertainty. For all his bravado and pushiness, for all his eagerness for a big case, the attorney is frightened. Blake shares all of these feelings. The two of them, as part of Donnelly's grand and unknowable scheme, will be wary partners in pursuit of truth, justice, and the American way, and shall be working together for the foreseeable future. At the door, Blake pauses; he wants to leave Halpern with some bit of fatherly advice, some expression of encouragement. But Halpern's phone is ringing, and Blake leaves without a parting word, which is just as well, because he really has nothing positive to say.

Outside in the sticky air, Blake grabs a hot dog from a street vendor and eats it while sitting on a bench in front of the Federal Courthouse. He needs a contingency plan; either Ellis, or Halpern, must just be a little too hot to handle.

●

Twenty-five minutes later Blake is at his desk reading an article he has found on his blue, government-issue blotter. It is about the conflict between the Department of Justice on one hand, pertaining to Ellis, and the Department of State on the other. A note in Campbell's handwriting is clipped to the margin. *Read it, Matty, and weep.* The usual skulduggery. Upper levels of State and Justice dispute Navy's assertion that Ellis is part of a far-flung network of Israeli spies operating in the United States. Ellis, avers State, is a onetime aberration in the generally cordial and mutually respectful relationship enjoyed by the two countries. The article is underlined in red by Campbell in various places, notations jotted in the margins. No evidence, says Bureau headquarters in an unattributed quote, of spy network. *Bullshit,* Campbell has written. Midlevel careerists in State in unattributed remarks nevertheless deemed worthy of reportage are offering opinions contrary. The Israeli embassy through its PR group is protesting its country's innocence. A onetime rogue operation. The attorney general, straddling the fence nicely and keeping his testicles off the pickets, speaks of the great damage inflicted upon national security and that, though there is no indication of a systemic penetration of American intelligence by people such as Ellis, that last phrase in cryptic quotes, he, for one, intends not to comment further until all the evidence is sifted.

Blake's reluctance to engage on Ellis is, once again, counterweighted by his growing professional interest. These cases, he tells himself, are provocative. Everyone will soon be at each other's throats, and the Bureau, he on point, in the middle.

Navy has its spy, a prime catch, and is digging in for a long war of attrition. There is a vast pool of a certain kind of sentiment lying just beneath the upper echelons of State and Justice that Navy might tap into. The fleet has its allies, senators and reps on different commit-tees—Intelligence, Appropriations, Weapons. They have their people in the administration, and on the Joint Chiefs of Staff. NIS works hand in glove with NSA, grudgingly with the CIA. They all have hidden agendas and want to take Ellis all the way, wherever the hell that is. And against these forces are others, equally powerful, exerting a con-trary push.

Campbell had even said it: stick it to the Israelis. It's about time.

Maybe it is, but in Hoover's day no one got the Bureau to do someone else's dirty work.

A shadow has altered the light and Blake looks up. It's Spanakos, an agent Blake has been mentoring. He holds out a handful of forms.

"The overtime cards."

Spanakos has placed the sheet in front of him.

"Thanks, Ed."

Spanakos, nodding, walks away.

Blake gives himself a few seconds of inactivity, then picks up the phone and goes about trying to locate Campbell, who is nowhere to be found.

# CHAPTER 10

It is an informal Postoperation Assessment get-together, known as a POP ASS, and were minutes kept they would show that present in lower Manhattan, in a stuffy, windowless room on Monday, July 23, are Murphy, Blake, Campbell, Halpern, and Spanakos. There are no minutes because, by decree of higher authority, Ellis no longer exists—at least for these participants. One needs a theological cast of mind to appreciate the nuances here, and Blake, given his affinity for the conceptual, comes close.

Murphy opens with a brief statement as to purpose and scope, expresses hope that following this meeting they will know what the goddamn hell is going on.

They all have identical files, thick and somewhat sloppy, and those of Spanakos and Halpern are still slightly warm from the copier. The covers are tattooed with all manner of stamps at different angles, and signatures have been scrawled over the stamps. Though technically Campbell should lead, Murphy begins and walks them through a quick chronology. Blake has done his homework and knows the macro aspects, listens with half an ear as he tunes into the nuances. They begin with the Ellis bio. Personal history, education, family background. Marriage. Hired by Naval Intelligence—isn't that a contradiction in terms, throws in Spanakos; it's an old one but gets a few chuckles— history of espionage: three years of passing secrets to the Izzies—

"Four," says Spanakos.

"That we know of," agrees Murphy.

He nods to Campbell, who steps in and takes them through the last six months, gives them a rundown on the field aspects of Operation Keelhaul. It was all very standard: Personal surveillance, telephone surveillance, photographic surveillance. In Bureau jargon it comes out PERSUR, TELSUR, PHOSUR. Only Halpern takes notes. This displeases Murphy, and he casts a couple of looks down the lawyer's way. He wants nothing on paper; Blake was supposed to have told him.

Says Murphy, "I still don't have a handle on this."

There is a resettling and shifting of everyone in their chairs.

"I mean, what kind of dreamland are we in?"

"More a nightmare," says Halpern.

"The man has access to programming manuals for two integrated cee-cubed-eye systems—I'm on page four." Murphy waits while they find the place. Blake has familiarized himself with the terminology. C-cubed, I: Command-Control-Communications Intelligence. It's the latest plaything of the Joint Chiefs of Staff, a state-of-the-art computer component of the Worldwide Military Command and Control System, the famous WWMCCS acronym, spoken by those in the know as Wimmex. Wimmex cost something like fifteen to twenty billion dollars, the exact numbers unimportant, and that's just for start-up. Congressional oversight committees have been giving the military grief on Wimmex for years. The system undergoes breakdown about 70 percent of the time, what the technicians call abnormal terminations, or spontaneous dysfunction, which sounds, to Blake, like something an internist treats.

"On the JTIDS," Murphy goes on, "our boy fed the Izzies a total of one thousand sixty-three documents, three hundred and ten of those from the operations manual." Halpern is checking the index; the acronym stands for Joint Tactical Information Distribution System. This is another devilishly complex computer multilink setup for battlefield Tactical Asset Management, TAM. It's the Army's newest toy, and undergoes the dreaded and hideous spontaneous dysfunction approximately 85 percent of its on-line time.

"We read," continues Murphy, working himself into a state of righteous disbelief as he turns the pages, "how our boy brings these documents out, just walks them right out in broad daylight, first to his house, where in a large walk-in closet he photocopies them—they bought him a copier just for that—and then delivers them in broad daylight to the apartment of the girlfriend of the military attaché." She is to be known in the future as the Girlfriend.

"They let the bastard walk out with the entire store," Spanakos says.

"I can't believe it." Murphy looks around, his stare almost as potent as Campbell's, though, without the alcoholic overlay, not quite as glittering. It's not yet possible to say precisely what the object of his disbelief is: the gall and nerve of Ellis, or the sheer incompetence of Navy.

"And get this." Murphy is flipping pages. "A year into the operation Navy decides to take away Ellis's clearance. It's been reported that his behavior seems erratic, whatever the hell that means, you can wipe your ass the wrong way and Navy thinks you're crazy. Page sixteen. They flutter him, and he fails, and Navy files for rescission of clearance. He's a civilian so they have to due process him. Ellis goes formal, grieves, says his wife's being sick made him nervous and depressed, and NERP restores his clearance. For the benefit of our young attorney, that's Naval Emergency Review Panel."

"Thank you," replies Halpern. Blake has passed him a note: *Flutter = lie detector*. Halpern pens a check mark on the paper.

"Not only do they restore him," says Murphy, his disbelief now taking on sublime proportions, "but Navy agrees to elevate him to SC."

"Special compartmentalized," Blake says quickly and quietly into Halpern's ear.

"Now. Navy's been putting out the word," says Murphy, "that they knew Ellis was involved with the Izzies all along and that they were just feeding him."

"That's a standard way out of an embarrassment," offers Spanakos.

"Right. But who are they fooling?" Murphy looks around the table; no one here, his eyes insist. "Because if they were, they fed him prime cut gourmet stuff. And we're talking about a lot of feed. Frank, you saw the vault." Campbell has. "We're talking a small truckload of paper."

Campbell amends that to a big truckload.

They all shift again, uncross their legs, cross them back. Halpern is sitting well back in his chair, his long fingers interlaced on his lap, very unimpressed.

"Okay," Murphy nods, "we'll give them the benefit of the doubt and say they were just being stupid. But then I have another problem: how Ellis was run. On both ends." He moves his coffee to the side, because when he gets excited he has a tendency to knock things over. "The operation is Mickey Mouse. Per se. I don't have to tell you that our friends"—here he sneers, for the friendship, if that is what he must call it, between American intelligence and the Israelis, is a forced one— "are professional all the way." He recites the Mossad's areas of expertise: they cover well—as well as anyone, considering—their basic fieldcraft is good; their signal security, when they use electronics, is adequate; they're next to impossible to penetrate. "Their screening used to be the best. They don't get caught."

"Until now," says Spanakos. Grunts all around; they are proud of the Bureau.

"You're saying," Halpern puts in, impatient, wanting, Blake suspects, to make his presence felt, "the level of Ellis's operation was too low?"

"Exactly. For instance, Ellis's bagman is the military attaché. He's accredited. A legal. Fine. They use their legals, who doesn't, as desk officers. But the Girlfriend? Who the hell is she? We still don't know—maybe an amateur. And then their field security is nonexistent."

Murphy shakes his head. It's too something, he doesn't know exactly what. There's nothing per se about it. He's flipping pages, pauses.

"Okay. They use no cutouts; they have a couple of dead drops, which Navy knows about, ditto their safe houses; Ellis uses open lines to the embassy. On our end it's just as bad. He's going back and forth with piles of stuff and no one cares. It's sloppy and it's dumb. But they got away with it for over three years, so maybe it's not so dumb."

"Maybe we're dumber." This from Blake, deadpan.

No one says anything.

"So Ellis is raiding the icebox and no one knows. Okay. Then we're tipped off by an anonymous letter. A cut-and-paste job using a newspaper from San Francisco, the letter can't be traced. Very professional. It comes into Southern, which gives it to Frank, and Frank drops it on Navy. You don't look a gift horse in the mouth, but no one likes it. Someone else knows—who? So Ellis's trailed by Frank with Navy riding heavy shotgun, Southern's case. For a couple of stupid but understandable reasons," and here Murphy nods in Halpern's direction, "Eastern thinks it has jurisdiction."

Halpern looks at no one, defiantly.

"Now we're all going merrily along." Murphy flips a page, looks it up and down, goes back to the previous one. "Ellis cleans out Navy, we're tailing the boy, everyone's happy. Navy's got a spy on the line, they just have to reel him in but they're enjoying it so much they want to play him along. Then something funny happens." He's looking for the right place. "Give me a minute, I want to get the chronology right."

"Fourteen," says Blake, and they all turn the pages.

"Okay. June twenty-eighth. The attaché is recalled. He's out on a seven-thirty flight. His wife leaves on the eleven o'clock. The Girlfriend disappears and we learn subsequently that's she's been ex'd through Montreal that afternoon. Ellis's handler, whom we've identified on signal just a week earlier but never make visually, code name Dipper, is gone the next day. We know this, Frank, don't we, because we've been listening to Ellis for months and the man has no goddamn concept of security. He thinks he's a talk show host. Okay, everyone's out but Ellis. He knows nothing yet but he's beginning to get nervous." Murphy turns the pages, paraphrasing as he scans, and they all follow. "Then another funny thing happens."

Blake, having read this earlier, knows what Murphy means. You can't put your finger on it but you sense it, all of a sudden there's a different order of operation.

"It's like dusk and day," says Murphy. "Two days we tail him around as he makes phone calls and acts very neurotic. There are signs all over the place that the relatives have activated a secondary and that Ellis is going to be taken out."

Here Murphy pauses and looks to Campbell. "Frank. Your team identified what they thought was a call signal."

Campbell looks up.

"What the hell was it, Frank? A nursery rhyme?"

Campbell talks about it, briefly. From all the ionospheric garbage up there, NSA pulled down a series of what they thought were code sequences. The Irishman shakes his head. No one could make any sense of them. Everything was happening too fast.

"Okay." Murphy continues. "They want to take Ellis out. They almost did. But they made a wrong assumption, Frank, didn't they."

Not a question, so Campbell does not respond.

"His wife," says Blake with sudden insight.

Murphy snaps his fingers near his ear and with the same hand follows through in a fluid motion to form a gun whose index finger is leveled at Blake's chin.

"Right!"

"The Israelis screwed up on their psy-pro." The psychological profile. "His handler," says Murphy, "thought Ellis was ready to go, but he refused. His wife is sick, some kind of internal organ problem."

"Lupus."

The table turns to Blake. Halpern has an idea what lupus is, but the others don't, and Blake explains the disease.

"And they didn't know she was pregnant. He kept it secret, we don't know why."

No one has anything to offer on this, and Murphy goes on.

"So he stuck with her. We knew that." Murphy's face shows his pride. "The boys at Number Two read him right."

Number Two, the Bureau analytical division, where they churn out the psychological profiles, the linguistic analyses, the socioeconomic, educational, ethnic background profiles. They tagged Ellis. He wasn't going to leave his wife. They call it the love factor.

"She, incidentally," puts in Campbell, "is not Jewish."

Murphy is sipping from his cold coffee. "Maybe it's not so incidental, Frank, we don't know."

Blake doesn't know either, but his instincts tell him there is a pertinence here, a factor yet to be weighed. Number Two will work on it. Halpern is leaning away from the table and crossing his arms. There is more talk about Jews, a great deal of it subliminal, and Blake, in a constant readout on the attorney—who is managing to look self-consciously defiant and defensive at the same time—is feeling very slightly squirmy for him.

"Okay," says Murphy, "I said I had two problems with Ellis and the first problem, as I have been trying to show you gentlemen," with a nod in Halpern's direction, "is that nothing fits." Murphy has closed his file, checks his watch. "And the fit is poor on both ends. The operation doesn't make sense on its own terms."

As Murphy talks, Blake appreciates his mentor's nonintellectual yet highly refined embodiment of the Bureau gestalt: nothing but the facts. Here's a man on whom the years of training and in-service upgrading have taken hold. In the beginning was the act. Goethe said that. Blake smiles to himself; his scholastic recall surprises even himself. First there is the thought, then the word, finally the act. That was what a Bureau agent was trained to uncover, the act itself. And that is what, as a special agent of the FBI, Blake has spent his life examining: the deeds of men. One must learn to look through them, as lean Cassius did, as he himself has learned. Whereas in Murphy the Bureau has created the kind of middle manager it wants. They're a dying breed, the old Hooverites, for whom the new, young, managerial types coming in have a thinly disguised disdain. They think it beneath their dignity and education to be government cops.

Blake has missed Murphy's lead in, and picks him up in midsentence:

"—and Navy's team is still working on damage assessment, per se, but we know it's pretty bad. Navy's looped into the integrated Wimmex, so you can figure that out yourself."

Murphy pauses to allow them to do this, and by the expressions on their faces they realize the implications, and Murphy does not have to say in so many words that the Israelis have access to the United States armed forces computer network.

"Now we all know, I assume, what that means."

As Murphy goes on, Campbell grunts, and glares toward Halpern, who rearranges himself but keeps his arms over his chest.

"They've been swamped with immigrants. The refuseniks, the religiously oppressed. Russian moles are coming in covered as refugees. And they've just begun to operate. They're ripping them to threads." Murphy is showing his anger in his hands, which are pressed hard and open on the table. Digressing, he makes a reference to the CIA, the b. s. boys he calls them, blue sky in polite conversation. Like most of the Bureau, Murphy has no love for the Company, in particular their counterintelligence division led, until recently, by Dryden and his gang of four; the Israelis were his special account. His unspeakable love, for which, it is rumored, he gave up all. Murphy throws out an opinion that maybe the only thing that Carter did right was sacking the assholes. Meaning Dryden and his cohorts.

"I ask you this." Murphy prepares his question by shifting in the chair, butting in upon himself, so to speak. "Why do you think the comrades put in such major efforts to penetrate the Izzies? Why?"

Clearly rhetorical, the question hangs.

"Because whatever they get from us, the Russians get from them. They're penetrated up to here." He holds his hand in front of his nose. "But that's not the worst of it. Do you know what you can do once you get access?"

Another rhetorical question, again unanswered.

"You bug the programs. It's the latest thing in overt ops."

Murphy's pitch has risen; his expression shows his outrage at such perfidy.

"Viruses," says Blake. He's read about this recently. "You introduce viruses."

Murphy rewards him with a second snap of his fingers, another finger pointed at Blake's chin.

"Right! Computer germ warfare. Little bits of programs that act as infectious agents. It's like genetic matching," he explains, somewhat unsure but looking now to Blake for confirmation. He might have seen Blake's assessment results, knew his general knowledge scores. "Once you know the program you clone a small section of it that then fits into the larger program, locks on like a parasite. The viruses grow around the program and cause it to self-destruct." He shifts his attention from Blake and moves his eyes from left to right, lingering just a while on Campbell, longer on Spanakos, come to rest finally, accusingly, on Halpern. "Let's say your system is coded to launch on condition Red Alert, well, you have that virus waiting there to destroy the program upon the appearance of the alert, and it goes, like that! Do you know what that means?"

His question seems to go mostly to Halpern.

The lawyer sits in defiant silence.

They do know.

"And where do these viral penetrations come from? Where?"

As if they didn't know. From the Soviets, that's where.

The comrades have always been lousy in computer science, Murphy says, and have for a long time concentrated their collection efforts on American computer technology, which they acknowledge, albeit grudgingly, to be the world's most advanced and sophisticated. So first they tried to steal our computer secrets. The Bureau has had a lot of action there. But lately the Russians have wised up and decided that rather than join us, it's faster and cheaper to lick us. They have a new section in their Science and Technology Directorate, Murphy tells them. DI-17, devoted to computer subversion.

Murphy doesn't have to draw the pathway: Ellis to the Israelis to the goddamn KGB.

"I know," he says. "Glasnost. All lovey-dovey. It's fine and fucking dandy, but let me tell you, it's not going to last. They're going to have a coupe de ville there, and we're going to be in the fucking well."

He shakes his head. They are all silent.

This is a natural break point, and by common and unspoken assent the five of them close their files and push up from their chairs. It's eleven-fifteen. Murphy wants to check in with his desk. Halpern, who hasn't had a chance to talk with Blake, sends him a few eye signals, but Blake pretends not to see and goes with Campbell on a bathroom run, leaving the lawyer with Spanakos.

●

"Matt," says Campbell, his eyes holding that blue glare in his fair, flushing face, "the politics are going to kill you."

And if anyone should know, it's Campbell, who's had, in this Ellis case, a close brush with death, professionally speaking.

"You're going to have half the Senate on your ass," continues the Irishman. They are washing side by side in the men's room. "Justice,

AIPAC. This isn't like chasing down some stupid Russian attaché just to score a few cheap points. You're talking about pressure you've never seen before." Campbell's pink cheeks have an extra touch of color. "And part of the deal that Newcombe worked out is that Ellis stops here." Campbell's hand comes down sideways to chop the air between them. "The deal, Matt. Now, listen. If you think you can reopen the case, if you've got a friend in high places, I mean high, Matt, hell, go right ahead. But don't get suckered in by a two-bit dandy looking for a goddamn killing so he can go out riding high." Campbell's glare is magnificent. "You're going to meet this hotshot in court, Matt, and he's not going to be on your side. Tell me another."

Campbell's anger puts him on alert. The man's protesting too much. But putting motive aside, for the moment, Blake knows Campbell is correct. Already there has begun a behind-the-scenes countermovement on Ellis, a big PR push to reduce the man to an inconsequential footnote in the annals of American treason.

For instance, this morning in *The Washington Post,* State had planted an article about the new breed of spy, the man who betrays not for ideology but for profit. Psychological studies by CIA assessment teams reveal that money was the motive. One of those venalities that everyone understands. Ellis wanted to raise his standard of living. Very human, you see, and comforting, because then you don't have to worry about all the ineffable and unfathomable urges of the human spirit. No questions of higher loyalties, more compelling passions. Forget values, you simply offer a higher price.

Reading the article, Blake knew it was going to fool no one; it was merely a necessary exercise in damage control. Keep it simple and clean: it's only money. Ellis bought a twenty-seven-inch Sony with a built-in VCR and stereo speakers—they had a printout of his purchases for the last five years—and that's fine, a good citizen's dream. Selling out for a new car. He bought a Toyota. With a sunroof. He was partial to the Japanese.

AIPAC had its hand in this. And what the State Department was doing was reassuring the concerned parties that no one was going to start, to be blunt, a Jew hunt.

"The point," says Campbell, "is that no one really gives a shit what he took. It'll be outdated in a year."

Blake understands.

"Just watch your ass, Matt," Campbell advises, and they step out into the hall.

●

The rest of the meeting is taken up with logistics. Murphy puts forth the
outline of what he expects to happen: the continuation of the Ellis case
as per the various caveats and lines of authority that have or shall be put
forth from time to time. Campbell, though technically off Ellis, and
winding himself down in contemplation of griping out, will be on call
to Blake and Halpern; Spanakos will work with Blake as required. He,
Murphy, will ride sidekick to the operation, Donnelly being very nervous. Halpern, it is understood, will do the preliminary interfacing with
Naval Intelligence.

"You'll move on it, Matt, but slowly."

Murphy makes it clear that at some point, and he doesn't know
where or when that point will come into being, Donnelly is going to
want paper, and he's going to want it on the proper forms at the proper
time so that it may be processed and acknowledged and sent up the long
vertical climb for further acknowledgment and processing, ending at
the director's office in the holy temple in Washington, at SOG.

Seat of Government. That's the great, upper synaptic nerve center of
the Bureau. Blake knows the paper route from his auditing days. At a
lower point, at the second deputy director's level, the horizontal run
begins, and the forms are channeled to the comparable levels of other
services, Defense Intelligence and their subclients, State, Navy, CIA,
NSA. They in turn will acknowledge and process, consult internally
and externally, disseminate minutes and prepare memoranda, offer
advice and suggest alternatives and demand changes. All this will be
done in quadruplicate and in color. From State Blake will get pink
forms, from Navy blue, from Langley a strange green. NSA is pink too,
a shade darker, more ominous. These will be funneled into Donnelly,
signed off by Murphy, who will send them down in Bureau triplicate.
Blake will get the brownish copy. The forms will be covered with
stamps, block stamps, signature approval stamps, time stamps. Each
stamp will have a signature. Every form Blake receives requires him to
prepare and submit a sequence of additional forms and memos indicating acknowledgment, implementation, progress, and results, forwarded back to Murphy, who then processes them accordingly,
sending them up and across in a grand and continuing cycle of communication. Thus does headquarters know to the last dotted *i* and crossed
*t* what its field operation is up to at any given time. This is Hoover's
legacy. The man wanted to be able to answer any question from the

president or any senator or representative about any investigation at any time. That's the theory. In practice what has been achieved is a vast, ceaseless paper dance choreographed by fourth-level Bureau management in which the slightest misstep—a misplaced memo, a late report—is grounds for a letter of censure in an agent's file. Blake has five such letters, many agents have dozens.

Anatomically, Murphy is the synaptic coupling midway up the Bureau's spine, which puts the field agent, Blake imagines, somewhere down around the anus.

"By the book," Murphy repeats, casting his eye this time upon Halpern. United States assistant attorneys are known for their enthusiasms, the price of which is too often paid by the Bureau.

"Matty, I want to see a flowchart."

Blake nods. It's going to be the three Ps: Politics, Procedure, and Personality.

"And I don't want any ruffled feathers, Matt, so we're going to channel everything through CI, just to make them feel useful."

Blake nods again. The counterintelligence people are the prima donnas of the Bureau, and have been known to throw petulant fits now and then.

"On second thought," Murphy grins, "maybe we won't."

Blake does not comment; Donnelly has his reasons; he knows what he's doing, and, at the least, even if he doesn't, the man will cover him.

Now Blake raises a few items, which he and Halpern have agreed need to be addressed.

"We need a briefing, a good briefing, on Ellis."

"We can do that. When do you want it?"

"As soon as possible."

Murphy makes a note.

"Also, we want to see the Ellis tapes."

Murphy hesitates. This is moving too fast.

Blake has to push. He has a good notion of Donnelly's approach here, which is to throw out a line and then reel it in very slowly. The dust on Ellis hasn't settled, and the Bureau isn't sure which faction is going to win. As Donnelly's gatekeeper, Murphy has to convert this policy—it's called the "wa-wa"s, watching and waiting—into operational guidelines. Donnelly's primary responsibility will be to assure his masters in Washington that there is no danger of his field men subverting the delicate balance so skillfully engineered by Newcombe. The case must yield just enough so that everyone doesn't feel useless, and just a little more to cover themselves should something break. And Murphy has expense lines to worry about; even a holding operation has to come within budget.

"George," says Blake, "we have to see those tapes."

Halpern seconds this.

Murphy scowls.

Out of the corner of his eye, Blake sees Campbell nodding.

"Matt," says Murphy, "I'll see what I can do."

From Halpern there emanates silent disapproval, and when Blake looks his way the lawyer is doodling dark, small cubes on his yellow pad. His eyes glitter with suppressed anger. He is the odd man out, nothing personal of course, purely generic. Blake's protective empathies are being stirred. He doesn't want his AUSA maltreated; it is a dimunition of himself. But he knows the fears such a young, aggressive litigator can arouse. It will be up to him to rein in the prosecutor, for everyone's good. It's one of his natural talents, making peace. That was one of his strengths in his assessment, he believes. But perhaps it is sometimes a weakness, for conflict has its uses, does it not? One must at times take a stand, if only to draw a line, and the line he has to draw now is somewhere between Donnelly and Halpern, and then he has to decide on which side to stand.

Murphy is ready to go. Outside, the corridors are noisy. It is 11:55. They all stand.

"So, Matt," says Murphy, "you'll start the paper."

Blake will.

"Tom gives you his completely revocable go-ahead." Murphy thinks this is very funny and is barely able to suppress his grin.

Halpern grimaces.

We wish you the best of luck; may you fall on your face.

Murphy and Halpern shake hands, the lawyer's long arm reaching across the table. Campbell leaves with Murphy, which makes Blake wary. "Ed," says Blake, "we'll get together after lunch and crank this thing up."

Spanakos likes that, and leaves.

"Richard," says Blake, and the lawyer follows.

The corridor is full of agents breaking for lunch, the elevators are packed, and while Blake and Halpern wait for another car the Bureau's press officer comes through the swinging doors. He's a young agent with a mustache and a very pleasant manner. He's due at the U.S. Court House where in about ten minutes Ricciardi is to announce yet another indictment of an insider trader, and, incidentally, to heap praises upon Southern, and by extension, himself. The press officer has a file folder of releases. Halpern takes one. Blake watches his face. His mouth has an envious pull. There's so much glory in the air, all you have to do is pluck it out. Blake wants it for Halpern because the AUSA thinks it will give himself some happiness. And maybe it will. They walk through the maze of desks towards Blake's.

There he and Halpern devise their strategy vis-à-vis Navy. They talk about solidification of jurisdiction. Halpern has to work his end. There will be problems. Blake will do his part. They have to see what Navy has. And keep this in mind, cautions Blake: whatever it is you have, the CIA has, and more. And they are a goddamn political bunch of guys. Halpern looks at Blake with appreciative eyes and nods.

For his part, Blake has to be careful with Campbell. There is in his fellow agent an undertow of resentment. And Murphy was too—too what? Too something. Too disinterested, which portends just the opposite. What does he know about Ellis that he, Blake, has yet to learn?

Well; Blake prides himself on his research abilities. Whatever is there, he will soon uncover. And though he will keep his disengagement plan ready, he is prepared to begin to open an investigation. But unlike this young prosecutor, Blake will hold himself in abeyance. That, too, is part of his training. The containment of passion. Halpern is talking with animation. Navy's going to give him everything; he has a contact, an old classmate from college who went to Annapolis. Great, says Blake. The lawyer is excited; this is going to be a good case, an important case, the best case he's had. Blake takes notes, asks careful questions. He uses a fatherly, almost pedantic tone to suppress the young man's rising swell of excitement.

Soon, he implies, soon, my fine young litigator, but not yet. Not for me is this glorious rush of conviction. No, not quite yet.

# CHAPTER 11

---

MEMORANDUM OF UNDERSTANDING

To: T. Donnelly
From: New York Field Office
    Matthew Blake
Re: Meeting of 23 July

Present were Messrs. Murphy, Blake, Campbell, Spanakos, and Halpern. Review to date on matters informally discussed.

Parties agreed further consideration appropriate. To this end submissions for warrants TELSUR, PHOSUR will be pursued. Approval was indicated on tentative basis.

Further actions pursuant to evidentiary collection re Operation Nova were discussed and tentative approval was indicated.

Mention was made of other governmental entities whose interests in this matter appear to be congruent to Bureau's, and it was discussed and agreed that at a future point cooperation with these entities in the matter will be solicited. Further, it was suggested after some discussion that the interests of security and efficiency would be best met by confinement of these matters within the circle present at this meeting. Indications were offered that any deepening of involvement in this matter shall require increased administrative involvement pursuant to Bureau Op Proc and Federal guidelines as contained in pertinent Statutory and Regulatory materials.

It was agreed that further discussion, dates unspecified, shall be arranged.

The meeting ended with a brief summary of points above, and with a reminder that all appropriate and pertinent guidelines were to be strictly adhered to.

Respectfully submitted.
M. Blake

●

That afternoon, Blake leaves work early and trains out to Carle Place, where he meets his wife and their lawyer in the offices of the funding company. It is a forty-five minute session of reading and signing forms, initialing changes and crossouts, all very much in keeping with what Blake does in the course of his workday. There are no hitches, and after all the fees and taxes and the outstanding principle of the original mortgage have been deducted, the Blakes are left with a little over thirty-five thousand dollars. The check is presented to Blake who, after a scowling perusal, passes it to his wife. Their lawyer, who handles all their legal work—real estate, insurance, the will—suggests coffee, but Blake, mindful of the quickly building traffic on the Long Island Expressway—it is a little after five—declines.

When they arrive home it is almost six. The phone in the kitchen is ringing and echoes in the bedroom extension.

His wife picks up.

Blake turns halfway to the bathroom.

Her hand is over the mouthpiece. "A Richard Halpern."

Blake makes a face. He had given the lawyer the number of his basement office. He'll mix family and paperwork, but he doesn't care to have his wife and daughters overhear Bureau conversations. "Tell him to call downstairs." He picks up his briefcase and heads for the basement.

Half an hour later Blake returns to the upper world. His wife is at the kitchen table, going over numbers. He stands in back of her and leans over. There is a faint perfume rising from her neck and hair. The bottom line, after all the give and take and consolidations of loans and outstanding credit balances, tax deductions, etc., is that for the next fifteen years they have to come up with about two hundred and fifty dollars a month more, net. That translates into about six hundred dollars on gross, per month. It doesn't include the inevitable tuition increases for Maureen.

"We should be able to do it," his wife says.

"I imagine so."

"Matt, your phone."

He hears it too, a distant, burring call to duty, to which, by training, he must respond.

"My hotshot AUSA," says Blake as he heads for the basement door. "Richard Halpern. Remember the name. You're going to hear it a lot."

●

"This is nice."

Maureen is speaking. It is nine o'clock. Blake's wife and daughter are side by side on the settee holding a thick loose-leaf binder between them. Nearby on the floor a hassock fan is noisily whirling the humid air.

"This isn't bad, either," says Maureen.

"Too hard to read," says her mother after a pause.

Blake stands behind his women, bending to look at the sample invitations. His presence is barely acknowledged. His daughter smells of suntan oil and soap. Her neck above the collar of her green T-shirt is a band of raw, red skin.

"Have you been using sunblock?"

Maureen turns her face up. Her complexion is slightly mottled, freckles prominent. "Yes, Dad, I have."

"You have a very fair complexion and I don't want you getting skin cancer."

"Dad, I use sunblock."

"We have to choose them tonight." His wife is the rule maker. "The printer has to know by next Wednesday."

"What does Meg like?" Blake asks.

"This one." His wife lifts two pages.

"It's simple," he says, approving. "Dignified." The name of this style is *Arnold*.

"Ugh, Dad."

Maureen stands. She is almost as tall as her father, and she shakes herself loose. She is wearing baggy shorts, and the skin between the cuffs and her knees is the same angry color as her neck.

"You have got to use sunblock," he calls to her back, very piqued. His downstairs phone is ringing.

"My prosecutor," Blake says, and heads for the basement.

●

"How much will the invitations cost?"

"Three fifty."

"That's not bad." Blake is finishing his supper. Against all rules, he has a file open next to his plate.

"Each," says his wife.

He looks up from the page. "That's about eight hundred dollars, with postage."

They need two postages, one for the reply card. He does the math again. Eight hundred thirty.

He's not going to make a fuss.

They are silent as Blake cuts up a few lettuce leaves and forks them around in the dressing.

"I'm thinking," his wife says, "of doing the addresses in calligraphy."

He closes the file and puts his elbows on the table. "How expensive is it?"

Also a thorough researcher, his wife has called half a dozen calligraphers; the best price is from a place in Brooklyn. "They charge a dollar for the outside address, three lines, black script. And an extra twenty-five cents for the name on the inside envelope."

That's about two hundred and twenty-five dollars.

Blake pushes aside the supper plates. He thinks of the proceedings this afternoon at the funding company, the ledger with their household numbers, thinks of his assessment, for the results of which he is still waiting, and of his conversation, just a half hour earlier, with Halpern, in which the lawyer, eager and excited, had told him how he is setting up a meeting with Naval Intelligence.

Blake supposes it's a nice touch, and not really that expensive.

"We can afford it, Matt."

He supposes they can.

Her silence says, especially after you get your promotion.

●

Peering down into the glass showcase, the young woman reads the typed card:

> To occupy their time on long sea voyages,
> often sailors would carve or engrave sperm
> whale teeth, whalebone, or tortoise shells.
> These works became known as scrimshaw.

Next to her stands another woman.

"How interesting," says this woman.

She is referring to a long piece of bone on which a whale-hunting scene has been carved. It is old, dating from the early 1800s. The knife lines of the waves are blue, the whale green, angry at the harpoon embedded in its hump.

"The details are quite wonderful," says the young woman.

"But so expensive."

"Here are more reasonable pieces."

The two women smile at each other, change positions. Each studies the items beneath the glass, bone medallions with faces, a long bone with a naval battle.

After a while, the second woman looks up, and the young woman has gone.

●

"Are you meditating?"

He has stepped into Maureen's room to follow up on the issue of sunburn, and finds his daughter in a modified lotus on the bed. Her shorts are crotch-tight, her back very straight, and her eyelids, loosely closed, tremble the slightest when he enters. He directs his voice to her upturned face. He talks about her fair skin, the well-documented dangers of sunlight. Her eyes remain closed, but fluttering. In this light he sees how burned she really is, her cheeks a hectic red, nose shiny with burn, and he carries on at greater, authoritarian length than he knows is good. With her back so straight her breasts push out the dark green cotton of her polo to smooth, rounded mounds of flesh.

"So please," he concludes, "use sunblock. You don't want to have skin transplants on your lovely face."

Maureen gives the slightest of nods. He notes the quiver of her pale eyelids.

"Have you started reading *The Stranger*?"

"Yes."

Maureen's hands, palms up, open, rest lightly on her knees, her thumb and middle finger forming delicate circles.

"I read it in college."

She opens her eyes at last, moves her hands from her knees.

"I remember the opening sentence." He speaks slowly, surprised that it comes back. " 'My mother died today.' " Long pause. " 'Or maybe it was yesterday. I can't remember.' "

He feels a thrill. "Isn't that interesting?" He repeats it more fluently, impressed with the words and the strangeness of the sensibility they convey, and how they open the book so well, so ominously.

"And there's a murder."

"Dad." The singsong she gets in the single syllable warns him off. She doesn't want to know the plot.

"Well," he says. "So, sunscreen next time."

He leaves, closing the door.

Twenty minutes later, having finished his bathroom tour, Blake gets into bed where his wife is reading.

She shifts the book slightly so he can make out the cover. *The American Wedding, Modes and Manners.*

"This is much more modern than the etiquette book."

"I'm glad."

His low-key sarcasm draws a quick look from his wife.

"We do have to be modern," Blake continues. "I would like us to avoid bankruptcy, too, but that's not modern."

His wife returns to the book.

"The way it looks," he says, carefully, gently, "it's going to cost about twenty thousand."

"About twenty-five, Matt."

"Well," he says.

After a pause she says, "We need a camera."

He knows. He will work on it.

"There was something on the news, earlier, Matt. About Frank's spy."

"Yes?"

It's actually more about the spy's wife. "She's pregnant."

Blake knows.

And she's ill.

Blake knows that, too. "Lupus," he says. "That means wolf." He's looked it up. "It's when the body's own immune system turns against itself. It's rare, but more common in women, young women."

"They said she's pretty ill. The pregnancy complicates it."

"Did they say anything about Ellis?"

"The show was about women's diseases and they used his wife as an example."

"I see."

His wife returns to the book, he lapses into silence. He is tired. His day has been full of aggravation and negotiation. Halpern has called at least half a dozen times, wanting him in Washington for preliminary talks with Navy, pressing. And rumors of the assessment results have been filtering down; a couple of candidates did very well. So much for the H'MP ASS. Lucky Campbell, checking out, starting his own company, Security Consultants Corp., Frank Campbell, president. My turn will come, Blake thinks, to check out. His daughter's wedding has prompted this turn of thought, which he does not pursue, for checking out is not within the realm of his possibilities, given all his givens, or even of his desires, which one day he will itemize but for the time being he will just accept and continue working and coming home to his wife and daughters. Correction, daughter. Very soon it will just be his wife, for already Maureen is home only during the summer and long weekends and holidays. Growing up. Blake turns over and arranges the bedding in the way he likes. His wife is propped up, reading about processionals. From his daughter's room there comes music, not disturbing in the least. Out of the blue comes his question:

"Did Maureen break up with Jonathan?"

"I don't think so, Matt." His wife holds herself ready to say more, should he ask, but he does not.

Ah, she was crying! In her room, before he came in, his daughter was crying. That redness about her nose, the luminosity in the eyes he had thought excess sun, was life's anguish'd glow. He has an impulse to go to her now. But there's nothing to be done.

Before he sleeps he repeats to himself the opening lines of Camus's book. How strange to begin a book in that way. It set the tone so well, so economically. A man who can't remember when his mother died. Blake remembers nothing but that, that and the end of the novel. The hero has killed a man and has been tried and found guilty and is about to die. It was an interesting, if absurd, courtroom case. The circumstances around the crime were confused, and the prosecution's case, both in evidence and presentation, were not in keeping with modern notions of criminal justice. Had the defendant had a better lawyer— Halpern, for instance—he might have got off. Today he would have, though of course the point of the book was not the technicalities of procedure but the confusion of motive, fact, and act. Camus was very effective on that. The hero on the beach, cornered by the sunlight, driven by the heat. Blake remembers too, though vaguely, the last pages when the hero awaits his death. He argues, if Blake recalls correctly, with a priest, actually strikes the priest. And then in the quiet of the summer night, a night much like tonight, the hero comes to terms with his own insignificance, and prepares, most willingly, for death; accepts his givens, if you will.

And how am I, Blake, he asks himself, able to bring this to bear on my own life? On my daughter's unhappiness? On my professional limitations and financial constraints? On my wariness of young Halpern, eager and striving, who seeks to drag me into uncharted waters where I will surely drown, much as the hapless hero in Camus's strange book drowned in the hot, blinding sunlight? How, he wonders, shall he apply this to himself?

And then, turning in the dark, the rest of that quote, the one about arguments and rhetoric, comes to him. Out of the argument with others comes rhetoric—was it Yeats? Yes, it was, he had used it so many years ago in a paper on modern poets—but from the argument with oneself comes poetry.

"Matt, would you stop tossing."

Blake apologizes; he was unware he was.

He once had it, the poetry.

Maureen's music is still playing. He turns, bends his other knee and moves it into the mattress's middle, encounters his wife's elbow and withdraws a fraction. She shifts too, adding a murmur, giving him permission. As he falls asleep he thinks of Halpern, of the attorney's leaping excitement. Unlike that young man, he has made a prudent, if reluctant, peace with himself, and no longer hears the siren song of his own soul calling him to battle.

# CHAPTER 12

**B**lood, thinks Dr. Starfield as he lifts the goblet of rich dark liquid and sips, blood is the wine of life.

He nods to the sommelier, who is waiting, bottle in hand. "This is fine," he says, and the steward half fills the three other glasses and places the bottle uptilted in its pouring basket, bows slightly, and leaves.

The four men lift their glasses to the center of the table in silent toast.

"Very nice, indeed," says Dr. Carroll.

"A fine burgundy," agrees another. "An eighty-three. Yes."

The four men are in Cologne, the host city for this year's annual symposium of the Institute of Applied Genetics. They are dining at the Hotel Briedenbacher Hof, which, as the hotel's complimentary stationery states, is a member of an exclusive European club known as The Leading Hotels of the World.

The men are all "Herr Doktor," though not in the medical sense; rather, they are doctors of philosophy: chemists and biologists, engineers and physicists. In Europe, most emphatically in Germany, where the university system was developed and perfected, and where the hierarchy of degrees was brought into being and declared good, the title of doctor or professor was just below that of God, or kaiser.

Dr. Starfield, hosting this luncheon in the chandeliered dining room of the Hof, is founder and principal owner of BioGen, Inc. The man sitting opposite him, Dr. Carroll, is professor of applied microbiology at MIT, and consultant to a number of American pharmaceutical houses exploring areas of industrial applications; he is here to tap German expertise. To Starfield's left is a young systems engineer, a free-lance wunderkind currently under sole contract to Thermo-dyne, Inc., an R & D company working to produce organic micromeasurement devices—biometrics, in short—to be used in detecting physiological patterns and changes. Body signatures, in other words. Thermo-dyne is under contract to another company, US TacTel, which in turn is a proprietary of the National Security Agency's Department of Research and Development. The science of biometrics is itself a subdiscipline of microbiology, and concerns itself with the detection and measurement of minute quantums of organic material, at times a mere few molecules' worth, at distances that on the molecular level are analagous to the spaces between stars. To Dr. Starfield there are certain philosophical ramifications here that pique the imagination. His work satisfies on a number of levels, and he spends many long days in his laboratory in the hills of Judaea, glancing up now and then to gaze at the parched, rolling land, and at the goats of the bedouin herdsman, barely moving on the distant slopes, strung like dark pearls upon an invisible thread.

The fourth man, Dr. Raphael Slavin, sitting with his back to the window—a pity, considering the wonderful view of Cologne's cathedral that most of the other diners glance at now and then, taking in the marvel of its massive, yet elegant, gothic elements—is a patent lawyer. He represents, in Europe, Dr. Starfield's company, BioGen, in negotiations with various corporate, educational, or governmental entities.

The waiters appear and set forth plates. Sitting through a long morning of academic monographs has made the men restless, and they eat with zest. Dr. Starfield requests a second bottle of wine. Slavin has put out a cigarette case of fine gold filigree which remains closed upon the white linen. Upon closer observation, it is seen not to be a cigarette case at all, but a voice-activated transmitter that will carry the conversation to a tape recorder in the lawyer's briefcase under his chair. This will insure that all proprietary information that passes between the parties, and surely protected information will pass, as it must in open and free discussion, will not at some future date become the source of unpleasant litigation, a patent-infringement suit perhaps. Minutes of the luncheon will be distributed to the parties present, annotated as to protected material.

But now, chatting casually, the men eat. They all have ordered poached salmon, lemon sole; the food is delicately seasoned, the sauces light. Dr. Starfield remembers to dab at his beard; he must remind himself from time to time that he has one.

This morning, to the two hundred and fifty members of the institute and their guests, he had delivered his first paper, "Applications of Membrane Technology in the Mass Production of Monoclonal Antibodies." Matters simple in theory often prove impossible in practice—a petri dish is far different than a factory—and his paper discussed the various engineering difficulties, and his proposed solutions. Later this afternoon, after an Italian biomedical team offers its research on template technology, Dr. Starfield will speak again, this time on the uses of long-chain polymers in site-specific delivery of medications. He has pioneered the use of microcapsules, lipoidlike packages of biochemical therapies. In essence these are organic bullets, fatty projectiles capable of slipping through the infinitesimally tiny gaps in the cell walls of body tissue.

At times Dr. Starfield himself marvels at his own accomplishments. Truly, there seems to be almost nothing beyond the reach of man. In this case, microcapsules are of great interest to the medical community, for too often chemical therapies relying upon organic bases—antigens, for instance—cannot be delivered to the target site before being destroyed by body defenses. Medicinally loaded microcapsules, when wrapped in properly coded, lipoidal polymers, will be able to slip through the defending armies of the phages—those lurking beasties so mindless, so voracious, they cannot distinguish the good from the bad.

And it all comes down to blood. Life's cocktail, infinitely more complex than this very fine wine, itself composed of over two hundred distinct chemical entities. The elements of blood, as the men around the table know, may be differentiated into two broad groups. There are the cellular components, dozens upon dozens of all shapes and sizes and functions, some highly specialized, others more generically constituted. The vehicle in which these cells are carried, the fluid, is known as plasma, and is a liquid mix of protein strands, organic groupings polymerized into long chains. Hemotechnology, involving the separation of these blood components, their purification and analysis, then their synthesis and production on a large scale, is of great moment and profit.

The men speak of this, of artificial blood. The military is exceedingly interested. It is a theoretical possibility, though its successful engineering is still years away.

Indeed, it is almost impossible, but Dr. Starfield will do it, given time. With a little luck and some cunning, he will do it first. And that is why, when he speaks, his audience of fellow scientists listens raptly.

But he is here for another purpose, as well. In addition to the academics and scientists that frequent these symposia, the intelligence community makes its presence felt. They arrive under many covers and titles, as attachés from ambassadorial units, officers of proprietaries established by intelligence entities, thinly accredited journalists claiming scientific specialties. The connections are many and intricate.

For instance, the research director of Botsch, a German biomed consortium under contract to the NATO procurement division responsible for medical supply and stockpiling of battle medicines, has sent a brief note to Slavin suggesting a discussion of matters of mutual interest. The Swedes, too, are very much interested in research on blood disorders of cold climates; in the latitudes of the far north blood components undergo great wear and tear, skewing the metabolic process and leading to a variety of circulatory dysfunction. Dr. Starfield will meet later with the research director of Ångström-Norde to explore the possibility of collaboration.

Their entrees dispatched, the waiters set down plates of greens before each diner.

Dr. Starfield has been silent for most of the meal; he is a tall, thin, dark-haired man, very erect. Behind his tortoiseshell glasses his hazel eyes make unblinking contact with the men around the table. He has eaten little, drunk less. He is thinking of the paper he will present after the Italians. He looks forward to Dr. Piro's presentation; he and his team are always so ebullient. He eats his salad, its dressing reminiscent of raspberry, a hint of vinegar coming through on the tongue, quite good. His thoughts have little to do with blood and polymers. Slavin has spent the morning receiving numerous communications, and Starfield has many people to see, events to arrange. He wishes to be in his home in the Judaean hills where the light plays in eternal hope, where his wife waits in her cold, dark world, and where, when he stands very still in the quiet dusk of the desert, he can hear on the evening wind the laughter of his child.

He remembers to wipe his beard. The salad was delicious. He checks his watch and signals to his lawyer.

"We had better finish up here."

The waiter appears. The gentlemen will not have coffee.

Raphael Slavin's cigarette case is returned to his pocket.

"Come, we must go." They have about fifteen minutes. "We don't want to miss the Italians."

●

Though Blake flies frequently enough, every visit to an airport stirs his amateur architect's soul, so that now, passing through the double doors, he feels himself entering a brave new world of magic and purpose. The red carpet welcomes him, men and women in uniform move about with a determined, smiling efficiency. And how various are man's creations! The plate-glass wall of the corridor looks out on to the airport's staging area, and he counts three sleek, silver creatures at rest, fuel trucks administering intravenous feedings. Luggage wagons, coupled like a wooden train set, snake in and out under the wings in tight circles. Every once in a while a muffled roar fills the air, and the very building trembles; one senses the immense activity, the ceaseless movement of men and women and their obedient machines.

Sitting now in a molded plastic chair in the central passenger lounge at La Guardia, Blake has positioned himself to see takeoffs and landings. Incoming planes approach from the east, over Queens, their lights bright in the overcast evening sky. Outside, a spoke of the wheel-like terminal cuts off the sight lines so that he can't see the planes land, but is able to follow them until just before they touch down. Then he counts slowly to ten, and sees the plane rolling by to the left, looking for its gate. In contrary movement, the departures first taxi slowly to the right, then roar past in the opposite direction; he watches a small jet gathering speed until it disappears behind the control tower, then sees it in the air at a desperate forty-five degrees, banking hard to the right, engines trailing heavy smoke.

He glances at one of the many display videos up against the ceiling. No delays, the shuttle is due in in fifteen minutes. He studies his immediate surroundings. The lounge is sparsely peopled; some young people are sleeping, two children and their mother are playing in a corner where a little playground of bright plastic climbing and crawling devices has been set up.

With a great and continuing effort he keeps at bay all thoughts of the postassessment analysis he has just come from, but knows they hover out there, evil spirits waiting to bedevil him with conjecture and despair. In keeping with Bureau nomenclature, Ms. Collins, a management psychologist, called it a debriefing. She spoke very much to the point, cautioning him about second-guessing, but Blake cannot resist. He sees, now, how he might have insisted in the case exercise on constitutional limits, for instance, that the warrant application was tainted, but he had deferred, against his judgment, to one of the more overbearing members of his team, the guy with the little bald spot—enough, he tells himself. Ms. Collins said not to replay the assessment.

Ms. Collins was about thirty-five, very attractive, very obviously efficient, one of the latest up-and-coming types of young woman, intimidating, yet not without an almost provocative allure. Quickly and succinctly she had reviewed the five categories of management behavior the assessment was designed to measure, had explained the weighting process and the method of ranking. One to five, five being the highest.

Kind of like an extended college grading system, Blake had quipped.

Yes. And his cumulative score was a solid, if lower than expected, two point six.

Blake was immediately thrown into a depressed turmoil.

Not good enough. Not good enough at all.

Her look direct, Ms. Collins had waited for Blake's response.

"Kind of puts me right smack in the middle, doesn't it?" He was trying to sound chipper, but he heard his own despair.

"It does, and it's interesting you put it that way, so may we talk about what the assessment might be saying?"

And so they did. Ms. Collins had his score sheet in front of her. Blake scored exceptionally well in the Stanford-Binet—top 4 percent. It doesn't put him in the genius category, but then, he wouldn't want to be.

"Vocabulary and word analogy are excellent and you're very high in reading comprehension. Also, you scored high in the general knowledge section—the ninety-third percentile. I mean," she had said, leaning forward and clasping her hands over the page as Blake noted the absence of a wedding ring, "it's unusual to find someone so consistently high-scoring in these categories. You must read a lot."

Blake admitted he did, and quite eclectically, mentioning in passing a few of the recent books he'd finished.

"So you're quite a Renaissance man."

Though he had been cautioned by Campbell not to argue in the postassessment evaluation, Blake had not been able to resist. He had thought, he said, the situations as they had been presented were somewhat inaccurate, in terms of Bureau procedure. Ms. Collins granted that. "We try our best to duplicate a work situation, not necessarily in all the technical aspects, but in the feel of it." Blake had hastened to assure her that he thought a number of exercises—the In-Basket, the Weekly Triage, the Hostile Interview—were indeed quite good. But, if he may offer an observation, he has never seen a correlation between the speed of a decision and its correctness. Over the long run, in fact, based upon his personal experience, the correlation is nonexistent.

That indeed is a good point, admitted Ms. Collins. But what they have discovered in their years of research and analysis and testing, is that a leader does not care about accuracy, or correctness. He has probably discovered himself that very often one solution is as good as another.

He has.

So what they are looking for is the type of personality for which decision making comes easily.

He lost a great many points in the exercise that measured how well he thought on his feet, the Mock Battle Scenario.

Blake squirmed, remembering, felt his body heat rising.

Ms. Collins had waited for him to speak, but Blake was too busy controlling his anger, his rising despair. A good, solid middle score; but there would be others, younger and swifter and stronger, to whom the prizes would be given.

"I can only think of Alexander the Great." Ms. Collins had checked her watch, which she had put on the desk next to the phone. "Some people attempt to untie the knot, others cut it."

Blake knows the reference. The Gordian knot. He assumes the cutters are in demand these days.

"It's a question of," Ms. Collins said, and she had snapped her fingers three times in rapid sharp bursts, "of being willing to take the risk. To decide, right, wrong, or maybe, always keeping in mind," and she had looked with a firm, impersonal, unblinking gaze into Blake's eyes, "that the name of the game is to keep moving. At the level at which we are assessing we are not concerned so much with the correctness of a given course of action, but with the ability to reach a decision. There is a very clear-cut distinction here," Ms. Collins suggested.

"Certainly." Blake had smiled. "That would make General Custer about your top candidate, wouldn't it?"

A smile played about Ms. Collins's efficient mouth, and they went on to discuss Blake's test results in other areas: Once more the despair returned as he replayed the events in the motel's parking lot, the room. The situation had been taken from an actual Bureau case. Damn it, he could have been better prepared. During the exercise, indeed, for the entire H'MP ASS, a group of evaluators had been following them, taking notes. Each participant had his or her own evaluator. Blake spotted his, a short man with bifocals who, whenever Blake spoke, wrote furiously. All the assessees, Blake included, were sweating like pigs. In one exercise there had been an argument between two members of his team that had almost come to blows—about whether to make a PC arrest then and there, or wait for a warrant—which Blake mediated. And then he had gone and lost his temper, his professional poise, in the motel room. Those goddamn actors; they forced him into it!

Ms. Collins then had brought up his Job Satisfaction Quotient.

"Your responses indicate a certain ambivalence."

Ambivalence? Yes, he admits to that, but who would not, if pressed? He repeats it to himself now as he sits in the airport lounge waiting for Halpern's shuttle, and wonders why he allowed himself such a public display, especially to this young, sexy Ms. Collins whose single strand of pearls lay warmly against her V of pale, clear flesh—this is what he said, as best he remembers:

"You get up in the morning and you come in and do your job, and that job consists of dozens upon dozens of other little jobs. You fill out forms, make telephone calls, interview all sorts of people. You're deciding what has to be done first and what can wait, what can be ignored and who is going to help you and who won't. You try to arrange your day so it's a mix of the boring and the stimulating. You look forward to lunch."

He went on, his fluidity and completeness surprising himself. He noticed Ms. Collins glancing at her watch. He was sure he was overrunning his allotment. "Part of your job is perpetuating your job." He talked about the many ways in which you learn to either make work or cut corners, ways to aggrandize whatever you've done, at times to minimize it. You try to get the praise while making sure that someone less deserving doesn't. There isn't that much to go around. As he spoke he became aware that his tone had become aggrieved, that he was beginning to sound, as Ms. Collins had indicated, ambivalent, if not downright unhappy. Wishing to correct this impression, he had made a conscious effort to inject more enthusiasm in his voice. It was at this point that a tiny but penetrating buzzing sound was emitted from Ms. Collins's watch.

Blake stopped in midsentence. Ms. Collins silenced the watch with a touch and closed the folder.

If he had any particular questions about what they had talked about, he should certainly feel free to call. Or if there was anything in general he wanted to discuss.

They both stood.

"Have you ever had or considered therapy?"

No.

She handed him a business card. MS. DEBRA COLLINS. MANAGEMENT PSYCHOLOGIST. GROUP AND INDIVIDUAL CONSULTATIONS.

Her hand was out over the desk. Her wrist was thin, and carried a thick gold bracelet. Her handshake was cool and firm.

"Good luck, Mr. Blake."

●

Now he looks out into the gathering twilight. He has been watching the incoming planes, on the lookout for the Eastern logo, but has let his attention lapse. He's probably missed it. He twists around and checks the overhead display. Not yet; a ten-minute delay due to heavy incoming traffic.

Good; he's not feeling chipper, not his usual alert, engaging, finely tuned self, not ready to deal with the young lawyer, who had called yesterday wanting Blake to meet him in Washington where Naval Intelligence was going to brief him with all sorts of exciting and secret things. Blake had declined. Halpern had pushed; he had been with Navy all day and things were moving, Matt, moving. Nothing hard yet, but soon. Blake suggested a conference call but the lawyer wanted a face-to-face.

Blake checks the display. The shuttle is landing. Time to go to gate fourteen and meet Halpern, the Boy Wonder.

●

At nine o'clock that night Dr. Starfield is in his suite in the Hotel Briedenbacher Hof. He has finished his meal and placed the tray with its empty dishes and utensils outside his door. He has drawn the curtains and now sits at the desk in the anteroom. He is in shirtsleeves. In front of him is a portable computer; under the scattered papers is his prayer book, which he uses infrequently and at certain odd hours not in keeping with the prescribed times of devotion.

He is intent now upon the computer's display, reviewing the data of a feasibility study for the production of human growth hormone. His laboratory has achieved the fusion of certain cell elements of the pituitary gland, where growth hormone is produced, with a rapacious cancer cell of extremely rapid reproductive capacity. This fusion, or hybridoma, as it is called, is able to produce tremendous quantities of hormone, which in the world of the cell is measured in milligrams. Growth hormone is in low supply and high demand, and is therefore very expensive; the company that is able to patent a production technique capable of turning out this hormone in commercial quantities will become very rich indeed.

Dr. Starfield scrolls through the data of the engineering projection. He has determined that when the chemical mixtures are subject to certain colors of light—near the yellow of the visual spectrum—the production equation is shifted to the right, increasing the yield of hormone. The key to the process, which will take place in huge vats of organic soup, shall be separating the hormone from the slurry. The problem was akin to panning for gold specks in the ocean, except that the hybridoma treasure was, unlike the stable metal, highly perishable, potently toxic, and invisible to the human eye. Dr. Starfield's task will be to construct the chemical equivalent of vision: he will use a polymer membrane.

Studying the data, he is a very still, intent man. They must set up a cost study, run a pilot. He needs at least a year. He knows others are working on it. Growth hormone is a sure thing, though there are dangers in making it too available, dangers of abuse, medical dangers. Its therapy requires a very high degree of monitoring, absolute and strict controls on dosage. He sees arising a quasi-illegal distribution system, a black market, in the drug. He closes his eyes and rubs his face. He exits from the program, shuts off the machine. With a tiny ping the screen dies into a charcoal gray.

Dr. Starfield stands, restless. As always, the conference had run over, the papers longer than allowed, the questions incessant. The Italians had been their usual lively selves. Led by Dr. Giovanni Piro, their team consisted of five men in dark dapper suits, white on white shirts, elegant silk ties, very elegant shoes. The lecture hall was full, as it always is for the Italians, regardless of the material.

Dr. Piro was a small, agile Neapolitan with a fine voice. He was an accomplished if amateur tenor, and his delivery showed this. His English was accented but quite idiomatic. One sensed the man's relish in being on stage and producing, even in simple speech, those ringing, open vowels that are his countrymen's specialty. His pleasure was shared by the audience, which listened as much for the man's style as his content. At the conclusion of Piro's remarks he and his team were rewarded with a long burst of applause. The Italians in the audience bellowed a few bravos. Piro waved, bowed, held his notes in the air and bowed again, then walked off without taking questions. His team members engulfed him, congratulating him on the beauty of his presentation.

The phone rings.

It is Raphael Slavin.

They are coming up now.

Dr. Starfield replaces the receiver without a word.

Half a minute later there are two knocks on the door, a pause, a third.

Raphael Slavin stands with Piro and another man. They enter without speaking.

●

From where he stands, Blake can see Richard Halpern striding down the long corridor in a gray suit. In one hand he holds a valet bag, in the other a bulging briefcase. Blake waits, motionless. The lawyer walks with strength and purpose, a happy warrior invigorated with battle, bringing tales of his and Navy's exploits.

"Let's find a place to talk," says Halpern, not breaking his stride.

Blake falls in step beside him.

●

The third man is as tall as Starfield. He, like Piro, wears a shaped dark suit and fine tie, is elegant in that simple, Continental manner.

Introductions are made. As Piro sits off to the side, the two other men talk, Slavin sitting between, his cigarette case on the low coffee table.

Starfield first thanks the gentleman for coming; Dr. Piro had been kind enough to suggest he might be of assistance.

The man smiles very slightly and remains silent.

"My company is familiar with your product line," begins Starfield, "and we wish to contract with you for representation."

The man stiffens very slightly, seems to push back into his corner of the sofa. He stares at Dr. Starfield, then for a brief moment looks to Slavin, whose expression remains unchanged except for the slightest movement about the eyes, a lawyer's acknowledgment.

The man returns his look to Starfield. "As you must know, we do a great deal of business with our regular clients." His voice is deep, his English excellent, the slight accent lending a sophistication to the words. "But it is to the trade only. How shall I put it? Wholesale, as you might say."

"We are aware of that. I believe Signor Slavin will assure you of my bona fides."

The man again looks to Slavin, who dips his head slightly. Piro is watching the three of them, smoking a long, dark cigarette with fine hand motions.

"I believe you will find our references impeccable."

"I am sure of that." Else he would not be here. The man frowns. "But you have a closer source of supply, do you not? A special relationship with some other company?"

"My request," says Starfield after pondering this question a few moments and deciding to sidestep it, "is for your assistance in locating a few old assets that were at one point held in common. Discontinued models, so to speak."

"How old, may I ask?"

"Prewar. Thirty-five, forty years. Forty-five."

"Dr. Starfield." The man is smiling, shaking his head, pleased, seeing how easily such a request might be refused. "I'm afraid you will have to go elsewhere. We simply do not maintain inventory that far back." He shakes his head, the smile slowly fading. "What you want is simply not in stock."

Now it is Dr. Starfield's turn to smile. He, too, picks his words with deliberation, and says how from his experience he has learned that very often stock can usually be found on back shelves, forgotten, dusty and old, but serviceable. He is certain they have what he requires and, if not, perhaps they might put him in contact with one of their own suppliers.

The man sits contained and elegant, the lines of his face and his thick wavy hair giving him a striking, handsome air. Piro, exceedingly curious, watches this elaborate dance of words and looks and silences.

"May I ask?" the man begins.

"Certainly."

"How quickly do you wish to proceed in this matter?"

"Expeditiously."

"Who will take delivery?"

"We will make the necessary arrangements."

Slavin's motion off to the side draws the eyes of everyone. He gives the slightest inclination of his head.

"We have limitations on transport." The man's reluctance will not abate. "Liability, border tariffs. My company is reluctant to go outside its usual shipping lanes."

"I understand."

"Dr. Starfield, I must remain hesitant." He refers again to what he assumes is their other, more usual source of supply.

Dr. Starfield explains that the company they have dealt with in the past has been undergoing frequent and unexpected changes in management, so that its day-to-day operation has been subject to a great deal of confusion and inefficiency. For reasons that he is sure the gentleman will appreciate, it has been very difficult dealing with such a company.

"At the same time," Dr. Starfield says with a smile, "they don't like to see us take our business elsewhere."

"Of course."

"They're very possessive, and we don't wish to jeopardize that special relationship, as you put it, or whatever remains of it."

The gentleman understands, and in turn points out that he, too, has a special relationship with the very company in question, one which he hesitates to put at risk.

Slavin interjects. "Dr. Starfield understands your concerns. They will be taken into account. We simply are asking for your assistance in reestablishing a previous business relationship that has been dormant for some time. I am sure that Dr. Starfield will at some future time be pleased to reciprocate, should the occasion arise."

The gentleman's silence, his slight nod, now bespeaks acquiescence.

Dr. Starfield is standing. Piro rises, as does Slavin, followed by the tall, handsome gentleman.

Slavin now speaks in Italian, and he and the man have a rapid-fire exchange. Piro simply stares. The gentleman then turns to Starfield, shakes hands, and is led to the door by Slavin, who goes out with him.

Piro remains for a few minutes, smoking, until Slavin returns and takes him out.

Starfield is at the window, silent and contained, staring out into the night.

●

"This isn't enough."

Halpern keeps his eye on Blake, whose face has taken on the slightest of deliberate frowns.

"There's more coming." Halpern's voice is low, urgent with promise, with hope. "Newcombe is giving them a hard time, it's taking longer than they thought."

"It always does," responds Blake evenly.

Halpern's mouth tightens; Blake ignores the young man's impatience and continues reading. They are sitting in a dark corner of the airport bar. The votive candle in its cranberry red jar with nylon mesh dances in the cold air pouring from the overhead vent. Blake takes the candle from another table and puts it on the other side of the yellow pad. The light flickers over the boxes with dates and names, lines drawn from one box to another. On another page are more names, circled and linked to others; arrows and asterisks are sprinkled like comets and stars on a yellow sky. In the top right corner there is a box with a legend: red for American, blue for Israeli, asterisks of appropriate color indicating a known intelligence association. The waitress stands over them but they don't want anything to drink. On second thought, two coffees, which, once brought, sit untouched.

"It isn't enough, Richard. I can't open a case with this." Blake speaks matter of factly as he peruses the material with a detached yet interested air; the field man is intrigued while the administrator balks.

"Matt, it's the tip of the iceberg. They're having a lot of trouble getting data."

"I'm sure they are." Blake turns the pages of the pad while Halpern watches for signs of enthusiasm. But Blake, still reeling from his post-assessment meeting with the spritely Ms. Collins, will play his cards closely. The dark room, its emptiness, the cool air blowing over them, and the flicker of the candle over the paper create a tangible aura of conspiracy. Blake turns back one page, studies something on it, goes on to the next, lingers, comes back to the first. Here, he says, first moving the coffee mugs to one side, then revolving the pad so that it faces Halpern. On a red box, his finger follows a pencil line to the arrow indicating the next page, which he turns to.

"This man here, Ephraim Hirsh." He pronounces it with three syllables, a long *a* in the middle. Eff-ra-im. "What's his connection with Ellis?"

"That's his cover name. Ephraim." Halpern pronounces it correctly, Ef-rime. "No one's sure. Navy thinks he's working in some capacity for the Lekem."

"What's that?" Blake is behind in background reading.

"Lekem's affiliated with the Mossad. It's a new branch, science and technology." Navy's given Halpern a crash course on Israeli intelligence and he shovels it back at Blake. He barely knows the names and lines of power himself, but offers an outline of their organization: the Mossad conducts foreign operations; Aman is the military intelligence arm; Shin Bet performs the internal CI role. Lekem came into being only a few years ago as the result of a power play between Labor and Likud, the Israeli hard-liners. To Blake the names are vaguely familiar. They are difficult to pronounce, impossible to remember; he's got his research cut out for him.

Blake turns the pad right side up again, and studies it; Halpern puts a hand on the top page.

"This is just a very brief synopsis of the computer analysis Navy is running. I've got a lot of material here. They're using data bases from the NSA, the NEXIS group—"

NEXIS, what the hell is NEXIS? He remembers. North European something Intelligence Survey.

"How current are they?"

"Okay, that's where the delay is. They're about four or five months behind. They have to kind of work backward on this before they can go forward." There's a name for the process, which he can't remember. "CIA has some of it. Navy's waiting for an update based on some of the Ellis stuff."

Blake thinks: it's going to be a long wait, we're all going to be running in the same place, and it's going to get goddamn crowded.

Halpern continues. "They're doing a link analysis on Ellis—that's where they trace movements and time sequences and names."

"I know what a link analysis is, Richard."

Indeed, as part of his career plan, Blake had taken a number of courses on investigative analysis, and knows the format. A link analysis or, as it is sometimes called, an association analysis, gathers the data on a subject's criminal, business, and family associations. These are displayed, on a spread sheet, with full documentation. Conclusions are drawn as to the subject's role in an alleged conspiracy, and determinations are made on the merit of continuing, or expanding, the investigation to include other associates or activities. To Blake's skeptical intelligence, it all seemed rather self-serving and circular. But the attorney is waxing enthusiastic.

"Navy's working on a computer model of the Ellis case, and once they finish that they'll tie it in to their bases, and we'll be ready to roll."

If Blake had a dollar for every time he had heard that, or one of its many variations, he'd be a rich man. He pulls his mug toward him, sips. Cold.

"Just slow down a minute, here, Richard."

Halpern leans back, his mouth showing extreme impatience.

"What you have here is a lot of names and possible associations, and that's fine, that's a beginning."

The lawyer is about to speak, but Blake lifts a restraining, fatherly hand.

"We're a case outfit," Blake explains, "not a target outfit." It is important to know the difference, and to behave accordingly. "We solve crimes. Specific criminal acts. Or those that are about to occur. Names matter only when they're attached to events." Halpern's reaction to this recital of the Bureau's self-imposed limitations is to frown. He doesn't want to be told what is not possible.

"Navy is pretty sure about this, Matt."

Blake imagines they are. He's worked with computer people. Their magic word is *printout*. Like Moses and the Tablets. I have come from the mountain and here are the printouts. They used to be called charts. Association charts, strategic flowcharts, operational flowcharts. Time-movement charts. Now they're churned out with computers, reams of data in those heavy dot-matrix letters that look like they were stamped out by angry robots. In that course on analysis he had been given the basic, apocalyptic NSA tour, had been shod with the special static-free shoes, taken to the rooms with all the lights and the buttons. He has breathed in the cold, damp, dust-free air that the computers, a special kind of animal, require.

"The data bases are amazing," says Halpern. Navy had done a number on him.

"Is everything fine here?"

Startled, they look up. The waitress is standing in the half-light.

Yes, everything is just fine.

Blake and Halpern are silent until she returns to the bar.

"Who's your contact at Navy?"

"I'm working with a guy named Tippet, he's a data analyst in Counterintelligence. Robert Lee Tippet."

"How do you spell that?"

Halpern gives him the spelling, Blake writes it down. "What's his rank?"

Halpern doesn't know.

"How old is he?"

Halpern says, "In his twenties."

A lieutenant, most likely.

"Who's the case officer?"

Halpern is uncertain.

Blake decides to display some impatience of his own, and says to Halpern with a well-modulated snappishness: "Someone has to be in charge. A data analyst just doesn't decide to go off on his own and start analyzing. Someone, especially here, coming off of Ellis, someone—a case officer, whatever Navy calls him, a coordinator—has to organize the damn thing. Who is that?"

"Ryan. Jack Ryan."

Blake writes.

"What's his rank?"

"I don't know."

"You met him?"

"Yes. Briefly."

"Was he in uniform?"

"Yes."

"How many bars was he carrying?"

Halpern's face is blank.

"They have stripes on the sleeve and the shoulder."

"I don't remember." Halpern concentrates. "One bar, I think. There was a lot of gold."

No, that's a commodore's insignia, too high; Ryan's going to be at least a commander, thinks Blake, but not more than a captain.

"The insignia. Do you remember, was it a leaf or an eagle?"

But Halpern can offer only a shake of his head.

Blake desists. It's not that important, just easier for the trace. Blake tries his coffee again and it isn't any better; he drinks it anyway.

"Matt, on the link analysis, they think they have a prime suspect, someone in on the Ellis thing. Navy needs a little more time to catch up on the data. Tippet thinks maybe a week."

Halpern starts as a big pink hand comes between them.

"Pay the cashier, please, and have a nice night. Thank you."

Neither bothers to even glance at the check.

"They need just a little more time, Matt."

Blake senses in the young lawyer an undercurrent of extreme excitement. His voice, his eyes, show a surging exhilaration barely held in check.

"No, Matt, Navy's not giving up Ellis. Not yet." He pauses, picks up the check and turns it over, makes a show of looking at it, returns it facedown. Halpern is developing a dramatic line. This is his strong suit. He has a reputation as a litigator, full of presence, poised, working the silences. Blake sees how effective he might be, tall and good-looking and not afraid of the dramatic gesture, capable of a little stage business, too, like moving the check around, lining it up with the salt and pepper. He knows, too, how to spin out the long pause during which Blake finds himself waiting for the lawyer's next word. I'm his jury, and he's playing me, and well.

"There's been movement out there, Matt. I mean, in Europe. They're not certain on the Ellis connection—Newcombe's deal kind of closed it off, but Tippet is running a back search through the files. He's got an in with NSA, and they're going to give him the old data tapes. The signal stuff." Halpern has already reached into his briefcase and is producing another folder. He moves Blake's coffee mug out of the way, sweeps the edge of his hand over the table to clear crumbs that aren't there. The folder is placed very precisely between them.

"Tippet's come up with names, Matt. They're in the files. He's been cross-matching them."

Blake looks at the folder. It is the link analysis.

Halpern's hands rest on the file. Blake notes the lawyer's long fingers, the clean line of his cuticles, the trimmed moons of nail.

"Let me show you," says the attorney.

●

"Well, Phillip, we shall see what they can give us." Slavin pronounces the name with a slight French air, stretching the *i*'s higher. "A week, maybe two. I would have preferred dealing with the British."

Slavin's primary contacts are with the British and Germans; he hasn't dealt with Arrita, Italy's intelligence service, and isn't sure of their procedures. For Starfield's needs, however, the Germans have little to offer and the British—those insular, peculiar, moralistic people—though indeed having greater access to the American market, are not to be trusted. Their sense of fair play might be activated at the oddest moments, the latent bigotries of class and religion surfacing at the most inopportune times. Their prejudices, like their moralities, are a matter of national pride, a heritage they trot out to remind themselves of their kingly history. Starfield prefers the Italians. They understand the Möbius twist and turn of the Machiavellian dynamic.

In the window, against the night, Starfield sees the tall thin man with a beard, and next to him the image of Slavin.

"I gave him the names," says Slavin. "They mean nothing to him."

There were four names on the list, the work names of old men, men of folly and of evil, men harboring secrets and nursing grudges, men with hidden loves and odd allegiances who for their own private, noble, or twisted reasons might be of assistance to men such as he. They were old and frail, and feared being undone. He would have to gain their confidence, connive and coax, perhaps threaten.

He turns at the sound of the closing door. Slavin has left. He turns again, sees his image in the window, alone, and behind him the reflection of the finely appointed room.

He shall leave Germany early tomorrow, and now must sleep at least a few hours; but he remains standing.

This time of night is dangerous for him, for he finds his thoughts turn, like waking dreams, to another time. As he stands his wife appears beside him, from out of the very air. For a moment he resists her, pushes her away, for he knows she brings their child with her. He resists mightily, bringing forth instead thoughts of work, of vats of slurry and dancing molecules, sees himself holding a flask of organic soup up to the light, searching for the faint, pale blue shimmer of emergent life.

But he cannot hold her at bay. Now they both are before him, in the flesh. He may talk to them if he desires, even hold them. His child shall be there for him, for as long as he shall live, and perhaps beyond, for he stands not in a room of man-made things, nor in a world of finite space, but naked upon a strand before an endless sea of time. Upon his feet he feels the ebb and flow, the soft gurgle of the washing tide. He wades in slowly, his wife beside him as he carries their child, time now lapping his thighs. Perhaps one day soon it shall be possible to be together, immersed in this soft, lapping sea of eternity.

For do not his colleagues, the mathematicians and physicists, the poets and philosophers, play with such notions? He knows the theories, the extraordinary chicaneries, knows the many blackboard proofs demonstrating how time curls in upon itself. He himself has scrawled upon blackboards symbols and squiggles, the final zigzag proving it is indeed time itself that creates that which it contains.

But there is neither comfort nor joy in the equations; he does not believe the formulae. He will not put into words that which he believes. Belief is not even the correct word. Simply, she is there, his child, somewhere, living in another place, a near world, a different configuration—however one wishes to put it—and he shall be with her again in that day when time and world shall join in the terrible fire of the future opening, the inferno in whose unbearable blistering heat the forces of another creation shall work their powers.

And in my case, he asks himself, looking at the thin man in white shirt and black trousers who stands so still in the reflecting window, an ascetic-looking man with glasses and beard, a man of unique passion about to embark upon a dangerous mission, when this judgment comes at last, what shall my fate be?

●

Halpern says, "They have evidence that the Israelis are going to try to get Ellis out."

Blake nods. "That's not unusual. A trade is pretty standard. There's that minister they have in jail. A bishop." Blake had scored very high on general knowledge, and now can demonstrate its professional pertinence. "The Israelis caught him in Jerusalem. He was running guns for the PLO. I'm sure the State Department will cut a deal."

"They're not going to deal, Matt. Navy wants to take him all the way, to the max. The way they're talking down there they're not going to give him up, not even to the president. And they have plenty of support on this.''

Blake is confused. What's the lawyer's line here?

Halpern has at last opened the file, turns a page, taps a line.

''They've been tracking him for a month, starting about a week before they caught Ellis. Tippet pulled it out of a slush pile of NSA discards—they have stacks of intercepts, Matt, rooms of it.''

The lawyer's finger obscures the print.

Blake is very quiet. The waitress looks their way again.

''I know,'' says Halpern, leaning now very close, his finger tapping the paper between them. ''It's unbelievable.''

A prosecutor is like a preacher delivering a sermon; he begins with the presentation of facts, worldly facts, mixes them with a number of unspoken truths that the congregation has long accepted as god-given—these truths referred to casually, subliminally, during the course of the litigation—then, taking them all by surprise, taking them by the hand, offers to leap with them into the realm of faith: you shall believe.

''Navy's about six weeks behind him,'' says Halpern. ''Tippet needs more time, a few more days, maybe a week. They're waiting for CIA station reports from Germany and Belgium.''

Whatever Blake's face is registering, it's powerful, because Halpern's look is one of fulfillment and vindication, of triumph.

''It's unbelievable,'' the lawyer repeats.

And so it is! It is unbelievable what this young lawyer is about to suggest. Blake doesn't want to believe, but it's here, on paper, in the printouts, in the boxes and stars on the long, yellow legal pad. His field man's gut is reacting. And Halpern—this young, clever, triumphant prosecutor—knows how to work him. Halpern's espousal of its unbelievability turns the thing around, and demands of Blake the counterargument. It's a standard courtroom trick that all prosecutors use: unbelievable, but you'll find reasons to believe.

''Tippet's tapped in, Matt, and it's perfect for us—jurisdiction, profile—just perfect. It's preliminary, of course, but I'm going back to Navy on Monday and we can start then.''

Blake is at a loss for words.

''Matt, the Israelis. They're going to take out Ellis.''

Carried by his own rushing excitement, Halpern grabs him by the sleeve. Behind the prosecutor's handsome face the lights from the bar are bright, and he is edged with the keenness of youth, the hot gleam of eager strength. He holds Blake's arm, not to be denied. He wants to bring Blake with him into the world from which he has just come, the world of Tippet and the little, blinking lights, the world where all things are possible, and hard political realities are held at bay.

"Tippet's linked him. It's preliminary, but they know."

Blake cannot shake the attorney's hand from his arm.

"Starfield."

Halpern has turned the legal pad around again and has flipped to another page.

"They don't know where he is right now. Tippet's tracked him from Israel, across Europe, to Frankfurt and Cologne. They think he's putting together an operation. No one knows who he is—Navy's running him through the data bases."

Blake looks down at the pad.

"It's this man, Dr. Phillip Starfield."

Halpern's voice catches.

Blake's blood rises in a sympathetic rush.

"The Israelis are sending in Starfield to spring Ellis."

# PART II

# CHAPTER 13

**B**ut I am not beautiful, yes?"

She had said this to him years ago, when he had already learned the metathetic syntax of her English and the way she mixed it with Dutch grammar.

"You *are* beautiful, yes," he corrected.

She told him stories of her childhood in Holland, after the Germans came. There was no before, only the after.

Soldiers. They watched her and her brother walking toward them. They were very tall and big, how do you say, she showed with her hands. Bulky, he said. Rifles were on their shoulders and ugly things hung from their belts, from hooks and catches on their uniforms. They stood in our way. My brother: I will show his picture to you. He is my older, by four years. One of the soldiers had pimples. She remembers that. They speak to us in German and we must stop.

*Halt, bitte.*

They are always polite to the children.

The one without pimples unslung his rifle. He stared at the bag her brother carried. What do you call such a bag—a Ladensack. A shopping bag. Their aunt had given them food.

*Was hast du darin?*

Grown-ups on the sidewalk did not stop. The thin winter sun was low in the sky. It was the time of year it is now, January. It is very cold and damp in Holland then, cold and damp and the sun is very—she searched for the word—*fahl*. Pallid. The soldier came closer and low-ered his rifle and held it near her brother's head.

*Was hast du, Kind?*

Her brother held out the bag. The muzzle moved in, poking, search-ing. Both soldiers leaned forward. They were hungry, hoping for her-ring, or a Dutch delicacy, a pastry. The black metal of the muzzle was an animal's nose sniffing at the Ladensack.

*Ah. Kartoffeln.* Potatoes.

The soldiers shook their heads. They, too, had all the potatoes they wanted.

That's all we eat for months, potatoes. Sometimes bread.

*Geh.*

A quick flick of the rifle, the pale sun shining meekly, all the grown-ups hurrying past, not wanting to notice.

Go.

And they did, her brother walking very fast, she running to keep up with him. He was ten, she only six and much smaller.

She sat quietly, a young woman with her memories, in a restaurant high over the buildings of Manhattan amid the pleasant sounds of men and women who had never had a German soldier's black rifle six inches from their faces. When the Germans came their tanks rumbled and smoked. They smelled of petrol and shook the houses. Sometimes, when they turned, a house was tumbled down.

"I was not made to wear a star." Now, after dinner, because of his steadily deteriorating hearing in his right ear—nothing serious, really, and something he had had since adolescence—he had arranged his chair closer, and leaned inward, presenting the left side of his face. Her parents and brother, yes, they were taken the next year. The aunt, the one from whose house they were coming with the potatoes, she too. Her uncles. She was hidden with a family. Like Anne Frank? It wasn't that bad. We could go out and play. I looked very Aryan.

"And after the war?"

"After the war there was much confusion. There is not left many of my family. I was nine years old. The family I lived with let me stay."

"And your parents? your brother?"

"Two years ago at the Jerusalem conference I went to the computer desk. They are gone."

Outside, thousands of city windows shone in the night.

"Do you want coffee?"

"Yes. And maybe some dessert?"

The pastry wagon was brought to their table and they made their selections. She was, indeed, very Aryan. *Fahl.* Her skin was fair, with two large circles of color high on her cheeks, especially in the cold. Her nose was long and thin, her eyes a pale blue. She had been spared, and was allowed to play on the cobbles of Amsterdam with the other little Dutch girls and boys while her dark-haired older brother was taken away. That was long ago, a lifetime past, and now she was in New York in this expensive restaurant watching the waiter maneuver with two forks to get the raspberry torte onto her plate. They had met six months earlier at the Weitzman Institute. She was a research librarian. They had spent time together, then he had left. She had a two-week vacation and at his invitation had come to the States. They sat looking out at the sky, a deep winter black, talking of her childhood.

"After the war many Jewish organizations came to Holland and wanted to help us. In 1948 I went to Israel."

"You were happy to go?"

"I was frightened." The memory does not leave her. "I was twelve. There were other children, older women. I remember. We stayed for a while in a school building while papers were made out. It was like a camp. The family wanted me to stay, but I could not. They were paid to keep me. From the Germans I was given, how do you say, reparations. I remember." It was a long trip, with many stops to pick up others. The train, then the boat. The Mediterranean. "It was hot and sunny and that was good. When we came to Haifa they took the young men right away and gave them rifles and put them on buses and drove them away so they could fight the Arabs."

"That must have been very frightening."

"I remember how I thought I should have stayed with the family. I yet write to them. I would have been a little Dutch girl. Holland doesn't get into trouble. They mind their own business and if someone like the Germans come they do what they are told."

Yes; the grown-ups hurry by on the streets while German soldiers stop little children.

"Instead I was in Israel, where people were trying to kill us again. It was not good for me."

The waiter had come again, asking if he might pour more coffee. "Yes, please," said Hans, speaking in her soft, serious voice. He filled her delicate cup.

"On the boat there were doctors explaining what had happened and how we would be safe now. They put me on a kibbutz with other refugees. They had two psychiatrists there. They told me to talk about my family. They told me that no matter what happens, if you are alive, it is good. If you are alive, there is hope.''

''I think that's true. Life is what matters.''

''Does Madam wish for anything more?'' asked the waiter.

Neither Madam, nor he, had any wishes.

''The torte is very good.'' She pushed the plate toward him and with his fork he took a piece of it.

''You haven't been married?'' he asked.

She shook her head.

He asked why and she smiled, very seriously, and shook her head again.

''Do you want to marry?''

She had nothing to say to that.

His look rested on her long, fair, and graven face. Could she love someone and have children? he asked. Could she do that?

''Children,'' she repeated.

''Can you carry a child?''

She was very still, her eyes upon him.

''They're life,'' he said. ''After what has happened you have to have children.''

She looked up into his gentle, hazel eyes. ''You are a very nice man.''

# CHAPTER 14

**W**hat do you know about Tippet?"

Blake asks the question as he walks alongside Halpern on a street in Alexandria, Virginia, where the Office of Naval Intelligence, Analytical Division, has one of its hidden residences. They are here to receive, among other secret treasures, the Ellis briefing. Suited alike in gray, though the attorney's cut is more shapely, both with red ties, Blake and Halpern are indistinguishable from any of the other assorted government types on the street.

"Not that much," admits Halpern. They knew each other in college, then went separate ways until the lieutenant, out of the very blue, made contact with him. "He's good with analysis," adds Halpern. "Knows his computer. Motivated."

"Yes, motivated."

Halpern already sensed, during the drive from the airport, a sharper than usual edge to the older man. Maybe it's the weather. This is the third day of a Washington heat wave and the city is smothering under a bowl of fetid, inverted air. Maybe it's the traffic. He's come to know Blake, psyched him out, as it were, and without realizing it, has come to depend upon the fatherly agent's quality of subdued engagement, of forbearance in the face of the world's contumely, of the man's intense but delicate balance. Halpern had been taken aback by Blake's distemper as they had driven through the city, Blake losing his way, finally getting on the Beltway then driving one exit too far. Halpern had the road map open on his knees but Blake was too busy fending off the other drivers—road morons, he called them—and they got lost again. The car was an old Volare from the Bureau garage and needed a charge of freon. Blake parked three blocks from the Navy house, as much to get out of the steamy vehicle as for security purposes.

Nothing like a novitiate to sing the praises of a newfound religion, thinks Blake as they walk in the humid heat. The lawyer has brought him here to meet Lieutenant Tippet, and his captain, and for Blake to be welcomed into the Chapel of the Chip, and inducted into the Faith, as has Brother Halpern.

"Motivated," Blake repeats. "He's very motivated." They are walking beneath oak and sycamore, their shadows mixing with the mottled, muted light that falls upon the concrete sidewalks. He's already given Halpern a few morsels from his serial search of the lieutenant: Tippet is a staff analyst, Office of Naval Intelligence, counterintelligence. It's a second-level assignment, nothing very elegant.

Blake checks the house numbers. They're looking for 135.

"Next block." Halpern knows the building. "It's got dark green trim around the windows."

"Robert Lee Tippet," says Blake. "Southern boy." As one may infer, with a name like that. "Comes from a long line of Navy men, four generations back. The Tippets. Grandfather was an admiral. He's got an older brother, a captain. Operational Command, Pacific. The seventh fleet. Is that it?"

They are a few houses down from what was once a stately brick residence. Its trim—shutters, cornice, sashes—is a deep colonial green that is in tasteful contrast to the earthen red of the unpainted brick. The windows are curtained with impenetrable gray cloth.

"We go in on the side." Halpern points out the path leading to a heavy planting of bushes hiding a tall chain-link fence.

Blake stops in front of the building. He wants to play this out in proper fashion, for he, as does the young prosecutor, has an appreciation for the dramatic.

"Tippet's father was killed in action in 1973."

Halpern takes this in, nodding as he runs a quick memory check.

Blake repeats: killed, October 1973.

The lawyer draws a blank.

Blake is heading toward the wire fence. He wants to teach this young, impatient prosecutor a very important lesson, which is to always, always know your source. Informants have their hidden agendas. Truth, of a higher sort, is in the details. Blake is looking into the yard. Behind the fence, its opening pointing directly to where he stands, is a birdhouse. Showing in the entry hole is the glass eye of a camera. A second lesson of Blake's is to never underestimate a Bureau agent; we have powers. There is a low, short buzz and they may push on through the gate.

"Who, Matt?"

Blake is already at the knobless door. He presses the white plastic button in the brass flange that has been mortised rather nicely into the dark green wood of the jamb.

Halpern catches up. "Who, dammit, killed Tippet's father?"

"Not just Tippet's father," says Blake. "He and a couple of dozen other Navy men. Their ship was shot up in the Mediterranean."

"I give up, Matt. I don't know."

Blake looks up into the lawyer's face, compressed with impatience and irritation. Blake won't tell him. He wants Halpern going on record as having said it himself, so that later, when he mulls it over and wants to blame someone for being the messenger of ill tidings, he won't be able to point his finger at Blake as the man who stripped him of his innocence.

They are waiting at the door. Halpern is staring at the agent. Blake sees a gathering of knowledge.

"Matt."

But Blake will say nothing.

Halpern looks away, then turns back, pain in his eyes.

"The Israelis," says the lawyer.

Bingo, thinks Blake.

Halpern, still not believing it, says it again, to himself, but out loud. "The Israelis killed Tippet's father."

●

The door opens soundlessly, and a woman in a brown suit stands in front of them. She beckons them inward, logs them in on her master sheet. They each sign two forms. She has their temporary passes ready, tells them to wear them just above your waists on the right side at all times while in the building. Halpern fumbles with his tag. The woman has a Southern accent with the slight up-pitch at the end of each utterance, half a question and an introduction to her next. She walks them down a corridor. Blake has been in similar buildings and knows their construction: a gut demolition followed by a complete rehab, thus allowing for the installation of all manner of electronic and security devices. Here secrets are incubated and plots hatched in a womb of anechoic darkness. Blake hates these buildings, especially the claustrophobic elevator the woman has summoned.

"Third door to the right, C-3," she says.

The doors of the tiny elevator slide closed. Blake notes the camera pointing its lens at them. Though Halpern wants to talk, Blake is playing the game to its bitter end, and will not meet his eye.

The man opening the door marked C-3 is a young lieutenant. He wears a white shirt and blue tie. The room is small and tight and crisp, its lighting without subtlety or shadow. The desk is a computer station. His officer's jacket hangs in a corner on a rack, his hair is cut close in a modified crew, and his face has the exceedingly clean, smooth freshness with which the military academies send their commissioned officers out into the world.

"Lieutenant."

"Sir."

Tippet steps forward a fraction, and for a moment Blake thinks he is about to be saluted, but the lieutenant puts his hand out. It grasps Blake's with strength and precision.

On the desk are photographs. Another young man, the older brother, in Navy uniform. And an older man in portrait. Finally, a large color photograph of a ship.

*USS Freedom. October 1973.*

Blake reads the words in the lower border. *They Gave.*

Blake stares in Tippet's face. His eyes, he thinks, are those of a child, like Maureen's when she was a girl. Yes, they remind him of his daughter. They are bright and intelligent and full of wonder, a painful, incomprehensible wonder at a world capable of visiting upon this young soldier's innocent heart the evil of a father untimely slain.

The door opens again. From the trace Blake knows the man, though the officer standing there looks older than his forty-five years and, at the same time, younger. Again, it is in the eyes. His are no longer innocent, their unblinking depths two icy points of deep and weary knowledge. He wears his wings, and there are ribbons on his breast, little pins, too, for his kills, but Blake goes back to his face, taut and strong and full of muscle around the jaw.

Blake knows the type, these hard-boiled Navy bastards with the fierce heart of the combat pilot and a raptor's killer instinct.

Blake has done his research. This is Captain Jack Ryan, ex-naval aviator turned counterintelligence theorist. He's called the Racker, and though now bound to a desk by age and orders, he will hunt, forever, the skys.

●

The congregation on the Lower East Side of Manhattan is a paucity of old men, not more than thirty all told, if that many. This weekday morning the ranks of the observant are further thinned by the hot and sultry weather.

He takes a seat beneath the cantilevered balcony, off to the side in the cooler shadow. His arrival is greeted by a few turning heads, a nod here and there; the rabbi looks his way, then returns his attention to the prayer book. They had spoken, briefly, when he made his first appearance weeks ago. I am a visitor, he explained to the rabbi. I will be here for two months, perhaps longer. It is his custom to attend services when he travels; at home he is not a practitioner. He appeared after that, always in the morning, for three days, then was gone for a week, returned for two more days. Now, after almost two weeks of absence, is here yet again. He is in his customary place beneath the balcony, sitting in the half-light. It is not a rich congregation, and the synagogue is old and decaying and in need of a massive infusion of funds; he will leave a large donation before he returns home, in the autumn.

Murmuring the invocation, he holds the shawl in front of him and with a practiced movement lifts and swings the garment up and over his head, casting it in a wide flowing motion like that of a matador opening his cape, or perhaps like that of a fisherman casting a net upon the waters. It settles softly upon his head, this gentle, white woolen cloth with bold black lines and hanging fringes, a rough comfort.

Thus shrouded, when he wishes to look around he must turn his entire head. This is by design, for idle sensation is reduced to a minimum, causing one's attentions to go first to the prayers and then, as the chanting rhythms of the ancient Hebrew fill the senses, to turn inward and focus upon what is in the heart.

In front of him the men are scattered loosely in the first dozen pews. A few also wear their shawls. Standing before the ark and facing the congregation, the reader moves quickly through the text. A murmurous response flows from the men, aging voices raised here and there in momentary passion, now a cry of an old man that trails off like an echo of lost lament.

He has one bad ear and no sense of pitch, and the melody is attainable only in his mind's ear. The reader continues his chant, the rabbi now at his side, contributing a light, easy voice. The singing continues and soon he is adrift on the soft sea of Hebraic song. The men's voices rise like offerings into the light, the only gifts they have. The sunlight touches the top of his shawl. He feels the heat, senses the light. His line of vision cut by the hang of the cloth, he lets his eyes close and soon finds peace. Once, looking up, he sees the rabbi's glance shift toward him. He hears the shuffle of a man entering a pew behind, the soft swish of a prayer shawl. He does not turn. The presence behind remains, waiting but not impatient.

"Those in mourning will now rise."

They all stand, for they mourn without exception relatives of the first degree, and recite the mantra of the Kaddish. Once, in slow curiosity, he turns to the rear and gives a casual look to whoever entered a little while earlier. There is eye contact.

In the shadow of the garment the man's face holds the gentle, impish smile of Ephraim Hirsh.

# CHAPTER 15

If clothing makes the man then, as usual, we're the slobs in the middle, thinks Blake as he and Murphy take their armchairs at the center of the mahogany table. Pitchers of water and ashtrays—contrary to government directive—sit at intervals on the burnished wood. They are on the fourth floor of Justice in a tight rectangle of a room taken up almost entirely by the large table. There is a large blinded window on the narrow end, western exposure, and the midafternoon sun is streaming in.

This meeting is the culmination of two weeks of intense interservice maneuvering by Donnelly and Mullady. The two of them have been working, if not quite in synch, at least not in contrary purpose, trying to put together a package on the post-Ellis material. Given all the political divergences and possible exacerbations—not to mention Don Ricciardi's hot breath blowing on the exposed neck of Eastern District—Blake takes his seat with wary anticipation. Donnelly is not averse to bargaining with the devil, but Blake doesn't want his soul in forfeit.

He is able to spot the affiliations before recognizing the faces. He doesn't catch all the names and titles on the first go-round, but knows he's in a strange ad hoc grouping put together by someone with a sense of incongruity and humor.

Occupying the head of the table in first power position, and one of the dozen or so assistant attorney generals, is the always natty William Roach, Billy to his friends, Wild Bill to everyone else. He is the only man with an empty seat on either side. He is backlit from the window. As the senior civilian present, Roach—one of Donnelly's supporters—will take upon himself the role of formal chair.

To his right is Harold Talman of the Espionage Prosecution Unit, Department of Justice. Rumored to be one-eighth or some similarly fashionable fraction Indian, he looks it: dark eyes, dark hair, dark complexion. His secretaries call him Chief; the young prosecutors, Geronimo. He's a notch or two below Roach, and of no discernible political persuasion.

Both Chief Talman and Roach wear gray suits of slightly different plaid, nicely muted, and the obligatory red tie. Roach's glasses are gold rimmed, and the cuff links peeking from beneath his sleeves have little red stones in them, garnets, Blake thinks.

To the left of Roach, on the table's other turn, and very finely dressed in a pin-striped, blue three-piecer, sits James Newcombe, assistant U.S. attorney, formerly of Southern District and one of Ricciardi's fair-haired boys. He's strong of chin, uses a pocket watch out of his vest. Having done the preliminary dealing on Ellis, Newcombe is now in Washington in some unspecified capacity awaiting his reward. His deal, however, is coming under increasing attack from all quarters, and part of this meeting's purpose is to work out a cease-fire before, as Murphy has put it, the whole hellish thing blows up in our asses. It is Blake's considered opinion, reinforced with Campbell's glaring wisdom, that Navy would not mind such an explosion.

To Newcombe's left is Halpern. He and Blake have just come off separate lunches, having finished their background session with Tippet. The young lawyer's lean, handsome face is clouded as he ponders his newly acquired knowledge. Halpern and Blake have nodded at each other, and are now carefully avoiding eye contact; in meetings of this sort there must be no question of one's loyalty.

On the other end of the table, second power position, though facing the window and therefore having to deal with the afternoon light streaming through the blinds—a tactical disadvantage not entirely accidental—sits the Fleet.

There is much to be said for uniforms, that dark rich blue that to Blake's eye is really black, the gleaming contrast of the gold piping, the ribbons and ornaments and buttons and insignia. In the center, sitting as only a career officer knows how, is Commodore Houseman, aka Roughhouse, a ranking officer from the Counterintelligence Command, Naval Intelligence. The commodore, roughly the equivalent of Roach, is present in a political capacity. Though he does not yet know what he shall be receiving from Justice, it is assumed that he has been instructed to receive it gracefully, though not entirely without a fight.

Flanking Roughhouse sits the Racker, the district intelligence officer of the 3rd Naval District, which comprises New York and environs. He has been transferred to Washington to oversee the post-Ellis intrigue. The captain was the field coordinator on Operation Keelhaul, interfacing with Campbell—whose inexplicable absence today gives Blake considerable pause.

On Ryan's left, in compact and fierce silence, sits First Lieutenant Tippet.

Without visible strain, the three officers remain at high attention. Their head gear is on the table, and the two older officers keep their hands there, too, showing their cuff stripes. On the commodore's breast is a broad spread of fruit salad, attesting to the many administrative battles fought and won. The captain has more than his share of decorations and Blake, coupling his knowledge of Navy insignia and the bio of Ryan's career, knows that many are battle ribbons received during combat duty in Vietnam.

It was there that the captain received his moniker, the Racker. Blake has looked up the word *rack,* and it means many things, from the gait of a horse to a medieval instrument of torture. In the captain's case it is derived from the vernacular of weaponry: to rack the action is to feed a cartridge into the chamber, thus to be ready for attack. The Racker had been shot down, wounded, and during his convalescence had taken a turn to the intellectual, publishing for in-service use a number of pieces on algorithmic applications in case management. Blake intends at some future time to read them.

Across from Blake and Murphy, and completing the table, sit two men of no discernible attachment. One of them Roach, clearing his throat, introduces simply as David, "the man from across the street." This might mean any of a great number of things, but Blake suspects it means the intelligence arm of State. When introduced, he looks at no one in particular and nods into the air.

"And as for our other observer today," Roach teases, "well, we won't tell you too much about him except that he watches our backsides in Europe, somewhere. Paris, is it?"

"Would that it were."

The present subjunctive springs into Blake's head, though he doesn't even know if it's correct. The man's use of it, however, brands him

immediately as CIA. Just the way he sits, insouciant but alert, aristo-
cratic yet not without a polite air of interested amusement, projects that
aura of mastery Company men assiduously cultivate.

Murphy has slid a small notepad in front of Blake. *Station chief* is
written on the page. *Frankfurt.* Blake looks up at the nameless man,
then covers the paper with his hand and slowly tears it from its binding,
takes the second sheet to get the imprint, and crumples both into a tight
ball.

Blake glances down toward the Fleet, which is maintaining a deep
and hostile silence. There's no love lost between Navy and the CIA, all
the way back to the forties when the CIA grabbed obscene chunks of turf
from the other intelligence services, particularly Navy. The enmity
between the two agencies was eternal; but then, there's no love lost
between Navy and anyone.

Roach has already launched himself into his presentation: difficult
situation, as we know, no one wants to waste time by beating around
the bush, "and I don't mean George." Chuckles from his gallery of two
AUSAs, Newcombe and Halpern. "We're not here to affix blame, just
to fix."

And it's a quick fix that he wants.

Silence all around.

David, the man from State, has put out a manila file. The flap is
embossed with the Great Seal. The incoginito station chief has pushed
back his chair, crossed his legs, and interlaced his hands over the
knees.

A slight movement from Navy's end, and a grunt, causes everyone to
look that way.

Roach speaks. "Go right ahead, Commodore. Unless anyone objects."

Real men don't object, and Roughhouse lights up.

"Jim, a quick review, legal wise."

Newcombe launches into his set piece on Ellis. He speaks from memory, very succinct. His hands rest open on their palms on the table, his
only display of nervousness a little sideways movement now and then
with his elbows, up and down, like a chicken airing out its underfeath-
ers. This material is unnecessary, but Roach has his methods and wants
the prosecutor to establish a government line.

Blake listens with half an ear. Navy, maintaining a pre-engagement
silence, puts out a palpable disquietude. Commodore Roughhouse is
smoking heavily, a battleship building up steam. The advancing line of
sunlight is about to touch the brim of Tippet's hat.

"May I?" The man from State has waited for a pause in Newcombe's narrative.

"Please, Dave."

"Jim, I think we want to emphasize the long-term strategic aspects here."

Newcombe nods, Roach murmurs. Everyone either nods or, by their interested silence, agrees.

State continues. They are concerned that Ellis is in danger of becoming a loose cannon, with the potential to damage certain long-standing foreign entanglements. There is the fear that intelligence interests will override diplomatic ones, which will prove embarrassing to the president who, as everyone knows, does not take kindly to embarrassment.

He wants to elucidate, but Newcombe takes back the ball. "We have a number of considerations here, as you are all aware."

Blake, and everyone else, knows the primary consideration is the goddamn Navy.

As Newcombe speaks, the Fleet maintains its silence, its battle readiness increasing. Roach, feeling the effects of the hot sun on his back, is beginning to sweat; the air-conditioning needs revving up. Halpern now catches Blake's eye, gives him the slightest of deprecatory movements about his mouth: Newcombe is overrated.

"I must point out," Halpern's rival is saying, cruising along smoothly, "how little room there is for negotiation." He alludes to a certain generalized sensitivity among various concerned and/or interested parties, pertaining to the Ellis affair. As the architect for the agreement divvying up the spy, Newcombe explains his methodology of compromise: basically everyone gets a slice, one or two slices held in reserve. Of course, it is precisely those remaining slices that everyone wants, and they are going to be apportioned by Roach. In a dig at Navy, which is acknowledged by the hardening of the muscles around the Racker's jawbone, Newcombe alludes to the string of security breaches that have been occurring with depressing regularity over the last five years: the ghosts of Pelton, Walker, Whitman, and one or two others. He must have received orders to hit Navy. He is good, thinks Blake, admiring the way the prosecutor avoids hard specifics while pointing them all in the general direction. A man like this can be used by others, and will go far.

"So we've reached a dead end, haven't we?" This from Murphy; Blake doesn't know if he means Ellis or this meeting. Murphy, too, knows the uses of ambiguity.

Roach allows the talk to alternate between broad policy and case details, seemingly without direction, but it is actually a display of high art, for the bureaucracy recognizes no higher goal than an intense and energetic pursuit of the status quo. It is apparent to Blake, however, that Roach wants to entice Navy into battle by allowing Newcombe a couple of hard, if cheap, shots. But the officers are refusing to engage. They, too, have their strategic considerations, and so far have withheld their fire.

"Gentlemen." Roach silences the table. "We all agree, I believe, that Ellis is an unusually convoluted case. We are under a microscope here, and one thing we want to make sure of, gentlemen, is that we don't—all of us, singly and together—find ourselves between a rock and a hard place." No one disputes this.

"Ellis," says Roach, and his tone tells them he is now going to talk turkey, "is one big sweet pie, and anyone," he leans forward, directing his words to Commodore Roughhouse, then moving on to the Racker, whose steely glance does not waver as the sunlight creeps up to the second button of his dress blues, "anyone who wants a slice is going to pitch in and show their cooperation."

Navy stirs.

"I have a memorandum—" He unsnaps his attaché case and pulls out a sheaf of papers. "Jim, would you?"

Newcombe doesn't bother to take one for himself but passes down the papers. State takes one, glances at it, puts it carefully in front of him. The Frankfurt man shakes his head and refuses to touch it. Chief Talman comments on the heat in the room. Indeed, the sun is streaming in, and the Racker's eagle and Roughhouse's star are ablaze. They should close the blinds, but no one does; let Navy suffer. Commodore Roughhouse takes papers for himself and his officers.

Having softened up Navy with Justice's heavy fire, Roach stands, looks at his watch.

"Thank you, gentlemen. Hal will take over. I expect you guys to come up with something workable on this. Hal, thanks." He looks again at his watch. "Jim, we'll talk. Gentlemen." They all murmur. Roach is gone.

Blake scans the memo, looking for the all-important clauses delineating prerogatives, parceling out territory. Chief Talman mumbles on. It's a standard document demanding in careful language obeisance to higher authority and subjugation of the individual will for the collective good. It is truly wonderful to see how one hand of the bureaucracy can undo in a day what the other has achieved in a month; wonderful to watch the low functionaries sabotage the high policy people.

State turns to the Racker. "Captain. I believe the matter of custody and interrogation has been worked out between the concerned parties."

The Frankfurt man speaks.

"I'm sure, Commodore, Captain, you will find something of mutual benefit in the arrangement."

The Racker clears his throat. "Our concern is with the integrity of the case. We are taking into account the porosity factor."

"Of course."

The Racker continues. Navy's point is, precisely, their informed apprehension that the foreign intelligence service in question has achieved a penetration of their security net and that the porosity factor has risen exponentially.

They all run a consecutive translation of this. Blake understands it to mean that the Israelis have turned the CIA inside out.

There are interjections of surprise and demurral from State and Chief Talman.

The Racker restates his assertion.

The tension around the table has leapt a quantum.

Frankfurt rebuts. "Come now, Captain, I believe your concerns are overstated."

The Racker speaks, his lips in sunlight. Lieutenant Tippet, who has yet to utter a word, remains upright, his neckline showing just a touch of razor rash. Murphy, listening and taking notes, will take this all back to Donnelly.

For his part, Blake wants to see Navy score a few hits on the State Department, represented by this smug David fellow, and score, too, on the smiling, nameless, present subjunctive bastard, the station chief from Frankfurt. Not that Blake wants Navy to win; he wants some blood drawn on the other side, just to make it easier on the Bureau.

The scuttlebutt making the rounds, which Blake got from Campbell, is that Navy was using Ellis as unwitting bait for a sting on the Israelis, but then were stung themselves when they had to move prematurely on the spy. It's all very conjectural, but the assumption was that Navy was goosed by the CIA, who have always had a soft spot for the Izzies, even though the Carter purges of the late seventies were reported to have cleaned out that faction. But the secret part of the Company's heart that still loved God's Chosen had yet to be completely excised. And never will, Blake suspects. It was a pervasive, though minority, bias that appeared to be ineradicable; wherever there were Jews, there would be those who hated them, and those who loved.

Frankfurt speaks to the Racker. "We are aware, certainly, that the territorial imperative is very much part and parcel of the intelligence experience.''

Blake feels a sharp sting on his calf. It is a kick. He glances to his left. Murphy is rolling his eyes at the ceiling: the blue-sky boys are at it again.

"Indeed, that may be," replies the Racker. He raises himself in his chair a fraction, and fires off not so much a rebuttal, because there indeed is nothing to rebut, but a digressive salvo into intelligence theoretics.

Now the Racker and the Frankfurt man are fully engaged. Acronyms of sundry and esoteric subgroups and methodology designations fly about, only a few of which Blake can pick out of the air before, like tracer bullets, they vanish into the thick argot. Op-54, which is the Security division of Naval Operations, goes shooting by, followed by a rapid burst of USASAC, which by the first four letters has to do with United States Army Security something.

Chief Talman waits for an opportunity to break in. Murphy is absorbed in a doodle. The sun's angle is now low enough so that Navy is in blinding sunshine, but, trained to composure under fire, the three officers sit high and tight. The Racker speaks with passion. It's very esoteric stuff, and the captain and Frankfurt are enjoying themselves.

Suddenly, like a firefight at sea, the table has fallen silent. Chief Talman is now pulling from his briefcase a file, from which he distributes copies of a two-page Justice Department memo.

Eastern District to be given primary jurisdiction. New York field office to work in conjunction with. All protocols and command chains to be observed as usual and customary. Paperwork as required.

Blake glances at Halpern. The attorney's eye is bright. Murphy is pleased; Donnelly and Mullady came through. Newcombe and State are giving each other eye signals. Navy is a study in inscrutability.

Blake, glancing down, sees Murphy's drawing of a cartoon face. The mouth has been drawn like a sphincter, round and puckered. A word bubble is attached, and inside Murphy has penciled in what can only be turds.

The Frankfurt station chief looks at it upside down, then reaches out a hand and, without the trace of an expression, tears it from the pad and tucks it into his side pocket.

Blake looks toward the Racker and sees a tightening of the powerful jaw muscles in the officer's face. They stare at each other. In the Racker's look is the hard, unblinking stare of the man who has met his enemy and discovers, not surprisingly, that it is his friend.

●

The two men sit in the cargo area of the blue van, which is fitted out in cunning and efficient fashion as a traveling workshop. Shelves lining both sides hold boxes of fittings and hand tools; an ingenious collapsible ladder is secured against the wall. In the front, just behind the driver's seat, is an industrial vacuum cleaner. The floor of the van is carpeted, and the ceiling has been dropped a few inches, but very discreetly, so that only a scrupulous inspection would reveal a concealed space. The cargo area is sealed off with a sliding steel grate just behind the front seats. Hirsh squats on his heels, adjusting his back against the shelving, and is ready to talk; Starfield sits on an overturned milk carton.

"So," says Hirsh. "It has all been arranged." He means his cover as Albert Deere, his worldly assignment. He takes cigarettes from his shirt pocket and taps the pack against the front knuckle. "I will start next week."

"How long will it take?"

Hirsh lights, blows out smoke. He gives a little sideways motion of his head. "Fishel." He uses Starfield's Hebrew name. "This is a three-week job, at the most. Maybe I stretch it out to four, maybe five."

"Then stretch it out. All contractors do. Talk them into more work. Windows, the fireplace. There's plenty there."

Deere pulls on his cigarette. The van is full of smoke. "It can be done."

They are silent while Hirsh carefully stubs his cigarette against the wheel hub.

"We have spoken of support," says Starfield. "Are you in agreement?"

Hirsh makes that little sideways movement of his head. "We will see what we need."

"I'm concerned about continuity. That's always the weak point."

Hirsh does not dispute this. "Everything will be done the way it should be. Even better." He lights another cigarette, aims a jet of smoke at the ceiling vent.

"Fine. Who are you using?"

Hirsh tells him names, gives their experience, their affiliations. Starfield nods. Hirsh has his own pool of talent.

"Now, your rates. I understand: five hundred per diem, plus expenses. Assistants, extra. What do you charge for them?"

"Two hundred, two fifty. We will see."

"Let me suggest that if you can accommodate us, arrangement can be made to have the fee deposited in your foreign account. I assume you have such an account."

There is a little smile which says, who does not? Hirsh is squatting flat-footed, his backside just touching the wheel casing.

Outside there are many people walking, talking.

"You have made contact with Anserman?"

"We have spoken." Hirsh exhales.

"You know how far things have gone."

"I am waiting for his report. He expects very soon a tap."

"You'll handle that."

"We will see."

"Do you have any questions? Any problems you can anticipate?"

Hirsh stubs out his cigarette; he never takes more than half. "There is interest being shown."

"Yes. It was anticipated."

Hirsh says nothing, but his eyes are upon the other man, his mouth holding his little smile.

"Are you concerned?" asks Starfield.

"It is always good to know who is working. There are different styles. With the Bureau we are not worried."

Hirsh shifts his legs, one knee pointing up, the other down. The street outside is very noisy with traffic.

"The wife of Ellis," says Hirsh.

"Yes."

"She is Jewish?"

"No."

"Catholic?"

"No. Protestant. Presbyterian."

Hirsh does not comment.

"You'll work with Anserman. Nothing fancy, please. We'll do it along the lines of Bar Kochba."

Hirsh gives his little smile again; he is familiar with that operation, if only through the legend.

Hirsh makes his way up front and slides open the gate to the driver's seat. When the van stops Starfield makes moves to the front passenger seat. It never looks good for a man in a suit to come out of the rear of a commercial van. They sit in silence, waiting for a woman pushing a stroller to pass. Hirsh is tense, wanting him out.

"Shalom."

They shake hands.

"Shalom."

The van pulls away and quickly merges into the traffic, followed by a little red car.

Starfield looks around. A narrow tree-lined street, expensive brownstones. He turns to get his bearings; the distant towers of the World Trade Center help. As Hirsh said, it will be done. Dr. Starfield walks north. He has much work to do.

# CHAPTER 16

—————●—————

A case always begins with a biography and a chronology, a study of a man through time and place. In the files and printouts and traces are found the building blocks of a universe, the panoply of beings and their positions and magnitudes. You draw up a flow sheet, which lists the types of requests and the dates they went out and when they came back. You make a chart of your particular heaven. The data arrives in fits and spurts, and you enter it on the maps and charts, which soon become, what with erasures and overlaps, illegibly complex. You are forced to eliminate and redefine, as Blake is now doing in the quiet of his home basement.

Above him, throwing off his concentration, is the angry staccato of his daughter's feet on the kitchen floor, followed by his wife's sharp voice, which she uses when she is at patience's end. Maureen's response is muffled, but loud enough to force him to listen.

Priority, however, must be given to the reading material on his desk. Beneath the hinged-arm fluorescent desk lamp, open to page three, is a thirteen-page Special National Intelligence Estimate, "The Decline of Israeli Intelligence in the Wake of Labor Party Resurgence." This study was undertaken at the request of the president's national security adviser and came grudgingly out of the CIA's Office of Near Eastern Analysis. The names and places in the report are unfamiliar, their pronunciations difficult, rendered as they are from the Hebrew into phonetic English. Though he is still in the introductory background phase, he notices a distinct before and after: the old-line operatives had European and English names, the younger ones more Hebraic. The sounds are driving him crazy. Shlomo, Mordecai, Zipporah, and his all-time favorite, Chaim.

Directly overhead his daughter thumps the floor sharply, and his wife, unconsciously, thumps back. He has half a mind to shout up at them but refrains, and returns his attention to the report.

He reads that various hypotheses have been offered in explanation for the general decline in the quality of Israeli intelligence, first evident in 1973 when their intelligence community incorrectly estimated Egyptian operational capability in Sinai and Syrian capability in the Golan. Among these many hypotheses are the following: generational differences between current intelligence staffs and their predecessors; political interference by the Laborites; internecine feuding among the various intelligence entities as to scope of activities and budget; et cetera.

More thumping above. His wife's voice loud, very sharp, accusing his daughter, if Blake is hearing clearly, of being stubborn.

It is apparent that one cannot underestimate the intensity of the involvement, bordering on obsession, that American intelligence operatives had, first, during the war, with European Jewry, and then with the Israelis. The origins of this obsession were part ethnic, part historical, part necessity. There was the grudging fascination the world seemed to have for all matters Semitic. Blake himself had been prey to it. There was that nagging notion that perhaps this tiny band of peripatetic scholars and warriors and philosophers and merchants and writers and doctors and lawyers carried the fire of a living god, though whether the sacred trust was for their good or their pain has not yet to this day, in Blake's mind, been made clear.

During the war, Blake reads, a good number of refugees were recruited by American operatives searching for talent. They found their agents among the Jews. The OSS—Office of Strategic Services, precursor of the CIA—officers cashed in, so to speak, on the ability of that unique tribe to occupy both the middle and the high ground and to hold it against the endless onslaught of history. How adept they were in a world of hard choices, how they transmuted themselves through time and space, submerging and surfacing time and again.

Above, the women have returned to the table. Their chairs scrape quietly. Blake reads on.

And now, in the endless pages of the files before him, a name keeps reappearing. Dryden.

Leslie Thaddeus Dryden, the guiding light, or should one say the evil genius, of the CIA's Counterintelligence Division.

Dryden, a fallen angel.

A young Yale scholar, a lit major specializing in textual criticism, Dryden was recruited by the OSS in 1938. The war was, his biographers say, his salvation, his escape from a dead and dusty world of library subbasements. In keeping with his academic training, he was put in cryptology, but soon, finding a desk too confining, got himself transferred to operations. Operations was the fun stuff. You got to shoot pistols, learn how to kill people with your bare hands, jump out of airplanes.

The novice Americans were trained by the British. They were flown to England and given the basic crash courses. Codes, deception, cover theory, camera work; the standard craft. After training they were sent into Italy and France and Holland. The British, always with an eye to the future, kept the Balkans and Greece to themselves. And Arabia, of course. All that oil.

Dryden spent most of the war in Italy, setting up spy networks, working his way into Greece, and from there into Turkey. He was the man who delivered the Mediterranean, in terms of operational intelligence, to the allies. It was then called the Golden Arc, a stretch of parched land that circled eastward from Greece into Turkey, curved down through the lands of ancient Mesopotamia, and moved westward into what was then Palestine. There was a large pool of potential spies out there, and most of Dryden's agents were taken from the roving bands of itinerant European refugees, many of them the aforementioned Jews.

The niggers of Europe, of Russia, the skeletal remnants of the camps, the men and women and children fleeing the centuries of hate and brutality, now clamoring for admittance into the tiny patch of land that no one really wanted until *they* wanted it. The Land. Israel.

Dryden foresaw that after the war Turkey was to become one of the main corridors for the overland run by European Jewish refugees into Israel. Istanbul and Ankara became the choke points of this human flood. One of the undertakings of the newly formed CIA was to establish a network of agents and officers that would monitor, and eventually direct, some of this traffic. Dryden's contacts in Italy, and with the Jewish wartime underground of Europe, were put to good use.

The British were not pleased.

His Majesty's Government, pressured by the many Arabists in their ranks and by the various shiekdoms whose anti-German stance had been purchased with bankrupting payments of pounds sterling and with even more lavish promises of future favor, turned their attention to fulfilling their secretly given undertaking to suppress Jewish immigration. With their holy regard for civilized behavior and the honoring of commitments, no matter how foul, the British did their best to appease the Arabs: limiting Jewish entry through clever interpretations of international protocols; banning the importation of all weaponry, though knowing well that the Arabs were well armed, often by the British themselves; refusing all property transfers from Arab to Jew, and in general favoring anti-Jewish groupings administratively, politically, legally, and financially. Reading all of this now, in the quiet of his basement, Blake sees how Britain had failed to comprehend that neither time nor tide was on its side.

Dryden and his British contacts had a falling out. They accused him of having picked up bad habits from the Italians. But Dryden, one of the charter members of the CIA, understood the flow of events and decided that the loss of British respect had more benefits than harm. He had formed relationships with the Jewish refugees who were later to become the leaders of the new Israeli state. He was an intimate of Begin and Shamir, helped train the Palmach, supplied them with weapons, brought in his own teams of instructors, taught them the art of the commando.

And then, because things were so loose and fluid in the postwar period, and because this new entity called the CIA simply had no idea what it was, or what it was supposed to do, Dryden was able to help himself to a big chunk of territory with the Company: he brought into being the Division of Research and Analysis. Given his background, it soon acquired a strong academic orientation. Business was conducted along the lines of a literary symposium. Dryden organized the staff in such a way as to put himself not so much at its head as at its nucleus, around whom all the agents and officers found themselves in orbit. He was the theorist par excellence.

Blake, listening with an attentive ear to his wife and daughter above, and hearing nothing, pauses in thought.

It seems to him, in hindsight, that Dryden had a very hidden agenda. He was a natural choice for the head of Counterintelligence. With his extensive contacts both domestically and internationally, he could consult directly with foreign intelligence services. He also demanded and got for CI an operational charter. Blake understands the implications of this autonomy. Instead of, for instance, having to go to the FBI for the field work—as, for instance, U.S. attorneys called on Bureau agents—

Dryden could do everything in-house. Surveillance, taps, interviews, break-ins, everything. In short, he answered only to himself.

It meant much more than anyone knew at the time. Dryden used his charter to send his own officers into the files of other divisions, to, in effect, raid their records. He had the power to recruit and hire his own officers, to task and target. He insisted upon and received exclusive vetting rights on all new recruits throughout the CIA. He conducted periodic and unannounced security checks on the other divisions, keeping them on their toes and under his thumb. He got budgetary powers for his counterintelligence division, thus avoiding the harsh infighting that so plagued the other security agencies.

Almost as an afterthought, and because it seemed so natural, given his contacts and the wartime networks he had put together, he was allowed to appoint himself the sole and exclusive liaison for CIA interests in the Near East.

It was soon to be called the Israeli Account. Dryden became the account executive. Indeed, he and his people had already played an important role, as Blake has read, in the formation of the Mossad. Philosophy, methodology, organization, theory—all had to be developed and implemented by the fledgling Jewish state.

He worked well with the Israelis. In Congress and in the other intelligence services there were those who suspected Dryden of certain affections and biases. But Dryden, a pure-bred Episcopalian of undisputed patriotism, paid no heed to the whispers that he was, putting it as kindly as possible, a Semitophile. Rumors, a few of which Blake has heard in the course of his career, circulated of vague Hebraic ancestry, that his mistress was Jewish, that he had in some manner been captured by these people, or blackmailed as the result of a particularly heinous, hidden crime.

At any rate, the man stayed in power for close to thirty years, until Carter purged the ranks of the counterintelligence division.

Blake rubs his eyes. Upstairs the silence is gratifying, yet in its own way a goad, for now he must contend with the files before him.

And now he sees clearly that there is more at stake here than another investigation and a possible prosecution and conviction.

It's not like being a squad supervisor or a section chief, checking the number-three cards, knowing where your agents are, signing them up for in-service courses, and making sure they get their firearms training. At the level to which he now aspires, the action is more political, more—and here he struggles to put it as precisely as his tiredness and irritation permit—more poetical. The three Ms, as Donnelly has said.

Maneuver, Manipulation, Make-do. You never really win victories so much as stave off defeat. Problematical, was the word. Even Donnelly, a man of great savvy, one of the old-time infighters, had his reservations about Ellis, and after high consultation and with some reluctance had given Blake his deniable go-ahead on Starfield. With the usual, implicit caveat. Cover our asses, Matty.

He sees what Donnelly has done: given him a test case.

For Starfield is precisely the sort of conundrum that Blake, if he were to be promoted, would have to deal with.

Blake's put himself in the middle, and he's got to hold both ends together. Halpern and his computer buddy, the young Tippet, had made their pitch. The lieutenant had sat at the console, logging on while pressing a scrambler key that covered his entry code with dark red squares. Eight elements, counted Blake. Another screen prompt requested his security level, and Tippet had typed in EAGLE, BLUE, hit the enter key, and zip zap, the screen had burst into a bright yellow triangle with the logo of the Naval Intelligence Command displayed in darker ocher. The computer room was very cool and low lit, antistatic pads on the floor, the hum of cleansing machines and humidifying devices coming from behind the wall panels.

Admittedly, the data had been compelling. Travel patterns, associations, contacts with various men and women entered on watch lists as possible agents. The classic link analysis. Halpern had looked on in approval, murmured at every hit. Tippet, full of a quiet, intense dignity, tapped out commands, making the screen come alive.

On the face of it, yes, Starfield is their man.

And on the face of it, he cannot possibly be.

There was so much that Tippet had, and yet so little.

It is a good case, a once in a lifetime, genuine spy case, a career-making case.

And one that, if Hoover were alive, would be avoided like the plague.

But Donnelly wants to see him in action. He's been H'MP ASSed, and found lacking, and he's being given another chance. That's the name of the game, action. Dad, Maureen might say, you got to go with the flow, hang loose, play it as it lays. Hearing the gentle murmur of voices above, he smiles to himself for the first time in hours. His wife and daughter are at peace.

●

His wife is outside, in the warm summer night, sitting in one of the chaise lounges. She turns as he slides open the patio door. Blake stops at the edge of the blue stone and looks out upon his neighbors' yards.

The night is quiet and all the backyards are dark except next door where a bug light shines forth with a garish, buzzing ultraviolet blue. It can't possibly be healthy. On the far side of the darkness another such light is piercing their rosebush. Blake looks away from its glare.

He speaks, says he will try to get a camera this week.

Good, his wife has a list for him.

They're both big on research.

"I'm working a case with Navy. I should tell you about this young officer, Tippet." He stands on the edge of the flagstone and speaks into the night. "His father was killed in 1973. Not just him, but others. Twenty-two, to be exact. He wants revenge. Maybe more."

You keep the memory alive, is what he means by more. The hate, when it's the only thing you have. "He was twelve, or thirteen. I suppose a hard time to lose your father. Adolescent adoration and all that."

He turns now and moves back into the light, stands above his wife, speaks.

It happened in 1973, October. The Yom Kippur War, history calls it. His wife remembers; the Egyptians attacked that day, very early in the morning on the Day of Atonement. The Israelis didn't expect it. He digresses for background: the Israelis had constructed these huge earthen hills in the Sinai as a defense line that was supposed to be unbreachable, according to their assessments regarding Egyptian capability. But their intelligence failed. Some say the failure was deliberate on the part of NSA, which was supplying them with satellite data. The Egyptians were able to move up two armies in three days—which is virtually impossible to do without detection by satellite reconnaissance; and then they brought up specially engineered water guns to blast through the defensive hills. They used water from the canal, and high-pressure pumps. They started the water blasting during the night, and by dawn two Egyptian armies, the Third and the Seventh, were pouring through the breach and on their way across the Sinai, toward Gaza.

He pauses for a moment, looking to his silent wife. Her eyes are on him, and Blake continues.

For the first two days the Egyptians had the momentum. They were unstoppable. The attack stunned the Israelis. Jerusalem was in shock. A paralysis in the Israeli high command set in. How did the Egyptians mobilize two armies, move them up in such secrecy, move up the materiel? What happened to their agents, to their vaunted intelligence? To NSA?

Blake now sits, putting his feet up on the chaise.

His wife waits.

"We had a boat, and it was called the USS *Freedom*. The *Freedom* was a World War Two victory boat that had been refitted as an electronic spy ship. They called them AGTERS." As does he, his wife likes details, and Blake slowly recites the full name. Auxiliary General Technical Research. "They conduct electronic surveillance. Telemetrics. The *Freedom* was attached to a small naval group that was in place in the Mediterranean two days before the Egyptians attacked. It had been ordered there by the Naval Security Group." His tone and pause indicate how curious he finds this part of the story.

Certainly, the Israelis found it curious as well. The *Freedom* had on board a large number of Arabic linguists. Not only that, but the National Security Agency, starting about a week before the attack, had thrown a lot of Arabic-speaking personnel into listening posts in Greece, Turkey, and Italy. You can't keep these things hidden, he explains. You have to pull people from other areas, there's a lot of paper involved, radio traffic. The Israelis learned this very quickly from their sources, one of which is the CIA. They then put two and two together, and came to the conclusion that NSA knew that Egypt was planning an offensive.

He rises from the chaise. Within the ordinary tapestry of their days, he is giving this story a special prominence. He's had an encounter, in part with himself; he now wishes to examine it, and wants his wife to be his silent control, perhaps to see if what he has found is of any significance.

So, to continue. The battle in the Sinai raged. Israel was fighting for its life. Look at the map of the Middle East, he suggests, bringing in a visual aid, as per his training. One sees the basin of the Mediterranean and the sickle curve of its eastern shore, the tiniest crescent of blue in a vast yellow. Geography is destiny: the Israelis don't get any second chances. They mobilized like madmen, and in the meantime called upon their air force to hold off the flying columns of Egyptian armor. By the end of the second day it looked like they were getting control of the air, but they were paying a very high price. For greater reality, and as a foundation for what he wishes to illustrate, he gives more details: "They were having trouble with a new Russian SAM."

"SAM," his wife says.

"Surface-to-air missiles," he interprets. "They—the Israelis—lost about two dozen planes the first day, and about that number on the second. For them it's a lot. For anyone. They put in an urgent request for replacements. Normally we fly them to England and the Israelis pick them up there, but they asked for immediate transfer of planes from NATO stock. They wanted the jets with a new jamming device—there's a package that attaches to the electronics that handles the radio emissions of incoming SAM."

Having consulted the sources and done a good amount of extrapolatory analysis, Blake can inform his wife that there was much argument within the administration as to how to respond to Israel's request. As always, the intelligence assessments were at odds with each other. The CIA insisted that the Israelis needed the planes, while the staff of the National Security Council disagreed. While this was being argued back and forth there were leaks and senators and congressmen began taking positions.

"In the meantime, Navy had the *Freedom* sitting nice and pretty out in the Mediterranean reading all the military traffic that was coming out of Israel. Of course, everyone knew this."

Here he pauses for effect, returning to the chaise, sitting.

"And it was also known that, given the realities, the hard realities, in a very short time the Egyptians were going to be fed some of those signals."

"What realities, Matt?"

He pauses, unsure of how to put it. He wishes to speak the truth, as he has learned it from the limitless files, as he has come to understand it.

"A lot of people—in and out of our government—think that Israel's defeat would solve a lot of problems. Short and long term. People are still looking"—and here he takes a sudden turn into a harsher reality than he himself thought possible—"for the final solution."

His wife remains silent, watching him as he stares off into the night. At last he speaks.

"There was resistance in our government to giving them the replacement planes, the parts. The package. The Israelis also needed some intelligence assistance; they wanted to know what the Syrians were planning, if anything, what the Soviets had up their sleeves. This request also encountered resistance. There was another faction in our government that wanted Israel to win, but not by much. Realpolitik and ambiguities of power."

His wife, also a follower of current events, has some knowledge of this, and murmurs her acknowledgment.

"They didn't want to see Egypt humbled and Sadat lose power, which would mean a coup by Arab fundamentalists or left-wing elements, you never know where it's going to come from in the Middle

East. This faction was counseling to send the planes, but to wait, let the Israelis sweat a little. Show them who's boss. Extract promises. Then of course there was the faction screaming for immediate delivery."

"Sounds messy."

"The usual. What's that?"

They both look up. From Maureen's open window comes music.

Almost immediately their daughter appears and lowers the window, and the sound diminishes.

"She's working on her paper," his wife says.

He picks up the thread of his narrative.

"So the Israelis were concerned, what with the *Freedom* out there pulling in all their military traffic. They tendered expressions of this concern. Our government reassured them. But they had contacts, people who were sympathetic; they remained concerned." How might he explain the network these people have? Their tenacious bonds of blood and history and suffering that cut across political and national boundaries? That cut across time itself?

"They had evidence that their signals were being given to the Egyptians. It's a standard telemetric." He lays out a quick, layman's explanation. "You set up a scam. Arrange a few plants, wait for the material to show up elsewhere, cross-check time and place, and you come pretty close to the source. It's called triangulation, I think." He leaves out the technical cant, a good bit of which, having just read it, he doesn't understand himself.

"The Israelis then asked for the removal of the *Freedom,* and they were again assured, at the appropriate level, that first, the *Freedom* wasn't in their territorial waters—which of course was meaningless, because the range of the signal catchers was more than a hundred miles—and second, the ship wasn't reading their signals, which of course was ridiculous, and third, that even if they were, not to worry, their security was being honored."

He pauses, hears the music from Maureen's room. She has it on louder than usual, but as long as he talks he doesn't hear it.

"Realize," he says, "all this was happening very fast. Twenty-four, thirty-six hours at the most. The Egyptians were using their SAMs, their Third Army was still rolling toward Gaza. Israel was very, very close," his hand is held up, thumb and forefinger barely apart, "to a psychological and military collapse. The Egyptians were gearing up for a second push with their Seventh Army. They were outmaneuvering the Israelis, which had never before happened. We assured them again that there was no break in NSA security. The evidence said otherwise.

They asked again, please remove the *Freedom*. It was a hard please. Very hard. They declared the Mediterranean a free-fire zone, which means—"

"I know, Matt. Shoot at everything."

"Right. They requested the immediate removal of all vessels from the zone. Navy said—to put it bluntly, honey—fuck you, these are international waters, no one tells the U.S. Navy where it can't go."

In the dark quiet of the night, his voice is a rough surprise. There is a long silence between them. They can just barely hear Maureen's music.

He finishes his story in short sentences, sketching in the attack, the bright Mediterranean sky out of which came screaming jets, the count of the wounded. The rest is a do-it-yourself project, and he lets his wife's imagination supply the flames and blood and death, Tippet's father upon the bridge, and the young lieutenant weeping, remembering.

There were inquiries. The usual committees took the usual testimony. Classified material relating to the activities of the USS *Freedom* were entered as evidence. The sessions were closed. Apologies were offered by all parties. All sorts of pieces were planted in the media. About a year later compensation was provided for the victims and their families. Three, four million. Our government said it was a mistake, all in error.

He stands once more and steps to the grass. From his daughter's open window the music, softer now, comes forth into the night.

After a minute's silence, his wife speaks. Her voice, light and quick, comes from behind and washes over him like the soft light from the living room. She is speaking of the wedding; the minister would really like to meet Jerry. There are certain requirements, one of them being the verification of his personal status.

"This is his first marriage," Blake says.

"That has to be verified."

"How's he going to do it? Run a computer check on Jerry?" Maybe the minister subscribes to a data base run by the clergy, new-age omniscience. A computer link to the divinity. Blake has put his hands in his pocket and is rocking lightly on his heels above his wife. He has an amusing thought: he'll put together a dossier on Jerry and Meg and bring it to the ceremony.

"Tell them," Blake says, turning back to the night, "that the groom has been cleared by the FBI."

●

Presently he hears his wife rise; the patio doors roll noisily, then close. After a few moments he moves once more to the edge of the grass and stares out across the expanse of yards.

From the rear of almost every house a light shines. From high bedroom windows, and from the lower, wider kitchen windows, from bright spots here and there, light is cast forth. The outlines of bushes and trees are black cutouts on the flat plane of black grass. Now that the bug lights are off and his eyes have adjusted, he is able to see his faint shadow elongated over the grass. From where Blake stands there is a part of his yard, off to the left, that is a black void. He has read about stellar phenomena, quarks and quasars, about such impossibilities as black holes. He would like to be, even for an instant, in such a void, would like surcease from the world of family and weddings, from his pushy AUSA, the endless files in his basement, the facts and conjectures that bombard him like a meteor shower. He stands very still, his hands still in his pockets, and feels himself, quite unexpectedly, tumescing. The air, the dense soft air rising from this yeasty, maculate earth, carries an erotic fragrance. He imagines himself in total blackness with his wife, in such lightlessness that one could not see one's hand before one's face, that one could not see the other person, only feel, hear, and taste. The black space out there in his yard might be suitable. One day he will take his wife by the hand and lead her to that dark fragrant patch of grass near the dogwood—surely, knowing the laws of physics, if there is no light, there can be no vision—and there he shall take her upon the dew-damp earth in splendid if cautious abandon. The grass feels soft and spongy as he steps off the flagstone. Another step and already the darkness is increased exponentially. Suddenly, from Maureen's room there comes a broad wash of yellow. His daughter is at the window. Uncertain whether she sees him, he gives a little wave and a smile, and she raises her hand. When he looks at the grass again the void is gone and he is casting two shadows, one long and pale, the other short and sharp. He lingers for a few minutes until his erection subsides, then he goes inside.

●

In their bedroom, his wife is reading.

He asks if Maureen is inviting anyone to the wedding.

"Not at this point."

"So Jonathan is completely out of the picture."

His wife says yes, and gives her attention to the book. Blake settles into the bed. Jonathan is out. Some other young man will soon be in. Jonathan was fine; he passed the security check. He thinks of Ellis's wife: the deal with Ellis offered leniency for her, but then something happened and the whole bargain fell off the wall like Humpty-Dumpty; Newcombe put it back together, but the cracks were still there. The woman paid the price for crossing over. It's part of the marriage package, join another's causes, fight their battles. Even more than politics, love makes for strange bedfellows.

"Matt, what would have happened if they had lost?"

"If who'd lost what?"

"The Israelis, to the Egyptians."

After a long pause he replies, "It's never going to happen."

"Suppose they did?"

Suppose. Arab tanks rolling into Jerusalem. He repeats: it's never going to happen. Before it gets to that, the Israelis would—what? What would they do? His wife waits for more, but he doesn't tell her what he knows, what he has learned from the background material, of the contingency plans the Israelis have. The mass burial sites in Jerusalem and Tel Aviv and Beersheba; the stockpiles of narcotic pain killers and other medical supplies—the blood and plasma and antibiotics; the bilateral agreements they have entered into with various other countries, including the United States, for full-scale evacuation of the civilian population. And other certain, secret contingency plans: the destruction by nuclear device of the Aswan dam; the destruction of Cairo in similar fashion; of Damascus, Baghdad, Amman, Riyadh.

He says, "It's widely known, you know, that Israel has the bomb. They have a small stockpile. The notion is that if they're faced with a defeat, they'll use the bomb. And they've let that be known, quietly."

His wife says nothing, and after a while he repeats that it's never going to happen.

His wife returns to her book, Blake to the cool of the sheets. Chances are, he thinks, that if it did happen, events wouldn't stop at those he'd just mentioned. He rolls over, ready for sleep. Instead he sees mushroom clouds rising. The world will go up in flames. God, talk about the Second Coming. They'll take the rest of the world with them; try it again, and this time you're all going to go. There is an undeniable, fearful symmetry there.

He keeps his eyes closed, but the light from his wife's reading lamp is intense and presses against his lids. Starfield, he thinks. A man, a shape; a presence, perhaps a mere configuration of the mind. Does he actually exist? Blake, his eyes still closed, stirs. Might he be a notional? He feels his heart suddenly beating. Starfield is a notional—a chimera created by an opposing security force in order to lead the Bureau astray, get us to squander our resources chasing a shadow. It's done all the time; anything is possible on paper. His wife has put her book down, switched off the lamp, pulling the light summer cover to her side.

Starfield, he reassures himself as his wife shifts about, finding her groove, Dr. Phillip Starfield, the man, exists. Halpern insists upon it. Blake will not question the premise, for his inclination, in spite of his agile, poetical turn of mind, is to the real, to the things of this world. And there is no arguing existence. In matters of this sort he has journeyed beyond doubt. He credits the Bureau, in part. Though he does have reservations, particularly from the so-called artistic point of view as well as from the administrative, for the most part he finds the Bureau a benign, reasonable, and moderate organization. Most important, for a man such as himself, a man given to speculating upon the imponderables, a man given to what his daughter might call the existential mode, the Bureau has trained him to focus on events; what people do, when and to whom. Gossip, as his wife and daughter accused. But a higher gossip. Nothing but the facts, Ma'am. In his half sleep he sees the montage of old Jack Webb clips shown to the trainees at Quantico. Facts and acts, the stock in trade of the Bureau. Starfield exists. Tippet proved it. Yes, the man was real, and alive, and though he appeared to be hiding within a black hole, the Bureau would find him. Blake knows this, now, for a certainty, and so is comforted, and sleeps.

●

One day, when their daughter was seven, he took her to Yad Vashem in Jerusalem. As always, Hans waited outside. In the memorial, among the displays of eyeglasses and shoes and letters, there were many photographs. There was one of boys and girls, their hands above their heads as German soldiers with rifles marched them through the street. A famous photograph. All the world knows it. His daughter looked at it for a long time and then, when they had returned to the hot, bright light of the Holy City, she asked about the picture.

What are the soldiers doing?

Why do they have guns?

Where are the children being taken?

In grave silence, Hans walked with them, listening to his explanation.

The soldiers, he told her, were taking the children away.

But Abba, where are their mothers and fathers?

They have been taken away, too, and are not there to protect them.

But where are the other grown-ups?

Hans now spoke. The grown-ups did not help, she said. She spoke in English, thick with a Dutch overlay. In their house they spoke English, not Hebrew or Dutch, so that their daughter would learn what Hans said was the more important language.

Their little girl was silent. He had told her, in the bright Jerusalem sunlight, that it will never happen again. Children will never be taken away.

Why, the little girl had asked, thinking of the photograph, grainy and glossy, why can't it happen, Abba?

Hans, returning to silence, let him speak.

Because, he said, there will always be your mother and father to help you.

But suppose they take you away?

If not us, then others, the grown-ups that live here will help you. Forever. There will be grown-ups with guns to make sure it doesn't happen again.

The girl, satisfied, put her hand in his.

It will never happen again, he repeated, and looked to his wife who, pensive, walked beside them. Men and women who will kill for you, he thought.

And now, thinking of that time, he sits quietly in the motel room, one of the many such rooms he has spent his nights in for too many years. His day has been long and he has letters to write. He needs a new power pack for his portable computer. He will purchase one when he is in New York next week.

He sits and thinks of his wife. He wishes to change what has happened, yet fears the irrevocability of time and event. But no, he reminds himself that he does not entirely believe that. There is some give, some elasticity, in the skin of time that shapes the world. He must enter soon upon a higher jeopardy, start events on a course the outcome of which he is not certain. Outer obstacles, his own inner resistance, must be overcome; he sees purpose and circumstance forming themselves, forcing events to a terrible, unforeseen climax. Dangers shall impede, loyalties are uncertain, men and women prove untrue.

Yet he must act. For should it come to pass that the men and women and children are led once again at gunpoint to the waiting cattle cars that will take them to the ovens, it shall not be without savage battle, and the blood of their enemies.

# CHAPTER 17

T hey have one photograph, and only one photograph.

It's tucked away on page three of the PI that just came in, which Blake and Halpern are going through as they sit in the lawyer's office at 225 Cadman Plaza East.

"I can't believe this, Matt. Is this it?"

"That's it," says Blake.

"You guys have been working on it a month, and this is all you can bring me? Man, come on."

Blake does not respond.

Halpern frowns, shakes his head, scans the summary sheet, frowns again. A PI, preliminary investigation, is taken in large part from the public record, which in this instance consists of school and employment records, credit card check, draft registration record, a computer scan with the National Crime Center in Bureau headquarters. It's a fairly low-grade report, and requires very few approvals. There isn't much, and the most current entry is four years old.

"He's been out of the country for fifteen years, so the record is spotty."

Halpern says nothing, flips another page. His office smells of paint, cartons of case files are on the floor. In the hall painters are spreading drop cloths. Blake checks his watch. He looks out the window and sees only a murky Brooklyn sky.

"This is back-shelf shit, Matt."

This is true, but Blake refrains from replying. The attorney, like just about everyone else, including his family, thinks of the Bureau as an omnipresent, omniscient Big Brother. It just isn't so.

"There has to be more," says Halpern. "Navy says that Starfield had been security cleared for defense work."

"We're trying to confirm that. We have TRs out."

"They've been prioritized?"

"Yes, Richard, the trace requests have been prioritized as high as humanly possible."

The lawyer looks up quickly, but Blake is a past master of deadpan and reveals nothing. Prioritize; one of the many new words in the manager's lexicon. As are every one of the hundreds of trace requests that the Bureau and other government agencies generate every week, Blake's are prioritized.

"Well, I'd wish they'd move their goddamn asses."

Blake shares some of the AUSA's impatience. The lateral flow of paper proceeds at a snail's pace. The Pentagon runs a clearinghouse on trace requests known as DIS, Defense Investigative Service, referred to as Deep in Shit by the more experienced, which is, in practice, a holding operation merely adding an extra layer of paper. The desk people at DIS are the newly hired, the punishees and the RIPs, Blake's designation for a unique class of government worker, the Retired in Place. They are the paper pushers and form shufflers for whom time flows like a thick, sweet syrup, men and women with no respect for the urgencies of others.

And part of the delay, explains Blake, is that we're trying to cover our tracks.

The attorney listens. You see, the trace requests are computerized. And that means that the programs are going to kick out anything relating to Ellis, and hold them. There are others who want to know what we're looking for. So he has people working on this, Blake says. We're doing it by hand. The old method. File cards.

"It's going to take a little longer."

They return their attention to the file. First, his age, fifty-two. Young, thinks Blake, for he is almost that age, to the month. Then, laid out in reverse chronological order, is the life of Starfield. Colleges, undergraduate, graduate, postdoctoral studies in microbiology, polymer chemistry, physics. These are high-powered subjects of which Blake, though knowing something about atoms and electrons and the periodic table, is completely ignorant. They continue reading until Blake, prompted by an item on the next page, asks, "What kind of school is a yeshiva?"

"That's a high school that gives you religious education half the day and standard academics the other."

"I see."

"I went to a yeshiva for a couple of years. My parents were religious." He offers this self-consciously, almost apologetically; pardon my differences.

For Blake, this is an opportunity to clear up a long-standing question.

"What, exactly, is a rabbi?" he asks.

"It's hard to explain." Halpern is thinking. "It means 'teacher.' Really, 'my teacher.' It's a person who knows the ritual law. It's not like being a priest." He smiles. "There are no special secrets or lines to God."

In a quid pro quo, Blake offers a bit of biography, and admits he went to Catholic school. "Until the fifth grade."

"Are the nuns as tough as I hear?"

As a child they were Blake's secret terrors, strict and angry, full of a deep preternatural fury. "Some of them were pretty bad." He adds, "I didn't send my daughters."

Blake senses the low-key wariness between then, a touch of mutual xenophobia; there is also a tenuous bond.

And then, when they return to the file, there is the photograph.

It's a copy of a picture from *Scientific American,* dated April 1979. It is of a group of scientists at a seminar in London. Blocked out in heavy marker, Starfield is on the edge, his face slightly turned toward the center of the picture. In the small photograph, his face appears dirty. Only in the grainy blowup, which the technicians have provided at Blake's request, does one realize the dirt is the beginning of a beard.

"He specializes in physical biology." Halpern is reading the copy that has been excerpted from the article.

"With applications to genetics," says Blake. It's a very esoteric field.

They both study the photograph. Then, with Blake insisting, Halpern impatient, they compare the image with the physical description on the draft registration records.

"He's tallish, about six one. Brown hair, light eyes. Hazel."

"Gray," says Halpern.

"He weighed, when he was eighteen, one sixty-five. And, judging by this photograph, he looks as if he's kept himself slender."

Halpern looks from the photograph to the draft report.

"And here," says Blake, indicating a notation on the medical report, "here we are lucky. He was deferred because of a medical condition. His right ear."

"Yes."

"A hearing defect, of unknown origin. It was confirmed by our doctors. The report of the medical examination is in there."

"Aha." Halpern pulls it from the back of the file.

"I did a quick check on it with our research desk, and they told me it was a kind of a chronic degenerative condition. So the hearing loss increases as he gets older."

Actually, what Blake had done was simply to call his wife, that very morning, and ask her to check their medical encyclopedia.

"And that's confirmed," says Blake, "by an examination two years after the initial one. The deferment was only good for two years. You can see by the doctor's report that he goes from a thirty percent loss of hearing—the cutoff for the Army is twenty—to a loss of close to thirty-five."

Halpern is not impressed. But at least it's a detail, an undeniable physical fact, which may or may not prove pertinent. And the more of those they get, the better they will know the man.

"I just can't believe that we don't have anything more," says the lawyer. "This guy is high powered."

Blake agrees, then explains that it's not a bad start. He's seen less. In fact, the paucity of data is, in a paradoxical manner, a good sign.

Halpern understands immediately: Starfield began his cover years ago.

"What about the tapes, Matt, can we get the tapes soon?"

"We're working on access," Blake replies. He refers Halpern to the page in the case file listing the forms and applications he has sent out. Here is his application for the transcripts, block stamped and signed.

"What about the actual tapes, Matt? Not the transcripts, the tapes themselves."

Blake is working on that, too.

"We really need those traces."

Blake does not respond.

"What about the contact reports?"

Again, Blake refers the attorney to the appropriate line in the case file. Requests have gone out to the Bureau legats—that's legal attachés—in Germany, Belgium, and Italy, who will contact the appropriate CIA field stations. A contact report is precisely what the name implies: the report of an agent's contacts with all and sundry individuals. The reports are prepared by the agent's case officer after intensive, regular debriefing sessions. But the contact reports are meaningless in their raw form; not until they are processed by evaluators, who cull, compare, and correlate, do they have any relevance. So it's the final product Blake wants, which is, as one might imagine, very difficult to get from the CIA. It's a very delicate liaison job. You have to know exactly what to ask for, and whom to ask; you have to offer something in return.

Again, Blake can only advise patience.

"Shit."

Though he will not display it, Blake shares Halpern's exasperation. His role shall be to play the older, wiser, more patient and moderate half of their unlikely union, until such time as he shall play otherwise.

"They must be in a data base, Matt."

Blake is sure they are, but there's an access problem there, too, as the lawyer can imagine.

"I'll get Tippet to work on it."

Indeed, the lieutenant is doing his part, hacking away at this very moment, Blake is sure, in his secure, clean-swept cubby in Alexandria, patching in to various bases, bringing in whatever he can lay his hands on.

"We need a break, Matt. Just a lucky goddamn break."

Indeed, they do. And when it comes it will be something very simple, very basic. The way Halpern brought it to him. A name. Halpern got it from Tippet. Tippet got it from—who knows where, but he got it. Out of the air, like a stone upon the tranquil surface of his life, Starfield had dropped. In unseen ripples the disturbance is now widening. Blake is on the fourth or fifth ripple, he figures, and if he can work backwards he might find the stone. The primal pebble, so to speak. *Ecce homo,* the man himself beholden; Starfield, their prime mover.

"We really need those traces," says the lawyer.

"Yes," replies Blake. "And we'll get them, Richard."

●

On his desk now, with the three photographs of his family in various stages of maturity, Blake has added a fourth. It is of Dr. Phillip Starfield, the grainy enlargement taken from the magazine. Until they get another, more current photograph, this will have to do.

The man's face presents itself in three-quarter view, the beard just showing, the hair dark, short. From the technical people he got two other copies. One will be for his briefcase, the other for his basement desk in Eastmere. And in this way shall Blake imprint Starfield upon his mind's eye, firing the man's features into his memory, like a brand.

# CHAPTER 18

From the hallway, Mrs. Greenspan watches as Albert Deere prepares to cut another length of stud for the framing. His pale, bushy eyebrows are aged even more by the fine plaster dust that seems to fall constantly. His leather tool belt hangs like a gunslinger's, the claw hammer with its fiberglass handle weighting it across the hip; in front he wears a faded-denim nail apron, its pockets bulging. She watches as he eyes a long two-by-four before rejecting it as warped. He takes another from the stack on the floor, tests it. It is acceptable; he gets ready to mark it for a cut.

First he looks up and gives the woman a half smile.

"It's coming along, isn't it," Mrs. Greenspan says.

Deere slowly nods and finishes the other half of his smile, and returns to his work.

Mrs. Greenspan enjoys having the carpenter in her house. He was recommended to them by a colleague of her husband, a man who had had Deere work in his house sometime last year. The Greenspans were quite pleased at Deere's estimate. They were much taken, too, with his gentlemanly ways, one of his charms being a heavily accented but proficient English.

He had explained to the Greenspans the schedule for their renovation. The work had a natural flow. First the demolition, which had taken, as he had predicted, a full week. Then the studding, which he is doing now, another week or so. The installation of the electric lines.

Then the Sheetrocking, the taping and compounding. That takes days, for compound must be applied, allowed to dry, then sanded, applied, and sanded again. If the humidity is high the compound will not dry and everything stops. Then moldings and fixtures, cutting and fitting. Priming of the unpainted surfaces. The painting. Floor scraping. Hanging the doors. Then you have to factor in delays. Delays for materials that are not available. Delays for mistakes and revisions of plans. Delays you create so as not to finish too quickly.

Deere works with two assistants. One of them is an American, a blond young man. He talks New Yorkish, very quick. The other has a foreign accent, like the carpenter's. The American's name is Danny. The other, the dark-haired assistant, calls himself what Mrs. Greenspan heard as Nathan, but he corrected her. *Natan.* The first *a* was long, the second short. Natahn. Both young men are strong, very quick, very handy with tools. They wear jeans and T-shirts and construction boots.

Mrs. Greenspan watches as Deere, having marked off three studs, prepares to cut. One end of the lumber is on the windowsill, the other rests across his thigh. He starts the saw, lets the blade just nick the wood, then backs it out and adjusts its alignment. Mrs. Greenspan braces for the sound. The blade spins, bites with a loud, high howl. Wood dust shoots into the air. In seconds, a length of wood drops to the floor. The next cut goes equally quickly, the loudness of the blade a little duller now to the overloaded ear. On the third cut he hits something hard in the wood, a knot, and the blade catches. Deere works the saw expertly, backing it out, holding it in a free spin to bring it up to speed, then advancing it with deliberation. His arms tense as the blade hits the knot again and screams in protest. He is aware of Mrs. Greenspan watching; he will put some style into it. Deere backs the saw off, keeps it running, then with a quick, smooth push forces the blade, shrieking, through. The pleasure of the silence is immediate and intense. Sawdust hangs in the air, as does the acrid odor of burned wood and seared pitch.

Deere shakes his head at Mrs. Greenspan, his imp's smile confessing his fault. He should not have pushed the saw like that. The blade, he tells her, hits the pitch in the knot, slows, heats up, expands, grabs the wood, and slows even more.

On the street, cars are blowing their horns. The carpenters are double-parked, and have to move the van.

Deere puts everything down, takes off his tool belt.

"Americans." He is amused, and smiles at Mrs. Greenspan. "You have no patience."

# CHAPTER 19

**S**tand back,'' orders Blake, and throws the match.

Behind the sheet of sudden leaping flame Maureen backs away; the tips of fire curl and snap and lick the air and whip off tendrils of black smoke. Holding his wine, Blake moves farther from the grill. He has used too much starter fluid and the low leaves of the maple are being singed.

They are having his wife's version of teriyaki, and the skewers of thin-sliced meat are on a plate sitting on the flagstone. It will take another twenty minutes before the briquets are ready, and, leaving his daughter to watch the flames, he carries the meat back to the kitchen.

●

"Was the traffic bad?"

"The usual horrible disgusting Friday mess. Maybe I should take the train on Fridays."

"Matt, you know how you hate the trains. The air-conditioning never works and half the time you don't get a seat."

"And when you do," says his daughter, coming in, her pale green polo shirt snug over her breasts, "you complain about getting wapped on the head with yuppie tennis racquets."

Maureen takes a can of beer from the refrigerator. Her dark green shorts are made of a shiny nylon with white edging, her feet are bare.

"What's this?" Blake asks.

Maureen leans over to see what her father is looking at. "Those are my three questions of the universe, Dad."

He reads them out loud.

*What does it all mean?*

*How long can this go on?*

*Why me?*

Maureen leans against the table, crosses one arm under her breasts, and takes a long pull from the can.

"Do you want salad, Matt?"

"Yes. Have you started your paper yet?"

No response.

"You're going to get caught short."

"Dad, I have it outlined."

"Matt?"

"Salad is fine—are you with us for the weekend or are you galivant-ing around?"

"Do you want it with dressing, or just plain?"

"I'm going to the beach tomorrow."

"With whom? Is it that low-cal Italian?"

"Friends, Dad."

"It's ranch."

"I'll have a little. Are you staying overnight?"

"We don't know."

"I want you to watch yourself with the sun."

"It's hard, Dad."

"I know it's hard, but getting skin cancer is harder and I want you to make the effort. Is that my phone?"

The three of them freeze. A soft burring comes up through the floor-ing.

"I'm going to let it ring." He knows who it is.

"Why don't you just turn it down, Dad, if you're not going to answer it?"

"He has an answering machine," his wife says.

"Yeah, but he doesn't use it."

"I turn it on when I need it."

"Talk about catch-22." Maureen has the beer pressed to her cheek near her ear.

The ringing has stopped.

"Tomorrow," says his wife, "in the morning, we are going to look for a gown for Maureen."

Says Blake to his daughter, "You're too old to be making faces like that."

"Maybe I'm not old enough."

"Apparently not. You're mother's right, it's only going to happen once."

"Yeah, Dad. IOGTHO."

Blake is puzzled.

"That's my acronym, Dad, for the wedding. You like acronyms. IOGTHO. 'It's only going to happen once.' "

"Yes, we hope, only once," he says.

"Dad, do you know what those dresses look like? I mean, you haven't seen them."

Blake looks to his wife.

"They're sweet."

"We're going to look like a bunch of housewives from Kansas."

"Maureen, whatever. It's your sister's pick, and it's only going—"

He catches himself in time; his daughter smirks.

"You'll do it, and that's it. You'll appreciate these things better when you get older."

"Right," says Maureen and raises her beer can to him. "WYGO."

Blake has caught on. "That's correct. WYGO. Remember you heard it here first."

"Right, Dad." She's using his tone.

"Right. And I commend you to studying your own three questions here."

His phone again.

As his wife tells him the coals are probably ready for the teriyaki, he dashes down into the cool mustiness of his basement office.

●

He catches the phone a split second after its last ring, hears the click of the receiver on the other end, waits, and sure enough, within a few seconds the prosecutor calls back.

Since their session with Navy, it seems that with every passing hour Halpern's sense of urgency is increasing, and Blake has to spend the next hour playing devil's advocate and fending off the lawyer's demand for immediate yet unspecified action. Halpern, excited, wants to put together a surveillance package. Blake agrees, a tactical concession, but counsels forbearance. Until Tippet produces something warrantable, nothing can happen. They will have to get the warrants through FISC—

the Foreign Intelligence Surveillance Court—and they don't have enough, yet.

"Richard. You know the guidelines."

Every prosecutor does, but they have to be reminded.

The evidence must be authentic and compelling; if your submission is based on a source, it must be a confidential informant of known reliability. All applications for domestic electronic surveillance by the FBI must be approved by the attorney general; in cases of espionage, the application for a warrant must be signed off by the internal security division of Justice and, finally, must be approved by a judge sitting in FISC.

But the young attorney is pushing, pushing, pushing. He wants to submit immediately. Blake, understanding Halpern's enthusiasm, and commending him on it, cautions against such an impetuous undertaking. The warrants manual, a four-hundred-and-sixty-page book from Justice, sets forth the requirements and proofs necessary. There are different levels of proofs for different kinds of allegations, all kinds of case precedents, statutory and administrative limitations, internal Justice guidelines to adhere to, not to mention the Bureau's own manual of proofs and requirements. Blake's position is that any submission, at this point, would be too circumstantial, really an overly intricate, yet incomplete link analysis, a mumbo jumbo of times, places, names, and events, and thus fatally flawed. And Halpern is bringing in new stuff all the time, adding to the confusion. Now he's got an insignificant character by the name of Deere, given to him by his sidekick wonder boy, Tippet. A carpenter, of all things.

"Matt, I hear what you're saying, but we have to move on this."

Above, as the lawyer reiterates his arguments, Blake can hear his wife and daughter crisscrossing the kitchen floor. The smell of the barbecued meat is strong.

Blake is not about to associate himself with a premature submission, and he doubts if anyone from Justice is about to either. "Richard, if we go into FISC now they're going to throw us out on our tushes."

Halpern rebuts: he has been making inquiries about judges and might have one.

There is a long silence between them. When it comes to a judge for a warrant, you look around. It's called shopping. Judges have their reps; you know who's a book man, who bends. If you look long and hard enough you can find a judge for anything. Blake's done it before and thought nothing of it, but now he's deeply offended. Halpern

makes it sound so cheap. This isn't goddamn Delancey Street, he almost says; indeed, there are many unkind, ugly comments to be made,
but Blake, a good and temperate man struggling against barbarism and
prejudice, forbears.

"Richard," he says, "we have to move carefully."

"Matt, Tippet's bringing in a hell of a lot on this."

"Damnit, Richard, we can't allow ourselves to be jerked around by
some young lieutenant sitting at a computer console."

"Tippet is good, Matt. You saw; he uses the new computer formats.
They're finishing their analysis of the Ellis operation. It's based on a
mathematical theory called cluster analysis."

"Look, Richard, you know goddamn well we won't get those warrants with a submission based on spread sheets."

Halpern, knowing how these old-timers fear anything but a pencil
and a three-by-five-inch index card, points out that the computer simply does what a team of collators does—gathers, categorizes, compares,
and connects—only it does it faster. "Much faster, Matt, incomparably
faster."

Blake cedes this point. What he finds exasperating is Halpern's in-
ability to get through his pushy, arrogant head the inbuilt reluctance of
humanity to surrender their god-given powers to machines. "The
courts will not recognize a computer-driven submission for a surveillance warrant," he says. "FISC wants the human factor prevailing."

"Informants lie, Matt."

Blake admits that.

"Computers don't."

Not so fast; Blake knows how these programs have their built-in
biases, and are often skewed to give out exactly what the programmer
needs. He throws out some of the jargon. Hits and matches. Patching
in. Biased response mechanism. He doesn't know that much and his
supply is soon exhausted, but he's made his point. Even with a computer there's the human factor.

On the ceiling above, Blake hears his wife's signal, two quick
thumps, followed by a delayed third, her peremptory summons to
supper.

"Matt, we really have to move on this. We have to force this thing
through."

Blake is tempted, so tempted; the clarion call to action is hard to
resist, but there are too many unknowns here. He's worked cases to the
edge before, but won't risk it with Starfield. The Bureau caught hell back
in the seventies when Carter found a moral lode to mine in governmen-

tal misdoings, and turned federal prosecutors loose on Bureau agents and CIA officers in an orgy of righteous cannibalism. Blake knows of half a dozen former colleagues who had been sued, censured, forced into retirement, or dead-ended for questionable taps and surveillances. If Halpern cannot be convinced, Blake will tie him up in knots on the technical end. But he won't have to. He has enough seniority and pull so that unless he agrees to a submission, Halpern's chief won't sign off on it.

By the lawyer's angry silence, Blake knows that Halpern knows this.

The main virtue of youth, thinks Blake, is also its liability: no doubts, no Hamlet-like hesitations about failure and lack of perfection. No thought, either, to consequences. Perhaps it's good that, for the most part, these prosecutors leave by their early thirties, before they start feeling sorry for the men and women they hound to death.

"Matt, what about a surveillance on Starfield?"

Blake is outright incredulous. All they have is that one old photograph. And Tippet's link analysis is still about a month behind. The last they know of the man, he was still in Europe. But Blake, hearing his wife tapping on the basement door, tired of fighting the young attorney and very hungry, expresses what he hopes sounds like cautious interest.

"What did you have in mind, a watch or a tail?"

"Just keep an eye on him, follow him around—a tail. Both."

"Richard. Starfield's a traveling man. We don't even know if he's in the States. There are a lot of factors here. Hotels, planes, cars. It's complicated." More complicated than Halpern knows. Technically, they haven't opened a case file on Starfield yet. And when they do, he's going to have to go into one of Donnelly's triage meetings and fight for a couple of budget lines. And Donnelly is going to ask some tough questions. This is not just to make life difficult; it's one of the maxims of resource management that people use the available services to the maximum extent possible—when there's unlimited ammunition you shoot at everything—so the Bureau induces a kind of self-imposed triage. Every agent he gets for his operation means one agent less somewhere else.

"We aren't ready, Richard. The other field offices are going to tell us to go to hell." The prosecutor has no idea of this. Blake needs the cooperation of the field offices; he has to respect the territorial imperatives. It's a question of professional courtesy.

"Then what about a watch?"

"Where?" asks Blake, suddenly very alert. Is this young, impetuous attorney keeping something to himself? "Do you know where he's going to be?"

Halpern denies any specific knowledge. "I was thinking, we could set up a passport picket, watch the phone lines—there's an office in lower Manhattan that his company routes calls through. On Water Street."

Blake is very quiet; how the hell does Halpern know that?

"So why can't we just put a couple of agents on him?"

"You're talking a SIP." Surveillance in place. Bucket jobs, the agents call them. You stand on a corner, sit in a car, or rent a room in a hotel and watch a house, a door, a car. For hours, for days, sometimes weeks. Blake tells him he is not going to call a watch.

"They're tedious, Richard, very tedious, and for the most part unproductive. I can't justify the cost."

Halpern has another idea. "What about the summer interns?"

"What about them?"

"The college kids. Why don't we use them?"

"Because they're all assigned to F and R." Files and Records. Because the Bureau is in constant and perpetual battle against the forces of evil and chaos which manifest themselves in misplaced and unalphabetized files. And because the summer interns are a bunch of kids who are more interested in having a good time than in carrying out assignments. There was a big flap last year, it was in the paper, Blake tells Halpern, *The Washington Post.* Halpern does not recall. Three summer hires in the Bureau's intern program had been assigned to baby-sit the apartment of a low-level Soviet operative attached to the economic mission. Those watches are the lowest of the low; nothing of any conceivable intelligence value is ever produced, but it's done to make life difficult for the Russians, and incidentally to keep open a few expense lines. The kids thought it was going to be fun, but it soon got boring, or maybe they became too enthusiastic. They started cooking up schemes, one of which was to deliver two pizzas to the man's apartment with the pepperoni arranged to spell CIA. Things like that. Harmless, stupid, collegiate fun. The Russians got angry. Then two of the interns, a boy who was a sophomore at American University and a pretty freshman girl from Randolph-Macon Woman's College—Blake has good recall for these kinds of details—were photographed in the backseat of a Bureau car in the parking garage of the apartment complex. The photographs were sent to the State Department. A cartoon and a sarcastic editorial appeared; *Doonesbury* ran a strip. So now the kids do Files and Records.

"We're not going to get much from a watch, Richard. At this point I can't justify it."

In the silence on the line, Blake hears the lawyer's unspoken criticism: he's afraid of getting burned again.

"We need those traces, Matt."

"They'll come in." Blake is an old hand, and very patient with the system. He knows, however, that the traces might come in too late, or not at all. And when they do, there might be little or nothing on them, and further, that even that lack of information might be disguised, for the absence of data is information in its own way, a starting point of another sort, and often a very telling one.

"Matt. I don't want to get frozen out again."

"Don't worry, Richard," Blake says, "I know what I'm doing."

●

When Blake comes up, his wife is in the living room, reading. He is not in a good mood. Teriyaki is one of his favorites, and now his skewer is cold and tough, the salad limp. On the kitchen table sits Maureen's copy of *The Stranger*, the beer can on top of it. He lifts the can. The condensation has left a wet circle on the cover. He shakes his head, disgusted, and wipes the book with his napkin.

Now, carrying his plates to the sink, he shares some of Halpern's fears. They are not unfounded. Nor are his, for that matter. He's got to keep himself alert, on point, so to speak, so that when the time comes, and come it will, he will know which way to jump.

He dries his hands.

He has to talk with Donnelly.

●

Whose bureaucrat's soul, when Blake gets in to see him two days later, is perturbed. The man has his lips together in cold calculation. Donnelly, second in command of the New York office, wants a big case too, but his reality is the political one. The institutional difficulties are beginning to mount.

Murphy, asked by Blake to accompany him, does the talking, while Blake stands in front of Donnelly's desk. Halpern is not there—the young lawyer drives Donnelly crazy.

Donnelly speaks. "Well, damn it, George, we can't carry this much longer."

"What do you have, Matt?"

Blake tells him. A few names, computer matrices; link analyses.

Donnelly sits hard and unsympathetic. On his desk is a file on whose cover Blake makes out the logo of the assessment center. Murphy, standing near the window, has his hands in his pockets, keeping in touch with his genitals. Blake gives a quick summary, the elements of the case, speaks to the next phase.

"There's an interesting link with counterintelligence that we're following up."

Donnelly, his lips still pursed, presses him on capability, and Blake, with a paucity of hard data, but calling upon his considerable verbal abilities, throws out a lot of material. But Donnelly knows when an agent is fudging.

"Matt, goddamn it. I don't like it."

"It's ticklish," Murphy agrees.

"Matt." Donnelly waits, a power wait of about five, six seconds. "You don't have enough to justify the line. You'll get your warrants through Internal Security, but those guys will sign off on their grandmothers. You know the sensitivities here, Matt. You're going to get your case stolen, or shot down—that's if you have a case, Matt, and I'm not so sure you do."

This is the realpolitik. Donnelly has to serve some very powerful and capricious masters in Washington.

"Matt, I shouldn't have to tell you this." But of course Donnelly will, and gives him a hard look, another power play. "You've been out in the field longer than me." A dig, and a reminder of past failure. They're the same age, Donnelly about four grades higher. "I can't carry it much longer."

"We need a month, Tom. Navy's pulling in a lot of stuff."

Says Donnelly, tight-lipped, "You know what these espionage cases are like."

Indeed, Blake does.

Murphy agrees; he's always had his doubts.

Donnelly relaxes his mouth. "We don't want Navy jerking us around on this. Who's your contact at Justice?"

"Wright."

"Jesus, Matt, that's like talking to the *National Enquirer*!"

Murphy seconds this. Wright's office leaks like a sewer.

"If you can't get me anything more, Matt, I'm going to have to ask you to double-four it." Designate it low priority. Which, of course, was the original plan, kick it around a little to satisfy Eastern District, let it die of benign neglect.

Blake agrees; he himself was going to suggest it. But he wants a month.

Donnelly looks at his calendar. He's got an upper-level case-management conference at the end of the month, and he'll put Blake on the agenda. Murphy nods.

"What else do you have going?"

Blake goes through a rundown of a few items, nothing important, the sort of cases every agent uses to keep his files full. You add an interview here, a computer check there, just to keep the case alive; no one expects too much, but these things generate expense lines.

Their fifteen minutes up, Blake leaves, but lingers in the corridor; in a few minutes Murphy comes out.

"Donnelly wants to play this very carefully."

Blake understands; the standard wisdom in the Bureau pertaining to espionage cases is that you can't win for losing. Also, though Navy is running point, he and Halpern can use them for cover for only a little while longer.

Murphy has more. "Donnelly has your assessment results. He just got them this morning."

Blake waits.

"Okay, look, Matt. You need at least a three point five. They put you on the list and they start moving you up."

"Listen, George. I put in twenty hard years here, I mean hard, and I can't see where four days, four goddamn days, are suppose to completely negate all of that."

Blake's voice quivers with anger.

"Matt. You don't have to tell me. It's off the ceiling."

Blake shakes his head in disgust.

"We'll work around it, Matt. Donnelly wants to play this very carefully."

●

Okay, thinks Blake, as he waits for the elevator, let's deal in realpolitik.

Suppose the unthinkable, the impossible, were to happen, and this man Starfield, whoever the hell he is, mounted a rescue operation and succeeded in plucking Ellis out of the lion's den, and we did catch him—what then?

Well, after the initial burst of satisfaction, and a prosecution of Starfield, all hell would break loose. Double hell.

Success would be a guarantee of nothing but trouble.

But, and here's an interesting question which Blake is sure both Murphy and Donnelly have asked themselves, singly and together, more than once, suppose we didn't catch him?

Blake smiles to himself as he enters the elevator. The finest and most excruciating forms of torture short of death would be visited upon at least a dozen heads of various intelligence agencies.

Blake, no longer smiling but feeling better, walks to his desk. Just as Donnelly is doing, Blake will protect himself. If they want paper, he'll give them paper. As much as they want, and more. He'll cover himself too deep for either of them to back out. But at the same time he doesn't want to protect himself too much. That would be disloyal, and if it's one thing the Bureau doesn't feel kindly about, it's disloyalty. What he must do, and which he has almost forgotten due to the various financial, personal, and professional pressures, is to go strictly by the book, and then some.

For the Bureau teaches, among other self-evident lessons, one crucial bit of wisdom: he who makes waves, drowns.

It's an apt aphorism, for later, back at his desk, Blake is just barely keeping his head above a rising sea of paper.

He's got manuals and supplements, addenda and extracts; piles of files, stacks of pamphlets, articles from the Bureau's clipping service, a half dozen books from the research desk. Of immediate concern, and spread before him, is a double-page foldout titled "Appendix VII: CIA Organization, 1984." Using this, Blake will chart his course through the labyrinthine underbelly of American intelligence.

He picks up a paper clip while he contemplates the chart. It is in the CIA where he will find the data on personnel, organization, and operational methods of Israeli intelligence, the Mossad Le Aliyah Beth. Formally known as the Institute for Intelligence and Special Assignments. He has to get into Langley, needs a sympathetic consultation, wants a few high-level brains. Those bastards won't give you the time of day; correction, that's all you do get. Files come back deleted of everything except for one or two words and the small, elegant black stamp proclaiming MAT DEL OP SEC. Material deleted, operational security. Okay, so the Bureau does the same. Or used to. Today it's supposed to be different. As Campbell would say, tell me another, Matt.

The chart is classified and he'd had to sign for it. Typical nonsense, but excellent first-line protection. They won't let you know who you have to talk to. The print is too small. He takes out his magnifying glass. Boxes with tiny names in them, lines running up and down to other boxes with names. Aha, it's got a hidden, triple fold. A goddamn

maze. There are four deputy directors—Operations, Science and Technology, Intelligence, Administration—each in a box, each with a thick
black line beneath, and a thinner black vertical line from which horizontal lines run to smaller boxes, which in turn have other lines leaving
on long sprints to other, even smaller boxes farther down and across the
creases of the page. Some of the boxes are rectangles, others squares.
Doubtlessly the shape has meaning, or maybe one is just supposed to
suspect this. Anything to make life more difficult.

Without thinking that he is defacing government property, Blake
circles in red the rectangle of Counterintelligence, Staff. CI, Staff is
synapsed, as they say, to the spine of deputy director, Operations. On
this spine are other synapses. Near Eastern Division is one, Special
Operations, another. He circles these rectangles in red too.

Under Science and Technology he finds no boxes of interest. S & T
provides the field hardware, the hidden mikes, pens that squirt foul-
smelling liquids to embarrass people you want to embarrass, cameras
that can be hidden in tubes of toilet paper. The in-service course given
by S & T is like a magic show, very entertaining and always a big hit.
Joined to the line for deputy director, Intelligence, are other boxes, two
of which he circles. Office of Near Eastern Analysis, and Office of
Central Reference.

He puts down his red pencil, looks at the chart. Here is where he has
to go, CI, Staff. It's there that he will find the people who can tell him
about Israeli intelligence, about the Mossad of a generation ago, about
the old-timers who came out of the German camps, and from there he
might be able to make the leap to Starfield. He takes up the pencil and
taps the point on the box, circles it again. He's got to get into Counterintelligence. And he knows he can't, at least not through channels. Because once he puts in a formal request for a background briefing he
loses all his protective anonymity. Blake now doodles small triangles
on the circumference of the red circle, more an ellipse. Turned vertically
it looks somewhat like a vagina with teeth going the wrong way. What
might Freud say? Never mind Freud, what might his daughter say? In
spite of his difficulties, he smiles. She'd connect it with his gun. Which
is in its holster, in the middle drawer of his desk, unloaded. He always
leaves the clip at home.

He looks at the little box again. Counterintelligence, Staff. Campbell
has warned him. It's not what it used to be, Matt. Now it's all very
formal. Submit your requests, clear them with the Bureau liaison, who
meets with the CIA liaison. No direct contact between Bureau agents
and Company officers. Too much potential for cooperation. Another

reason why the big Irishman is getting out; everything is on paper. You used to be able to sit down in Carlyle's, a badly lit, seedy restaurant with decent food on the southwest edge of the capital. You sat in the rear, near the windows overlooking the parking lot. You faced the door, the men's room off to the right on a corridor that led past the kitchen to a fire door that was never activated. You saw everything, had your escape routes. You called a certain number and left a standard message. After a few minutes of sitting and drinking the Carlyle special, a very dry Manhattan made with overproof Wild Turkey and a twist, no ice, another man sat and ordered the same thing, and you talked. It was the old-fashioned way, face to face, in the dark. They were professional, very sharp, and paranoid as hell; now all they were was well paid.

So that's the way it used to be. Now it's back alley all the way, which isn't such a bad thing except Blake's area of expertise and most of his contacts are in Banking and Fraud. So he will have to rely on Campbell, the only problem being that Campbell's CI contacts at Langley had been decimated during the Carter purges. The old-timers who managed to save their hides have been shunted off to those tiny boxes lower down on the chart and are in deep hiding, having lost their support, their courage, and their clearances.

The Mossad had been handled through the counterintelligence division of the CIA, Dryden's personal fiefdom. After his fall, the Account had been transferred to the National Security Agency, given to their Near East desk. Whatever files still exist, if any ever did, are buried deep in the Black Chambers at Fort Meade, where the NSA is headquartered. Where is Dryden now? One rumor has it he is sick and dying of some kind of cancer. God, does anyone escape? Another is that he is under house arrest in his forest home in Pennsylvania in the Lehigh Valley, under twenty-four-hour surveillance by a triumvirate of watchers from the CIA, the NSA, and the Defense Intelligence Agency.

Blake will have to work his own contacts, the few that he has, and go to Campbell for more. There are two distinct eras, grand epochs, in the life of the CIA, and Blake needs the officers who served before Carter came in, before the Halloween Massacre. Carter, called the Deacon by the intelligence community, had an especially deep disdain for Dryden, almost a hatred. So there was B.C., before Carter, and A.D., after Dryden. Blake needs B.C. And only God knows in what dark little rooms those men and women, trembling and fearful, are hiding.

●

The names of the dead are carved in alphabetical order on the polished marble walls, and the portly, well-dressed gentleman stands before the ones beginning with *S*. The morning light is angled so that he must stand away, a little to the side. Of the others studying the names carved in the granite, there is a tall and bearded man who wears a little hat of the sort religious Jewish men favor when they are out in public. He carries a *Washington Post* folded so that *ton Po* shows. The gentleman and this man are almost touching.

William Smith, the gentleman says. I knew his family.

The tall man must bend and turn his head to catch the words. Yes, I did too, he says, and, after a moment, walks away.

The gentleman follows at a distance of about ten paces. Against the fencing, a throng of tourists have queued for the ferry to the statue. The sky is hazy, the light reduced to a dull glare that bounces between water and sky, forcing one to squint no matter where the eye is cast. At last, near the western end of the park, near the van with Hebrew lettering that seems to have acquired a permanent home on the edge of Battery Park, the two men close their distance and begin to talk.

The gentleman, and it is Raphael Slavin, brings news. Intermediaries have established contact with the party in question, and an exchange to arrange a meeting has begun. Representations have been made that the interest is personal and private, and that the party in question is not working under the auspices of any governmental entity.

They stroll side by side, two men in conversation, the taller inclining his head, favoring his good ear. At the water's edge stands the old and abused boat house; the fireboat—used only for ceremonial purposes these days—lies in the scummy water, tethered to the pilings with thick twists of rot-blackened rope. The Mitzvah Mobile is a clean, shining vehicle in the flat, glaring light.

Lawyers are skilled at these sorts of things, and Slavin assures the other man that no names have yet been exchanged. The father of the party in question—there is no mother involved—has had enough of life for the time being. His daughter's marriage to this Ellis fellow had been just another unlikely piece in the curious puzzle of her life, which was now, apparently, in its final phase of dissolution. As the father's lawyer put it, they are a curious and distant family not given to display, and the father has his own preoccupations. That is the way they are.

As they walk along the wide footpath, circling back toward the Mitzvah Mobile, the gentleman continues. The woman is in temporary remission, though her condition remains precarious. The level of care required remains high. A visit may be arranged. They will work with our people. He, Slavin, will undertake the arrangements.

Standing side by side and gazing out to the statue, Slavin waits for a response from the bearded man, who remains thoughtfully silent. Then, the two men, by common accord, turn to each other. A nod is given.

"Thank you, Raphael," the tall man says. "Next week. Friday."

"Is that certain?"

"Yes."

"Fine. You will contact us in the usual fashion."

With another nod from the tall man, they part, each going his own way into the thickening crowds of rush-hour pedestrians, disappearing.

# CHAPTER 20

O n tape, Ellis is not a compelling person.

He is a youngish man with glasses, jowls that always need a shave. The camera angle is not conducive to cinematic excitement: it's a straight frontal shot, no variation in distance, and the man's facial planes are reduced to a pasty flatness.

The tapes are grainy, so that prolonged viewing is impossible. This might not be purely the result of poor technique; rather, poor technique as a means to another end. The light is intentionally too bright. On the television screen Ellis appears small, drawn; his voice quality is subdued. The unrelenting light does something, too, to the sounds, or perhaps it is the acoustics of the room or the microphone, but Ellis's words come out inconsequential, illusory.

•

The tapes had been put into a Navy van and expressed to New York, where Blake and Halpern were to take possession. In the parking lot of the Bureau's Long Island field office they'd had a last-minute standoff with a Navy security officer who insisted that Blake's papers were not certified with the proper signatures. An hour of intense, mannerly argument was unavailing. The sticking point was that specific operational material, in this case the Ellis tapes, was not covered by inter-agency protocols, and required a higher level of clearance than that possessed by Bureau agents. Blake, on the contrary, maintained that his security was generic, and entitled him, and his young AUSA, to view the most highly classified documents and that, further, requiring agents to obtain case-specific clearances would subject them to countless delays and impossible requisites.

This, of course, was precisely the point.

Calls were put in to Murphy, to Navy, to Walsh at Eastern, who kicked it up to Mullady. The officer, a lieutenant commander, presented a pinched and morose aspect; his raison d'être was to limit and deny and retain. Halpern's temper, always simmering, threatened to rise to a furious boil. *Fucking anal-retentive asshole,* the attorney said, sotto voce. Blake put out a restraining hand, but even his customary equanimity vanished in the face of such adamantine and mindless resistance. At last Donnelly, his fury aroused at this encroachment upon his fiefdom, intervened, and Blake and Halpern were allowed to take possession of half a dozen large cartons sealed with a special government adhesive tape and stamped on every available square inch with cautionary imprecations.

●

Except for a glimpse of their hands as they push documents at him, one after the other, in an endless stream that Ellis is required to identify as those which he passed to his controller, the inquisitors remain invisible. You see their hands as they light cigarettes, lift cups of coffee, unwrap a sandwich or a bagel. Once, just once, Blake catches a flash of chin and mouth—something has gone wrong with the camera and one of the men has problems adjusting it. But except for that brief moment the only image is that of Ellis.

●

Interrogation, Blake explained to Halpern as they were opening the first carton, is an art. Few people really understand it or do it well; those who do cannot explain it.

In Campbell's time things were simple, as they always were in the old days. You brought in an M & S team, muscle and smile, who did a B & C, beating and confession. It was basic abuse, with variations both obvious and subtle, physical and psychological. Sleeplessness, hunger, thirst; praise, sympathy, humiliation, anxiety. The old standbys work best: pain and fear. But never too much pain, or too much fear. The old saw that with enough pain you can get anyone to confess to anything is true, and precisely what you want to avoid.

Whatever; within the limits allowed by law, they tortured Ellis. In a civilized manner, of course.

They used four teams of two interrogators each, and worked Ellis in continuous three-hour sessions that began at six in the morning and did not end until just before midnight. Time, you see, was of the essence. There were fifteen-minute breaks for breakfast and lunch, and half an hour, at seven, for supper.

●

The interrogation uses a very standard approach. The teams go over the same material, each time going in deeper, each time the questions more specific, more challenging. There is a back-office team of analysts sitting through the night with tapes and transcripts of each day's take, feeding the stuff into computers, evaluating, comparing, and correllating, checking for discrepancy and corroboration. Before they go in, the interrogating teams are briefed for their attack.

The psych people put their two cents in too. Blake knows their advice. Try yelling at him, try not yelling; smile more, frown occasionally. Praise him. Tell him you love him, hate him, despise him. You can hear the role-playing in the voices; they sound like amateur actors, hamming it up for effect, but you had to be there, in Ellis's shoes, in the harsh, cold light, Blake supposes, to find it real. A lot of the time is taken up with cajolements, what the psych people call positive inducements. You are supposed to make the interrogee love you and fear you at the same time. You are supposed to show him that you are his only hope, his last chance. And yet, at the same time, you have to be very, very careful not to compromise the government's legal position by implying in any way, shape, or form that you have the power to absolve him of his guilt. You offer no deals, give no quarter, yet you are his friend, his savior. You actually begin to believe it yourself. That's part of the process. The training warns you: you will identify and sympathize with the interrogee. It's inevitable, something about the social response. The training will allow you to give in to all these contradictory impulses and, at the same time, permit you to control and direct them. This, too, is part of the process.

In the Ellis tapes one sees the training applied. The teams take turns attacking. Frontal, flank, from underneath—known as kicking ass. Or from the top—the appeal to the higher faculties. Come, let us reason together. The voices seem to come from all directions; Blake notes the shadows, the shifts in Ellis's eyes.

By the afternoon of the second day of viewing, Blake is able to pick out the teams, their individual members, their styles, and is able to determine, by their questions, their affiliations. The first team, the breakfast boys, are Tom and Hal. Tom sounds about thirty-five, Hal older. He sounds bald to Blake. He has a school ring on his right hand, and if Blake is interested, and for a while he thinks he might be, he can request a freeze-frame blow up and use that to begin a trace on the man. It would be an interesting exercise; he's worked with less. Tom and Hal are technical specialists from Navy. Did Ellis pass document such-and-such? What was the sequence of acquisition and transfer? Did his handlers express interest in such-and-such a manual? Did they give the impression of understanding the workings of the Wimmex system's interface with the IC-3 Command Sequence in case of nuclear attack? Did they have follow-up requests? What were those requests? Did you expect them?

At one point, in a discussion of a piece of cryptological machinery, a KWR-37, which had been mentioned a number of times in passing, and which later Blake, doing his research, discovers is one of a series of coding machines in wide use by NSA, Tom asks whether or not he, Ellis, had been tasked to obtain the series of key lists without which the machine is meaningless. Ellis's reply that no, they weren't interested, leaves both Tom and Hal speechless. You can hear their silence. Blake would like a quick cut to their faces, the reaction shot. He is sure they have gone pale. He explains it to Halpern. If the Israelis' weren't interested, it meant they already had access to the key lists, which meant they were getting them from someone with a spec-cat clearance—special category—which meant, finally, that they had a source within the ultrasecret K Unit at NSA.

The second team, the after-lunch boys, are hard bastards. Blake thinks of them as Rambo and Son of Rambo. Rambo smokes; you hear the cigarette in his mouth, see Ellis blink back from the smoke. They are Company men, a new breed of toughie of which Langley has lately become enamored. The ashtray is sometimes in frame and you see Rambo's hand, hairy with a thick gold watch, flicking ash or stubbing out a butt. By accent he is a Southerner, and judging by his fleshy wrist, big.

They are interested in tradecraft and identifications. Who did you meet and what was his name and where did you meet him? What was your travel route? What were the signals you used for contact? Did your handler talk about himself or his family or his job or his country? Did he have any hobbies or interests that you could pick up on? They show Ellis photographs, fire off lists of names. And here is where you sense

Ellis lying. Or not so much lying as holding back. Blake senses it by the pauses, the look in the man's eyes. Halpern agrees. They play these sections of the tape back and forth. The two inquisitors know it too. They want to break the man, but there are guidelines and agreements, and they have to be gentle. But they drive him crazy. They make Ellis trace his movements and his wife's and those of the people they know. They make him repeat himself. They call him on contradictions, on lapses. Pages are heard turning. Their voices have no forgiveness.

These are unedited tapes. They contain all the pauses, hesitations, repetitions, and silences of ordinary conversation. And it all happens in very real, very excruciatingly slow time. With nose blowings and coughings and yawns and itches. An occasional bathroom run. The tapes go on, and on, and on, and neither Blake nor Halpern has the patience or the fortitude or the plain dumb animal perseverance to take it for more than three days.

Nothing happens. In his training Blake had seen videos of good interrogations: there was movement, direction, purpose; a certain subtle passion. Not with Ellis. The tapes have no form.

At one point, during the morning of the third day, Halpern breaks into hysterical laughter. It is during a long sequence in which a technical team takes Ellis through an entire maintenance manual for a machine that produces another machine used to configure a ultra low-sound-signature submarine propeller. Page by page. Halpern, staring at the screen in the dark room, sniggers. Blake looks his way, puzzled. The lawyer begins to laugh. And Blake, after an alarmed moment, joins him. They can't stop. It is hilarious. Ellis doesn't know what the hell these men are talking about. They are showing him pictures of propellers, talking about screws, and Halpern is pointing at the screen and laughing hysterically like a crazed donkey. Blake has to wipe tears from his cheeks.

The transcripts would have been better, but not by much, for though they have none of the long silences of the tapes, they form a stack of papers about six feet high. Anyone who could read through that wouldn't have the imagination to do anything with it. It would be like sifting through a garbage bin looking for a piece of candy. The goodies are there, and you know that you will find them eventually, but the problem is that some of the candy is not healthy for you. In fact, it is poisoned, planted there by an evil magician. And you need the specialists from the CIA to tell you which is the good candy. If you eat the bad stuff, you can become very, very sick.

What Blake wants, what he needs, and at last Halpern is beginning to appreciate this, is the analytical product. Forget this bullshit, these ridiculous tapes. We need the extracts, the annotated and cross-indexed transcripts. That's where the names and dates and places are all linked with colors and boxes and asterisks and lines and brackets and arrows, and that's where we're going to find the names, codenames and worknames, surnames, given and middle names.

Which means that Blake is going to call on Frank Campbell.

And the prosecutor is going to go to Tippet, and Tippet is going to hit those keys and not stop until he pulls something hard out of that damned machine of his that Blake can bring to Donnelly at his case meeting, barely a month away.

●

"Frank, what the hell."

Campbell, glowering at his desk, has just informed Blake that his retirement has been brought forward by about a month. Midnight, September 30, Matty boy.

"Goddamn it, Frank." Blake's assumption is that Donnelly is forcing Campbell out.

Campbell says nothing, but he displays a face full of anger.

"Just leaving a little sooner, Matt. They sweetened the pot."

"Frank."

Nothing to be alarmed about: a revision in the retirement plan had come down the other day giving Campbell an extra couple of thousand on his pension if he left by October 1. Blake is shaken. They are planning to party the big man out in style, at McMann's. He is organizing the affair, has been collecting for the gift, contacting the supervisors Campbell has worked for over the years. What might this portend for himself? Campbell hadn't H'MP ASSed too well. In more ways than one. Goddamnit. At the banquet, Blake intends to give a comic overview of Campbell's career, then present the watch engraved with Campbell's favorite expression: TELL ME ANOTHER.

Blake will have to spread the word, get moving on changing the date. McMann's might be booked up.

"Frank, just when I need you."

Campbell thanks him with a glare.

"You still working Ellis, Matt?"

"It's not Ellis anymore, Frank. He doesn't exist."

Nor, for that matter, Blake fears, does the elusive Starfield.

# CHAPTER 21

Lupus erythematosus. In the vernacular, wolf rash." The young doctor wears whites, and a stethoscope shows from a low side pocket. He is giving a mini presentation to his visitor who, as the doctor understands, is a consulting physician brought in at the request of interested family members. All professional courtesies are being extended, and he feels obliged to be sociable.

"The disease hasn't captured the imagination of the public or the medical establishment, the way other diseases have. Cancer, for instance. The way polio did. AIDS, of course."

There is nothing particularly distinguishing about the doctor's physical appearance except his almost total and premature baldness. In manner he is pleasant, if slightly officious, and seems quite capable of carrying on a conversation entirely by himself. This suits his visitor perfectly, who has to merely smile and nod for the doctor to feel his comments have been reciprocated.

"Did you know that Flannery O'Connor died of lupus?"

Yes, the tall, bearded physician knows, but had not recently thought of it, and is pleased, by his smile, to have been reminded.

The doctor is leading them down a long hall toward a bright but diffuse block of sunlight. He speaks of the complications of lupus's more advanced stages: edema resulting in severe weight gain; kidney damage; loss of protein due to this improper kidney function. All in turn leading to more complex systemic malfunctions. They walk side by side. The hall is very long and the light seems to collect at the end, near the elevators, a distant and discrete oasis of life. The doctor talks on. The treatment of lupus is not amenable to the high-tech approach; drug therapy is primarily employed, prednisone, a cortisone derivative, being the drug of choice. In this case the pregnancy limits treatment, naturally. But it is not, the young doctor assures his visitor, at all unusual for women to carry to term. In fact, many women find that the hormonal changes during pregnancy exert a salutary effect. This is not altogether surprising, he continues, since lupus itself is a kind of internal, self-generated cannibalism in which the body produces antibodies directed against its own organs. And in pregnancy, you see—the visiting physician nods, for he wishes the young doctor to talk on—the body undercuts, you see, its own rejection mechanisms, the fetus being, in the strict biological sense, an invading organism. Somewhat paradoxical, is it not? In the present case, alas, this has not been so. In addition, it has been made clear to him, through other parties, that the health of the unborn child is to be considered paramount, and, therefore, treatment has not been as aggressive as he himself would have recommended.

The doctor and his visitor now stand in the light, waiting for the elevator. The doctor presses the elevator button again and continues talking.

"Unfortunately, lupus doesn't have a lobby behind it." He wishes to draw from the older, more reserved physician more than a smile, more than a prompting nod. He feels that there is something to be said about the politics of lupus that is important, considering how often doctors have been maligned as sexist and unresponsive to women. He doesn't consider himself a feminist, he says as they wait for the elevator. Feminism, for some reason, strikes him as an inappropriate posture for a medical practitioner. But, compared to the general state of political reactionariness—is that a proper construct?—in the medical profession, he is a flaming radical. A disinterested observer might say that this young doctor appears to be striking a defensive position, though it is unclear from which quarter he expects an attack. One can see that he has been bothering himself on this issue. Perhaps he has had a number of arguments with his wife, perhaps he has been disputing these points with colleagues. You see, the disease strikes mostly young women of child-bearing age, and of course one has been sensitized to the gross and perpetual injustices visited upon that particular demographic group. He is now rambling on, as the older man simply offers an encouraging silence. But at last the elevator arrives.

"Please."

They ascend in silence. The doctor has decided that his quiet visitor is simply not going to be drawn out. He is obviously a self-contained gentleman, a well-practiced doctor. Well, the woman's family has money. His thoughts turn to the past weekend during which he and his wife had socialized with colleagues at a surgeon's home in Westchester. About three quarters of an acre and an in-ground pool. Talk had turned to money, as it always did. There was an arthritis man, the head of rheumatology in an upstate hospital; he was talking shop with the surgeon who, during the week, had performed three hysterectomies, at four thousand per, two lumpidectomies and a radical. The surgeon spoke about a tennis court. Twelve thousand, was the quote. "Just have to whack out a few more uteri." It was that phrase that, overheard by some of the guests, later led to a ferocious argument between the doctor and his wife, and which now causes him to offer a contrite silence regarding the impending tragedy that shall be the Ellis woman's fate. They stop in front of her room. He hands his visitor a face mask.

He taps lightly on the door, opens it.

"After you, Doctor."

●

"Have you ever been in after an S and D?"

Blake is slowing for the exit on Interstate 95. Halpern isn't sure to what Blake is referring.

"Search and Discover." He takes the long curving ramp, stops at the stop sign, flips his left flasher on. He drives by the book, the way the Bureau likes it, albeit with more verve.

"No," replies Halpern. "We don't usually visit any of the scenes."

No, indeed, thinks Blake. That would be too real.

He says, turning the Ford into the far lane, "The teams usually go through like Rambo."

Halpern has heard that.

They are heading north, into Fairfield County. Blake watches for the turnoff. Campbell had told him that it comes up fast.

"What are we looking for?" asks Halpern.

"County Road 311." Blake glances down at his yellow pad. "It's right after a big red sign. Jack's Hardware."

Blake keeps an eye on the gauges. The Ford is from the Bureau pool, government olive, no chrome, basic interior, underpowered, and totally lacking in road status. It's two in the afternoon, very hot, disgustingly humid. The air-conditioning is on high, the engine straining on this dippy, curvy road. Both Blake and Halpern have their jackets off. Blake's sunglasses are on the dashboard of the family wagon—he never has them when he needs them—and he has to squint against the glare slanting off the hood. The lawyer has on a pair of spiffy aviators.

"There is it." Halpern is pointing. CR 311. Blake slows, turns. They are on a narrow road without shoulders that takes a long S curve up to the right. The Ford strains to pick up speed. Blake flicks his eye to the temperature gauge, then to the yellow pad. About three miles to go.

He picks up the thread of conversation. "The S and D teams are professionals. You'd be surprised at what they find, and where."

"I'm sure."

Blake throws a look at the lawyer. He's not in his good and aggressive spirit, probably doesn't like to leave his office on a hot, muggy day to take a trip in a lowly vehicle with crummy air-conditioning to see a house that's been gone through by a bunch of Bureau thugs. He'd rather be on the phone, pushing and badgering, using his government-issued powers to terrorize the citizenry.

"It's good to get out in the field now and then," Blake deadpans.

Halpern does not reply.

A flash of color in the rearview mirror catches Blake's eye: there's a low-slung, red car tailgating. Blake tries to coax more speed out of his four cylinders but they're going uphill, and the Ford just doesn't have any reserve. Ignoring the little red car, Blake keeps his eye on the road as they approach the crest. It's a pleasant part of Connecticut. A narrow road, pretty facades flashing behind the thick summer foliage.

"Nice houses," he offers.

Manifestly, Halpern's interest doesn't lie in suburban residential property, but he's willing to make conversation. "Yeah, pretty expensive out here."

"Yes. Fairfield County. Greenwich is only three or four exits back. The closer to the city the more expensive. Every exit is another fifty thousand for the same house." He knows, he and his wife having priced the real estate when they moved back on his last transfer and upgrade.

"How did he afford it?"

"His wife's family is wealthy."

"So money wasn't really a motive?"

"Money's always a motive."

Blake checks the mirror. The red car is riding tight. It's making him nervous. The Ford's license is marked, white with blue lettering, standard government issue, GS 11, but this doesn't prevent the driver of the fast little car from tailgating. No respect. On the gauge the needle is swinging up to HOT. They're chugging up the hill. He's not going to turn off the air. He checks the odometer. They've gone about two and three-quarter miles, the road is still curvy, solid double lines all the way, and the pushy little car in back is hugging their rear, waiting for its chance. He can't make out the driver through the heavy tint of windshield glass. They crest, and the Ford picks up speed on the downhill run, the gauge drops, and the red car falls back.

"Keep your eye out for a white and green wooden post."

"Right or left?"

Blake looks at his yellow pad where he has Campbell's directions, can't find the line, catches the Ford in a swerve. "Right. It's going to be coming up any moment. The moron in back'll have to wait."

Halpern turns to look. The car is just about touching their rear bumper. The manual has a suggestion for just such a situation, and Blake reaches to the dash and pulls out the headlight switch, which turns on his brake lights. The red car drops back with a quick deceleration; he must have downshifted. Then the car honks and zooms up to the Ford's tail. Blake's face is tight.

"You just passed it."

"Shit."

"White pole," says Halpern. "Green on top. It was hidden by some bushes."

Blake lets out a breath. No shoulder, only a grassy, weedy dip about three feet wide. He slows and pulls carefully to the right. The little car swings into the left lane, pauses for a long moment alongside the Ford. A young man with dark glasses. With a long angry toot and a burst of exhaust the car roars away. The driver's hand is out the window, his finger raised. Blake blasts back.

Halpern has his head out his window. "Fuuuuuck you!"

Blake puts the Ford in neutral. There's no room to turn. According to the manual, the driver shall proceed to the next available safe turning area and shall there execute a full reverse turn. "I don't like doing this on a curve, but . . ." He twists around, backs up with just a bit of a weave. The white post with the green top approaches and Blake stops, shifts, and turns into the driveway.

The house is set in a clearing; pines and maples form a perimeter around the grass, and a pin oak with its compact, conical crown stands to the side. There are rhododendrons and lilac bushes in front of the trees, azaleas line the bluestone path to the entrance. The earth has been dug up along the foundation and some of the shrubs are uprooted, their leaves a dying, dessicated brown. The grass needs mowing.

Blake pulls the Ford to the closed garage. When he turns off the ignition the engine keeps chugging, then stops with a sigh. They get out. Halpern's back has a big damp splotch on it. The lawyer puts on his jacket, straightens his tie. Blake opens his attaché case, straps on his pistol. God knows why he brought it, the clip is in his basement desk. He puts on his jacket. They close the doors, roll up windows, all buttons down. Regulations. He should raise the hood, let some of the engine heat escape, but that's contrary to the manual. He's going to do it anyway; he unlocks the driver's door, releases the hood lock, and lifts the hood. The engine is ticking.

"Nice little house," says Blake.

It is. The windows are sealed, shades down, curtains closed. The clapboard's white, the trim around the windows and entry door a deep mauve, a more pleasing combination than one would think. Except for the upturned earth, which has long lost its ugly rawness, and the bushes lying on their sides, the only sign that the premises have been subject to government attention is a big shiny padlock and a block-print notice on the door. PREMISES SEALED PURSUANT TO COURT ORDER. There are no sounds of cars, trucks, people. The sun is bright and hot in the clearing.

"They have about an acre. It's appraised at three fifty." Blake is amused at himself; he sounds like a broker. He has the key out. "Let's go in and see what the boys did."

●

The woman in the bed breathes with an easy, shallow rhythm. Her face is bloated and her hands, relaxing on either side of her hips, are puffy. Her bed has been cranked, and she reclines very gently, a sea-foam-green blanket covers her upswelling abdomen. Tilted the wrong way, the blinds hold back the light, and the room is lit with a dull and pale wash of no particular color.

The young doctor stands at the foot of the bed; his visitor, after a moment of indecision, moves closer to the window, coming between the woman and the light. She stirs, rising slowly through a fretful sleep. He waits, and at last his presence wakes her.

"You are here." Her voice is hollow.

She keeps her eyes closed and carefully turns her head upon the pillow. Her medication, the doctor has explained, makes for strange dreams.

"Rachel," the visitor says.

"My husband?"

Her eyes open for a moment, her hand comes up and wipes a fleeting chimera from across her forehead.

"Are you my husband?"

He says nothing. The untinted light in the room is like the cool filtered air blowing from the ceiling vents, a light that is like the air itself, producing no shadows, having no substance.

She is beginning to wake, and looks at the man. The surgical mask covers his lower face, and for a long while they stare at each other. He is not her husband. The doctor watches them, wondering.

"I bring you love," says the man at last. His words come through the mask clearly.

"Love?"

"From your husband."

"My husband? You've seen my husband? When did you see him?"

Her questions are fitfully spoken; she is impatient with this man's parsimony, his quietness, the eyes that never leave hers, probing for her innermost secrets. Standing very still in the pale wash of light, he seems to be part of her dream.

The woman is now, at last, awake. The man has called her Rachel. That is not her name. Why has he done this?

"When can I see my husband? They said I will see him. Can you bring him to me?"

"Yes."

"You will bring him to me? When?"

"Soon. Very soon."

The doctor standing at the foot of the bed takes all this in. He is puzzled, but sees no danger to his patient. He watches the man sit on the bed and take the woman's hand in both of his. He is removing his surgical mask.

The woman's regard is long and silent.

He has called her Rachel. This is what they agreed to, she remembers. She was to be Rachel.

"I know you."

Wide awake now, and fighting off the effects of whatever drugs they have given her, she searches his eyes. The puffy skin of her face is radiant with a false health. She studies his face, the eyes behind the glasses. The beard is not familiar. Perhaps they have never met, but she knows him. He has said he comes from her husband. But when will she see him again? There isn't much time.

Suddenly she withdraws her hand and hides it under the covers. She tries to sit up but the slant of the bed and her distended abdomen prevent her.

When she speaks her voice is cold and bitter.

"What do you want now?"

●

For a full minute they stand in the entrance foyer of what was once the Ellis home. Blake has been in other premises after an S & D team has gone through, but this is breathtaking in its utter destruction. The house has been closed for months, the electricity off, and the heat and stench are overpowering. Halpern doesn't move from his spot. Someone, one of the wreckers, maybe someone from the Ellis family coming in later, had, with a broad horsehair broom which is propped against the wall, pushed a swath through the debris to the base of the interior stairway. Blake takes a few steps on this path and looks through a doorway. The dining room. Halpern is still in the foyer, unable to move. Sometimes the team takes pity and stacks the breakables out of the way, will roll up the rugs and carpets before attacking the flooring, but not in this case.

Blake turns and steps over a mound of broken pottery. The living room. Unconsciously, he makes a noise in his throat. Evil forces have swept through. Like torn animals, the long green sofa and two matching chairs have been left to die, their innards ripped out. Near the window the baby grand piano is a mess of wire and wood. Its key are on the floor. Ugly, thinks Blake, like teeth smashed from someone's mouth. The heat is truly unbearable. He looks again at the dining room: plates on the floor, a large vase in pieces, a side butler with its doors broken, linens strewn about in heaps.

The walls, all of them, have been smashed through to their hollows. The heavy plaster, and the underlying lathing, had provoked the searchers into a frenzy, and they have broken everything looking for hiding places. Pictures have been taken down and ripped, flooring has been pried up. Lighting fixtures dangle from the ceilings, and there are large holes around the electrical boxes.

There is an intermittent buzzing off to the right, like the alarm of a clock radio running out of power.

Blake turns to look at the attorney. Halpern, pale, sweating, is moving gingerly through the debris.

"Fucking animals," he says.

Reality, kid.

Blake moves to the right, where the buzzing comes from. The kitchen. He stands on the outside of the saloon doors and looks in. Halpern makes his way over. Food everywhere, refrigerator open, not running. Flies and heat and feculent rot. A small heap of what were once lemons are a squishy mound of fuzzy green mold. The flies are buzzing loudly in languorous circles. Blake should have remembered to bring a couple of cans of insecticide.

Blake leading, they go through the living room and stand at the stairs leading to the upper floor, the bedrooms. In layout, it is a house not unlike his own. The carpeting, of the same color as his, has been torn from the steps. The treads and risers have been ripped off, the wood thrown haphazardly to the floor. He's been on other sites when the teams were working. They came in with jackhammers and crowbars, sledges, power saws. They carried upholstery knives, magnetic probes, plumbing tools. He never cared to hang around. The S & D team, Search and Destroy, the scavengers. In this case, they were furies. Espionage cases did that. Faithlessness seems to bring out the demon in some men.

They stand at the foot of the stairs. They don't have to go up to know what's there. The mattresses would be torn apart—more than torn, disemboweled—clothing would be everywhere, all seams would be ripped open and linings torn off; drawers pulled out and overturned, back panels of chests smashed. Bottles and tubes of lotions, creams, perfumes, medicines, and toothpaste would have been smashed or cut through, emptied in the bathtub or, in this case, most likely, on the floor. Books would have been given the full treatment: pages ripped, bindings slashed. Bathrooms are the playgrounds of the S & D people, the resistant tiles a challenge. Blake doesn't have to go downstairs, either—the basement will be in the same state.

"Let's go." Halpern is at the door.

Outside, the sun is a clean relief. Blake replaces the padlock carefully. Halpern stands near the car, holding his jacket. His shirt is wet front and back. Blake closes the hood, unlocks the car, and opens all the doors to let out the hot air.

Halpern, grim, is looking at the house, expecting the wild monster who ravaged it to rush out. Blake slips out of his shoulder holster and puts it back into his attaché case. When he looks up, Halpern is standing in front of the entrance door.

Blake joins him. The attorney is staring at the jamb, the slab of wood that forms the outer frame of the doorway. There is something attached to the wood, nailed, and painted over with the rich mauve of the trim.

The lawyer is working a key under this thing, prying it up. "They missed this," says Halpern. He's got it off and shows it to Blake. It's a thin tubular casing about three inches long, metal, kind of like a big capsule with holes on either end where nails or screws are inserted. Turned over, there is a flimsy paper backing, which Halpern removes. Inside is another piece of paper. With his key, Halpern gently lifts the paper and unrolls it. Hebrew letters in black ink fill the paper. The lawyer turns it over; more Hebrew writing.

"Parchment," says Halpern. A mezuzah. He spells it for Blake. Jewish people put it on their entryways. Blake turns the paper over in his hands. Incomprehensible scribbles. "Ellis might have used the mezuzah as a drop, if that's the right word," says Halpern.

It is, Blake says. A drop, a place to leave a communication. But you can see by the paint that it hasn't been disturbed for a while. Well, it was worth a try. Halpern takes the parchment and reads it to himself, his lips moving slightly. No, nothing. Anyway, it's good to know about the, how do you say it? Mezuzah. The team missed it.

"Well," says Blake once they're out on the winding, dipping road. Halpern's face is set in an expression of distaste. Blake talks in a professional voice. "What they look for, you see, is evidence of tradecraft. Code books, cryptograms, cameras, instructions. You'd be surprised how important those things are for a case." He's watching the gauge, doesn't like the way the needle is hovering around HOT. "It's the stuff that the counterintelligence people want. They want to know the mechanics of the operation because very often that tells them who's running the spy. Tradecraft—it's a signature." To himself, he sounds like an instructor in a training course.

"The dining room." Halpern's voice is pinched. "Did you see that?"

Yes, Blake was there and saw it.

"And the kitchen."

Blake saw that too.

"Fucking unnecessary."

For the briefest of moments their eyes lock before Blake returns to the road; this hotshot bastard in his fine suit and his righteous indignation. Very, very sensitive all of a sudden.

The needle is already in the red. He shuts off the air conditioner. They open the windows to the hot, noisy rush of air, and drive back in silence. It's an unpleasant drive, very slow going, hot and smelly. In Blake's pocket is the disassembled mezuzah. Not that he doesn't trust Halpern, but he wants his forensic people to check it out. Also, the boys on the S & D teams ought to be told; every little bit of tradecraft helps.

Later, having dropped Halpern off at City Hall to catch the subway to Brooklyn, he regrets, for a moment, having confronted Halpern with such ugliness. But they had been looking too long at words, at computer printouts, at reports and forms, and it hadn't been real. The house full of flies and smells and destruction was. That was how it's going to be, and it's time to face it. If and when they nail Starfield it is going to be ugly, too.

●

What Blake had not noticed was the young man in the small red car watching through a pair of binoculars as he and Halpern had gone into the house. The man was slender, dark haired, and had pulled off the road, climbing to a hill in the distance from which the little clearing in front of Ellis's house was visible. He watched them go in and then, after their fifteen minutes, come out, had watched while the taller, younger man had fiddled with the key on the door jamb. The binoculars were quite powerful and he was able to capture in his field of vision the two sets of hands as the men passed the parchment between them.

And with his long telephoto lens, which he is now detaching, he was able to capture, in more permanent fashion, the faces of the gray-haired, older agent, and his companion.

That, together with the license number of their chugging Ford, shall provide much information. For everything, everything, is on paper.

●

A little after four, sitting at his desk and going over his chronologies, Blake gets a call from Halpern.

"Matt. Navy's picked up on Starfield. He came in about three weeks ago."

Halpern's voice is trembling with excitement. "I want to do a break and enter."

Blake is silent.

"What do you call it, Matt? A black bag job."

"What, exactly, Richard, do you want us to break into?"

Halpern names a few places. Tippet has just begun tracking him in the States—Starfield's little downtown office, one of his hotel rooms.

"We have to be aggressive, Matt, rather than the opposite."

"We need a warrant, Richard. What's the PC?"

"The probable cause, Matt, is that I can make a pretty good case that our target is acting in the interests of a foreign power. I bet we can get him on agent registration, at least."

Blake isn't so sure, but he doesn't argue.

"I've spoken with Wright at Internal Security and he'll sign off on the warrant. He thinks we have enough. He's got a judge, too."

Where does Halpern come up with these people?

"I can get the warrant signed by Monday. So how long? A day, a week, what?"

Blake explains that a surreptitious entry is complicated. The Bureau has very, very strict guidelines on black bag jobs. There's a lot of preparation. He will have to arrange a pretext visit—fake a utility call or a telephone repair, send out a few agents pretending to be one of those cable TV companies scouting sites. Then he's got to do a T & P—time and person—surveillance so they know who's coming and going. He has to line up his people. They'll need a good picks and locks man; he needs a forensic agent—a physical evidence man—to go in with a camera. They'll need an agent riding shotgun outside, probably two. A van or car with radio hookups. Then there's the paperwork: everything's got to be requisitioned and signed out. The agents will be on standby, ready to go in when the premises are vacant, which means a lot of overtime and that makes him uncomfortable. If it's a weekend job everyone, including himself and Halpern, will be pissed.

All this is obvious once it's explained, but like most U.S. attorneys, Halpern doesn't want to know. Like the Ellis house, it's too dirty. Leave it to the guys with the polyester suits and the guns, the lower classes.

"Time," Halpern is saying into Blake's ear with an imperious tone, "is of the essence."

Well, it always is. Blake will make a point of scheduling the break-in on one of Halpern's Hamptons weekends. A nice, sunny, beach Saturday. Another dose of reality.

Closing off, Halpern wants to know if Blake will go down to Washington with him for another briefing with Navy. Thanks, but no thanks. He's got a lot of paper to get through, a lot of family business. Yeah, says Halpern; he's busy too, it's his weekend at the beach. They'll stay in touch. In the meantime, let's work on that break-in.

For a number of minutes, Blake sits very still at his desk, mulling, working a clip into a square. After a while, not quite satisfied with the angle of the bends, he discards the wire in his wastebasket and rings Campbell, who has a minute and tells Blake to come down. Blake finds the flushed Irishman in the midst of cleaning out his desk.

"Frank."

"Yeah."

Blake watches the big man put papers into an official Bureau storage carton. The boxes are the size of milk crates. There are three of them on the floor.

Blake is stunned.

"Frank, goddamn it."

Campbell continues packing.

"Donnelly," says Blake. "The bastard."

"Tell me another, Matty," Campbell replies. "Just tell me a fucking 'nother."

Blake watches him pack. The Irishman's face is red, as always after lunch, his mouth tight. His eyes are full of glare and, in this light, just for a brief moment, overflowing with loss.

●

When Blake gets back to his desk his phone is ringing. Murphy's on the other end, glad to have caught him. He got a call a while ago from Williams, over at I-DAC, who's ticked up, as Murphy puts it. "Your boy is trying to pull rank on a bunch of traces."

Blake thinks: I-DAC? Inter-Data Access Center.

My boy, who's my boy?

Who else?

Murphy goes on. Everyone wants to jump the line, but your prosecutor rubbed Williams the wrong way, and he called Walsh at Eastern. Halpern's a pushy kid.

"That's part of his charm."

Murphy says yeah, but remember there's an agreement on Ellis.

Blake knows that.

Murphy wants that knowledge in writing.

"I'll memo you, George. Give me a day."

Murphy reminds him that Donnelly will carry him only so far.

Blake knows.

"Call Walsh, will you. Keep me informed." Pause. "On second thought, don't."

Half a joke; they chuckle.

"We'll talk on that memo, Matt," says Murphy, and they hang up.

Blake's first reaction is to pick up the phone and bawl out Halpern for being the pushy kid he is, but he refrains. He wants to give this some thought and work out the angles. He swivels his chair to the window. Outside the sky is promising one of its most glorious sunsets of the last seven years, and Blake appreciates this beauty as a fitting backdrop to his growing sense of satisfaction.

He doesn't like his name being used without permission, though one can argue that permission is implicit. By making it known that he's working the Ellis case, Halpern has stripped him of some, though not all, of his protective anonymity. Donnelly, perturbed, wants a memo indicating that Blake's push on Starfield doesn't vitiate the agreement Justice and Navy have hammered out on Ellis; fine, they're covering themselves.

Blake puts his hand out for the phone, again to call Halpern, and again withdraws.

Some good, some serendipitous good, has been accomplished here.

I've got all the time in the world, he tells himself, as long as I do it before Donnelly's triage meeting, to disown Halpern and abort the investigation. It is not that time, yet. Let the boy push a little more. Ruffle a few feathers. He's young and aggressive and hungry and he wants a case. Let the word get out that a hunt is in progress and that Blake is one of the hunters. Good. He likes that. Perhaps this is just the right moment to apply a little devious pressure. It's been his experience that a short period of initial and intense uncertainty does wonders in the opening phases of an investigation, especially one in which in-house political considerations tend to subordinate substance to mandarin form. He rocks in his chair and watches the sky over the harbor. The air there has a dusty thickness that traps the tilting light in the west, and is just beginning to redden. Halpern has actually done me a favor; he's put me on the map without revealing my exact location.

Someone watching Blake would wonder if the man was going through a strange, compulsive ritual, for he reaches for the phone again, thinking to catch Walsh, but again withdraws his hand. He knows Walsh; Walsh likes his AUSAs pushy. If Blake comes in with the right tone, they'll both chuckle and agree to let the problem solve itself in the interagency marketplace. It's another version of the squeaky hinge getting the oil. He who asks will sometimes receive; but he who demands, usually does. Looking westward, he sees how the red leaches through the higher blues, the colors bleeding downward in wispy tendrils of dense orange and lighter pinks. He will call Walsh, but not before Monday, most likely late Tuesday or early Wednesday. Chances are that by then, the point, whatever it was, will be moot. That's another bit of wisdom that Blake has acquired over the years: procrastination has its own rewards.

As for Williams, his complaint is one of those petty grievances that the RIPs over at I-DAC are famous for. Are all your forms in? Is every *t* crossed? Are they block stamped? They're file clerks glorified with security clearances needing a bit of massage now and then. Like all paper pushers, however, they can make you or break you. Blake will sweet-talk this Williams on Monday. But not too sweetly; they have to know they are there to serve.

Blake reaches once more for the phone and this time dials Eastern headquarters. Halpern's line is busy. Probably lining up the judge for the break-and-enter warrant. Blake cradles the mouthpiece between neck and shoulder, watching the sunset. He doesn't mind the wait; the traffic will be thinner for it. As for Murphy, his once-upon-a-time mentor, he's going to run him around just a bit on that memo. Let Murphy and Donnelly sweat a little. Let them think they might have created a monster, the sort of beast which wrecked the Ellis house. He smiles at the thought and leans back in the chair, still cradling the receiver, thinking that Halpern shall be his bush beater. He will encourage the young man, albeit carefully, to keep thwacking the drums and stomping his feet, just to see what comes running out into the light of day.

●

The Greenspans think Albert Deere is doing an excellent job. He and his assistants work at a steady, determined pace. The studding is almost complete, and the electrical wiring will soon be in place. Soon they will begin the Sheetrocking. He warns Mrs. Greenspan, however, that the last quarter of the work often takes more than half the time.

Until the walls are finished, they cannot put on the baseboard and the moldings and trim. They have to scrape and refinish the floors. The American boy, Danny, is assigned the task of preparing the new doors, and is kept busy mortising out the lock holes and hinges. Natan does not come often. When Mrs. Greenspan asks Deere where his young man is, he smiles his impish smile and tells her that he has already begun another job, and will be bouncing back and forth between here and there. Soon Danny will go there too.

And, for himself, once he is finished here, he will join them.

"But you won't leave until you're done?" Mrs. Greenspan is worried; she has heard horror stories from their friends about contractors who, leaving too soon and promising to return, never do.

"I stay until we finish." Deere's freckled face was reassuring. "Even if I move in with you."

●

A little before seven, Blake pulls into the driveway of his split ranch in Eastmere. Due to an especially irritating delay caused by the usual convocation of road morons at the Elmhurst tanks, he is foul of mood and unfit for family intercourse. He finds his daughter in the living room, and they manage to get into an argument about, of all things, the digital versus the analog approach to life. It's for her term paper, apparently. Wedding music is a soft background. Life, she says, can be seen as analog—bumps and dips on the winding road of existence. Blake, standing in his steamy suit, thinks digital is more accurate: tiny blips of experience, the data all the same but strung out in different sequences.

"Very Skinnerian," counters Maureen.

"Don't try to put me in someone else's black box."

Maureen appreciates this, and then remembers: "Dad. One of your lawyers called."

"Richard Halpern."

"Yeah, he said he's going to drop something off."

"Did he say what, when?"

"He said about eight. It's on the note."

He is standing over her as she lounges on the couch. "Maureen. Use sunscreen."

"I do, Dad."

"Your mother said we're going out for supper. Are you going to be home?"

"I don't know."

"You have something planned?"

"Dad, I don't know."

He goes to the refrigerator and jams a glass into the ice dispenser. God, it's loud.

Maureen follows him into the kitchen.

"If you're not sure you'll be home I'll leave a note, he can slip it through the mail slot, though I don't like that."

"Top-secret stuff, Dad?"

"No, it's not top-secret stuff. It's just that there's—"

"—no substitute for hand delivery."

"That's right, Maureen."

"I'll be home."

He drinks the water.

His daughter says, "I think you're going out for Chinese food. With the Swains."

"You think or you know?"

"A strong think, Dad."

He looks at the clock. "I better wash up. When did the lawyer call?"

"About half an hour ago."

He'll be here soon; he's going out early for his half share of beach weekend. "You're sure about the Chinese food?"

"Pretty sure."

"Where's your mother?"

"The caterers, I think."

"Okay, I'm going to shower. Where will you be?"

"Downstairs."

"You'll get the bell, then?"

"Yes, Dad, I'll get the bell."

He looks at her. She's got enough on, certainly; but in some way her body's latent charge has rendered the satiny fabric of her shirt and shorts permeable to her flesh, so that she seems naked, not to the eye, but to the other, higher faculties.

"Maureen, I want you to use sunscreen."

"Dad."

●

The voices reach the upper floor indistinctly; the baritone is Halpern's. Blake dresses quickly. The attorney is standing near the couch. Blake's wife is on the love seat. Maureen has put herself in the doorway between the kitchen and living room drinking beer from a can. Her polo is now tucked into her shorts and her hair has been put up into a thick, quick pony tail.

"Matt."

"You've met my wife and daughter?"

"I have."

On the coffee table is a big manila envelope. Halpern hands it to Blake, who moves off to the side near the window. The attorney follows. They converse. The women observe, interested. From their quiet huddle one hears affidavit, probable cause, least-intrusive, agent of a foreign power. The men are out of their professional context, and there is a palpable awkwardness between them, exacerbated by the silent women. Halpern is facing the kitchen, and his eyes keep shifting over Blake's shoulder and back again. They soon finish their conversation and return to the center of the room. Maureen is gone. Blake's wife offers Halpern a beer, or a glass of wine, and there is a hesitancy for a moment, but no, he has to drive and should be going. He and Blake speak briefly at the door, agreeing to talk again, soon, or whenever necessary, whichever comes first. Blake closes the door after him.

"So, are we having Chinese food?"

"Yes, with the Swains. We should get going."

"The Jade Teacup?"

Yes, his wife replies.

"Thanks for entertaining Halpern. How long was he here?"

"Five minutes."

"How were the caterers?"

"We have to decide on the hors d'oeuvres."

Blake thought they were going to go with the Continental smorgasbord; whatever, they will talk about it in the car.

From a window upstairs, where he has gone to get his wallet, he sees Maureen standing at the curb speaking with Halpern. She has one hand across her stomach, the other holds the beer. His car is a small, black, sporty, foreign thing.

Blake's wife is calling. When they step outside the car is gone and Maureen is coming in.

"Are you staying home?"

She doesn't answer until she's gone past. "I don't know."

"Don't you have finals soon?"

The question bounces off the closing door.

Blake drives. Their conversation is disjointed and never really gets going. There is too much to talk about, they both want their say, every topic has its side avenues, they are in the parking lot too soon. The Swains are already seated at a window, and wave to them as Blake pulls in.

His wife says, as they walk to the entrance, "Your lawyer is a very handsome young man."

# CHAPTER 22

**C**an you give me a close-up?"

The Marine guard works the controls. The sound of the lens turning causes the man on the bed to open his eyes and Blake has the uncomfortable sensation of being stared at. He can't see me, Blake tells himself. The image zooms until the face fills the screen. The man has grown a mustache; he's dark, dark hair, dark eyes, dark life.

"Thank you," says Blake, "that's fine. Thank you."

He could have had the spy brought out, but decided, instead, to see him in his cell. There is an impulse of hospitality he wishes to engender in the prisoner. The Bureau psychologist, Dr. Bauer, had agreed. Perhaps, Blake had ventured, there was a clever stratagem that might be applied to the man. The psychologist did not think so. Ellis exhibits all the characteristics of the unbreakable spy. He turned once, Mr. Blake, he won't turn again.

In the argot, the man possesses an intact superego. Ellis believes in what he's done. Not that there are no fears and misgivings—no sane man can avoid going just a little bit crazy after being in a cell more than a week—but he has acted in accord with higher and more compelling moralities, as he sees them. And there is the special circumstance of the wife. Dr. Bauer thought it interesting, in a literary sort of way. One saw the paradox therein, the dying woman carrying a new life, yet one was unclear of its pertinence, or how to exploit it. It was an unsatisfactory consultation. Good luck, Mr. Blake.

While the Marine guard waits, Blake takes a few minutes in the corridor to prepare himself and then, signaling to the soldier for Ellis's cell to be opened, presents himself carefully, cautiously, just inside the door that then closes with a silent, gliding finality. Calling once again upon his latent talents as an actor, Blake has dressed himself with the affect of an intruding, yet diffident guest. He and Dr. Bauer had discussed various postures: he might have come in like a master, hard and righteous, demanding tribute; perhaps a friend. Or a relative—the psychologist suggested that a perusal of the profile might reveal someone in Ellis's life that Blake might want to imitate; they had had much success with fathers and brothers. None of these were Blake's choices. Instead, he stands patiently, waiting for his captive host to welcome him.

Ellis has sat up on his mattress. Their eye contact is long before Ellis breaks off. His hands lie loosely across his thighs. Ellis knows who Blake is—his lawyer has insisted on certain protocols—but now Blake formally introduces himself and offers his hand, which is taken softly. Good, a semblance of normality.

Now Blake must do something with his body, which, though fine and slender as it is, intrudes with a gross presence. In this small room, where is he to go? He cannot sit on the floor, there is no chair, and he cannot join Ellis on the edge of his bed for the mattress will sag, surely, and they will be too close. Nor can he sit on the toilet—there is a seat, but no cover.

He will stand.

"It's a warm summer day out there," says Blake.

Ellis looks up, then away, and Blake says nothing more. The silence, the stillness, rather, is total; the air is clean, very cool, coming from a ceiling vent. The bulb above is enclosed in a wire mesh. The cell itself is about ten by ten, its walls white painted concrete, not unpleasant.

Blake knows this man, has seen him on the tapes, read the profiles, conferred with Dr. Bauer, come to certain conclusions. Ellis is intense, sorrowful, frightened, brave. A man who has jumped his own time to come. Blake and his daughter have bandied the existential truths about, but here, before him, is truly a man without future, without time. And he's not a criminal type, a vicious felon. Ellis is educated, holds a degree in literature from Columbia. His field of specialization was modern American poetry. How the hell did he come to this pass?

Blake has his pitch. It's complex, and not completely thought out, but he's sure that once he begins, and Ellis responds, the thing will form itself. He begins by talking about his family, and his older daughter's upcoming marriage. He mixes the general with a few specifics about the wedding, its cost. Ellis, sitting on the bed, does not look at him, but seems to be listening, if his unblinking eyes and the position of his head mean anything.

"I remember," says Blake, "the birth of my children."

He talks about that, about how his life was changed, in an instant. How he wanted to live forever. He feels he is striking the right tone, conversational, yet heartfelt; a touch of self-conscious passion, a bit of legitimate exasperation. He's run some of this past Dr. Bauer, some he has not. He stares at the bald spot on the spy's head.

"Your wife is going to give birth soon."

The man's eyes are fast upon him.

"Daniel, you're going to have a child."

Still Ellis does not speak.

Blake hesitates. He has to be careful here. He wants to offer hope, but everything he says is being recorded and, as an official representative of the United States government, he is constrained. In his briefcase there is a photograph which, he had been told at the last minute, he is not allowed to show. He had certain questions he wanted to ask, which, too, he cannot. That's part of Newcombe's deal, part of what Ellis's lawyer insisted upon.

"For the sake of your child, I want you to help me."

The spy continues staring at him, and for a brief moment Blake thinks he has broken through. There is a subtle shift in the depth of the eye, a movement about the mouth signifying contact.

"Daniel."

But a strange thing is happening. Blake is losing control. Above the door near the ceiling the camera, on it's wired mount, is focused on him, the nearest living thing. It's got an infrared activator. Ellis continues staring at him, waiting. Blake has lost his train of thought. He's made a mistake coming into the cell. He should have known what to expect, because he's interviewed enough prisoners to know how intense the physical aspects of a cage are, how after only a few minutes the space becomes more poetic than real: a sense of deprivation so eternal as to be almost incomprehensible except in the abstract. Adding to his confusion is an intense and overwhelming sensation of déjà vu. He's back in the motel room with the two actors—what were their names? Mel and Alice—and the woman is pointing her pistol at him. He's in hell, locked with this spy in a self-contained void. He has nothing to offer. There is no hope he is allowed to give. For a wild moment, he panics. No hope, no escape. He is trapped in this pleasant whitewashed room forever, Ellis staring at him, his dark eyes like the muzzle of Alice's automatic. He feels the sweat break out on his forehead, and a feeling of dizziness, almost nausea, rolls over him.

As quickly as it came, the feeling passes. Ellis is still watching him. What can I offer him? thinks Blake. My goodwill? A smile? He sees how futile, how amateurish he has been, with his little bag of actorly tricks. How much a fool!

Ellis waits; indeed, can he do anything else?

After a brief interval of silence, Blake apologizes for the intrusion, signals to the camera, and in a few moments, immensely disappointed in himself, yet profoundly relieved, is out.

●

"Matt."

Blake, back from Washington an hour, looks up from his desk. It's Spanakos, holding a file.

"A quick job," says Spanakos. "Research cranked it out."

"Thanks."

"Sure. Interesting."

Blake opens the file, scans the summary. Preliminary spectroscopic analysis indicates specimen as having been written not more recently than seven years ago. Material is sheepskin. Colorants, solvent vehicles. The text: Old Testament; Deuteronomy 6:5–9.

It is the translation of the parchment that Halpern took off the doorjamb.

> And thou shalt love the Lord thy God with all thy heart, with all thy soul, and with all thy might.

"Thanks, Ed."

Spanakos is already walking away.

Blake puts the translation on his desk and, picking up a paper clip, reads.

> And these words, which I command thee this day, shall be in thy heart.
> And thou shalt teach them diligently unto thy children, speaking of them when thou sittest in thy house, when thou walkest by the way, when thou liest down, and when thou risest up.
> And thou shalt bind them for a sign upon thy hand, and they shall be

as frontlets between thine eyes. And thou shalt write them upon the door posts of thy house and upon thy gates.

He closes the file, puts it in his desk. He makes a mental note to thank the technical and research people; they're always so responsive.

# CHAPTER 23

———————•———————

**B**lake, not being a drinking man,
has no affection for bars, nor does Halpern, but McMann's, with its
rough-hewn planking floors covered with sawdust, the high, dark ceilings, the long run of polished bar, and the stacked rows of glinting
liquor bottles, has a rugged and manly appeal. Tucked away on one of
the narrow off-streets of the financial district, just a long stone's throw
from 26 Federal Plaza, McMann's caters to a Bureau trade. When Blake
arrives the air-conditioning is turned up high, every table is occupied.
At one of them Campbell sits, his glaring eye upon the entrance. The
table has three other chairs; on one of them is a suit jacket. Halpern is
late. Blake, spotting Campbell, crosses the floor on a diagonal, but
before he reaches the table he feels a hand on his arm just above the
elbow. Murphy. He's just coming out of the men's room, all smiles and
handshake.

"Matt."

"George."

They take their chairs. Campbell has two red spots below the eyes, the
flush of hard liquor; his beer color is brighter. Amazing, thinks Blake,
and he is sure Campbell is thinking the same, amazing what a difference a few days make. Campbell's an ex-agent, with all the rights and
privileges and liabilities attached thereto.

Their waiter's Jimmy, an older man with a butcher's apron.

It's white wine for Blake, Murphy the same; no, make it red.

Campbell nods at his own glass. "Another, Jimmy."

Blake asks how the consulting business is going, and Campbell tells him that his company is still in the formative stages, but he's got a number of things going, one of them being the security contract, believe it or not, for the AFL play-offs.

Blake is genuinely impressed, as is Murphy. There is life after the Bureau.

Their drinks arrive and they raise their glasses.

"The Bureau."

"The goddamn Bureau."

Said with the proper inflection, it makes them feel good.

Murphy glances at his watch. This conference has been called by him, at Donnelly's behest. Nothing formal, just a quick review and progress report. Their window looks out on a dark gray building across the narrow street. Red-checked curtains cover the lower third, and Campbell has positioned himself to be able to look out between the panels. From time to time his blue eyes flit to the left, to the entry. In front of him, mounted low on the wall, is a mirror in an ornate gilt frame that provides a reflection of the doors to the men's room. It's been a couple of weeks since Campbell left, but as an ex-squad supervisor he's getting any number of calls about cases. He's wearing one of his favorite grayish-blue suits, his dark blue tie, a handkerchief in the breast pocket. And also, showing its grip high and nickel plated in the waistband, his .38. Once an agent, always an agent.

"Here's your boy."

Blake turns. Halpern is coming through the door.

All assistant U.S. attorneys carry a touch of majesty and are treated with an unconscious reverence; Blake stands, as does Murphy. Campbell remains seated. Halpern's glance goes quickly around the table, beginning and ending with Blake, who offers the slightest of raised eyebrows.

"George is stopping in on us," says Blake, with a tight smile.

"Observer status," responds Murphy. Jimmy is upon them immediately. Halpern wants sparkling water.

Campbell glares. "Bring him a scotch."

Blake remains poker-faced. Jimmy is gone before Halpern can object. He slips his sleek leather case under the table.

First things first; and the men turn their attention to the chalkboard menu above the bar. Campbell orders a bacon burger with hash browns; Blake, having indulged at the Jade Teacup a few nights earlier, goes with the spinach salad, blue cheese dressing. "Hold the bacon bits,

Jimmy." Halpern springs for the steak. Murphy asks about the fish, is told by Jimmy that it's whole red snapper. Murphy wants it. Fish is the new power lunch; brain food. When Jimmy leaves they spend a few minutes discussing cholesterol and weight, a conversation that for Halpern, at his age and physique, has little interest. Then Blake, having touched bases separately with everyone, starts the ball rolling with a question to Campbell.

"Frank, can you put us in touch with someone in CI who's up on the Israelis?"

Campbell, having been prepped, doesn't hesitate. "Ben Glauber. Our legat in Haifa. We liaisoned with him on Ellis."

"The man's been transferred," says Halpern. "Chicago."

"Jesus, tell me another."

It might mean anything; Bureau policy on personnel deployment has always been capricious.

"Who else, Frank?" Blake asks.

"There's Hanson, at State."

"Hanson," repeats Murphy. He doesn't know any Hanson.

"Anyone else who might be more aggressive?"

Campbell's flush is getting deeper. "Matt, I thought you were going with Navy on this."

Halpern pushes aside his glass and leans forward. "We find it hard to believe that the Bureau doesn't have anyone inside."

Campbell glares. "We don't have any luck doubling their people." He drinks again, his lips wet with liquor. "They don't trust outsiders. They stick with their tribesmen."

Halpern doesn't take Campbell's bait. He finally reaches for his scotch, sips it with a face, takes a long pull of soda water.

Blake watches the Irishman, ex-agent, still a power, carrying around a lot of knowledge, some of it dangerous, which he will dole out a little at a time in return for favors from his agent friends. He shouldn't have left, didn't want to. Ellis did him in, Donnelly forced him out.

Their food arrives. Silence reigns as Jimmy puts the plates on the table.

Campbell, who hears everything, puts out the rumor that Newcombe is about to be promoted to U.S. attorney for the District of Columbia. This is a dig at Halpern. Newcombe even held the ground against his own Justice Department. Blake has to give Newcombe credit: he agreed to be screamed at by everyone. Crunching on his croutons, Blake glances at Halpern working his knife around the T-bone. Rare; the young man likes the taste of blood.

Halpern, finishing a mouthful of steak, turns to Campbell.

"Look, I have to say. The Ellis thing just doesn't make sense."

Campbell refuses to address his reply to the lawyer, looks instead to Blake.

"Hey, Matt, don't say I didn't warn you."

"You did, Frank, you did. But I'm too dumb to listen."

Campbell likes this, as does Murphy, not because it's true but because it strikes a chord on the strings of his field man's heart. You play the hunch; you're not supposed to listen to reason. Campbell, a lifelong alcoholic and not really interested in food, pushes aside his plate and centers his glass of liquor over the shamrock on the cocktail napkin. Murphy pauses between bites, turns to Blake.

"What do you have, Matt?"

Blake lays down his fork. One of his strengths is his ability to encapsulate, and he lays out his case, shading everything toward the potential. They have managed to avoid Donnelly's scrutiny on most of their warrants, using Navy to cover their submissions, and Blake sees no need to offer any of this. He gives some background material, a few biographical tidbits. Not too much detail, but just enough; he'll give more, if he has to, as footnotes in the question and answer period that Murphy will hit them with.

"Okay, Matt."

Murphy's first comment is a restatement of the premise of the Starfield case, posited from a skeptical angle: he doesn't see how the hell Ellis can be sprung.

"I just can't buy into that, Matt." Nor, by implication, can Donnelly.

Blake and Halpern exchange glances.

Murphy clears his throat. He's got a maxim, he says. "If it's unbelievable, Matt, I don't believe it." He has in the last weeks given this much thought, and has come to a slow but sure realization of the impossibility of this man Starfield being what Blake says he is. It is a realization that strikes, at this very moment, with such force as to be almost sublime in its intensity. The notion that an Israeli agent is coming in to spring Ellis, is actually going to remove the man from a naval prison, is just too far-fucking-fetched for words.

"Don't get me wrong, Matt. We understand how these things happen." As related by Blake, Halpern's postulation was without a doubt the sort of grand and genuine leap—give the young man credit—too infrequently encountered. Even he, Murphy, hearing it secondhand, had responded, as had Donnelly, at one further remove. He understands, per se. It's a wild notion, springing Ellis, an irresistible one.

And have they not all been, thinks Blake now, in situations in which a similar, incredible idea has taken hold, and how the participants, by common and unspoken assent, have agreed to cast off the bonds of reality that keep them tethered to this mundane earth of triplicate memos and signature approvals, allowing them to soar into the azure skies of possibility? How more beautiful and lush the earth appears from such flights of conjecture, how pregnant with promise. You come up with some fantastic hypotheses which have their own logic and plausibility, undeniable in the heat of their creation, later viewed with a certain bemused embarrassment. This, too, is expected. Reality exerts its moderating influence. As does a few nights sleep.

Thus, today, here and now, Donnelly no longer believes, at least in its pure form, in the notion of springing Ellis. By extension, neither does Murphy. They assume Blake does not either. It is merely a starting point for opening a case, a motivating premise, the crank-up assumption that energizes the body bureaucratic, to be later discarded once everything is in motion and running smoothly. And so he had assumed that once they, that is, Blake and Halpern, were fully out to sea on Starfield, they would abandon the hypothesis. Yet, from what is happening—the trace requests, liaison requests, reports here and there from other, competitive parties—it is apparent that Blake, goaded by this eager AUSA, himself prodded by Navy, is preparing to take this thing all the way.

"It's like Gretchen's law," Murphy says. Halpern refrains from correcting him. "Bad money drives out good. There's a fair chance that Ellis was jettisoned. So why risk everything—we are talking, Matt, very heavy flap here—why risk so much for an agent they willingly sacrificed?"

Blake goes on the defensive. "George, we don't know that."

"There's a hell of a lot we don't know, Matt." Murphy has a few talking points, and, while Blake picks at his salad and Halpern cuts up his steak, he addresses them.

First, the link analysis. Fine and fucking dandy, Tippet did a good job. A great job. Murphy opens a folder. Cities in Europe, dates, coincidences of time and place admitting a certain apparent pattern. Starfield has been traced as far as Stockholm, which was about a week and a half ago, and now they're waiting for an update—but Murphy's point is that the subject's appearances in these various cities are easily accounted for on the basis of his work. For instance: he attended the conference for genetics in Cologne; he was in Frankfurt at the invitation of ChemTech, the West German industrial consortium; and so forth.

Halpern ripostes that Tippet has more, much more—

So far, replies Murphy, he has yet to produce.

Halpern replies: they are experiencing difficulties in accessing the data.

"Yeah," Campbell glares, "difficulties."

Murphy takes another forkful of fish, then lays his utensils down like oars. He wants to talk operational reality.

"Do you know what it would take to get access to Ellis? Just to penetrate the holding area? Hell, Matt, it would be like abducting the goddamn president."

Blake agrees; indeed, that was one of his unspoken reservations from the first.

Murphy goes on. "Assuming they're crazy enough to try it—another Entebbe, though this isn't Uganda—and assuming they have something absolutely amazing in mind: cloaks of inviability, a machine that allows them to pass through walls, whatever."

Halpern scowls.

"Assuming that Starfield is even going to try it, let's walk it through just to see what's required from the operational point of view, okay?"

"Let's, George," says Halpern.

Murphy and Blake exchange looks. Blake puts out a hand toward the attorney, signifying that his tone is bringing him to the edge. Murphy, after an intense silence, speaks.

"Okay, right away you've got problems with support. Assuming you spring the man, and I think that's a false assumption, what do you do with him? Hail a cab? Put him on a bike, what? You're talking about split-second coordination. Everything has to be ready to go. Transportation, covers, cutouts, vehicles, switches. You're talking about penetrating a secure government compound, removing a heavily guarded prisoner and bringing the son of a bitch through at least four layers of security. You are talking impenetrable here. You don't do this without heavy communications. Basic plumbing, surveillance teams, technical support. I don't see any of that yet. And then what do you do with the man when you get him out? Where do you hide him? You need storage. Safe houses, travel arrangements, backup. You need people all over the place. Matt will tell you they don't materialize out of the air. They're specialists. You use your best people because if you don't it isn't going to work. They're professionals. Experienced. And there aren't that many of them. A couple of hundred, at the most, probably two or three dozen who are capable of this kind of operation, who are chartered. We know who's working and can find out where they are—not all of them, but most—and we can trace their movements because we know their covers and their methodology. They have to put themselves in place. They have to meet and talk with each other, which means they have to establish communications. You can't keep it secret."

"But that's my point, George," exclaims Halpern. "Matt, damnit! We uncovered them."

Campbell scoffs, shakes his head.

Halpern is clearly daunted, and Blake, in spite of himself, is gratified; Murphy is putting it precisely, correctly, in a way that Halpern will understand, will see as clearly as he, Blake, now sees, that the lawyer's hypothetical case contains within itself the seeds of its own refutation.

"What he means, Richard," says Blake, "is that they're already blown." He speaks kindly, didactically. He likes the attorney, wants him to see the truth.

"It's too easy to be true," says Murphy. "It's too good. For all we know, it's a trap."

This comes from him unexpectedly, and it's got that ring of sudden and insightful truth. He can see how both Blake and Halpern are considering this.

"And if it is a trap," he says, "I ask you—who's the hunter, and who's the prey? Listen guys, you don't want to wind up being the bait."

But Halpern is shaking his head. He is a United States prosecutor, one of the chosen, and he counterattacks.

"You're putting us in a catch twenty-two here," he begins.

Murphy frowns, as does Blake. The last thing either wants is a semantic argument.

"George, you're tying yourself in a knot."

Murphy controls himself, but barely: this snot-nosed two-bit lawyer.

Halpern is sitting very tall and confrontational. "Okay, look, I understand. You're saying that the operation has to be secret."

"Secure," says Blake.

"And that the security validates the operation." *Validate:* a new-age word. "So what proves the operation real is its security, and once the security is broken the operation cannot be real, even retroactively."

Murphy is confused; his mind had just wandered for a moment.

Blake is listening.

Campbell glares.

"What you're really saying, guys," and here Halpern has a little smile, so smug and amused at catching these older agents in a self-evident contradiction, "is that if the operation was real we never would have found out, and that because we did, because Tippet was able to zero in on Starfield, it's not."

Murphy blinks.

"It's a catch twenty-two." Isn't it amusing, Halpern's smile seems to imply. "It's an interesting takeoff on the Hegelian dialectic," continues the lawyer, "because how the hell can you investigate anything since the mere fact that you uncover it means it doesn't exist."

Murphy frowns again.

"And it leads us around in a big fucking circle back to ourselves."

Murphy, struck dumb, cannot refute.

Blake, following the lawyer's argument, sees how they've become entangled in a self-perpetuating solipsism. Halpern has struck at the very core of Bureau methodology. Blake understands the seriousness of the charge and its implications in terms of operational strategy and case management. He is, frankly, stunned, though it is a few moments before he knows this, and a few more moments are needed before it registers on his face.

Campbell is glaring at Halpern.

A goddamn clever lawyer, thinks Blake.

Halpern wants to say more but holds off. He's pushed enough. Blake knows what the young man is thinking: these older men need a kick now and then. We tend to become complacent, and sit around waiting to collect our pensions. To be honest, he's right. Whereas the lawyer can't sit still. He's mentally hyperactive, if that's possible. Blake knows, too, that Halpern wants a big case, and he wants it now, because he's tired of having to shop very carefully for his expensive suits, going to the annual sale at Barney's, having to skip every other weekend at Quogue. God knows what else he wants; one assumes there's much more. Whereas I, thinks Blake as Murphy continues his thoughtful silence, I only want to keep my job.

But Campbell is shaking his head. He's their control.

"How the hell are they going to spring the son of a bitch!" The thought is ridiculous, and Campbell signals Jimmy for another round.

"Unless it's an inside job."

All of them look at Halpern.

"Look. Guys: You don't mount an operation of this kind unless you know you'll get inside help."

The enormity of this suggestion, the audacity that Halpern would even voice it, reduces the table to silence.

"Richard, damnit." Blake is embarrassed for them both. Halpern is his protégé, whether he wants him or not, and he doesn't want the lawyer spouting this sort of thing. "Your premise is very, very problematic."

It's a good word, a perfect word, suggesting complex and impersonal difficulties.

"Ellis is not getting out," Murphy offers. "We've got a tamper-proof system, checkpoints and security lockups."

"That's my point, precisely."

Again, the table is silent.

"They need inside help. Unless they go in with Uzis."

The three of them look at Halpern. He's only kidding.

But now Murphy, alarmed, wants both Blake and Halpern to walk him through a hypothetical operation to spring Ellis, just to see for himself how impossible it is.

"Give me the model," he says.

And because Murphy is echoing Blake's own misgivings, Blake is pleased. He wants to see how Halpern handles this.

Halpern has a kind of smile on, it's hard to tell if it's a superior or a frightened one.

"People are funny," he begins. "They think that because you can't show them a working model, it can't happen." He pauses to push away his plate, arranges his silver neatly. He takes another sip of liquor, this time doesn't make a face.

"It's what I call the fallacy of demonstrability."

Campbell is glaring, but interested, as is Blake.

Murphy's nose is pinched in.

"What they're trying to do is to throw us off balance. It's part of their operational cover. I've been reading a lot, Matt." He says this almost apologetically, not wanting to admit to greater knowledge. "Navy has analyzed the patterns of Mossad operations. They call it the unbelievability factor. If you don't believe it, it doesn't exist. That's what I mean by the fallacy of demonstrability. You can't show a model for everything. These operations are one of a kind. That's what they specialize in, the older operators, out of Europe." He turns to Blake. "Tippet's working a connection with the British. They think they have something on Starfield. It's going to take a little more time."

Murphy looks at Blake; doing a little back-channel maneuvering, eh?

"The old days," continues Halpern. "Dryden's men. They improvised. They had no patterns. If we keep looking for the pattern we're not going to find it, and that's just what they want. So there's no model for this. They'll put it together as they go along."

Okay, thinks Blake, he handled it better than I thought.

"And who is they?" asks Murphy.

"Starfield," puts in Blake. "And whoever else he's working with."

Murphy, as Donnelly's man, here playing the court skeptic, is not convinced.

"But what's the prize?"

Blake and Halpern are caught off guard.

"There has to be a prize, and it has to have value, and the value has to be obvious." This is Donnelly's credo Murphy is putting forth. He shakes his head. "One low-level spy—Ellis—who's been selling technical data that's already outdated, and you have this world-famous scientist—a member of the National Academy, a possible future Nobel Prize winner—coming in to spring him?"

Blake and Halpern exchange looks; he knows more than they thought.

Murphy is shaking his head. "No. From the point of view of what they've got to spend and what they're getting—no. It's not cost-effective."

Spoken, thinks Blake, like a true middle manager.

"They have a different bottom line."

Halpern's ball again.

"They don't think about cost-effectiveness. They're not looking for a bargain. They'll trade a hundred prisoners, a thousand, for one of their pilots. That's why they take so many Arabs. One flyer. Crippled, burned, maimed, arms shot off, a leg gone, but they'll bring him home."

Campbell's mouth is pressed into a thin line. "Goddamn better than we do."

"It's part of their Holocaust mind-set. They have no choice," continues Halpern. He wants them to sieze upon the intangibles as he has done, to use their imaginations. "Think of Entebbe." They do. Blake remembers the excitement, the sheer amazement of that rescue. "They take risks we consider too high. I don't mean they squander their lives." The young lawyer shakes his head; he means something else. "It's an Old Testament outlook."

Blake understands. They are a tribe; they bring out their people from the camp of the enemy.

"And they'll come in shooting." The lawyer means this, Blake assumes, figuratively. Halpern's addressing his remarks now to Campbell, because he knows if he can be convinced, Murphy will fall into step.

"Over our fucking dead bodies," says the half-drunk Irishman.

A busboy arrives during the long silence, and they wait while their plates and utensils are collected.

Then Murphy, still unconvinced, continues. "Gaps," he states. Donnelly doesn't like all the gaps. He's looking at Blake when he says this, the prosecutor being beyond reason. Biographical gaps, history-of-recruitment gaps, association and motivation gaps; gaps everywhere.

Before Blake can offer anything, Halpern jumps in. "You expect gaps."

They are stunned into silence.

Halpern becomes even more peremptory: "Damn it, we can't waste time on this. We want to go for the broad picture. We have to make some assumptions. The details are not important."

"Christ," mutters Campbell.

Murphy is beyond words.

Halpern is speaking like an apostate, voicing all these heresies. Make assumptions? Details not important? How the hell can gaps not be important? You study the record, go over the details, until you know what side of the bed the man sleeps on and the make of his underwear; you know everything. No gaps allowed, because the person who falls through them is too often yourself.

But Blake sees how the prosecutor's argument can beguile. They would save a hell of a lot of time and effort if they were willing to assume some natural, God-given givens. Just take some things on faith. But the manual of field operations does not allow leaping until you have looked both ways, covered your ass with a multitude of forms, and then looked again.

"Guys," says the lawyer. His eye is bright with belief, and he recites his articles of faith. "Starfield's a pro. He operates in Europe. He's coming in to take Ellis out. We have to stop him."

Mea culpa, thinks Blake, watching the lawyer's eager face. I have sinned the sin of doubt, of growing old, of consorting with known sinners of similar persuasion.

To his credit, Murphy is thoughtful for a few long moments. He wants to believe too. Then his managerial instincts take over, and he frowns, sips the last of his wine. He has to bring something back to Donnelly. He needs more than these elegant postulations of a heretical AUSA. He wants something he can put on paper, he wants dates of birth and social security numbers, times of recruitment and names of recruiting officers, he wants to see motivations and opportunities, travel logs and contact reports. He doesn't want any gaps. But Murphy is going to let that go for the time being; he has another item to discuss.

And that's the embarrassment factor.

"It's not just the logistics. We are talking here blowback, Matt. A hurricane. You're talking about major upheavals in some long-standing alliances." Murphy shakes his head. "Anyone involved is going to be dead history." Halpern smiles; Murphy has two teenage sons who bring home the slang, which he rearranges to suit himself. "Meat. They're going to be meat."

Blake has to agree; he offers the point that perhaps it's precisely for the embarrassment factor that the operation will be allowed, by various and interested parties, chief among them Navy, to go forward.

Campbell grunts, Halpern nods. Murphy's interest is aroused.

Blake amplifies. Anything that makes the Israelis more tractable—a backlash in their own country, encouragement of the anti-Jewish forces in the United States, a field day for the media—is definitely a plus.

Halpern says, "So maybe Ellis is a dangle. The bait in the trap."

Murphy showing interest, Blake and the lawyer play this between them; Campbell joins in, glaring his agreement.

"Okay," says Murphy. "Okay." It's a bit circular, but it's something he can bring to Donnelly. Any attempt to maneuver with Ellis will be the beginning of a huge, intragovernmental contretemps, with the various agencies and their people ripping each other apart. There are the international aspects too. Donnelly would definitely like it. The spin is fantastic.

Jimmy breaks in by asking for dessert orders, and when he leaves a thoughtful silence descends.

Campbell is nodding at Blake, glaring at Halpern. Murphy is preparing his briefcase for departure. The busboy lays out the coffee mugs for them, puts sugar and a creamer on the table.

"Well," says Murphy as he lowers his cup to the saucer, "you have a week."

"We need more time," says Blake. "George. I think something's there. Navy thinks it can deliver. But I don't know if we'll be ready."

Murphy hesitates. Donnelly has given him specific instructions; he's not authorized to grant an extension.

"I'm sorry, Matt. No can do."

Blake looks at the man as Campbell glowers.

"And Matt. Donnelly wants to discuss some personnel matters."

●

Murphy has another meeting, and leaves in the middle of coffee; he wants something in writing from Blake. Blake promises: Monday, George.

With Murphy gone the atmosphere lightens. Campbell, even by his standards, has drunk too much.

"Asshole." Campbell says this without inflection. Halpern stares at the Irishman as if he's from another planet.

"Frank." Blake is very pleasant. "We need access."

Campbell wants to be told another.

Blake presses. "Frank, you interfaced with CI. Who can we talk to from the old networks? Dryden's time."

Jimmy is passing, and Campbell gets him by his apron. The waiter nods.

"Frank, you've had enough. Jesus."

"You got to go through channels, Matty. Talk to Andretti." Andretti is the New York Bureau liaison with the CIA.

"Damn it!" Halpern can hold back no longer. "No one wants to talk, man! They're hiding out behind their goddamn telexes waiting for their pensions!"

Blake puts a hand out toward the lawyer, doesn't quite touch his arm, but the gesture is enough to silence him.

"Frank." He speaks softly, moderately. "We want to get in, quietly. We want to see the files, if there were any to begin with."

"There are always files, Matt."

Spoken simply, drunkenly, this is nonetheless a great truth. Even Dryden in the days of his dictatorial glory had his lists and files. There's no other way for an organization to create itself; the paperless bureaucracy is impossible to imagine. One has to know where the people are, their titles and responsibilities, their phone numbers. Give me the organizational charts and personnel lists, thinks Blake, and you give me power. For someone like Dryden, impenetrability was the last, the best, the first, the only defense. Within the universe of American intelligence he had created his own black hole; nothing ever came out. Until the very end, that is, when the fat man sat dazed and confused on public television, spilling his guts into the hot lights.

"You have to go through the liaison, Matt."

"Damn it, Frank!"

Blake's anger is immediate and hard. He pushes his cup and saucer to the middle of the table, disgusted. "Frank." He doesn't have to spell it out; it's too damn obvious, even to a man as drunk as Campbell. If he has the slightest hope of maintaining his contacts with Blake, and to make use of him for his own goddamn private security firm, he had better be forthcoming now.

"Matt. Your man—Starfield—he's on the list."

"What list?"

"The untouchables."

Blake and Halpern exchange looks.

"He's got protection," says Campbell.

"Who's protecting him?"

"Who do you think?" The glare is back.

"Newcombe?"

Campbell glares harder. Blake is playing out his naiveté too finely, but he's committed to the position even though it makes him out as too much of an amateur, which Campbell knows he is not.

"Use your fucking imagination."

At this point Jimmy places a check on the table. Blake puts his hand on it and slides it under his coffee mug.

"For what it's worth to you, Matty boy."

Blake has turned the check over and is reading the total. Seventy-eight dollars.

"Harrow."

Halpern's eyes are bright.

Maxwell Harrow.

One of the gang of four, Dryden's henchmen. Executioners, some might say.

"Where is he?" asks Blake.

"Archives."

Blake shakes his head. That's like being banished to Duluth.

"How do we get access?"

Campbell glares. "Pick up the goddamn phone, Matty, and call the bastard."

●

The stretch of lower Broadway onto which Blake, Campbell, and Halpern emerge from the darkness of McMann's is a clotted mass. On the outer edge of the sidewalk, obstructing the pedestrian flow, are push-carts selling slushy lemonade and hot dogs and Mexican specialties; other stands sell nuts and fruits and incense and books; still others, the ubiquitous Koreans, display sunglasses and cassette tapes and batteries and women's stockings. The heat is unbearable, the humidity a disgrace. Blake loves it, the slow-moving, teeming crowds, the high facades and gleaming glass, this glorious dirty, crowded, noxious city. Campbell, flushed, fishes for his sunglasses.

The three of them walk slowly, silently with the crowd. The big Irishman leads the way, his arms slightly out in front, running interference.

Blake misses a step.

He turns his head, still walking, and with his eye follows a man disappearing into the sea of shuffling, shifting backs.

It is a tall man in a small hat and a dark suit. A beard. He is just visible, then is swallowed by the crowd.

For a moment Blake has lost awareness of his surroundings, but returns immediately, and is already in adrenal alert; he continues walking, but more slowly, Campbell ahead, Halpern alongside. Now he's got Campbell by the arm, turns him into an entranceway. Halpern follows.

"There." They turn to follow Blake's look.

The man with the hat, crossing the street.

Halpern is looking.

"The beard," Blake says.

Campbell is looking with steely pale eyes.

"Starfield," says Blake.

The photograph is imprinted in Blake's mind; the overlay is perfect.

Blake and Campbell exchange a split-second look.

"Let's go," says Campbell.

Blake pulls Halpern close and, while Campbell keeps his eye on the target, gives the lawyer a thirty-second course in street work. "I'm the tight tail. Frank will be across the street. You're in back of Frank. Pick out something on the target that's visible and keep yourself positioned so that you see it at all times." Halpern swallows, nods. "If he stops, I'm going to pass; you stay behind, I'll cross over, come up behind, we switch. Don't avoid eye contact, but keep it brief. Natural." Halpern nods again, but he's confused. Campbell is ready to move out. "If he turns you keep walking. Don't reverse yourself whatever happens. I'll pick him up. Crowds this thick you can stay four or five steps behind. Frank?"

Campbell grunts.

"I'm going to move out ahead. I want to pass him face on."

"What's happening, Frank?"

"Going south."

"Richard." Halpern swallows. Blake talks quickly. "If we separate, use a pay phone, call my office, leave the number." Blake is spitting out the words evenly, cleanly, in a low, intense voice. "Stay on it. I'll call in. The switchboard knows the game."

"Matty. Damnit."

Blake thinks. One last thing: if he stops at a window, stay back. Glass is a mirror.

"Take off the goddamn tie," says Campbell to the lawyer. Suddenly he's not drunk anymore.

Halpern unknots it with one hand, stuffs it in his pocket.

"Okay. Stay on my right. Frank."

Campbell is already on the sidewalk, cutting in and out. Blake steps into the flow, slips past a woman in very high heels and catches up with Campbell. Halpern is a couple of yards behind.

Blake and Campbell move quickly on a slant across Broadway. Campbell gets on the sidewalk about ten feet behind the man with the hat while Blake scoots along the street hugging the line of vehicles. It's an ABSOLUTELY NO PARKING zone but the curb is jammed with trucks and livery and cabs and vans so there's more than enough cover. Blake moves quickly. He wants to get ahead and turn and pass Starfield head on; he has to get a fix. A few streets up horns are blaring, behind that there's a siren. Fire truck. Blake scoots along, gets to the corner just as the light changes, stands in the crosswalk.

He can't see Campbell, doesn't bother to search. The target is crossing. They close. Blake maneuvers to the inside.

Tall, thin, beard. Dark glasses. No tie. Little hat.

Passed.

Was it him?

Keep walking, resist the urge to turn, resist, you never know who's spotting.

Campbell passes. Step on the curb. Keep walking, turn in here. The siren is loud, but stationary—the fire truck can't get through. Blake steps out into the crowd, moving south. Across the street Halpern is standing on the corner, peering around like a nervous ostrich.

Blake's almost caught up with Campbell, sees him maneuver his gray-suited bulk through the crowd, slowing. Blake slows too. Campbell turns out to the curb and, as Blake passes, signals with an open palm. The target has stopped.

Blake walks to the corner, turns right on Pine Street, then jaywalks across. Not half as many people here. He makes another quick turn and returns to Broadway. There's Halpern on the corner, intent and searching. In the heat the lawyer has taken off his jacket, incidently changing his cover. Goddamn it, he's got on flaming red suspenders. The siren is going strong, trying to blast through the traffic. He can't see Campbell, then does as the big man takes up position on the corner diagonally opposite. His sunglasses, his slick, gray suit, his beefiness, make him look exactly what he is, a tough fed on a close tail. Halpern has wandered down the street, pretending to be doing nothing, and looking very purposeful.

Campbell is their spotter, and Blake watches him. He's just lifted his hand to his right cheek, scratching. But when Blake looks he doesn't see anyone. The big red fire truck is stuck between Wall and Exchange, shrieking at the reluctant traffic. Horns are blaring. A police car has come down a side street and is spinning its roof lights, blasting out loud, intermittent whoops. People are holding their ears. A gray limousine is outside 120 Broadway and a mail truck is on the other side of the street and nothing is moving. The sirens are screaming with that piercing vortical force that makes the air spin. Someone is yelling at the limousine driver.

Blake has made a mistake. There is no target. He crosses the street. He thinks he spots Halpern's back disappearing into the crowd, looks for red on the shoulder. Too many men in dark jackets and hats. He's about to head south, feels a hand on his arm, a body drawing close. North, says Campbell. They turn as one, causing a minor pedestrian jam.

Blake crosses in the middle of the street. The fire truck is wailing and the police car is whooping and flashing and other cars are honking. The noise is painful. It's only on the extreme outer edge of the sidewalk that Blake can make any progress at all, yet through the thronging lunchtime crowd and the sidewalk vendors the slender Matthew Blake moves in an easy gliding silence.

Aha.

The target is crossing at Cedar.

Blake crosses a dozen steps behind. The limousine has finally moved and the mail truck has squeezed closer to the sidewalk. The tall man with the hat walks north. The beard is just visible as two raised streaks of black on either side of his face. He carries a small briefcase, on which Blake now fixes. He fixes, too, the high tilt of the man's head, lack of dip in the shoulders. Campbell's backing him and he doesn't bother to look. Halpern, good boy, is across the street; Blake catches his red verticals in a window.

The target turns on Maiden Lane. Blake, eager now, makes the turn about ten, twelve feet back. The side street is less crowded. But the man has made a quick reverse: he's either gone the wrong way or changed his mind. For too many long moments they are face to face. Eye contact, thinks Blake, make eye contact. It's been so long since he's been out in the field like this. Do not avoid eye contact, the training admonishes. Then the nose, always the nose, then the shoulder. They are closing. He looks up. Beard, passing, eyes, hold a moment, one two, he cannot spot their color; glasses. No discernible scars. Passed. Safe.

Was it Starfield?

Yes.

Maybe.

The man shouldn't have turned, Blake should not have been so close. He continues about twenty paces, stops.

Where's Campbell?

The target is standing on the corner of Nassau and John streets.

Where's Campbell?

And is it Starfield?

Is it the same man he spotted on Broadway?

That briefcase. He doesn't recall its size and color. Paid too much attention to the fire truck trying to get through.

Blake has to move. Men in business suits don't hang out in front of stores selling women's lingerie and skimpy, black lace leotards. At least he doesn't, and they teach you to do only what you normally do, but with purpose.

The man steps off the curb, then back on.

He's just a businessman, like Blake, walking about after lunch, not quite sure how to spend a few minutes.

From behind a hot dog vendor's shiny cart on the other side of the street Campbell steps out. He's got a dog with all the trimmings. He stands against the window of a shoe store and begins to eat, holding the dog away, bent slightly at the waist so as not to spill kraut on his suit.

Where the hell is Halpern?

Aha.

Look at this.

There's another man, a portly, well-dressed gentleman crossing the street and not watching where he's going. Blake sees what's going to happen. The portly man, carefully not paying attention, is looking over his shoulder. Starfield on his corner is gazing down the street, away, and is taking a step in the opposite direction.

Watch.

Blake feels the impact when the two men collide. They go through a quick pantomine on the edge of the curb. Blake notes the body language that allows them to engage, then very quickly separate, apologies spoken, and the portly gentleman moves on, toward Fulton.

And when he looks up Starfield is walking west.

Blake crosses over to where Campbell stands with his hot dog.

"Brush contact," says Blake. Very well done, very professional.

Campbell agrees.

"Anything exchanged?"

Campbell can't be sure. They were carrying the same case, and the switch, if there was one, was too well executed. He's no longer drunk, if he ever was.

"Where's our boy?" asks Campbell.

Blake shakes his head. Halpern's lost. They can see Starfield on Broadway, pausing at the corner; the other, the portly man, is still in sight.

They have to split.

Campbell takes off after portly.

Blake, hurrying, sees Starfield just turning the corner, south on Broadway.

Blake knows these streets like the palm of his hand. He rushes east on John, turns south on Nassau, is slowed by the throngs of meandering shoppers. Sweating now, almost running, he twists and dodges, turns west again on Maiden Lane and dashes pell-mell down the narrow, uncrowded Liberty Place, his wing tips loud on the cobbles. And collides with Halpern in front of the Chamber of Commerce building.

The impact is glancing, but throws the attorney off the sidewalk.

Goddamn it.

"Matt, I saw him."

"Where?"

"He went into 160 Broadway."

Halpern, lost, had called in to the switchboard, waited, then, deserting the phone, had taken up position on the corner of Broadway and Cedar, spotted—lucky chance—the target under a marquee. He thinks it was him. The man was holding a briefcase, had a beard. Tall. Went through the revolving door.

160 Broadway.

Blake passes the entrance, where a young man is handing out blue fliers. He reverses at the corner and, while Halpern waits across the street, goes back for another look.

A small, metal sign is affixed to the granite. CITY CAMERA AND ELECTRONICS.

Blake takes a flier. Electronics, Photography, Computers.

In front of the revolving doors Blake makes a show of reading the flier and peering in through the flat plate glass on either side. Too many turns and dark crannies in the lobby. Elevators and stairwells. A newspaper stand, brightly lit.

A man walks by; Campbell.

Blake falls in step and they turn quickly into a doorway. Campbell has his glasses on. Facing the street, not looking at each other, they talk.

Campbell's man, the portly gentleman, went into 110 John. Fourth floor. Three offices listed.

They'll check it out later.

"Starfield's in 160."

Campbell, looking out into the street, his dark glasses hiding his eyes, nods. City Camera. It's one of the stores he recommended to Blake for the electronics, good prices. He knows the building. There's an exit from the lobby onto Maiden Lane. City Camera, the store itself, is in the rear lobby.

Halpern is standing across the street, watching the two agents.

From the pay phones on the corner, there is a view of 160's exits on both Broadway and Maiden Lane. Campbell will occupy this position. Campbell signals to Halpern, and, as Blake pushes through the revolving door, the lawyer moves, as Campbell directs, a few yards north.

The front lobby is marble and brass, art deco and faded glory; a couple of quick turns—right, straight, then left—brings him to glass doors, behind which is City Camera. He enters. There are three lines of customers; on instinct, as well as craft, he chooses the middle one. The man at whose back he stands, a business type in olive poplin, does a quarter turn; Blake offers the slightest of acknowledgments. On his right, another man glances at him, then away. Blake draws a breath, lets it out, and takes his bearings.

He's in the customer holding area, a small clearing in a sea of merchandise. Floor-to-ceiling shelving holds cameras, radios, personal stereos, clocks, tape recorders, and audio components. To the left, stacked against the walls, are large cartons marked IBM, Panasonic, Leading Edge. The cartons are block-inked with pictographic instructions and caveats, kind of an international Swahili: the outline of a cocktail glass indicating fragility; an open umbrella cautioning against moisture; a hook with an overprinted X.

On either side of him the customers stand patiently, a broker-lawyer-corporate crowd. The lines end at a long glass-topped counter. In back of this counter are more shelves with more equipment, mostly cameras. The counter itself, all glass, holds video games.

For an out of the way hole in the wall, City Camera is very busy. Behind Blake another man has joined the line; to his left has been added a woman. One of the lines is now out in the hall, and from behind the counter a worker—in vest and skullcap—comes out and wedges one of the glass doors with a triangle of wood.

Like the other men behind the counter, he is a Hasidic Jew. They seem to favor the electronics trade. In the heat the men have removed their jackets and are in white shirts, no ties, black vests. They have beards of varying color and length and curl. Thickish lengths of hair are wrapped about their ears.

Carefully, casually, slowly, having given the herd time to accept him, Blake runs down the customers on his right. His target, the man who he thinks, hopes, prays is Starfield, is two customers down. Now Blake checks the line on his left, just for balance. He gives a little sigh of forced patience, then looks around again, finds the stacked boxes of monitors just beyond Starfield's head of great interest.

He tries to match the man to the photograph, but is not sure.

On his left, a man leaves with a package and the line moves up. The customers stand very still, shifting their weight to the creaking of shoe leather. Blake has Starfield's left cheek to watch, can make out the tip of his nose, his ear. Height about six one, weight about one-seventy, slender. Beard dark, close-trimmed, tight. Glasses with black frames.

After a short interval Blake's line advances. More of Starfield's face, nose, cheekbone comes into view. He is looking straight ahead, his briefcase in hand, very patient, very still.

This will take a while.

Fine; Blake has the time.

Campbell's covering the side exit, Halpern the one on Broadway.

And if he knows anything about the Irishman, he's certain that Campbell has already put a call in, and there will be half a dozen agents waiting when they come out.

And Blake has his cover, a perfect, made-to-order cover. He couldn't ask for anything better. His wife has been after him to buy a camera and now, at last, he's going to.

The lines are moving. From his, a woman leaves with a portable typewriter. To his left, a transaction is being completed. Starfield is still two ahead. Ideally, chance will favor him, and they will arrive at the counter together. His line is up again, but so is Starfield's. The Jews in their skullcaps are deliberate and mannerly, very calm; faith seems to impart patience. The lighting is fluorescent, just a bit garish, excellent for details.

Blake reduces his level of tension a couple of notches. Nothing very alarming is going to happen. Starfield is unaware, by all accounts, that he is being tailed. This is a first sighting. There'll be others. But now he wants a number of items. He wants the man's voice, his tone and accent, he wants his gestures, what he buys, how he pays for it, and the name he uses. And they will follow up the brush contact on John Street with the portly gentleman.

The next customer on Blake's line is told that City Camera does not sell Nintendo, only the games, and he moves up again. He and Starfield are now almost side by side. The tall, erect, motionless stance of the man bespeaks discipline and concentration. Starfield's left hand holds the briefcase, and the fingers are neither too tight nor loose around the handle. There is a gold ring on his finger. Blake makes an attempt to match the man to the little he has learned from the files: age fifty, biophysicist, married to a Dutch woman, one child.

The customer in front of Blake wishes to exchange a battery charger. The give and take is courteous. The Hasidic counterman goes into the back area for a new charger. In front of Starfield a customer is having his order written up for a combination clock-radio–cassette player.

Blake prepares. Removing his wallet from his inside breast pocket, he takes out the folded piece of notepaper on which his wife had listed, in her neat hand, the requisite features of the perfect camera. He studies the list with great and genuine concentration. The essence of cover, as the instructors many years ago were fond of repeating, is to live it: how simple it is, how existential; you are what you do.

And that is what I am. A man buying a camera.

In fact, that is why I have come here, to 160 Broadway, to City Camera and Electronics, this very day at this particular hour. That is why Campbell and Halpern and I had lunch at McMann's, why we happened to step out onto the hot, bright street at the moment we did, just when Dr. Phillip Starfield was passing. But Starfield no longer matters. The fortuitous confluence of chance and event that have brought me to the edge of the counter where a black-garbed Hasidic Jew waits to serve with a little smile is nothing short of remarkable—and yet, quite in keeping with my needs and intentions.

There is no way this could have been planned; it's one for the training books.

●

Who is this little man?

The small, slender man, gray suit, gray hair cut short. He's been with me since Broadway and Cedar. With the other men, the bigger, fair man with the gun, and the tall, young one, he has not left me in peace. I had to ask Slavin, there in the street when we bumped, to send a decoy, just in case. I expect he will arrive shortly.

But now the little man is here, again. They're doing very well.

●

Blake and Starfield reach the counter at the same moment. He has the slip of paper in his hand, puts it on the glass and looks up into the eyes of a short man whose beard is a curly iron gray.

"I want to buy a camera."

"Ah." The Hasid has a twinkle in his eye, and makes a gesture in the air that seems to imply that it's quite obviously a camera that Blake should want. "And in what kind of camera are you interested?"

"It's really for my wife."

"Ah, so, what does your wife want?"

His English is precise, a trifle overenunciated, but facile. The twinkle in his eye bespeaks a good-humored gentleman.

Blake looks at his list. Ease of use is the first item. Automatic focus and shutter-speed settings. It's got to be less than a fancy complicated and expensive camera, but more than a cheap amateur's box. Next to him, Starfield is talking to his salesman, a short man of Orthodox mien and garb. Blake hears surge suppressor, power pack.

"My wife wants automatic advance and rewind."

The Hasid turns the paper around with two nicotine-stained fingers. His hand motions are the equivalent of his speech, precise and defined.

"This one we don't carry." His finger is on his wife's second choice. A Ricoh.

"Why, not good?"

"It's a good camera. We just don't carry it."

Blake buys that with a smile. "We don't want to go more than a hundred, a hundred ten."

"I will show you two cameras, both good," says the Hasid in fine, soft articulation, and goes off to the left.

Blake waits. On his left another customer is buying a computer; it's going to be used for word processing and the salesman is putting together a package, hard disk, expanded memory, printer. On his right Starfield and his Hasid are consulting a catalog. The man is bending low, turning his face so that his left ear is close to the other man's

mouth. He is hard of hearing on the right. Blake stares straight ahead, picking out Starfield's reflection in the chrome trim of an automatic coffee maker on a shelf. He moves to the side, a fraction closer. He wants a mental print, what they call an auric impression. There is the sense of great reserve and restraint, of intelligence. An obsessional quality. The man serving Starfield is stout, his cheeks ruddy over a reddish beard, like a Santa Claus. They are looking at a piece of electronic equipment.

"Here we are." Blake's Hasid has returned with two boxes. "I will show you both cameras, and then you will decide what your wife will like."

It is amusing to them both to focus on Blake's wife.

The Hasid is opening the boxes, talking, his dark-stained fingers nimbly undoing the packaging. The first camera, a Minolta, has many sliding surfaces and clicking latches. Here, you see, the Hasid's index finger touching it lightly, is the lens, here the electric eye. Flip door for the batteries. Film-winding switch here. The shutter, the focus. Slide-out flash. On his right, Starfield will pay with plastic.

"Everything automatic. Everything. Your wife, your children . . ."

A pause, and Blake's smile affirms his parental status.

". . . will like it."

"How much?"

"Eight-ty nine fift-ty." The man speaks his *t*'s with emphasis.

Blake gives a little nod of approval. His wife had seen it listed at over a hundred.

There is a card is on the counter. Barclays. Excellent. Yes, it is he. At last, a confirmation in embossed, black letters. He knew it all along, of course, but it is a thrill, a genuine, blood-tingling thrill. He hasn't had one this real in years.

"Now. This camera is not as fully automatic, but its lens is finer."

The Nikkorflex.

"Well, we are interested in quality," says Blake.

"This is one hundred and five dollars."

Still, twelve dollars better than his wife's lowest.

The camera is demonstrated. Here are the buttons, the catches; here the battery compartment.

Starfield's Hasid has left with the card.

Blake now puts on an elaborate display of urgency. He looks at his watch, fidgets on his feet, checks the time again. Finally he interrupts.

"I'm sorry." He's very sincere. "I'm running late." Speak calmly, be firm. Smile. "I'm going to take the Minolta. Could you load the camera and show me how it works exactly? Batteries, film. I'd like to be able to show my wife."

"Certainly." The Hasid turns to his left.

"Moishe." The Hasid writing the sales slip for the computer package grunts. Blake's man asks for something in another language, Yiddish, Blake assumes, and Moishe—is that a name or a title?—bends low and comes up with a roll of film, which he puts on the counter.

Starfield's salesman has just returned, and pulls a gray metal crank box toward him.

Blake's Hasid is nimbly loading the camera. He turns to Starfield's salesman, speaks. "Chaim." With the same unlooking disinterest as Moishe, Chaim places two AA size batteries on the counter.

Starfield is very still, very patient, as his paperwork is completed. Blake fidgets some more, scratches his nose. He puts an elbow on the counter, leans over, picks up the box, and reads the warranty inside. He wants to generate some energy, wants Starfield to react to his presence. But the man remains oblivious to Blake's fussiness. The camera is being loaded, the gray strip of film pressed upon the sprockets of the uptake reel.

"Ah. We are ready." The salesman holds the camera between himself and Blake. "Here, very simple. The lens cover, like this. Then, this slides open, like so. Now." He raises a finger. "The flash is activated. You set this little slide, here, for the film speed." He consults the box of film. Ah, good, preset to 100. He presents the camera to Blake. "Press this button." Blake does. There is an internal whirring sound as the film winds into place. "You have just advanced the film. See, in this window." Their fingers touch, their faces are very close. There is the faint but pungent odor of cigarettes about the man, also an odor of soap.

"Now you are ready to shoot. This button is pressed."

Blake hands back the camera. "Take a picture of me." Keep your voice calm. Be deliberate, as you always are. Be polite. Smile.

Starfield, waiting for Chaim to get an approval code—there is the usual delay on the phone—is very still.

"Certainly."

The salesman backs off, pressing himself against the shelving. He aims, presses. Nothing. Not a click, not a whir, not a flash.

Goddamn it.

"The batteries," suggests Blake. "They might be weak."

"No, they came in last week." The Hasid speaks in quick Yiddish to Moishe, who, without saying anything, reaches out his hand and takes the Minolta. Starfield stands very contained, exuding patience; he has not moved, it seems, a muscle. Moishe is turning over the camera and looking at it in a way that Blake knows is not going to do a damn bit of good. He points the camera to the ceiling, presses. Nothing. The two Hasids now look at the camera together, each with a hand on it, and speak rapidly in a leap-frog exchange. The customers in back are getting restless. Starfield's Hasid is still on the phone. Blake pretends to a fit of amusement and shakes his head, smiling, at the intractability of mechanical devices.

And then suddenly he senses an increase in tension. He glances up, then away: Starfield is rock still, his face in steady profile. But the energy between them has leapt a quantum, which means that they have, at last, engaged: "mutuality of affect" is what the psychologists call it, and Blake has just experienced it.

The bright flash makes him blink.

"The film wasn't advanced enough," Moishe explains. His voice is straight New York. "They added a new magnetic catch that is deactivated by a digital code on the first frame."

Blake takes the camera. Starfield has signed the slip.

"May I?" He points the camera at the Hasid.

Chaim is pulling apart the copies.

"No, please. We don't take pictures of ourselves."

The equipment is being bagged.

Blake makes a show of aiming the camera around, then points it up at the ceiling. He presses the button. The flash bounces as the lens clicks, the whirring mechanism advances the film.

Starfield has his hand through the plastic hoop of the bag.

Blake, his heart strong, steady, has his camera ready.

He wants a full-face shot.

They are too close.

He presses back, against the customer on his left.

"Excuse me."

And, now, finally, compelled by Blake's will that he react, Starfield at last turns to see what the quiet, intense, prolonged fuss that this little man has orchestrated is all about.

For a long instant the two men are staring into each other's eyes.
*Flash.*

The shutter clicks, the camera whirs, the film advances.

Greedy, Blake is about to try for another shot, but Starfield has quickly turned away.

Blake's hand trembles as he puts the camera on the glass.

"You take MasterCard?"

"Certainly."

With shaking hands, Blake produces the card. He is in a daze of success. He has to bring himself down, and quickly. The training is explicit: always follow up. He should, for instance, pass a comment to Starfield pertinent to their mutual presence, something about lines and waits. He should say something in a casual and disinterested but mildly friendly manner about surge protectors. He should, of course, apologize, thus continuing their silent, unwitting interaction, give it a greater, more mannerly completeness, ending this first encounter with, so to speak, another beginning. But he doesn't trust himself; he is trembling with that heady mix of exhilaration and exhaustion that is the aftermath of a successful field operation. He has the touch, still.

"Excuse me, I do need disks."

Chaim, having thought the transaction complete, was about to take the next customer. He looks up at the tall man.

"Yes, how many?"

"A dozen. Formatted. Double density."

Chaim goes off to get them.

All of sudden, it seems to Blake that his salesman is moving glacially, laboriously penning in the make and model of the camera, taking his particulars, checking the serial number of the camera and noting it on the top copy of the slip. Hurry up, man, he wants to tell him, hurry up and get me out of here. The tall bearded man is still at the counter; what is he doing? Blake is reacting too strongly. It's the lack of recent field activity. He has the photograph, and he has numbers, and he knows what Starfield has—the equipment for his laptop— his credit card, and from this they will work backward, and then forward. For certain, the man works with a modem, and with a tap on his line that modem is going to tell them a great deal. He tells himself to relax, to focus on the details of his salesman's penmanship as he fills in the charge slip with his nimble nicotine fingers, asking in his precise English if Blake wants an extra roll of film, which Blake does not. He wants nothing at all but to leave, now. Starfield is talking very quietly with the big, happy-cheeked Chaim. Hurry up! He doesn't want to press his luck. This was a propitious, unsought encounter from beginning to end, demonstrating how a combination of training, experience, and attitude can turn a seemingly chance encounter into a successful field operation. It's one for the books, a display of the improvisational skills of the complete agent. Blake will write Technical Services and suggest a video. Luck, Blake tells himself, itching to grab his package, grab it and run, luck is the residue of design. He doesn't know who said it, but

it's probably the same man that said chance favors the prepared mind.
Maybe a football coach; that's my one area of weakness in general
knowledge, he tells himself with a smile, aware that he is on the edge
of a fearful mania, sports.

●

Starfield doesn't want to use Yiddish, for it is too close to English in
certain words, particularly the semitechnical terms for camera and film
and photograph, so he bends down and leans with his elbows on the
glass countertop and asks Chaim, softly, if he speaks Hebrew.

*M'daberet evrit?*

The red-cheeked Hasid, pen unmoving, lifts his untroubled eyes into
the hazel-gray irises of the tall, bearded gentleman.

*Ken.* Yes, he speaks Hebrew.

The dapper little man has given himself away, at last. When he came
through the glass doors there was that hard, determined air of the
hunter about him. Then, in the curved camera lenses pointing out from
the shelving one was able to watch his casual yet too obvious interest,
his careful, patient posturings. The slip of paper with the cameras had
fooled him for a brief interval, but then there was a long series of
gestures and glances and nervous little jerkings that had culminated in
the blinding flash not two feet from his face. Clumsy, but effective.

Now he speaks to Chaim. This man has taken my picture. *Tazt-lote,*
a photograph. Hebrew is an ancient language, an inflected, expressive,
emotive tongue economical and forceful, partaking of the rough but
energetic cadence of the Bible, a sprung rhythm, and conveys the urgency of Starfield's predicament. Wide-eyed and innocent, Chaim listens without a single twitch of his red, full lips as this tall man makes
his request.

You shall do me a favor, a great favor—*chesed, chesed gadol*—and not
allow this man to leave with the photograph.

"*B'va ka sha.*" Please.

Chaim's glance goes momentarily to his right. Blake's Hasid is taping
the camera's box. Chaim stares into the eyes of his customer bent low
over him. He understands: it is prohibited to take pictures. And now the
man requests of him a favor, a *chesed.*

"*Ken.*" He barely moves his lips, puzzled. Yes.

"*Todah.*" Thank you.

The tall, bearded man puts twenty dollars on the counter and without
waiting for his change takes his bag and leaves.

●

"You, or as the case may be, your wife, will fill out the warranty card. In addition, we give you a thirty-day one-hundred-percent guarantee."

"Excellent," exclaims Blake.

Chaim has put his hand, lightly and quickly, on the salesman's arm. The two have a rapid-fire exchange in guttural Yiddish, their faces close.

"Ah." Blake's salesman makes a sorrowful sound with his tongue.

"Chaim tells me we have a problem here." He is seemingly amused by this, as he was by Blake's wife's vicarious presence. "He has to check your camera against our stock lists. I was unaware of the fact that this particular model sometimes has a lens-mount defect. It will take only thirty seconds."

Blake wants to object, but the baby-faced Chaim has already disappeared with the camera. He is on instant alert; there is a set of inserts, another of cubbies, and Blake is fitting one into the other: Starfield and himself, Chaim and the other Hasid, the camera, its supposed defect. Adrenaline is pouring, as is his sudden sweat. I am alone among these people. They shall conspire against me.

More quickly than he expected Chaim has returned. He places the box on the counter. "It's fine," he says, without a glance at Blake. The box has been opened and the camera is tilted up out of its Styrofoam packing.

"What was done?" asks Blake.

Blake's salesman speaks to Chaim in Yiddish, and gets in return a quick blast of words. "Ah. This little attachment over here." He indicates with his pencil point a tiny screw on the face of the camera. "This has sometimes worked loose. A factory defect. But your camera is fine."

Blake bets it goddamn is; as soon as it's packed he double-times it to the street, coming out on Broadway sweating, disgusted, and furious. Halpern is in red suspenders, jacket over his shoulder, loitering under the marquee.

"Where's Frank?"

Halpern said he went inside.

"Did you see Starfield come out?"

"He didn't come out the front, Matt."

The sun is bouncing off the hard reflective surfaces, glare everywhere. Squinting, Blake looks up and down the street and then goes to the phone and calls, hangs up after a quick exchange.

"Frank's on his tail. Starfield's gone south. Heading into the park."

Blake's cover has been blown. It's a whole new game.

"Richard, let's go."

Hurrying down Broadway's gentle, curving descent to Battery Park, Blake stays on the left side of the street; Halpern, about twenty feet back, keeps up on the right. At one point, at the corner of Broadway and Morris, Blake glances back. He should have told the lawyer to put his jacket on, those suspenders are like a flag.

It's almost two, and the crowds are thinner, but there's enough humanity on the streets to make Blake's progress a cut-and-dodge operation. At the triangle of Bowling Green, Blake crosses over to the corner of Broadway and Battery Place. Halpern stops at his side.

"We're going into the park." Halpern, sweat on his upper lip, nods. "Walk slowly to the firehouse, then toward the ferry. Stay on the right, near the water. I'm going up State, then down. We meet at the eagle."

They split. Halpern disappears off to the right; Blake crosses to the park side of State Street and hurries along, all the time looking into the park. He's angry with himself; he should have held on to the camera. He's making elementary mistakes at every turn; ridiculous. Now, searching the winding paths, he is unable to distinguish from among the citizenry anyone resembling Starfield. There are dozens of men fitting his broad description, but he has lost the power to see. They plotted against me, spoke in an ancient tongue, a code. Where is Campbell? He turns into the park. Here, beneath the canopy of trees, the hot blaze of sun loses its blinding intensity, the air is cooler. He stops, breathes deeply, loosens his tie.

And spots Starfield.

It is unmistakably, definitely his man.

He's got the bag with the equipment, and he's got the briefcase, and he's got the hat. He's heading back toward South Street, blending in with the crowd on a curving path leading away from the water. Blake moves quickly, catches up, holds at about thirty feet. The crowd is just the right density. He knows his man now, the erect posture with the head tilted slightly up, the line of beard that forms a black shadow at the jowl line.

A whole new goddamn ball game.

From the left, a bright X of red cuts across his field of vision. In a moment the prosecutor falls into step. Halpern speaks without turning his head.

"Target's down by the ferry."

"Goddamn it."

Blake is trying to keep an eye on Starfield; Halpern says he saw him at the ferry.

Blake stops. Did he have a bag? a briefcase?

Halpern hesitates.

Blake has been looking at him while they spoke and when he looks back Starfield is gone.

"He's not at the ferry. I was on him."

Starfield is gone.

"Matt, I spotted him at the ferry. Frank's there."

Blake shakes his head, turns, and looks toward the ferry terminal.

"Did you see him? Actually see him?"

"Campbell?"

"Starfield."

"No."

"Frank's there?"

Halpern hesitates. Blake shakes his head in disgust. Maybe it wasn't Campbell. Maybe it wasn't Starfield. Maybe no one exists any-god-damn-more.

"Richard." Blake looks around at the men and women passing, the bums lying on the grass under the shrubs. He looks out toward the water where the statue is a green-gray colossus in the bright sky. Halpern is squinting at Blake, waiting for the agent to suggest a course of action. Where the hell did Campbell disappear to? Hell, the man's no longer on the payroll.

"Matt."

Halpern is gesturing.

There's a man on the far side of Battery Park striding, almost running it seems, toward a long, low van.

Tall, hat, a bag in either hand, dark clothing.

Thinks Blake, as he hurries along the path, Halpern with long strides keeping abreast; it ain't over till it's over.

Dead end.

The man has dashed into the large tan van that has been an established presence in Battery Park for most of the summer.

The Mitzvah Mobile.

Blake, emerging from the park, had caught a glimpse of briefcase, the dark legs of trousers disappearing through the van's door.

Okay, Mr. Dr. Starfield, you're goddamn cornered.

●

Time: 2:37

Blake stands in the shade of the Russian olive trees that line the edge of the grass and looks at the van standing in the hot sun. It's about thirty feet long, and takes up the space of three parking slots.

I'm going to wait for you to come out and I'm going to take your goddamn picture whether you like it or not.

●

Time: 2:52

Halpern stands at his side.
"He's in there?"
Blake nods.
No, it ain't over till it's over.

●

Time: 3:06

Halpern, at Blake's instruction, calls into the Bureau switchboard and leaves a message for Campbell.

●

Time: 3:10

The Irishman hasn't called in. At Blake's instruction, Halpern calls in a message for Ed Spanakos. Using hand signs, Blake positions the lawyer across the street on the other side of the van. Blake continues signaling and, after much confusion, the attorney puts on his jacket. He finally grasped it: the suspenders.

●

Time: 3:15

As per training, Blake conducts a thorough visual inspection of the vehicle. It is a recreational van. It's got a sloping windshield and two rectangular, tinted-glass side windows. The cab area has triangular side windows. The body of the vehicle is light tan with dark brown trim around the lower third and along the base. There is only one way in, other than the driver's entrance, and that is, as far as he can tell, the only way out. Beneath the lettering that identifies the vehicle as a Mitzvah Mobile there is smaller print, some of it in Hebrew. Around the word MITZVAH there are drawings of various religious objects. At the level of the door's handle is an air-conditioning sleeve cut through the skin of the vehicle. Mounted in the other side window is a drawing of a man praying, big Hebrew letters saying, Blake supposes, something pertinent. Planning a contingency attack, he notes the thin black wire leaving the top of the van and dangling it's way to the base of a lamppost. If he has to, he'll get them on that, theft of government services. It sounds flimsy, but he's fussed his way into places on less.

●

Time: 3:22

From the phone Halpern gives a thumbs-up signal: The Irishman's on his way.

Blake, having crossed the street, is peering up into the side window.

He whirls around, sensing the presence, the danger, before the contact.

The man is burly, looming. His hand is on Blake's arm, a very light touch that does not disguise the great strength.

He has asked a question which Blake has not heard, and he repeats it now.

"*Villst du daven?*"

There is a furtiveness in this, put there by a millennium of caution.

"Do you want to pray?" he asks, reverting to English.

The Hasid is a giant of a man, a full head taller than Blake, with a long black frock coat and full beard, and a big, round-brimmed hat.

"Come."

The man has placed a hand under his arm.

"Come, please."

He gently coaxes Blake to the van's side. Come. He has had experience with the reluctant.

He urges him up the steps. From inside someone must have been watching, for, as he ascends, the door opens and Blake, to his own amazement, steps into the cool quiet of this traveling synagogue.

Of the interior details he will recall little; they are unimportant, though he will recollect that the van is partitioned into three sections. In one, there are two chairs and a narrow table. Sacred objects are present: a candelabrum, books, shawls with fringes. In the area where he stands, there is a tall cabinet with double doors, gold Hebrew letters in columns on each door.

And there is another man, the man he saw running in, standing with a book in his hands.

Blake is being spoken to by the large Hasid, but he is disoriented and begs the big man's pardon, and the question is repeated.

Blake shakes his head. He has not been bar mitzvahed.

The Hasid's expression does not indicate disapproval. He is holding what appears to be a small pillow made of blue velvet, decorated with gold stitching. From it are taken two black, wooden cubes wrapped around with thin black straps. Blake's camera is placed on the table and his jacket is arranged on the back of one of the chairs. He is profoundly relieved not to be wearing his gun.

Another question, which he hears the first time.

Blake responds. No, he cannot read Hebrew.

The big Hasid is not discouraged. Men come late to their destiny. He unwinds the leather in a deft, practiced, counterturn of hands. As instructed, Blake has rolled his sleeve and bared his left arm. One of the black cubes is placed on his arm, just below his elbow. The straps attached to this block are wrapped around his arm, and with a quick loop and a twist down again to his hand, woven in and out and through his fingers. The Hasid has thick, soft hands, fingers plump and gentle. His beard is brown; he is young, thinks Blake, not more than thirty-five. The air conditioner blows upon Blake's feet a coolness that is not unpleasant. The Jew is placing the other box upon Blake's forehead, *frontlets between thine eyes*. He wraps the leather around and around his temples, and lets the ends dangle.

Next, the prayer shawl. The Hasid holds it open, mutters a line of strange sounds. Then, in a sweeping, rising motion, he places it over Blake's head.

I am alone in the camp of my enemies, thinks Blake. Yet I feel no fear. They think I am one of them. The other man, facing away, is reading from his prayer book silently. Through a wide slit in the curtains people can be seen walking in the bright sun; inside, the van is cool and quiet. A tugboat has blown a long loud blast, like a ram's horn, a faint summons to prayer. The Hasid stands close. His breath, of no discernible odor, is on Blake's face. A book has been placed in his hands. Here. The man indicates a passage with a thick finger.

"Thank you," says Blake. It is in English. He cannot focus. He looks up, studies the other man. He is standing to the side, facing the window, and the shawl covers his face. Blake looks down. Dark trousers, black shoes.

Blake stares at the book in hand. Afternoon prayers. It is for the novice, for beneath the English are phonetic renditions of the text into Hebrew. Blake does not attempt it. Again, he raises his eyes to the other man, and tries to pierce the thick shawl that obscures his face. And at last, feeling another's gaze, the man turns with a slow, stiff movement of the head, and Blake looks into dark eyes that wear no glasses, a beardless face that unsmiling, turns away.

Too late he offers to this stranger, having it fall into the quiet air, the trace of a smile.

He is, of all things, relieved.

He looks down again at the book.

*The beginning of wisdom is the fear of the Lord.*

Raising his eyes, Blake can see two men through the curtain. He transfers the book to his left hand and reaches out and parts the curtain further. There in the sunlight stand Halpern and Campbell. At the curtain's movement, they move a half step closer and peer in. Blake parts the curtain even more. They see him now. Blake returns their stare and notes quite clinically, as he has been trained to do under all field conditions, that the faces of the eager young lawyer and the blustering Irishman are configured with amazement, absolute and uncomprehending masks of astonishment.

●

From where he stands at the ferry terminal, Dr. Starfield trains the powerful, public binoculars upon the van. Using the fine focus, he cuts through the intervening blur of moving heads and waving trees. The binoculars cost ten cents for three minutes, truly one of the last bargains of the western world, and he spends almost a dollar in dimes before he is satisfied, waiting until he sees the small man emerging from the van, his pantomimic conclave with the tall dandy and the beefy blond man. He tracks them briefly with the glasses, then, at a moderate pace, strolls through the park and the streets, and is able to catch the two older men—the tall, young one has spun off—standing in the sunken piazza of 26 Federal Plaza, where they remain for some time in intense conversation. He watches until the bigger man leaves and the smaller enters the building.

For a full minute Dr. Starfield takes the measure of this structure. It is a great, modern mediocrity, a bulking tower of metal and glass unredeemed by grace of concept or beauty of material. A brutal building, as befits its function.

His has been a minor victory, perhaps unnecessary, perhaps even counterproductive. Yet he is gratified that he has been able to serve notice upon the small, slender man—actually, more average than small, but the compactness of his frame and purposeful, efficient bearing produce an impression of littleness—that life is, indeed, tough, and replete with chance, and that which works to one's advantage one moment will not the next, and that even a special agent of the Federal Bureau of Investigation is subject to another's will and purpose.

And, finally, that it was the height of impoliteness, truly barbaric, to photograph him in public in that fashion.

The little, dapper man shall have to learn some manners.

At last he leaves his corner post. From a phone on the corner of Lafayette and Duane he dials a number in midtown Manhattan. A woman answers.

*I have a message for Mr. Anserman.*

She requests him to proceed.

He speaks his few words, quickly rings off.

It is time to begin providing for contingencies.

●

''Fogged.'' The woman's voice on the phone is emphatic.

''Shit.''

The silence lengthens.

Blake apologizes for his French, asks for an explanation.

''The compartment was opened.'' The woman, one of the agents in Technical Support, says this matter of factly.

''So there's no image?''

''No.'' It's obvious beyond question.

''And there's no way to use that process—?''

''Salvaging?''

''Salvaging, yes.''

''No. We tried. There's a hot spot on the emulsion. It was opened under a bulb.''

''I see. Thank you.''

''By the way, the lens-connecting screw was loose. We tightened it.''

Blake has no further questions. ''Thanks again.''

Blake stands at the window, his usual pleasure in the skyline over-clouded with an intense anger. He returns to his desk and calls Spanakos, and in a few minutes the earnest agent appears.

Blake wants a sanitation job. It's at City Camera, Broadway, south.

Spanakos knows the place; good prices.

''It might involve some overtime.''

Spanakos never minds overtime.

''The usual, Ed. Get the carter, I think it's Gambini Brothers down there. Time of pickup, truck number, driver.''

Spanakos will arrange it. He and a couple of agents will pick through the garbage for pertinent scraps.

Does Blake want a four-o-six on this?

Blake says no, then reconsiders; if Spanakos wants his overtime they have to put it on the book.

"No problem, Matt."

●

Blake sits for a while, his anger only slowly moderating. He should write that memo for Donnelly. He pulls from his desk drawer a legal pad, but before he begins he takes out the pink sales slip from City Camera. His Hasid is named Avram, but it was the other man, Chaim, who pulled the fast one. Chaim, the red-cheeked man who opened the camera under a bulb. They stick together, don't they? A very nice trick. He arranges the pad at the correct angle, sharpens his pencil for the first draft. Well, Blake has a whole bag of tricks at his disposal and it's about time he used a few of them. He shifts the angle of the pad again. One of them will be to blackbag the son of a bitch, as Halpern has been pushing for. And another will be a shooting expedition, the photographic kind.

Yes, a whole bag of tricks.

●

**MEMORANDUM**

To: T. Donnelly, Assistant Deputy Director,
     New York Field Office
From: M. Blake, Special Agent
Re: Operation Nova

Present were Messrs. Donnelly, Murphy, Blake.

Pursuant to our discussion of 17 August, formal applications have been made to various services requesting pertinent data re target(s).

As required, applications as made are listed in Addendum 1, attached hereto; notice of any such additional applications shall be provided in timely manner and similar fashion.

Discussion regarding Operation Nova was limited to general case guidelines. It was noted that a preliminary review of the extant material indicated possible warrantable activities on the part of target(s), and that such warrants would, at the appropriate time, be pursued with vigor should further information, if any, become available.

Misgivings as to the indictability of aforementioned activities were expressed, and note was made by M. Blake for further review of case elements with appropriate legal parties regarding this matter.

It must herein be noted, however, that preliminary, informal review does indeed indicate that the alleged activity(ies) of Target(s) is (are) indictable under present Statutory and Case Law relating to Espionage and/or Foreign Agent Registration laws. Relevant statutes and pertinent commentary may be found in Addendum 2, attached hereto.

Discussion of principles of case management ensued; concerns were expressed, both generically and specifically, regarding proper application of such principles to all investigatory phases, both in-field and ex-office. Final reiteration was made of the necessity of strict adherence to all relevant guidelines.

Meeting concluded with reference to anticipated discussion with M. Blake re H'MP ASS results and future career enhancement. M. Blake expressed eagerness to proceed on all such matters with dispatch and diligence, and does indeed anticipate a prompt, and mutually satisfying, conclusion thereof.

Most cordially submitted:
M. Blake

# CHAPTER 24

—————————●—————————

First the two men come, ringing the doorbell at nine-thirty in the morning. Deere, on the job since eight, hears Mrs. Greenspan talking in the entry hall. The men are from the New York City Department of Housing, inspection division. They wear no special uniforms, their ID cards hang from their shirt pockets. They are on an inspection tour of Cobble Hill brownstones, they tell Mrs. Greenspan. Some of the houses; hers for instance, have not been inspected for over fifteen years.

It takes them half an hour to do the house. They are in the basement for ten minutes. On the parlor floor they give the rooms a quick eye sweep, then step out onto the deck and check the backyard. Deere has come down to the kitchen, is busying himself with a cup of coffee. He puts out his cigarette by holding it under the faucet.

Then, while Deere returns to the middle floor, where he has been lacing BX cable through the studding, the two men go up to the roof. Deere stands among the wood and his tools, smoking. Natan comes in, but Deere sends him out again. The men stay on the roof a long time.

"How did we do?" asks Mrs. Greenspan when they finally come back down to the parlor floor.

"Very clean." She has only a few minor problems, nothing to worry about. For instance, the television antenna wire on the roof must be moved, and there is an opening in the basement ceiling that must be sealed, as per fire regulations.

On the way out, they pass the carpenter. Deere offers no smile, only a guttural vocalization that, though not intelligible, contains all the disdain, and the fear, that contractors the world over have for the representatives of a petty but powerful bureaucracy.

But that is only for show. He knows very well what a building inspection is. And he knows that these two men are on a mapping run.

They will return, he thinks.

And very soon.

●

"If cover, Matt, is what our man is living."

Among the many files and appreciations and background materials Halpern has been accumulating, and which Blake now takes from the lawyer's hand, is an interesting piece on the Mossad's philosophy of cover, entitled "Small Differences: Camouflage Theory and Cover Applications."

Its author, Halpern points out, was a British intelligence officer during the war, a man by the name of Maurice Levi-Smythe. "That was his nom de guerre, Matt. He was a comparative zoologist, a don at Cambridge. He had a side interest in Elizabethan politics, specifically the secret service of Queen Elizabeth during the time of the armada." How's that for an eccentric Englishman? As Blake skims, Halpern throws out background. The queen had a very extensive network of spies, foreign and domestic, inherited from her father, the amorous Henry, who was a matchless intriguer on more than just the fields of matrimony. The British had been practicing the art of spying for a millennium. This don, Sir Maurice Levi-Smythe—his grandmother had been Jewish, which gave him a certain cachet in English social circles, being as he was a combination of exotic Semite and country gentleman—had been placed in one of the war offices and told to study the science of camouflage.

"You can see it fits right in with zoology."

Theories are curious things, thinks Blake as the prosecutor goes on, in that they generally are of two kinds: those that link esoteric facts into a complex formulation that only experts appreciate, such as Einstein's special theory of relativity, and those that, on the other hand, state what anyone with half a brain who has given the subject any thought already knows. The theory of small differences was of the latter kind. After the war, when Levi-Smythe returned to academia, he was called upon from time to time by various secret services, the CIA among them, to contribute his special brand of eccentric thought. His theory was seen to be applicable to clandestine operations, specifically the production of agent covers. The CIA always had appreciation for this kind of eclectic thinking; the Mossad was also very interested. Indeed, Levi-Smythe's ancestral affiliations were invoked on more than one occasion, and he is regarded as one of the many unsung heros of the neonate Jewish state.

The theory is obvious in application. In camouflage the object's visibility is reduced by minimizing the differences between it and the environment.

"Small differences, Matt. Keep the increments of disguise as small as possible."

The best cover is that which comes closest to the truth, but never touches it.

"An asymptotic reality," suggests Blake.

The lawyer does not know the word. Blake, glad to display some erudition, explains. Halpern, impressed, nods, continues.

"So, Matt, in practice, this links up with long-chain theory." Halpern repeats the phrase, pulling from his briefcase another sheaf of papers. From source Tippet. Extracts from the operations manual of the Mossad, out of date by almost twenty years, but the real thing.

"It's part of the larger science of information theory, and it's right up Starfield's alley, Matt. I mean, think of it: he's a microbiologist, a geneticist, and he can incorporate all this into his operation." Halpern raises his hands and holds an imaginary ball between them. "It all just fits."

Halpern talks on. Blake is impressed with the outreaching, all-grasping quality of this young man's mind; he's not just another pretty face. Sequence theory, the lawyer says, postulates that with every pass of data between an agent and the agent's contact there is a loss of both quantity and quality. Studies of data transport bear this out. The loss occurs at the connecting terminals. In physiology, it is referred to as "synaptic dimunition of signal strength." It's what happens in field operations. The experts call it loss of content validity.

Meaning the goddamn message is garbled.

Now, in the Bureau, which is bottom heavy with field agents, as they both know, there is the belief that the more cutouts you use, the more switches and drops, the more secure is the transfer of data. Which explains why every FBI operation is like an anthill, dozens of agents crawling over each other.

However, data-transport theory states that diminishing data accuracy—DDA—is directly proportional to the number of transfers made.

In translation, this means that the more cutouts you use, the more mistakes you make.

So, since the Israelis always had limited resources, they conveniently applied this theory to their operational approach. Budgetary considerations, Matt. The Israelis believe the optimum is three intervals. They rarely use more than two cutouts, sometimes only one.

Meaning the obvious: they keep their operations small.

Halpern makes another related point. In keeping with the small-difference theory, the Israelis prefer to use natural cover. In the Bureau they call it clean cover. A sales rep for a pharmaceutical house, for instance, will double as a source of information on drugs applicable for military use; an Israeli air force officer on a visiting scholar's program studies for a year at MIT under a professor of computer science, who just happens to be one of the consultants on the new Integrated Defense Communications System.

"Starfield is living a perfect cover." Halpern is sure of this. "He's got dual citizenship, travels with an American passport. He's all over the place, Matt. He's got carte blanche. Europe, the States, he's got entry into the higher circles of academia. A lot of connections, Matt."

"Richard. All this is fine." Indeed, it is. Blake has an affinity for these sorts of concrete-abstract dualisms. But the Bureau loathes them. "When I go into Donnelly, I have to show him something hard."

"Tippet's working on it."

Blake doesn't doubt it.

Halpern is impatient.

"Matt, Navy's on to him. Starfield's been operating much longer than we think."

●

The Greenspans' brownstone is in the middle of the block, between Henry and Clinton streets, and from the rear window on the top floor there is a clear view of the long valley of backyards onto which the row houses face. At two o'clock in the afternoon—it's a good time, most people are working—two telephone repairmen show up.

They work at a leisurely pace. They arrange their straps and belts. First one goes up the pole, then the other. They strap themselves face to face, then open the junction box.

At the first sighting of the linemen, Deere sends Natan to a public phone on Atlantic Avenue. From there Natan calls back immediately. There is a great deal of static on the line. He hangs up. From the window, standing, Deere rests his binoculars on the sash. Mrs. Greenspan has left for an hour or two of food shopping, and he is alone in the house. The powerful glasses cut through the blurry green of trees and vines to show the man's hands as he runs his fingers over the T-splices with an artist's touch. This is standard work, and a good wire man does it with his eyes closed.

Through the glasses, Deere sees the hirsute hand using the pliers to remove the terminal splice from its clips. These days everything is modular, for ease of repair, so it will be a simple, quick task of cutting and refitting. Deere is smiling his lopsided, gentle smile. The man on the other side of the pole is smoking, enjoying the sunny day on his perch. He is one of the men who had come around two days ago for the inspection. He wears a headset, its mouthpiece a capsule mounted on a thin, bent wire. In his hand is a little box with wires which the other man is connecting to other wires in the junction box. It is pleasant work; a breezy summer day, nice gardens to look down into.

Deere squats on the floor of the Greenspans' library room and rests the twin barrels of the binoculars on the windowsill. He enjoys watching a craftsman at work. A plastic sleeve is slipped onto the wire, then slid down around the splice. The ring on the man's finger holds a blue stone. His fingers move swiftly, cutting and turning, now taping. Almost finished.

Deere has taken the telephone off the desk and placed it on the floor by his side. His hand is on the receiver, his other steadies the glasses. The moment the man touches the wire Deere lifts the phone. The hairy hands freeze. Counting, Deere watches the immobile hands; at eleven he replaces the receiver. The hands move again. Natan calls just as the men are going down the pole, using their straps in a lift-and-slip maneuver. They will need just a little more time to activate the tap, but already there is a very slight drop in signal strength. By this evening they will be recording. He tells Natan to return; they must begin the Sheetrocking for the Greenspans.

# CHAPTER 25

———————————•———————————

**W**ell, maybe it's about time, thinks Blake, as he sits in the window seat of the commuter train that clicks through the early evening dusk, about time to confront some of the problems out there. He is not quite sure where these thoughts are coming from, and he looks out the window at the passing greenery. The lawns are lush and inviting. Problems; they wait, like beasts in the jungle. Case problems, he means, operational decisions. Choices of the sort that that poor spy in the cell must endure, of the sort that Starfield will make. And which in turn shall force him, Blake, to make his choices. For the greater part of his career he has been spared the truly difficult decisions, and, as he glides gently eastward, into the diminishing light, he is thankful.

And regretful, too. For he has not yet passed through the fires of consequence, the flames that give one the burnish of achievement, set one glowing with the luster of hard-earned truth. There are those men and women possessing the fine, supple strength of the victorious, of passion honed to a fine edge. His younger daughter will possess it, he thinks; she will become an artist of sorts. Most likely a writer, taken as she is with words, searching for her truths.

Blake stares out the window. He is feeling at a loose end. He'd fired his gun today, and perhaps that is what is putting him on edge. The noise, the quivering, pulsing shock of the Sigsauer spitting out the bullets, the recoil. The slide action was too rough. He doesn't fire it enough. And then, walking off the range, the gun had pressed against his ribs like a live creature, adding an extra, unaccustomed warmth. And he had been embarrassed. His score was very low. The firearms agent at the range had admonished him, but gently.

He stands, shakes out his legs, positions himself for a quick exit. His briefcase is very heavy, what with all the files he must go through in preparation for Donnelly's triage. The train slows, stops smoothly. His station wagon is just where he left it this morning. The air of Eastmere is soft and fragrant with the perfume of freshly cut grass.

Yes, he thinks, the good are sometimes punished, the evil escape, and the Bureau works on.

●

Before descending into his basement dungeon, Blake treats himself to twenty minutes of radio news. His wife is out. Maureen is at the sink, cutting into a tomato.

"When are your classes over?"

"Next week."

"How are you doing?"

"Fine."

"What about that paper?"

"I'm working on it."

She holds the tomato up and bites into it. Its scarlet pulp squirts out over the sink.

"You're doing it on *The Stranger*?"

"Yeah."

He watches her finish the first half of the tomato. "Is that tomato good?"

"Hint, hint, Dad. Here." She cuts him half of the other half and holds it out.

"Thanks."

"Ugh, Dad. What's that smell?"

"What smell?"

"On your fingers."

He holds his hand up as Maureen leans over. She wrinkles her nose.

"Right," he says. "I took target practice today."

He had forgotten how powerful the lingering odor was, and had not scrubbed hard enough.

She makes a face, and then they both turn.

From the doorway, Blake's wife has been listening. "Target practice?"

"You know, bang-bang."

His wife is looking at him, and he bites into his tomato.

"Very sweet," he says. He, too, smells the cordite on his fingers.

And because his wife is still looking at him, he says, knowing that he's making it too much by trying to make it so very little, "My yearly qualifier, honey."

●

Later, just before he goes down, he steps into the kitchen again. His daughter speaks.

"I might go away this weekend, Dad. To the Hamptons. With Elaine."

"Who's Elaine?" He doesn't remember any Elaine.

Maureen explains: "Elaine is someone I know from school. She knows someone who has a house in Westhampton. It's called the DoubleDiamond, Dad. It's a famous house."

Blake remembers—it had been a feature in the Sunday *Times* a few years ago, two squares balanced on their edges, connected by a glass-walled living room.

"Is this a coed house, or what?"

"I don't know, Dad."

He has a devious turn of mind, part of his training; Maureen hardly ever reveals her plans with such abandon and detail.

Before he can reply, Maureen has a question.

"So, Dad, how's your big spy case coming along?"

"Fine," he says, startled, but showing nothing. He never talks about cases with his daughter, barely ever with his wife. He cannot recall mentioning, ever, the Starfield case in Maureen's presence. "It's the usual sort of thing," he says.

Maureen walks across the kitchen. She's in her usual mufti of shorts and polo, barefoot, drinking from a juice box. The backs of her legs have a glossy finish, and by the way everything under her clothing moves he knows she's not wearing underwear.

"We're getting responses back," says his wife when Maureen has gone.

Blake says something benign and pertinent. His mind is not on the wedding. He's thinking of Maureen's question. He has already leapt to all sorts of conclusions, the most obvious of which, and therefore probably the most accurate, is that she's heard about his big spy case from a third party.

And that party, of course—and he will bring this up later with his wife; he's certain that she knows—is, damn his youth and good looks and his insecure mouth, Halpern.

# CHAPTER 26

**A**t a late hour, Dr. Starfield sits at a desk in a motel room not far from Princeton. Before him is a closed file, which a few minutes ago had been delivered by special courier. Soon he will open and study it. But now he writes in a bound composition book of the sort that schoolchildren use, black cover with white, amoebic squiggles. His entries are for the most part professional in nature, though at times he puts down more personal thoughts, notes of his travels, conversations of interest.

He writes now of his late afternoon talk with one Dr. Kirov, professor of biology at the Institute for Advanced Studies. Until his defection in 1982, Kirov had worked at the Leningrad Institute. There, in the capacity of senior scientist of the Soviet Union, he had devoted his energies to recombinant technology—in popular jargon, designer genes. Kirov, until his defection, was head of a unit researching application of this technology to communication science.

The Soviets call it cryptogenetics. It has many applications in both civilian and military areas, and Dr. Starfield has in mind a number of avenues of exploration. He notes them now in his composition book. Tomorrow, he and Kirov will tour the laboratories, where Kirov will demonstrate his modifications of a Sam-1, a DNA synthesizer and a standard piece of machinery in genetic research. The Sam-1 arranges, as the technician directs, the four chemical bases—adenine, guanine, thymine, and cytosine, known acronymically as ATCG—that form the covalent backbone of the DNA molecule. One takes, then, a primitive form of life, a simple bacterium, one such as *E. coli*, for instance, which lives in the intestines of Homo sapiens, and imposes this structured DNA upon the bacteria which, obeying the imperative to multiply and be fruitful, replicates it accordingly. The possible combinations of the four bases are endless, and a communications code based upon a bacterial encoding will be, for all intents and purposes, unbreakable. Of its use in cryptology, no more need be said.

Dr. Starfield pauses in his writing, puts his pen down. The file he will soon open sits on his desk. It has been procured at some cost and will return, he hopes, fair value. Soon he will read it, but now he stands, shuts off the light, and goes to the window to look out upon the night.

In return for Kirov's confidences, he had offered the Russian a few tidbits of his own. His company was developing a membrane diffusion process as a means of treating certain cancers of the lymphatic system. The difficulty of such treatment lies not in what to do, but how to do it. The medicines, usually in the form of radioisotopes carrying chemical therapies, must be made to attach themselves to the cancer site. The attachment must be specific, durable, timely, and concentrated. He was attempting, he explained to Kirov, to engineer a package whereby the medicine traveled with its doctor, a delicate molecular membrane that would monitor and dispense dosage as required. Kirov was most delighted.

He returns to his desk, sits in the dark, still, the closed file waiting, and thinks of his day with Kirov. They had met when he had taken the Russian biologist through a series of technical debriefings, first in Vienna, for the Lekem, then in Frankfurt, for the Americans. They had conversed at length on matters both professional and philosophical. The defector's English, adequate for most technical discussion, was not always up to the idiomatic shadings required in more abstract conversation.

Today, Kirov had waxed philosophical. His long absence from his homeland was taking its toll. Kirov had a love of theater, of drama, and he spoke of life as a play, of acts. Of the final curtain, and how that which has no beginning and no end does not fit into the human mind.

Birth and death, said Kirov, they make life more human.

Starfield smiles at the recollection of the Russian's impassioned silliness. With drunken humor, he had inveighed against the notion of eternal life.

If we lived forever, where would everyone fit! Indeed, where? Will there have evolved a self-limiting quota? Would we two gentlemen, sipping vodka among the test tubes and bubbling flasks, have made it before the cutoff?

Kirov had waved his hands in despair.

Dr. Starfield had sought to cheer him. Existence is a circle upon whose circumference we travel, the circle of time. The trick, dear Nikolai, is in speeding up or slowing down the voyage. This, Einstein proved possible.

Ah, my Phillip! Kirov had exclaimed, his eyes brimming over his beaming cheeks, if only we on paper lived!

Starfield now rises again. It is very late, he must work. Standing over the file, he now opens it. His contacts were most obliging, and were able to procure, from the office of Ms. Collins, a copy of this very interesting assessment.

And now we will see, at last, just what this Mr. Blake, special agent of the mighty FBI, is all about.

# CHAPTER 27

O ver there, Mr. Blake.''

The cameraman directs him to the table where the photographs are arranged on the dark, wood-grained Formica. Spanakos stands at his side. Halpern, experiencing a traffic delay coming in from Quogue, has not yet arrived.

He looks down at the image of a thinnish, pale man, slightly stooped. Two younger men, one dark with curly hair, the other blond. They wear construction garb. Blowups of their faces. The dark boy has lips, lashes, eyes, and nose Mesopotamian in their full beauty, like a face in an ancient mosaic. The other boy is all-American, nice looking too, nothing striking.

Back to the older man, he of the pale face.

Spanakos recites what he found. Albert Deere. Carpenter. Legal entry. Citizenship unclear. They're running a pedigree through Navy.

"Tippet thinks he's got something."

How does the lieutenant do it?

Blake picks up the photograph of the carpenter. In the blowup it's hard to tell if the spots are freckles or the emulsion's graininess. His eyebrows are tangled, hair crimped-looking, thinning. Why is he smiling?

The photographer wants to talk technique. Luckily, he explains, the way the Greenspan house is situated, they were able to set up their blind in a Brooklyn Union Gas truck a few houses down. We used T-Max, one of the new emulsions.

Three days, the photographer says, two technicians. This shooting expedition has cost Blake a little over eight hundred dollars. Time and material. It's government money, but Blake will have to sign the vouchers. Three days worth of meals. If the Bureau is willing to pay, they'll stay a month. It's an example of unobtrusive surveillance, and does not require a warrant. The Bureau manual describes such a surveillance as anything that does not penetrate an imaginary line over which the target's constitutionally protected space exists. In essence, anything that an agent can see from the street is fair game.

He and Spanakos turn; Halpern is behind him. He hadn't heard the attorney come in.

"Very crisp."

The photographer is pleased at the lawyer's praise.

There are other photographs. The mail carrier, a UPS delivery man. A woman, Mrs. Greenspan. A man, presumably Mr. Greenspan. On the back of each is the time, place, and date of exposure. Every subject is given the full treatment. The photographers are technical people, they shoot at everything that moves. But the goddamn mailman? Eight hundred dollars.

"Thank you," says Halpern.

"Yes. Thank you very much. Excellent work."

When the man leaves, Blake, Halpern, and Spanakos study the faces. Spanakos has already run them through the Bureau's photo-ID files and come up with nothing; Blake is neither surprised nor alarmed. He doesn't expect anything on the Greenspans. Also, the images will be sent this morning into the I-AIS, the Interagency Identification System, which uses a computer-imaging process to match the photographs to the file descriptions.

"What about Starfield?" Halpern asks.

Spanakos replies, "We're trying to catch him."

Halpern shakes his head.

Before they leave, Blake takes the images of the older man, with the slight stoop and freckled face, and the two young men. My new family portraits, he thinks with a wry, inner smile that is almost an exact duplicate of Deere's lopsided grin.

●

They have another photograph, another man, which Blake and Halpern study as they sit in Halpern's office on Cadman Plaza. The different divisions are switching floors—for the third time in five years—and the halls are obstacle courses of file drawers and boxes. No security, but no one cares.

The image is of a fat, dark man with a pencil-thin mustache.

Leslie Thaddeus Dryden.

It is Blake's contention, Halpern agreeing, that Dryden would not have fallen had he been more telegenic. Small, fat, swarthy men with dirty-line mustaches and funny names do not do well on television. God knows what unpleasantries were visited upon him during childhood, those cruel years. Watching him sweat and fret, as Blake has on the tapes of the Senate hearings, it is hard to imagine that a man of his roly-poly physique and uninspired physiognomy could have so much brilliance in him.

As the lawyer puts it, if Dryden was so fucking smart, why was the man on national television being so fucking dumb?

There are a number of theories to account for his fall, and Blake and Halpern discuss them.

One, put forth by the clever and brilliant people who take these things seriously, is that the man was playing a very devious and extraordinarily complex game based upon his own theories of counterintelligence. Not a double or even a triple cross, but a furious zigzag run across a line drawn in the sand, on one side of which was truth and reality, and on the other, lies and fiction. These same, clever people are quick to point out that for a man like Dryden, such a line did not really exist. This was part of his downfall, for it rendered him an easy mark for the senators: Americans insist upon lines. Blake understands this. We want to know where we stand. For America is Eden, a land of primal innocence, and one is either in the garden, or out of it. And Dryden, Leslie Thaddeus Dryden, the self-appointed keeper of the Tree of Secret Knowledge—as one TV commentator described him—had turned out to be the serpent in his own garden.

Another theory, which Blake advances, is that Dryden himself was the very mole within the CIA that he claimed all those years to have been looking for, and that his search—conducted during the last fifteen years of his autocratic reign—had been but a smoke screen for his own treason. And now, carrying this to its logical and absurd conclusion, Dryden was, incredibly, and driven by some mad necessity, putting himself up in front of the firing squad. Blake suggests an uncommon wisdom: the man's sense of guilt, revealed in his lifelong fascination with religious metaphor, provided the imperative for self-immolation. For one knows, does one not, my young and handsome lawyer, that the value of a crime, its true value, as opposed to the public, wordly price one pays for it, is one's intense, internal guilt.

Halpern, sitting silently, appears about to blush, or perhaps protest, but Blake, aware of the delicate balance of their relationship, and reluctant to point an uncertain finger, brings the discussion back to the matter at hand.

No, he says; Dryden as his own mole is an interesting, teasingly circular hypothesis. But we are looking, Richard, not for philosophical confirmation, but for operational direction. We are seeking to know what he did, when he did it, and how.

As were the sleek senators of the Intelligence Oversight Committee. At the hearings, Dryden had spoken of Plato's cave analogy, perorating at length while the senators, a line of well-groomed rectitudinal gentlemen, received notes over their shoulders from their young aides. Dryden had droned on, unheeding of his lawyer's cautionary scribbles, until, at last, he was interrupted by the distinguished senator from Idaho, a Midwesterner of extreme impeccability and faultless pronunciation. In twangy mellifluosity, he had put the question to Dryden: had he, indeed, in fact, authorized the use of torture—the senator believed that Agency parlance referred to it as *duressful data extraction*—and had he, in fact, indeed, been present when such extractions were effected? Here the witness was admonished to answer yes or no, and not blur the moral line with a too-finely drawn verbal fuzz.

I ask you, Leslie Thaddeus Dryden, yay or nay. Sir, yay or nay?

And Dryden had sat there, one hand delicately touching his water glass, the other drumming ceaselessly upon the table. Blake squirms even now for the man. He has looked at the tape, gazes now at the photograph. Behind that furrowed brow was reputed to be a mind possessing a photographic memory. On the operational level, this meant that he was able to remember all his lies. For a man of pronounced religious sensibility this was not an advantage. Dryden had sat there while the senators took the slips of papers from their staff and nodded, then hunched up to the microphone to fire another shot into the fat man.

But now, the lawyer, his imagination racing in high gear, advances another theory, which is that Dryden's tumbling fall was engineered by the Russians.

Blake's heard it before. It's quite an improbable and breathtaking notion, and therefore quite beguiling. One may reject it out of hand as prima facie nonsense; or, on the other hand, admit it contains an undeniable plausibility.

The two men talk the theory over, more as an exercise in dialectic than anything remotely real.

For the sake of argument, they agree on the notion of Soviet duplicity. Though one may think of the Russians as crude and boorish and not given to subtlety, they are really, by all accounts, a patient and complex people. Mother Russia may never triumph, but she endures. Think, the lawyer puts forth, of their mastery of chess.

Blake is thoughtful. If indeed the KGB brought Dryden down they laid the trap fifteen years ago, probably twenty. He explains. Little bits and pieces of the puzzle are strewn about, in order to be picked up and sorted out. A defector showing up in Berlin, for instance, is followed up by a fortuitous bit of collateral brought in by the French in one of the sting operations they do so well. In turn, this is certified by the British, whose verification process is conceded to be one of the best. Then another tidbit is thrown to the Army's intelligence division two years later in a contact report filed by a low-level agent regarding the pillow talk he has had with a junior coding secretary working for some hostile intelligence service. And, by definition, any service but your own is hostile. The chain goes on and on. Intercepts are brought in by the NSA telemetry station at Trabzon, a small Turkish village about seventy miles from the Russian border, and through whose air space the Soviets are known to communicate with their case officers in Vienna. Another defector is sent in, sometimes not quite knowing his own role, convinced his own defection genuine—which it surely may be; in the great game of spies, as in chess, one will give up a pawn to get a knight—and the field station in Brussels or Prague or Frankfurt is in ecstasy. This is the stuff of which careers are made, promotions granted, bonuses awarded.

Thus the Russians gave Dryden no choice, and of course, he took it.

Blake nods, agreeing with this line of argument. He likes the complex balance of contrary forces, and allows himself to be pulled in by its elliptical rush, first riding in close toward certainty, then back out to the beguiling reaches of conjecture, here to touch, just, the far edge of credibility until, smiling at his own silliness and not a little fearful of the ever-increasing velocity of his thoughts, leaps clear of the hurtling premise: the Russians did not do it.

And, more important, even if they had, we chose, Richard, not to believe it. It has no pertinence to our scheme of things.

As your behavior with my daughter has none to mine.

So, thus, we shall discard it. Dryden's world was much like a Möbius strip. Ours, Richard, is a place of law and linear order, a world of manifest truth and certain, if hidden, consequences. A Newtonian world, wherein one progressed from one point to another in precise and careful steps. It was the world as created by Hoover, overseen and maintained by the Bureau.

When he looks up, the attorney's eyes are upon him, steady and deep; is there embarrassment there, or triumph? Is it just my imagination? By common accord, they both look away immediately, and return their gaze to the photograph of the short, fat man with the dark eyes and mustache.

●

Before Blake leaves they view one more photograph, this in color, quite recent.

It has been acquired through one of Campbell's old connections in Division 5, the Bureau's counterintelligence section.

"What is he, seventy-five?" Halpern is genuinely surprised; anyone that old can't possibly be alive, much less functioning.

The full-face photograph clipped to the top sheet shows a man with wisps of graying hair combed across a bald pate. The image is that of a wizened old man. There is a congestive quality to the features, a quality of anger, of loneliness.

Reading the file, they progress through Maxwell Harrow's life.

Like Dryden himself, like most of the OSS operatives, Harrow began his career as a field hand. He was in southern Europe for the last year of the war, was transferred to Greece, and from there to Egypt. He kicked around various departments, from cryptology, where everyone began, to research, and wound up, finally, in the psychological warfare division.

"That's the section," Blake tells the lawyer, "where the OSS hid its unofficial assassination unit."

Halpern makes due note of this on his copy.

Like many of the people in clandestine work, Harrow's background was liberal arts; another lit major. Shakespeare. Would have got his doctorate had not the war intervened. Stayed on when the CIA was chartered in '47. Became Dryden's special assistant in the late fifties.

Harrow's title was Head of Operations, Counterintelligence.

Harrow implemented the methodologies. He took the world that Dryden had created, a world of smoke and mirrors, a world which, for all Dryden's brilliance, was a world without form, and ordered and arranged it. He oversaw the paperwork, approved the identities, planted agents, doubled the opposition, and sowed the lies that years later they would all reap in a devil's harvest.

All this, the files only hint at.

And to every man, thinks Blake as he and Halpern pore silently over the pages, to every man his modus.

Harrow favored certain points of entry, brought in the field teams in a certain order, set up courier routes along certain lines, preferred one set of crypto over another. Campbell, having worked with him—rather, with some of his secondaries—knew the man's craft.

Harrow preferred, for instance, on text codes, to use children's nursery rhymes.

*If wishes were horses, beggars would ride.*

*Sing a song of sixpence.*

You start your coding from the second word, skip every other, go backwards at the end of the line. As to which rhyme to use, you signaled your agent through various means: a newspaper of a certain date indicating page number, the last digits of a telephone number left on a message slip, sometimes transposed. Standard craft, simple and secure.

Blake's childhood memories are jogged.

Here's that old one about about children and the days of the week: *Tuesday's child is full of grace.*

And this one:

*One, two, buckle my shoe.*

Easy to remember, diverse, and unsuspected. Perfect for scheduling meetings.

He gave his agents names taken from the rhymes. Cock Robin, Little Miss Muffett, Hector Protector. He once ran an operation based on "The Queen of Hearts." The king and queen, the knave. The tarts, thus, were the goodies.

That was Harrow's trademark, children's nursery rhymes.

And there was more; Campbell could only point Blake because he knew so little of it himself, and even that was secondhand. He was never comfortable interfacing with Langley, had a field man's bias against their academic, blue-sky stuff.

"A lapsed atheist," says Blake.

Halpern nods, though not quite certain what the older agent means.

Harrow needed Dryden's secularized religiosity, his purity of methodology, to get him over his occasional yearning for a diety. Further, Blake suggests that Harrow had a love-hate relationship with Dryden.

The lawyer agrees. How could it be otherwise? They, Dryden and his cohorts, the gang of four, had iron holds on each other. They had shed blood, run the gauntlet of fear and hate and despair, had seen each other do things of which no man can be proud, at least no normal man. Dryden, like other gods, was covetous of his worshiper's devotion, and had grappled his men, and an occasional woman, close to his bosom, holding them in a secret, unbreakable embrace.

Maxwell Harrow and Carl Landis, John Whitman, Martin Carr.

The gang of four.

"All dead," says Halpern, looking up from the page. "Or close to it."

Yes. Landis in a car accident, Whitman by suicide, Carr by disease. All within the space of two years. And Dryden, dying of an unspecified illness, a prisoner in his country home.

So Harrow was, at last, sole survivor. All the lies and secrets, the dark treasures, were his and his alone.

●

With Dryden overseeing, Harrow's last assignment was to handle the Israelis.

The Mossad trusted him; he had Dryden's blessing, and some of his curse.

"Dimona." Halpern has been reading ahead and now he looks up. The name rings a bell.

"Dimona is an atomic energy plant in Israel," says Blake.

"Wasn't something in the papers about it?"

Blake's fund of general knowledge is ready with another payout. "A technician was arrested for leaking the news that the Dimona reactor is producing plutonium for atom bombs. They arrested him on a boat in the Mediterranean." They lured him with a woman. Never fail, those potent pheromones. "It began way back in the fifties."

Blake tells Halpern the story. A large amount of enriched uranium, or maybe it was plutonium, was missing from an American plant in Pennsylvania. "There was a story about it, a few headlines, and then it was hushed up." Trucks loaded in the dead of night, armed men, missing invoices. The plant owner—the government contracted out its uranium needs—claimed the missing poundage was consistent with acceptable process loss. "It was eventually traced to the Middle East. Assumed diverted to Dimona."

The usual denials were issued. The government—the Atomic Energy Commission, State Department, FBI—put out contradictory and accusatory press releases.

At the time no one thought of Dryden, much less Harrow; they weren't onto them quite yet. Later, when the bits and pieces were being put together by enterprising journalists, many of the participants were no longer to be found, and the trail was cold.

They return to the material. Blake studies the photograph. An interesting man. These bored academics were all interesting. Rumor had it that Harrow was, perhaps still is, an alcoholic. He was also a man alone. No marriages, no children. An island unto himself, full of unexplored latencies.

Homosexual, wasn't he? That was said of him, but Blake thinks not: more of a celibate, one of those ascetic, asexual creatures, passionate, brilliant even, but whose spirit is held in thrall by an evil magician such as Dryden.

"Seventy-five years old." The lawyer is amazed.

"He knows, Richard," says Blake, recalling Campbell's words, "where the bodies are buried."

●

Holding the knife so that it follows him as he walks backward, Deere leaves a long, deep incision in the panel of Sheetrock, finishing the cut with a practiced twist of his wrist. With Natan holding one end, they tilt the Sheetrock onto the floor, cut side down, and then, with a sure, quick lift, Deere snaps it at the cut. Natan, stepping in, then runs the point of his matt knife along the crease, cutting the paper layer. From her post just outside the door, Mrs. Greenspan marvels at the clean cut they have thus achieved, and rewards their prowess with a smile.

They have just begun this phase of the work. After an absence of two days—they were on another job, Deere told Mrs. Greenspan—Natan and Danny had shown up yesterday afternoon with the blue van full of panels. The two assistants had spent a good hour carrying up the Sheetrock, two panels at a time. She knew how heavy the sheets were by the taut ripple of muscle on Natan's arm, and by the way he and Danny scurried through the halls, not wanting to give themselves a chance to tire.

They did the ceiling first, because, as Deere explains to her, that is the hardest part. They use long-snouted drills with magnetic tips that hold long, black drywall screws. Mrs. Greenspan is interested in all these things, and Deere is pleased to demonstrate their use.

They had begun early in the morning, to avoid the heat, and by three o'clock most of the ceiling is done. One of the corners is left open, as well as a small square where the overhead fixture is to be installed.

Before they leave for the day, they put up one panel on the wall stud-ding. Just to have it started, says Deere. So when they return tomorrow morning they will have something to work against.

"In a few weeks, maybe less, we finish," says Deere.

Mrs. Greenspan is very pleased. As is her husband. They will, of course, recommend Deere to their friends.

Deere smiles his lopsided smile, and thanks her.

He's always looking for work.

# CHAPTER 28

**G**ood morning.''

Blake and Spanakos stand in the lobby of 225 Cadman Plaza East, Halpern having just come up from his office to save them a trip down into the basement. Spanakos and Halpern shake hands.

Spanakos holds out a file.

"They went in last Thursday. It was a clean job."

The three of them move to the rear, past the reception desk, and stand in the light that comes through the yellow-orange checkerboard wall. Eager, like a kid unwrapping a new toy, Halpern opens the file and scans the inventory sheet. He closes the folder.

"Let's go down."

●

It's a standard bureau report on a surreptitious entry. There are photographs and diagrams that show the position of everything from the insides of drawers to the layout of the room. The suitcases have been opened and photographed, contents inventoried. Again, the photographs are excellent, black and white and very crisp, lighting arranged to cast only the thinnest of necessary shadows, because without shadow there is no depth and the images come out too cartoonish.

Spanakos has typed out the summary, which states that though there were indeed high expectations of discovery, subsequent inventory and analysis shows little that is applicable to the ongoing investigation for which warrant was issued, etc. Blake's signature approves.

Halpern asks: What about these?

Spanakos replies. "He carries small batches of biological materials. One of the things these genetics companies do is trade samples. They're very gentlemanly about it and consider it a professional courtesy. So he's got these sealed vials of, I guess, mutations. They were all matched against his inventory sheet. No discrepancies. If this is his cover, he's living it like a second skin."

Halpern goes back to the first page and reads the report again.

"What about these?"

Spanakos looks at where Halpern is tapping a finger. A long list of books and magazines and professional papers.

"What about them?" Spanakos counters.

"Could they be code materials?"

Spanakos looks to Blake. To be honest, after reading Spanakos's summary, Blake had merely scanned the inventory. The books were listed separately, as were the clothes, the toiletries.

"It's possible," says Blake.

"So shouldn't we run them across a computer, see if they match up with some kind of code?"

Blake lets the junior agent respond.

"No, Rick, it's not done that way."

Then Blake explains how you don't run a book across a computer code check without having something—a possible cryptogram, a message that might have been encoded using one of these books—to match it against. Otherwise it's like analyzing the alphabet.

"Yeah. What about this?"

Halpern's finger taps once on the last page.

A tin of earthlike substance.

The photograph shows a metal container the size of a cigarette pack; the photographer has been thoughtful enough to place a quarter—the standard comparable—nearby for scale.

Inside the tin a dry, brown, granular substance.

"They don't know," says Spanakos. "They took a small sample for the lab."

"Whatever is it," says Blake dryly, "it's not a breakthrough."

●

Later that afternoon Halpern calls to arrange an impromptu meeting. It's with a liaison officer from the CIA, arranged courtesy of the Racker. Navy will be there, too, says Halpern over the phone.

When Blake arrives, there are not two but three men sitting at the table in the small, sound-secure room in Eastern's headquarters. The lieutenant is not in uniform, but Blake picks him out by his lapel pin, a magnifying glass crossed by what looks like a feather, an intelligence technician's insignia. The CIA liaison is an older man, incongruously youthful in affect. Their eternal youth is the objective correlative of their function: they have little substance, only form, for their responsibility is not disbursement, but containment, and to this end they are given no secrets of their own. In short, they are package without content, all Dorian Grays; somewhere deep in the netherworld of Langley, thinks Blake, must be the repository of all their portraits, walls of vile, ugly images.

The third, unexpected man, is indolent with the superior ease of the higher managerial type. It takes Blake only a few moments to recall that he is the unnamed chief from an unspecified European field station. The Frankfurt man.

Before he begins, the liaison wishes to tell them that, having made inquiries through channels, he is able to assure them that Israeli intelligence reaffirms, for the tenth time or whatever, that they have no operatives in the field at this point in time.

This is a pro forma denial that no one need take seriously.

Halpern wishes to put his skepticism into the record. "They want us to think it's a rogue operation, a bunch of amateurs."

It could go either way, agrees Blake; and he is sure it will.

"God spare us," says the liaison, "from another gifted amateur."

The Frankfurt man smiles, finding all this very amusing.

The liaison has placed upon the table his thin portfolio and now unzips it. A file is produced, opened, and is turned toward Blake and Halpern.

"Aha."

A pale face stares at them, freckled, unsmiling. On the other half of the file is the typed bio. Ephraim Hirsh. Age sixty-one. As they read, the liaison offers a running commentary.

"The British know him. He was interred in Cyprus in '46. We have no trace of him in a professional capacity in the States. He's got a history as long as your arm. Early forties, in Europe, parents on the run from Germany. As a teenager he was infiltrated into Palestine, the usual route. Ran guns for the Haganah, then later joined the Irgun. Was on the wanted list of the British high command. Served a year in prison, was freed when the Stern gang blew the walls out. Went back to the Irgun and terrorizing the British. Didn't stop them from using him in a joint Israeli-British commando unit against the Egyptians in '56 when they took the Canal. After that, the British lost track of him, or rather, didn't bother to look. He works under names that are variants of Hirsh. That's German for deer. Hirshman, Deere. Stagman. Harte, Hartman. Also Zwieman.''

"Zvi is Hebrew for stag.'' Halpern pronounces it with a long *e*.

The liaison waits for questions; there are none. A long pause ensues during which the Frankfurt man, relaxed and smiling, takes a pipe from one pocket, from another a tobacco pouch, and goes through his business of packing the bowl.

"We believe that in the sixties,'' he says as he tamps the tobacco with his thumb, "Hirsh was employed by the Shin Beth. That's the CI grouping of the Mossad. I say employed . . .'' He puts the pipe in his mouth, holds a match a distance from the bowl, unstruck. "What we call an independent contractor.'' He strikes the match, sucks the flame down. They wait. He is in control, wants to set his own pace, wants everyone to see him playing with fire.

Halpern stirs, impatient. "What are your sources, if I may ask?'' The tone is too blunt, adolescent in its challenge, and smashes through all the protocols.

Good boy, thinks Blake.

The liaison and the lieutenant are studiously unreactive.

"We have them.'' This with a smile, a nod, a return of the pipe to the mouth, its removal after a long inhalation.

"In 1972 we believe Hirsh was made a section leader for a newly formed counterterrorist strike force. The impetus for the creation of this force was, in part, the Munich massacre.''

Halpern's expression is that of a perplexed student.

Says Blake, "The '72 Olympics. Munich.'' He looks to the pipe. "They killed seven athletes.'' The pipe nods.

Twelve years old at the time, the lawyer's face shows the struggle of recall.

"It was the Black September group,'' the liaison explains, eager to contribute. "Arab terrorists. Ragtag sympathizers joined them in Europe. Japanese, Red Brigade, German radicals. The Israelis formed an intelligence unit to identify them and a strike force to search them out. They were known unofficially as the Sword of Joshua. They operated in three geographic sectors.''

Off to the side the Frankfurt man is studying his pipe, pulls at it, looks in the bowl, presumably checking the evenness of the ash.

"Middle East, Eastern Europe—including Greece and Turkey—and Western Europe: France and Germany, Belgium and Italy. The Sword of Joshua."

Blake's attention is on the photograph of Hirsh, or Deere. It's not one of theirs. It's a formal frontal shot taken in a harsh light that washes out the humanizing curves and creases and makes the man look more like a thug, or an animal.

Liaison continues. "Three sectors, each with a unit of two teams. Each team had four or five men or women, teams alternating between operations and support."

The pipe is in and out, suck suck, and the air is full of spicy, sweet smoke.

"They traveled light and fast. Made contact with their general networks only in emergencies, used them for occasional support—documents, travel arrangements—but in general kept their operations separate."

Silence once more as Blake and Halpern study the photograph.

"How effective were they?" asks Blake.

Silence. The liaison is befuddled. He knows nothing, operationally. The pipe is taken out, the man trains his eyes on Blake.

"In all honesty, gentlemen, we don't know."

Their ignorance, thinks Blake, is a measure of the operation's success.

"We assume they had a fairly high kill rate."

Certainly; bodies are found in the street without identification, people die in their beds, there are automobile accidents. The targets might have violent lover's quarrels or indulge in mutual perversities that have fatal consequences. A favorite is the self-administered, lethal overdose of drugs.

The plainclothes lieutenant continues his total silence. He is much like Tippet, a boyish officer from the Racker's stable of young, fresh lieutenants, and is present in observer status.

"In '74 Hirsh's team was kicked out of France. They killed a waitress and a sous-chef in a Paris bistro." It was in the news, and a couple of magazines ran articles. Mistaken identity, it was said. "The usual diplomatic noises were made." Frankfurt recrosses his legs and leans back. The pipe is resting on the table. "They were asked by the French government to refrain from further activity. Interpol escorted them to the border, and they disappeared."

Silence while the pipe is relit. Blake uses the pause to compute the variables: How much does the CIA know about Hirsh's whereabouts? What can he hide? What do they know we know? The CIA is very territorial, and there is a real danger that the operation will be stolen, or blown, accidentally or on purpose. God knows what they're after or what devil's bargain has been made with Navy. There is the long arm of Harrow in this, reaching out from the dusty stacks of his archives.

The pipe is cradled in Frankfurt's right hand. "We assumed Hirsh returned to contract work, but he hasn't been spotted in Europe for years. Frankfurt was his staging area." He pauses, then adds a little bit of incidental knowledge, as if he's talking about a friend. "Hirsh was never a formal employee of the Mossad. They kept away from the Irgun. We insisted upon that, you know, as a sop to the British. They didn't want to have to be polite to the men and women who assassinated their officers in Palestine." A long pause. "Understandable, of course."

Another reflective pause ensues. Blake, should they pursue him on Hirsh, is planning his defense: stonewall all the way. Once the CIA gets their claws into this, the Bureau's going to be pushed aside. Halpern's posture, one hand holding his chin, the other strong and tense upon the table, shows he is equally aware of the danger.

Says Blake, "This group, the Sword of Joshua . . ."

"That's the informal name they were given by the media." The liaison speaks brightly. "Their official code designation was Group Ariel." After he says this he looks to the pipe for approval, and gets it in the form of a nod.

"Ariel." Blake can't resist adding a bit of general knowledge. "That's the name of the fairy in one of Shakespeare's plays."

"*A Midsummer Night's Dream*," says the lieutenant with happy certainty, his first and only contribution.

"That's Puck," corrects the liaison.

Blake seconds that. "Mickey Rooney played Puck in the movie."

The pipe comes out of the amused mouth. "Ariel is in *The Tempest*. I believe he's the spirit that works for Prospero."

"Ariel is one of the moons of Uranus," adds the liaison, keeping the ball in play.

"It's also the name for Jerusalem."

They turn to Halpern, their Old Testament specialist.

"In the Bible." He's sitting up very straight. "Isaiah. In Hebrew it's two words. *Ari* and *el*."

They are listening.

"It means," says Halpern, "the Lion of God."

"Ah." The Frankfurt man nods; yes, at last something he has wondered about for years is explained.

The Lion of God.

"We were curious," says the liaison, "just where you dug him up."

Blake says, "We're not sure ourselves. This is a casual contact we came across that we ran through our files. We have no serial on him." All this is true, technically; he's quite comfortable with half lies.

Frankfurt has used up his quota of smiles. Navy is very still. Halpern is tense, his fingers pressing the tabletop.

The pipe speaks with more formality and less smile. He doesn't have to point out, he points out, the delicacy of the situation. He is suddenly angry, though it isn't clear why. His pipe punctuates his words.

"A man such as this, this Hirsh is, of course, quite serious."

The liaison keeps his eyes on Blake.

"You are aware, I assume, of his work?" The question is rhetorical.

Now the pipe is very steady, held near his mouth. "Very simply, gentlemen, group Ariel was an assassination squad. Every Arab operative has a price on his head."

The liaison is upset. He wants Blake and Halpern and the lieutenant to know how serious this is. "Interpol keeps a special watch for him."

The Frankfurt man speaks.

"He's no amateur, Mr. Blake."

No one says anything while the tobacco pouch is put away, the bowl tapped lightly on the table's edge.

"It's very simple."

And now the Frankfurt station chief seems to be amused once again as he looks first into Blake's eyes, and then into Halpern's.

"Hirsh travels around the world, Mr. Blake, Mr. Halpern, and kills people who hurt Jews."

●

Mrs. Greenspan thinks Albert Deere is doing his best. During the last two weeks, he and his two assistants have worked at a steady, determined pace. As the carpenter had predicted, the last quarter of the job takes more than half the time. The weather slows them. They have had a week of late summer rains, so that the compound has not dried. Deere has brought fans in, blowing air over the walls, but the humidity is much too high. Until it dries, the compound cannot be sanded, so the last coat is delayed.

And until the walls are finished, Deere cannot put on the baseboard and moldings and window trim. Instead, he busies himself with preparing the new door for sanding, mortising out the lock hole and hinges. Natan does not come often, and Danny hardly shows. When Mrs. Greenspan asks him where his young men were, Deere smiles his impish smile, tells her that he has already begun another job. They are doing the demolition.

# CHAPTER 29

G aps, Matt? You wanted to fill in the gaps?"

Blake, at his desk working a paper clip, stares up at the tall AUSA. "Here are the fucking gaps."

The lawyer throws the file so that it skitters across the desk, knocking Blake's magnetized clip holder aside. Halpern, breaking protocol by coming into Manhattan, has caught Blake by surprise.

"Where'd you get it?"

Halpern brushes the question aside. He has his contacts.

"Four years ago," he says. "Starfield's daughter."

Blake reaches for the file.

"In Israel—terrorists," says Halpern.

The lawyer is in extreme agitation, barely controlling his voice which, as he speaks again, breaks into a tremble.

"Matt. The evil bastards. They killed his little girl."

●

Blake holds the file, but doesn't open it; Halpern brings himself under control. The trace requests came in through Navy just a few days ago and the Racker had Tippet put a package together.

"This is just the synopsis."

As Blake leafs through the material, Halpern talks the highlights. Starfield had a family connection with the Irgun through an uncle, one

of the family's few surviving relatives of the camps. Sternfeld, a German name. Starfield is the straight English translation. The uncle's
work name was Fielding. The records are spotty, but the assumption is
that he was connected, at some point, with the CIA.

"Is there any basis in fact for this assumption, Richard?"

"Damn it, Matt, the files have been scrubbed. We're going to assume
it. He worked for the CIA. Low-level stuff, maybe."

Blake accepts it. They'll treat it as an unacknowledged truth that is to
be accepted—or denied—as needed.

"We're going to assume too, that the uncle pitched the nephew, and
brought Starfield in. Because we do know that when Starfield was
younger—our Starfield—he did a few things for the Israelis. When he
was a graduate student. On the scientific end."

Blake has found the reference on the third page of the file.

"And Matt, his connection with the Mossad ends about the time that
Dryden was kicked out. About when he marries the Danish girl."

"Dutch."

"Dutch." Details unimportant; those little European countries are all
the same.

"It all fits. Look at the chronology." Halpern lays out the sequence of
events. "He's an only child. His parents got out in time, in the late
thirties. They came to America. Everyone else was killed in Germany,
everyone, except this one uncle, Sternfeld, who after the war runs the
blockade and becomes a charter member of the Irgun and fights the
British. Okay, he comes to the States—it's all there, travel dates—
pitches his nephew. Through him Starfield makes his contacts with the
Mossad and through them with the CIA. We're not sure about this, it
might be the reverse sequence. He does his thing for a while, scientific
stuff, scouting for the Mossad at conferences, kind of doing the same
thing for us. Working both ends. He's based in the States, travels a lot,
has dual citizenship. Not unusual, Matt. His father died in the forties,
his mother about fifteen years ago. He's alone, Matt. Okay, then he
marries this Dutch girl who's a refugee and they go to Israel to live, and
he starts his own company there, becomes very successful. He's combined a number of disciplines. Physical chemistry, biology, genetics.
He probably keeps the intelligence connection alive but doesn't really
get involved in a heavy way. An occasional consultation, a contribution
on the scientific end. Maybe in his travels he acts as a courier, facilitates
an exchange, helps attract talent to Israel from Russia, from the United
States. He's tops in his field, and they use him to debrief defectors.
Okay?"

Blake nods; he likes it: the intelligence connection through the uncle, the connection with the CIA, possibly, probably; a hiatus when Dryden is forced out, coinciding with Starfield's marriage to the Dutch national, then the death of his daughter providing the impetus for a reactivation of Starfield's agency; a secondary recruitment, as it were.

"Navy thinks Starfield was Ellis's handler. In Europe. On the scientific end. Tippet's working on that. They think he was about to come in and take Ellis out. They think, too, he was involved in another operation, and they're trying to access some files. And Ellis; remember, he had that magazine when Campbell arrested him?"

Blake remembers. The recognition signal. Navy's checked it out, and Blake can find it, on page four. The cover of the magazine is a photograph of a spiral nebula.

"And this, Matt." The lawyer is very excited. "Look."

He flips the pages of Blake's file.

"Tippet's done another link analysis. Navy thinks the uncle was handled by Harrow. There are just too many coincidences, Matt. Fielding and two other refugees were a network. Do you know what they were called?"

Blake can look in the file and find it himself, but he lets the lawyer tell him.

"Three Blind Mice."

Harrow.

"And do you know what Starfield's call signal was when he was signed up?"

Blake waits for Halpern to speak.

"Little Boy Blue."

●

Halpern continues. "They—Starfield and the Dutch woman—have a kid, a girl, and life is fine for them, very safe. That's what his wife wants, safety. Then, Matt, it happens."

The prosecutor pauses, one of his dramatic stops.

"We should have known, Matt. It's in the files. It was in the newspapers."

Blake makes an effort to recall the event but, most unusual, comes up blank.

"She was with her class on an archaeological dig."

Again, Halpern stops. It's not for effect—his voice catches.

"And some crazy Arab terrorist threw a bomb at their bus when it went through the Old City in Jerusalem. She and about twenty others. Mostly kids. It was in the newspapers.''

Now Blake remembers the headlines, the thirty-second bites on the late-night news.

''They went wild.''

Blake remembers this too.

''The Israelis, Matt, went fucking crazy and tore up southern Lebanon.''

●

''Think of it, Matt.''

Blake does.

''I had a session with the psychologists when I was down there.''

His tone is apologetic, thought not by much. Professional courtesy dictates he should inform his case agent of any contacts with other Bureau personnel. This spares everyone, especially Blake, duplication of effort and much embarrassment.

Halpern pulls a chair to the side of Blake's desk and sits.

''He's obsessed, Matt. His world isn't safe anymore.''

Indeed; for such a man there is no longer even the comforting notion of mere, random violence, chance encounters with evil people. On the contrary, the threat is real, the evil directed and inevitable. It certainly would motivate one, would it not?

''Everyone he's known is either dead or has come close to death. And his wife—Matt: it's in the bio. It's part of the psy-pro they worked up.''

Halpern reaches a long arm to the folder and opens it, finds the place he wants, puts his forefinger on an asterisk in the margin.

''She's gone catatonic.''

His hand remains on the page.

''It's a different kind of posttraumatic stress reaction. Extreme withdrawal. Catatonia.''

Blake doesn't bother to read it.

''And Matt.'' The lawyer taps the page, at another asterisk. ''Starfield, Matt.''

The lawyer leans back, crosses his arms over his chest. Blake reads. When he looks up Halpern has a bright gleam in his eye, like he had that night at the airport when he showed Blake a similar file and brought Starfield into their lives, a sudden creation. No one believed, not even Blake, and now here it is in black and white. The Racker pulled strings, bribed or blackmailed the right people, and got the files from a

CIA vault in Langley. Halpern has worked it around in his mind, understands the symbolic significance, wants Blake to understand it too.

Halpern leans forward. "Matt, he's pathological. They don't say it in so many words, but the man is borderline psychotic."

Halpern's voice holds a plaintive passion Blake had never expected to hear.

"Matt, damn it. The psych people said we have to be careful."

Yes, thinks Blake, as the image of a thin, bearded face appears before him, very careful.

"They think," says the lawyer, referring to the psych people again, who know these things, and with whom he has spent a good half day dissecting Starfield, "we have a mad scientist on our hands."

Blake, silent, has his own thoughts. You're wrong, he thinks, but doesn't say it; Halpern won't understand. He stood next to Starfield in City Camera, looked into his eyes for an eternal moment. No, Halpern and the psych people are wrong. The man isn't psychotic, or crazy. At the most, as Blake knows these things, Starfield is only half mad.

But that, surely, is mad enough.

●

Just before he leaves for the day, Blake has an apparently chance meeting with Murphy. He drifts by Blake's desk just before five, stops to talk. On second thought, the meeting is not entirely unplanned. Murphy asks if he would be willing to relocate.

Blake stares, hoping thereby to convey his utter disbelief.

No, George, we are not willing to relocate.

"Matt, I was just in with Donnelly. We were talking moves."

Rumors are rife; the New York office is being blitzed with changes and reassignments. It's nothing new; ever since Hoover went to the great file in the sky, the restructuring had been ongoing and endless.

"I've put my time in, George. Up to here. And I've been moved around like a checker."

"All of us, Matt."

"And I've been jumped, too many times."

"Matt. We have a lot of good people here."

"Goddamn it, George. If Donnelly can't or won't get me a promotion, tell me. Don't string me along."

"No one's stringing anyone along. You know how these things go, Matt."

Blake goddamn right knows.

"George, that assessment was a one-shot deal. I've got a record that puts me up there with the best of them. A couple of mistakes, I know, but still, up there. Now, I've made plans and I've got commitments, George, and I don't want to be jerked around." He was as close to exploding right there in public as he can ever be. "I'm no Frank Campbell, George."

Murphy grimaces. The Irishman's inebriated ghost stalks the washrooms, pointing an accusing finger.

"What's happening with Starfield?"

"It's coming along."

"Donnelly wants a four-oh-six on it before you come to triage."

Four-oh-six, a preliminary presentation.

"Fine, George. You'll get it."

Unspoken fuck-yous are exchanged and then Murphy returns to Donnelly. A lot of ass there to cover.

●

"What's this?"

At the dining-room table, Blake is looking at numbers. His wife is just coming down.

"We're going to go with the premium," she says.

Blake is in his suit, his briefcase in hand, and bends over the figures. These are the bar costs for the reception. The difference between name brands, which come with the package, and premium, is four dollars a person.

That would be about eight hundred dollars more.

"Is it necessary?"

His wife stops.

"I mean, is it really goddamn necessary?"

He turns to face her.

"I've gone along with a lot of this. The flowers, the—goddamn, whatever it's called, the professional handwriting—the scriptology. We've refinanced. Maureen's tuition is up. We're going to need another car. I'm doing my best to get a goddamn promotion, and who the hell knows what's going to happen, and I come home and see that we're going to spend a thousand dollars so that someone can drink goddamn Black Label instead of Red!"

Maureen comes in through the patio doors and stops in the hall.

"Look," says Blake. "We really have to get control of this."

●

Later, he apologizes. It's just that he's concerned about the money. He tells his wife, at last, about his assessment, and what that has done for his chances of promotion.

Having never really spoken with her about the actual events, he now gives her some of the details of the exercises, how he did, what his strong points were. He tells her, briefly, about the mock arrest in the motel.

"I got the results last month. I didn't tell you about it." He apologizes for that.

But his wife had suspected; prepping his clothes for dry cleaning, she had come across Ms. Collins's business card.

"Ah." The corporate psychologist. He tells his wife about that.

"So you came out in the middle," she says.

Not quite; it's not like his high IQ and general knowledge scores cancel out his poorer showings. These things are weighted.

"All things being equal, a good assessment would have put me over the top." He shakes his head. Now he's just running with the rest of the pack.

"These things come in cycles," he explains. Within the next month an entire slew of promotions and new assignments are going to take place in the New York office. He's got to be among them. A promotion will mean, on top of the usual salary-grade jumps, another eight thousand a year. And that will be factored in to his pension calculations. It has to happen now, or it never will.

He doesn't tell her that he might even be transferred out of New York; he will spare her that aggravation until after the wedding.

"Is there some way, Matt, the assessment can be ignored?"

"No. The high scorers are putting on the pressure."

His wife is thoughtful.

"What about that case with Navy?"

"Yes, that could make a difference."

"When will you know?"

"I don't know." He speaks after a pause, amending, "Soon."

Later, passing through the dining room, he pauses to look again at the figures. His wife has left her loose-leaf open for him. They are back to the name brands. She has made a point of crossing out the premium surcharge.

As he heads down to the dark cool of his basement, Blake notices a green duffle bag near the door. Maureen's. He had forgotten; she's going out to a beach house. The zipper is open and he glances in, sees, on top of the variously colored items of clothing, school materials—

papers, a couple of books. Good. He goes downstairs, thinking of his wife's question. What about the case with Navy? What about it, indeed? He finds his way in the half-dark to his desk, presses the button on the fluorescent.

His papers are spread on the desk; circles and colored arrows cover the pages.

The photograph of Dr. Starfield.

A mad scientist.

And my one shot at redemption.

# CHAPTER 30

$\text{A}$ lapsed atheist, Blake repeats
to himself as he and Spanakos sit across the table from the old man,
and, therefore, like all who have given up their doubts, impregnable.
While Harrow fusses with his papers, Blake allows himself to read into
the man that which his research has revealed: his celibacy, his lack of
children or wife; his lack, now that one sees him in the flesh, of love.
His is a desiccated soul, dry like the bones of the dead, much like these
old records piled around him, the archives of a distant, bloody past.

He knows, Campbell had said, where the bodies are buried.

And without a doubt, a pro. One senses Harrow's delicacy of touch,
his mind so carefully, so expertly, examining the materials that Blake
has put before him on his polished table, here in this little airless room
of the sort the CIA provides for its exiles.

One watches Harrow's eye judiciously moving from line to line,
absorbing, integrating and matching, correlating. He turns the page,
reaches out a palsied hand to pull the desk lamp closer a fraction. Blake
enters into the play, offering a very delicate crossing of his legs to add
a touch of silent movement. Spanakos remains immobile, watching the
progress of Harrow's eyes, which are holding now at the abstracts of
contact reports from the Istanbul field station, the old stomping ground
of Harrow's early years. Spanakos guesses at the place, marks his own
copy with a check in the margin. The silence continues. Harrow turns
each page with a trembling finger placed carefully, delicately on the top

edge. He doesn't want to leave any fingerprints, thinks Blake. The old man neither smiles nor frowns; his eyes move at a steady pace, sometimes backreading, pausing, but never for long, always moving on, taking everything in on the first go-round.

It's taken Blake a good three weeks to arrange this tête-à-tête. The first phase was spent establishing contact through intermediaries. Campbell supplied the leads. It was kind of silly. Blake made calls from designated street phones, ringing on and off at prearranged intervals. He received, at home, half a postcard and was required to return mail it to a postal box number. The typed note he received a week later was most likely composed on a typewriter rentable by the hour at the New York Public Library. The man's fucking crazy, said Spanakos. Agreed; but professionally crazy. These things can't be rushed, Blake explained to Halpern, deflecting the chronically hyper lawyer.

Harrow was conducting his own back-channel inquiries; he doesn't want to fall into any traps. God knew how many he had rigged himself. Blake was not optimistic; what did he have to offer? But whatever it was, Harrow wanted it, and Blake, in a little box ad in the *New York Times* real estate section, was so informed.

The old man, however, insisted, first, on a showcase presentation. This was a standard procedure wherein Blake was to appear at a particular time and place—in this instance, to the right of the left lion on the steps of the New York Public Library at precisely 3:15 on Tuesday afternoon. As instructed, he wore a gray suit and blue tie, and held a red book. Harrow wanted to know who he was, wanted to be certain that when he showed up at the meeting he was the same man; wanted to be certain, too, that Blake wasn't any one of dozens of men he, Harrow, did not care to meet.

Standing at the lion, Blake had felt intensely vulnerable. The day was cloudy, very muggy. The air was full of static. He suspected everyone, from the beggar reeking of urine to the tall, attractive woman with a butterfly pin on her lapel who loitered on the other side of the lion but who finally went off with a blue-suited man who carried an attaché case. Blake waited half an hour, then, as per instructions, left. He was apparently judged acceptable, for the next day he was informed by a quick phone call to his desk that Harrow would meet him the following week.

There were to be certain rules of engagement. First, one meeting and one meeting only. Second, no tape recorders and no note taking. Spanakos thought that ridiculous but Blake acquiesced; they had no choice. The old man, his capacities failing, was limiting his liability. Third, the meeting was to be between Blake and Harrow, man to man. Here Blake objected. He wanted a control, someone with whom he could do a postmortem, double check his impressions. Harrow, after two days of silence, agreed to clear Spanakos.

Through all this, Blake was uncertain as to just who he was talking to. They were using a voice disguiser; perhaps it was even a woman. Among the many caveats and prohibitions, Harrow reserved the right to terminate the meeting at any time. All these rules were subject to change, of course, without notice. Halpern was piqued at being passed over. But Blake wanted someone who knew how to follow rules, and whose professional advancement was in his hands. In addition, Spanakos was interested in moving into counterintelligence, and needed the experience.

But now Harrow is finished, and his speech is as deliberate as his reading.

"Very interesting, I must say, Mr. Blake."

A short, trembling eternity passes as he pushes his chair away from his desk and stands, using its arms for support.

He's an old, sick man, Blake tells himself with a twinge of disappointment and self-reproach. He's lonely, and palsied, and we are here to harangue him.

"Refreshments, gentlemen?"

●

An array of miniature pastries is produced. The tea service is silver, elegant in the simple Revere style. There is a porcelain creamer in the shape of a cow, and it is held by its curved tail and tipped so that milk comes out of its mouth. Spanakos wants to catch Blake's eye for a reaction, but Blake avoids contact. There will be no looks, jokes, or sarcasms at this old man's expense.

As in a tea ceremony, everything has import, the selection and arrangement, the offering and acceptance. Spanakos takes a petit four, Blake a tiny tart with a shiny strawberry on top.

Harrow pours from the Revere; the tea is very dark, fragrant, English. "Thank you."

While Blake and Spanakos nibble, Harrow prepares his tea in the more elaborate British manner: one sugar, cream, a stir of the spoon, a touch more tea.

Goddamn cat and mouse, Blake is thinking, thinking, too, with a touch of despair, that Harrow has to be broken, and that old and lonely as he is, he won't break. We know a great deal about him, and he knows that we know. And we in turn know that, too. In this fashion one may extend such mutual knowledge ad infinitum until, standing between double mirrors, we reach the point of infinite removal, becoming specks in a perspective so great that relevancy vanishes. The Ultimate Know—he stops himself in midthought, pays attention to his tea. He notes a smaller chamber off to the rear of the room, whose entrance, ajar, is a door made of bookshelves. He can see a kind of kitchen arrangement: a double-burner hotplate, a half-size refrigerator, the corner of a sink. Wonder where he has put the microphone. Blake sips again and Harrow, noting his reaction, suggests sugar, which Blake adds. Yes, that does the trick.

●

The have agreed on an agenda and Harrow, his remarks prepared, begins.

The Mossad.

He gives a quick overview of its corporate culture and product management. Its operation standards are very high, very precise. It covers well; personnel exceptionally well vetted. Very motivated, as one might expect. Fairly commonplace tradecraft, with its own nuances. For instance, they have a tendency to go for biblical coding. Understandable. If they can be faulted it is for their aggression; they put a premium on risk-taking.

As he speaks, Harrow's voice takes on more color, his trembling begins to slow.

"They collect primarily in the Middle East and the United States. What they don't use, they sell. We used to piggyback a great deal, but they always had reservations about what they perceived to be our low standards of security. They have an inbred distrust of all foreign intelligence services and I believe that these days, from what I have heard, we have experienced difficulties in liaison."

Harrow pauses to top off his cup, offering more tea in a trembling hand to first Blake, who accepts, then to Spanakos, who declines.

As one imagines, Harrow continues, Mossad requirements are military-driven. The Israeli concern for their perimeter, what Harrow calls their window of vulnerability, is absolute and unconditional. "Theirs is a small world, physically, and this translates into a mind-set that mirrors that. Geography, I have always said, Mr. Blake, is destiny."

Blake has heard this before, and recalls where: from Dryden himself at an in-service lecture.

"They perceive themselves as having no grace period in terms of military options. If they are slapped, they return with a bomb."

"The cornered-animal syndrome," offers Spanakos.

"Quite. The air life of an unidentified flying object approaching their border is measured in seconds. When one knows that the overfly time from their farthest border to the Tel Aviv–Jerusalem corridor is approximately four minutes, and that a single nuclear device detonated within that corridor will annihilate seventy-five percent of their population, one begins to appreciate this clarity of strategic vision."

"Very much so," Blake throws out.

"And we see that clarity informing both their military and intelligence operations." Harrow's voice has taken on some fire. "When they decide to move," and here he makes a fist of his right hand, at the side of his tea, "they move with determination and skill." The fist tightens, then is released and embraces the other hand, the fingers meshing in quivering repose. The man is old, and suffering from Parkinson's. His voice returns to its lifeless mode, the voice of the archivist burrowing among his beloved dead.

"Yes. Quite. Their vision was very clarified."

And from the point of view of the Ellis operation?

Harrow is not intimate with Ellis, but from what he has heard he has to say the operation was of a very basic sort.

"Collection, removal, processing. The inside man—this Ellis gentleman—is tasked by his handler. Couriers to move the product, one or two drops. What we used to refer to as a 'call and haul.' Operations in friendly countries will have the case officer in situ. The risk is regarded as minimal." Harrow shifts, reaches out for one of the petits fours and puts it on his saucer under the cup. "They have an unfortunate penchant for taking too much. From what I hear," and he nods to Blake, his Parkinson's, "they simply told Ellis to go in and raid the store."

Spanakos speaks. "Would you say then that Ellis was not up to their professional standards?"

Harrow does not respond immediately. No matter how innocent, the man cannot bring himself to answer a direct question. That's the first rule of resistance: don't answer the first question. The psych people warn you; after that it's an avalanche.

Prepping for this meeting, Blake and Spanakos have agreed to work the old man between them. They know when they will be silent, when they will speak. Now, they keep their eyes upon his wrinkled visage, and wait. It's a tactical truth, silence prompts. The seconds tick away as they play their tripartite game. Harrow bites into his pastry, brings his embroidered white napkin to his mouth. He knows the tricks, yet cannot resist. That is the wonder of it. Research has shown that the inevitable will always occur.

Thus, Harrow allows himself to be compelled. "Generally speaking, their modus is somewhat different from this Ellis business." He goes into detail, speaking quietly, pedantically, reciting from a prepared script. It's like a lecture. They have their operation team, their support people, the technicians, couriers. What the Bureau refers to, he believes, as the plumbing. As one expects, their line people are very mobile. In operations on American turf they don't require especially deep cover. They have access to and use American passports. Politically, the environment is relatively safe, so they have few reservations about who they pitch, given the usual prohibitions, of course.

"They cover their middle very well." Harrow goes into their organization, giving Mossad equivalents to CIA levels, field and staff, ranks and titles—about four strata. "They tend to allow their field people considerably more autonomy than, for instance, the Bureau." He gives a tremulous nod to Blake, then Spanakos. "They have more of a battle mentality that you do, I believe." He has heard, however, that their training is not as good or intensive as it once was.

"And the American connection?" Blake has been given to understand that the liaison was very intimate.

There is, Blake imagines, a fleeting but unmistakable irony on Harrow's lips.

"Oh, I daresay the bonds were very strong. All that came to an end, of course. It's quite different now, I understand."

The irony persists; Blake matches it with just the tiniest of smiles: yes, quite different, the agent is sure.

"May we ask about recruitment?" prompts Spanakos.

"Certainly." Harrow ticks off a quick list. Politicians, not only the Jewish ones, but those who had a constituency of such. Legislative aides, of course; all the lawyers and research assistants and media people that government cannot do without. The Mossad tended to stick to the middle level. They felt the higher you went, the less return you got, in terms of usable material. It was their notion that anything higher than, say, under secretary of state, was too high. Even that was pushing it. They understood the difference between the appearance, the trappings, if you will, and the reality of hard political power, and knew that in any bureaucracy the power was, for practical purposes, concentrated in middle management. They had a theory for it, which they called Middle Might.

Of course, they worked the higher ground too, as well as the low; secretaries, clerks. Anything, actually. For instance, there was an extensive education exchange program between services, in seminars, show-and-tell conferences; graduate students, scientists, business people, that sort of thing.

"And the pitch?"

Oh, the standard lure. Help us. You're part of a greater whole, do your part. One easily imagines; indeed, Blake does. The world's biggest yet most exclusive club. You have been chosen; help us.

Taking another pastry, Blake works in an observation: he imagines Ellis's wife was a concern.

"Not necessarily, Mr. Blake."

Though they had a hard and fast rule, under pressure they relaxed its application. Middle-ground theory again: they needed outsiders to hold the terrain. Harrow can speak authoritatively that this was one of the ongoing, acrimonious disputes among the Mossad theorists and psychologists. Considering that loyalty and betrayal are but the two sides of a single coin—forgive him, please, Harrow begs of them with an old man's ironic smile and an offer of the pastry tray, this rather hackneyed allusion!—one sees how confusing, delicate, and ambiguous many such distinctions become. As are love and hate, good and evil—again, forgive him this recital of the great dichotomies! The personality inventories, the review of the record, the clever insightful tests and interviews by the clever and insightful psychologists, the weighted score sheets, only take you so far. The human factor, unknown, prevails.

And now Harrow asks in quivering voice, asks rhetorically, was there a bedrock aspect to this, a terra firma of the human soul that one might say, aha, upon this we may safely stand?

"They had a word for it, Mr. Blake." Harrow speaks it, in Hebrew, hard to translate, but it means, roughly, as he understands, tribal affiliation. When the crunch came, and they always assumed it would, you trusted your own. One could find a few exceptions, but they were so rare as to be aberrations, the exception that proves the rule. The fight was over whether and when to go outside the inner circle. On this question the Israelis were forever at their own throats.

Spanakos asks another question about Ellis, a technical one about call signals, and Harrow responds, very carefully. They are at the outer limits of the briefing. Harrow is giving them some claptrap about telemetry, about how they, meaning the Americans, used to clear the airways for the Mossad: you gave them a frequency and a time and then you suppressed other traffic so they could punch through all the electronic garbage up there. Blake reaches for a miniature éclair and then, with some of the crumb still in his mouth, asks as if he really doesn't care, as if the answer could be of no possible consequence, "Could you tell us who handled Starfield?"

It's a bomb, totally off the agenda, and one Blake and Spanakos had decided would be dropped at Blake's discretion.

To the untrained eye Harrow seems not to have heard, but Blake notes the man's micro responses: a solidification of the facial muscles about the mouth; a movement of his right hand, trembling, to his groin, seeking anchor, his left remaining shaking on his thigh.

Blake is watching Harrow like a hawk; thrown off by the old man's silence, he tries to compute the variables. They had talked about possible answers, and this—how dumb could they be?—was not one of them.

As the pause grows, the three men go through their own reactive body English. Blake has a way of pressing back with his lower torso at the same time his shoulders come forward; he gains an extra inch of height this way. Spanakos, tall enough, slouches, hunkering down. As for Harrow, the man adds an increment of solidity to the lower portion of his face, his mouth setting itself over the shrunken bones.

The silence lengthens. Blake will not break it. Spanakos follows Blake's lead. Harrow waits. The question, so good when it came out, is useless now, hanging as it does between them, a dead conjecture.

I have nothing, thinks Blake, that Harrow wants. Money, position, immunity—nothing.

Unless, thinks Blake, unless it's love.

"Tea, Mr. Blake?"

"Yes, thank you."

But the tea has lost its heat.

"Someone had to handle him." Blake is perplexed, wants simply to clear up a confusing minor point.

Spanakos stirs, contributing a bit of tension off to the side; everything helps.

"What we've been hearing," says Spanakos, now putting forth what he and Blake have worked out as their line, "is that this man Starfield was used for low-level work. Courier service, a cutout here and there. Casual, free-lance work." This of course is not true. They have assumed that Starfield, if he was anything, was fairly high in the ranks. But they have decided to construct one version of the truth, and see how Harrow deals with it.

Blake takes over. "You see, Max, everyone"—and Blake will let

Harrow wonder just who he means by everyone—"insists how absolutely and extremely casual he was."

"He barely did anything." Spanakos puts a naive surprise into his voice. "He practically doesn't exist!"

"Yes, Max. The casual spy."

Harrow's face shows only the increasing firmness about the mouth. Look how he has his pastries and tea, something to eat and drink during an interrogation, very clever protection: keep your mouth moving without saying anything.

"Max. The man was with your group in some capacity from the mid- or late sixties until the late seventies."

Spanakos chimes in. "And do you know how we know, Mr. Harrow?"

Blake will answer the question himself, but first he pauses. This is their big gun and he wants to fire it himself. For a few moments he watches Harrow work his tongue against the inside of his cheek. When Blake speaks his words are sharper, faster.

"Because we've done our homework, Max. We know where he got his doctorate and with whom. And we know who among his thesis advisers were spotting for you. Barnett, for instance, in microbiology at UCLA. And we know that you had some S and T people out there. We can put together quite an impressive *little* biography."

This, indeed, is true. Tippet had done a yeoman's job during the last two days, and Blake and Spanakos have studied the printouts and made the matches.

"We have the records, Max. His side trips through the academic centers, and just who he might have been with in Europe at the time—all casual, of course, and purely coincidental—but we can match names, I mean work names of course, Max, and places and dates and specialities. Casual, of course, coincidental."

Spanakos's turn. "We think we can come up with four or five names, or maybe one or two, one of whom, Mr. Harrow, I'd bet my balls on was his handler."

Another pause. Harrow's lower face is taking on the appearance of a bulldog.

"But we don't want to turn everything upside down, do we, Ed?"

"No, Matt, we don't. And we won't, unless."

"That's right, unless. Because we don't know where it will stop. We want it to stay here, Max." Blake's hands are open and his fingertips press the table. "Among us, Max. Friends."

Blake is immediately embarrassed; a goddamn mistake, he shouldn't have put that in. It cost.

Harrow has not moved, and Blake has to make an effort to control his rising frustration. He wants to throw an accusation that cannot be denied at this decrepit old gentleman, an ancient, incontrovertible truth dragged from the jungles of his bloody past, something that will spring a trapdoor beneath this complacent son of a Dryden bitch and drop him into a freefall of uncertainty which only he, Blake, can arrest.

But he doesn't have anything. One shot, and it's a blank. And it doesn't matter. Like Ellis, Harrow is not going to break. He, too, possesses an intact superego, whatever the hell that really means. He's ready for anything I can throw at him. He's been hit before and he's ready to be hit again. That's why he's survived, living like a monk on bread and water—only it's expensive continental pastries and tea—in a little cell with dead books and a meager faith, praying to his god, living with the memories of a man he wanted to love but was not allowed to. Dryden knew what he was doing. Harrow is his left-behind agent. They wanted someone in place when the CIA officers ran, their hearts liquid with fear, before the looting politicians. And Harrow was chosen to be the keeper of the flame. So maybe Harrow is the mole, the penetration agent for Dryden, and therefore the Russian sleeper—Blake forces himself to stop. This will get him nowhere.

"More tea, Mr. Blake?"

There is that ironical glint in the old man's eye.

He wants me to come at him again, thinks Blake; the old bastard hasn't had this much fun in years.

Harrow's mouth has relaxed; he is suddenly nothing but an old, tired man with a plate of pathetic cookies, hands atremble, sitting before an old cow creamer with a chip on the spout.

He and Spanakos have other signals, and Blake checks his inner breast pocket for something he doesn't find, looks at his watch, turns to his agent, who has no further questions.

After a few minutes of very idle chitchat they are out in the sunlight, looking for a cab to take them downtown.

●

As they ride, they do a postmortem.

"What do we have, Ed," Blake asks, "what do we have?"

"I'll tell you," says Spanakos. "It was one long, fuck-you."

"Yeah." He stares out the window as the cabbie jerks and cuts through the traffic. As with Ellis, he had gone in expecting that his considerable psychosocial skills would get him through, only to discover they were inadequate. Out loud, Blake castigates himself for not handling Harrow more deftly.

"We lost him, Ed."

"Matt, we never had him."

Blake appreciates Spanakos's candor. We thought we were going in for a quick win, but the old man invented the game, and played us against ourselves.

"He just didn't fucking care," adds Spanakos.

Blake agrees with a grunt.

They are riding down Lexington Avenue, crossing Forty-second, and Blake stares out the dirty window at the city. He is not pleased; though he had scored well in the assessment in negotiation and interrogation, he suspects he needs to develop his interpersonal skills, and should check out the in-service offerings. He had set himself up for defeat. Damn Newcombe; he took everyone's bargaining chips, left me with nothing to give. Unless it's love. Love is all one has.

They bounce along in the backseat of the taxi.

He smiles to himself, extending his thoughts. Love, the coin of the realm; so many currencies, and yet all the same.

And the rate of exchange always favors the house. And in this case, I, Blake, special agent, am the house. And the beauty of it, the real and amazing beauty, Blake thinks as the cab hits every pothole on Second Avenue and he searches vainly for the seat belts, is that the premium always increases. The economists have a term for it—inelastic demand. The quantity stays the same but the price goes up. It's a perpetual mortgage. You never make the last payment. The manual speaks of that. Never complete the deal; when questioning a suspect, always ask for more, and you'll get it. So maybe that's what the Bureau is selling; we're agents of the heart, brokering deals, offering love. Not really a specific love but love in general, love that no matter how lavish and unselfishly bestowed is never, by definition, enough. Neither you nor your god nor your mommy or daddy nor your dog nor your children can supply enough of it.

# CHAPTER 31

I t's dirt.''

Blake is writing out a summary of his meeting with Harrow, which is strictly off the books, and looks up from his desk. Spanakos has a file in hand.

''I sent a copy to Halpern,'' he tells Blake.

It's the lab report on that tin of earthlike substance from the Starfield break-in. Chemical ran an assay, a qualitative analysis. Organic and inorganic compounds, elements, ash content, micro-organic content. A photograph of a mound of grains resting on a white circle of filter paper. A full page of chemical names. A lot for such a little heap.

''It's a soil sample,'' says Blake.

Blake is going down the list, though it can't possibly have any meaning to him. He's looking, he says as he reads, to see whether they were able to determine from where the earth came. Nothing in particular, the assay report says, renders it site-specific. Blake studies the photograph of the container in which the soil rests.

''Jerusalem,'' Spanakos says.

Blake doesn't get the reference.

Spanakos says, ''I spoke with Halpern. The earth comes from the Mount of Olives.''

Damn it, is the lawyer a wizard? How does he know that?

''It's a tradition.'' Spanakos repeats what Halpern told him. ''The Messiah will ride into Jerusalem on a white donkey and will proclaim himself as the messenger of God. He's supposed to come in through one of the gates. I think it's the Dung Gate, Matt. Yeah, the Dung Gate." Spanakos feels a little self-conscious saying all of this; it's not his myth. "And once he proclaims himself the dead are supposed to rise. Now, the land facing this gate is the Mount of Olives and the people buried there are going to be the first to see the Messiah so they'll be the first to rise again. You know, the story of the dry bones." This Blake knows. The wind shall blow and the bones shall rattle.

"Jeremiah," Blake says. "The prophet."

Spanakos goes on. "So anyway, on the hillside, that's where religious people wanted to be buried. When Elijah blows the ram's horn and the dead rise." Halpern told him all this.

"They put the earth in the eyes of the dead. Sprinkle it."

Blake and Spanakos nod at each other.

"So he carries the earth with him. Religious people do that. If the Messiah comes when he's not there he won't be left out. It's just a custom, Halpern said."

Blake looks at the photograph of the heap of grainy soil, the scrapings of the holy hill Starfield carts around with him. A custom; just a myth. No one believes it, of course, especially not young, aggressive prosecutors.

Spanakos is saying how it makes sense, in a way. It does to Blake, too.

They mean the psy-pro is growing; they are beginning to know the man.

The end of days. His dead shall rise, thinks Blake, and Starfield wants to be there, just in case his child shows.

# CHAPTER 32

A t ten o'clock that night at home
in the basement, Blake takes a break and considers his work. In spite
of the circumscription of his days, the endless paperwork and perpetual
pettiness, the ignominy of serving too many unappreciative masters—
not to mention his daughter's nocturnal ramblings, the caterer's unc-
tious demands, and Murphy's suddenly harsh and calculating eye—he
allows himself a few moments of cautious satisfaction.

The puzzle is almost complete.

Of course, the pieces that are missing will be the ones Donnelly will
want to see.

Blake's system is a loose one. He uses colored markers and a black
felt pen. He has little round stick-ons color-coded for the principle
players. Black for Harrow, the primaries for the others. Starfield is blue,
Hirsh, red. He has small rectangular strips indicating place—New York,
Washington, Israel, Germany. He will add Italy and Belgium as the
night wears on. He will use a large sheet of oaktag to draw columns and
boxes with lines crisscrossing and snaking.

When he began, last week, his voluminous data was without form.
He had to pull files on the run, grabbing whatever he could, and what
he wound up with was an unholy mélange of originals and abstracts,
raw field reports, intercepts, contact reports. He's got personnel evalua-
tions, which Tippet was kind enough to pluck from the computer files;
there are government employment forms and clearance searches, many

of them diligently mined by Spanakos from the vast storage area where the interagency reference material lies in undisturbed dust. He has printouts of telemetric intercepts, which again Tippet has been good enough to provide. And also from Tippet, whose bright, mourning eyes remain focused on a distant goal, Blake has obtained a treasure trove of materials from the administrative side: budgetary items, receipts and bills for travel expenses that detail the dates and places where various men and women have gone on their official and sometimes unofficial trips, printouts of telephone traffic, copies of telegrams and telexes. He's got papers everywhere, each with a color code, an index card clipped to each, scribbles on each card, numbers in circles indicating appropriate references, and two yellow legal-size pages telling him what all these colors and numbers mean.

How impossible this would be without a supply of his beloved paper clips.

And a lot of what he needs he doesn't have. It's not on paper. It's in the hearts and minds of old and dying men and women scattered over the face of the earth, and in other less accessible realms. Dryden and his people. Maxwell Harrow, for instance. He thinks of Harrow in his office, offering them cookies and English tea. The quivering repose of the fingers on the tabletop, the old man's rigid mouth, his tongue working the inside cheek. An arid man, yet bloated. Blake wants to pin Harrow to the wall and throw darts at him and watch the man deflate, all those secrets rushing out in a foul flatulence.

Had his wife come down during the night, or had she a secret peephole in the floorboards of the kitchen through which she might spy, she would have seen her slender, middle-aged husband with his iron-gray hair and black bifocals pacing. He's of the old school that insists upon having everything in view. He works on large, flat surfaces. He can't work from a computer screen. He has to be able to see and touch and lift and carry pieces of paper from one place to another. Thus, he walks from one end of his basement office to the other; removes papers from one stack, puts them on another. He holds a piece of paper with an interesting tidbit and wonders where to put it. He will start another pile, and shift and rearrange all the others. On occasion he throws a piece of paper away, but that is rare. He should throw more away. That's the secret: discard, discard, discard. He's learned the hard way: the more you keep the less you have. Sometimes, and he berates himself when he does this, he picks up a scrap, uncrumbles it, and places it on a stack again.

And always, always, he keeps moving, stopping only briefly to ponder a blue circle, wonder over a piece of paper. He will traverse the western hemisphere without ever leaving his room. He will talk to himself as he does this. I am Deere, now, and I have fled Paris after killing a waiter and a sous-chef, and I want to hide for a while. I will go to the United States and become a carpenter. And now I am Dr. Phillip Starfield, in my desert home with my poor, soulless Dutch wife. I have been in Frankfurt, perhaps at the same time Deere has. And I have met, perhaps, Ellis in Brussels. And now I am in the United States, waiting, planning.

Where are the missing pieces?

The so-called plumbing. Communications. How they talk to each other.

And another piece: Starfield himself.

Donnelly is going to want to see capability, and Blake has nothing to show.

He has been working on this for days and nights. There is only so much the human brain and body can take, and he's already exceeded the limits. Much of the material is prolix and unendurable. Every half hour or so, notwithstanding his disdain for gadgetry, he berates himself for his lack of computer literacy. The success of his search will turn on the least little thing, a word or phrase, a date or a place; and computers are robots that make almost no mistakes, can be programmed to select or ignore, whereas the human eye—his eye—oftentimes looks without seeing.

What he is conducting tonight is, in effect, an experiment in physics. All these papers, these files and intercepts, are his building blocks, his primal bits of space and time that he uses to create a world. He will follow Starfield through time and space, careful all the while not to fall prey to what Halpern has called the "evidentiary fallacy." Meaning, in layman's terms, that merely because you cannot find the needle, you must not assume it is not in the haystack. One must make assumptions; indeed, the world turns on them; one knows, assumes, that entities exist beyond one's sensory apprehensions. Yet operational methodology requires at least one precise and irreducible bit of physical evidence, some one thing of mass and volume. This creates space. Two such bits, so that one may go from one to another, bring forth time.

But what he has achieved here is timeless. For the briefest of intervals—and he cannot here refer to time, having just annihilated it—he has slipped the bounds of physical constraint, leaped outside the construct known as the present. And he is gratified at the sheer pleasure of the experience, the ease of the escape. Everything has stopped; he studies the photographs on his desk, these men into whose universe he has been unwittingly drawn.

See this picture. It is of the man with the smiling face and freckles, but whose smile is not a smile at all but the lingering, lopsided result of overenthusiastic British interrogators, and whose freckles were not the real sort that Maureen had, but were liver spots due to advancing age.

A man who killed a sous-chef, by mistake.

What did they say he used?

A target pistol, silenced, shooting .22 longs, hollow-nosed. The weapon of choice for Group Ariel.

Together with Starfield, he will bring Ellis out of bondage. They will move fast, with an appropriate level of violence. And if need be, over dead bodies.

●　　✦

Here is another face, that of the old man, Harrow, Dryden's right-hand man, second in command.

Blake has been thinking about both men, and now, at this late hour, tired, hungry, and irritated with the intractability of the material, knowing that his time is running out, he attempts to force the matter to a conclusion.

He has a thesis about Dryden, which is that it was neither the Russians nor the American Senate who brought him down—though they all might have had a hand in it. No, Dryden was destroyed by the Israelis.

His special account.

Blake, standing too long, sits in his uncomfortable desk chair.

In goddamn cold and cynical blood, they shot the man down.

And Ellis, he tells himself, whatever else Ellis was, was used to administer the coup de grace to the remnants of Dryden's counterintelligence network.

But they're not working on their own. Damn them: the Israelis had been given the go-ahead.

But by who? The administration? The Bureau? Factions of the CIA? Enemies within Dryden's own counterintelligence group? Perhaps Dryden himself, who in a last spasm of suicidal penitence was prepared to destroy everything, like a god visiting destruction upon his ungrateful creation?

And once Dryden was eliminated, the Account must be closed, lest it fall into other, less friendly hands.

Or transferred.

Thus, the Mossad, Dryden's brain child, is passed on to Harrow.

But then something goes wrong, dreadfully wrong.

Ellis.

Blake stands stock-still. He wants to force a rising revelation, like a hidden sun, through the dense, obscurant mass of detail.

They are going to bring Ellis out.

There is Starfield, his dark, bearded face undeniable, mounting an operation.

And Navy on to him, immediately.

The phone rings.

Tippet's big find, the impossible needle in the haystack.

The phone continues. He will ignore it.

And Navy finds more needles, like Hirsh and his two assistants, who are being planted in the most unlikely of places.

The phone will not quit—

How will Starfield do it?

Do what?

The goddamn phone!

What was he thinking?

The phone dies as soon as he picks it up.

He rubs his face and lets out a long breath. His concentration is shattered. He is suddenly very tired, and though he wants to try again, he hasn't the energy to start from the beginning. He almost had it, a radiance that a few moments ago was about to fill his mind, but whose light is now in fragments, scattered in the angry glare of his desk fluorescent.

And now, from upstairs, he hears the kitchen phone ringing. Hears his wife's thumping barefoot run across the ceiling. The phone caught in mid-ring. Her muffled voice through the floorboards. Her feet coming to the basement door. The turn of the handle.

"Matt?"

"Yes."

"It's Richard Halpern. He just tried your work number."

"Yes."

His wife's silence, then her question. "Should I tell him to call you downstairs?"

Blake sighs. No, he will come up.

When he takes the receiver from his wife's impatient hand, he hears the attorney's voice shaking.

His wife listens.

"Okay," he says.

Then, "Anything broken or bleeding?"

And, then, "Have you called anyone yet?"

And then, "Don't."

Finally, "Give me an hour. Don't touch anything."

As he unrolls and buttons his cuffs, Blake turns to his wife. Halpern was calling from a pay phone on the corner of Remsen Street, in Brooklyn Heights. That's where he lives. He had arrived home, gone into his apartment, and interrupted a burglary.

Her face shows concern. "Was he hurt?"

"They roughed him up a bit."

●

It's 1:00 A.M. when Blake pulls up at the corner of Remsen and Hicks. Beneath the tall sycamores Halpern waits in the mottled lamplight. He's wearing a pair of running shorts and a polo shirt.

"Rick."

"I'm okay." He looks it, except for a touch of pale beneath his tan. "I called the cops."

Blake wishes he hadn't. "Have they come yet?"

"No, they said they'd be here in about an hour."

They turn as a car pulls up. Blake talks to the driver through the window. It's a Bureau forensics team he called before leaving Eastmere. A man and a woman, each with a sizable attaché case, more like a toolbox. Halpern leads them all into his building. In the company of the three agents, the lawyer shows some humor. He comments how he's sorry to have brought them out so late, but apparently burglars these days have no respect for working people. It gets a brief chuckle. He lives on the third floor. The door is unlocked, slightly ajar, and he's about to turn the knob when the woman grabs his wrist.

"Fingerprints," she says.

Halpern apologizes.

Blake enters first, reaching up high with his arm and pushing the door open swiftly and smoothly. He hasn't brought his weapon. The room is dark. He steps in. The light from the hall falls a short distance onto the orangish floor planking. There are a few books lying in the light.

"There's a lamp a couple of steps in, to the left. It's a pull chain."

Blake finds it.

They follow, stand in the middle of the mess.

"The fuckers," says Halpern.

●

After a quick tour, and while the forensics agents work the apartment, Blake sits with Halpern in the kitchen, the room most intact, and questions him. He had come home late, about 9:30—he's only about six or seven blocks from his office, very convenient—had changed and gone out for a late-night run. He usually runs over the bridge and back. Jogging back to Brooklyn, there's a big clock on the Witnesses building, so he knows he came off the bridge at 10:15, give or take a few minutes. On Montague he had bought a quart of orange juice and a pint of Häagen-Dazs. He got home about 10:45.

His building is a co-op. There are five apartments, one to a floor. There's a family on the ground floor, with two young children, and they keep a stroller and toys in the hallway. Just below him lives a couple, and they're away this week, on vacation; he's taking in their mail. Above him lives a girl who travels a lot doing political research on third world countries, and this month she's been in Honduras. She has friends who use her apartment when she's gone. And the owners of the top apartment are always coming and going. There's a lot of activity in the halls.

There is a loud, crackling sound in the stairwell. It is the police, big and blue, their radios putting forth loud, static-filled voices. They stand in the entryway, taking in Blake, the man and woman with their guns and open suitcases, the mess. Blake shows ID. Halpern explains that he is an assistant United States attorney. There is some tension as the parties confront each other, but in a few minutes, once the police adjust, and the forensic team returns to their dusting, they sit with Halpern in the kitchen, their black radios on the table, and ask him the same questions Blake did, and get much the same responses.

Actually, this isn't that bad, the cops tell Halpern and Blake. They have seen, believe them, much worse. Blake agrees, it's more mess than destruction. Judging from the pattern of debris, mostly in the living room, and in the little room off to the side, the lawyer's study, the perps, as the cops refer to the burglars, weren't here long enough to do a complete job. In a way, he was lucky to interrupt them.

And unlucky, too.

Or maybe, thinks Blake, luck had nothing to do with it.

Halpern describes how it happened.

He had come in, his juice and ice cream in one hand, his key in the other. He remembers, he tells them now, that he was the slightest bit puzzled to discover the door was double locked. Because usually, when he goes out for a run or for food, he just closes the door, let's the spring bolt catch on its own. But this time he had to turn the key twice. He gave it a second thought, but was tired, had things on his mind, and simply went in.

Of course, the burglars had double locked it from inside to give themselves a few extra seconds should he return.

Anyway, he stepped in and headed, as always, for the floor lamp that's about five or six paces in. He never leaves lights on.

The forensic people, now in the kitchen, listen along with Blake and the two cops.

His foot hit something on the floor. There was movement behind him. And then the door closed very, very quickly.

"I knew what was happening, I knew it."

But it happened so fast that he was reacting a beat late.

The lawyer describes being grabbed from behind. Hands came out of the dark. An arm around his neck. His wrist grabbed and twisted. A man in front of him too. Though he does not refer to his fear, one hears his absolute panic. The lawyer stands at the sink, speaking with great control. His long legs are hairy and muscular, as are his upper arms. His suits, dark and well-tailored, hide his power. It happened so fast. You can see he is still confused. A few moments of struggle. A couple of blows, not sure where he was struck, feeling only a general impact. He was in a state of shock. Then he was pushed hard enough that he lurched across the room, fell over a chair. Then the flash of hall light as the door opened and closed, and his entire being, abused and terrified, was left trembling in the dark.

There are more questions from the cops, who are very cautious. Did he see faces, hear voices? How tall—you see, Halpern is about six feet, and so to be grabbed from behind with an arm around his neck requires someone of comparable height—how tall did he estimate his attacker? And what about the man in front of him? Any distinguishing facial characteristics? Any weapons?

Halpern has very little to offer on any of this. It happened too quickly. His entryway gets no outside window light, and once the hall door is closed it's almost pitch black. He saw nothing. He apologizes for having so little. Their radios are crackling again. They flip their books closed, stand, mention in passing that this is their fourth burglary this evening. Just giving a little perspective.

They speak professionally. They can send a detective team, who will ask the same questions. Or, if Halpern wants, the detectives can come to his office. That'll happen in about a week or so.

Because it's an assault, technically, they can do more. So if he wants to work that angle, they can also send a forensic team, though that usually isn't done.

Halpern looks to Blake, who suggests that the duplication of effort involved in that would most likely not be cost-effective.

The cops leave, clumping down the stairs, their radios crackling. By now, the woman on the top floor has come out, and the couple downstairs are standing in the vestibule, looking alarmed. The woman is holding an infant, and asks the police what happened.

"Break-in," they tell her.

Blake talks with the forensic team as they pack. They've lifted a few prints, but it seems like they were gloved. Even in the kitchen, where you usually find something, there was nothing. Blake thanks them, and they go.

He stays for a few more minutes. The cops were right, it's mostly mess, books and clothing strewn about, papers on the floor. He takes Halpern on another run-through on the time elements, concludes that the burglars had, at the most, fifteen or twenty minutes in the apartment.

Blake questions the lawyer as to what case materials he had had at home, but Halpern assures him that he follows, quite strictly, the security guidelines. Living so close to his office, he'd rather return there after supper, if necessary.

Was there anything of particular value, or special significance, either taken or damaged?

Halpern hasn't had a chance to look, but, offhand, no.

"Take an inventory," says Blake.

Blake uses the bathroom, then finds Halpern in his study. He is holding a picture frame. On the wall, Blake sees where other frames have been pulled down. Broken glass and strips of wood and metal litter the floor.

At the door, he asks the lawyer if he's all right.

Halpern says he is. You can see he's tired, and edgy, and his face has a sheen of oil and sweat. But he seems to be taking it well.

Says Blake, "Your ice cream."

On the Indian rug is the squashed container, and an amoeboid pool of thick, white cream.

"Shit."

On that note. Blake leaves.

●

Most of the road morons having long gone to garage, Blake's drive home is uneventful. He drives with barely a movement of the steering wheel, a few miles over the speed limit. He is tense, keeping two particular thoughts at bay. Arriving in Eastmere a little after 3:00 A.M., he briefly fills his wife in while undressing at the foot of the bed.

Sleep comes almost instantly, and he is gratified that he hasn't had to give any thought, on the conscious level at least, to any parallels between Halpern's burglary—if that indeed was what it was—and the destruction of the Ellis household.

He will save for a future date the thought of that book on the young attorney's floor amid the debris. Halpern had been in the bedroom with the cops, and Blake had caught the book's title: *The Stranger.*

A popular book, no doubt. But this one had the wet beer circle enclosing the man's face, like a bull's-eye on a target.

It had just fit into his deep pants pocket. Now it was in his briefcase. She would need it to complete her assignment; there were notes in all the margins, yellow underlinings everywhere. He would decide later how to present it to his daughter, if ever. But now he had a certain knowledge, which he would use not to his advantage, for he sought none, but for her good. He might have mixed feelings about her bedding down with Halpern, but nothing he could not, as she might put it, deal with.

But on the matter of her safety, he would not compromise.

●

Richard Halpern had lied to Blake. Something of significance had been damaged, but nothing quite tangible. He has just finished picking up the many bits and pieces of the frames that had been torn from his walls. High school diploma, college, law school. Certificates of achievement. Letters of appreciation from the justices he had clerked for. They had been smashed on the floor, desecrated with footprints and slashes.

What he had been holding in his hand when the older man had come into the study was his Hebrew school diploma. They had left that on the wall, intact. And he had taken it down to hide it from Blake's sight. That was the thing of significance they had damaged, by not touching it at all.

And he didn't tell the agent other things. How, in the first moments in the dark, when they had grabbed him, he had felt a terror such as he had never known. He was tall and strong, but they were stronger. He was being held from behind in an unbreakable grip. The man had stood before him in almost total blackness. They had flashed a bright flashlight into his eyes. He had turned away, as if the light were a blow, or a shower of cold contempt. The light, more than anything, was terrifying. He was naked in front of them, his face, his fear.

He had struggled very briefly, but the man holding him was expert, and simply increased the pressure on his neck, squeezing hard, and Halpern stopped. His eyes were tearing. The man in front of him was a presence, his outline edged in darkness. There were no words spoken, only the heavy breathing of the three of them. For a long moment nothing had happened.

Then he felt wetness on his face.

The man had spit on him.

Without a word they had flung him to the floor and were gone.

Now, showering, the young lawyer is scrubbing his face hard with the washcloth. The water is hot, the soap thickly lathered. He has decided he will not pursue it any further with the police. There is nothing to be gained by bringing in the detectives. The police advised him that should he wish to file an insurance claim for damaged or stolen property, he must report same to the precinct, and he will be issued a form that he may submit to his insurance company. A quick inspection indicated he had very little monetary loss. The diplomas and certificates can be patched or replaced, he is sure.

The older agent had asked him if he was all right, and he was. Now, his primary emotion is fury, which he will nurture to a proper prosecutorial pitch, if only to keep the shame at bay.

# CHAPTER 33

F rank, what's the procedure on an interservice target?"

Blake is paying a first-time visit to Campbell's new corporate head-quarters. He's got a three-room suite in an office building on Forty-second Street just east of Fifth Avenue. He's got two desks in each room, three phones, and a water cooler. There are two women at the desks, and a man who Blake remembers vaguely as having retired from the New York office three years ago. The carpeting hasn't been installed yet. He's been in less than a month, and there's a lot happening. Paperwork all about, a phone ringing. The Irishman is his blustery, red-faced self.

"We don't work an interagency target," Campbell says. "We pass it along to their internal people."

"Come on, Frank, you can't tell me we never tapped or tailed another service."

Campbell gives him one of his fighting glares.

"What are the protocols, Frank?"

"We request very nicely, and they tell us to fuck off. Nicely, some-times not."

"And?"

"And sometimes yes and sometimes no, Matt. It depends. Who's the target?"

"A man by the name of Harrow."

"Tell me another, Matt. Jesus."

Campbell gets up and closes the door.

"Harrow's an old-timer. Jesus, Matt, he's been out of it for years."

"Very much out of it, Frank."

"He must be about seventy-five."

"About that."

"Usually we pass anything we find along to the service of employ and if they want us to follow up they let us know."

It's too dangerous, bureaucratically speaking, to allow a rival into your files; if you've got a problem, you handle it yourself.

"A man like Harrow, Matt, goes back a long way." A phone rings. Campbell hits a couple of buttons. It's his wife. He assures her that he won't stop off anywhere this afternoon. He tells her he's in conference, hangs up.

Blake and Campbell let the silence do its work.

They reach an understanding very quickly. Campbell will work Harrow. Hell, it's only a stone's throw from his office. He knows the man, has his old-line connections. He is pleased beyond measure, Blake sees by his happy glare, the energetic anger around the man's mouth, to be back in the field.

# CHAPTER 34

**C**anceled due to unfathomable administrative requirements, Donnelly's triage meeting is rescheduled a week later; that's fine, Blake needs all the time he can get. He wants to come in as thoroughly prepared as possible, but doesn't want to lose his edge. He finds that his timing is just a little off. Late August is bad because vacations are heaviest and the paperwork piles up. You'd think that with everyone away there'd be less of it, but it's the opposite, one of life's vexing paradoxes. And Donnelly will be away in Denver at the Annual National Conference of Law Enforcement Administration, so that Murphy will chair. Donnelly will, however, remain in his hotel room, hooked into the triage by speakerphone.

The meeting will begin at 8:00, Tuesday morning, and Blake and Spanakos meet an hour earlier for coffee and review. Halpern is supposed to be there, but isn't. He's been in Washington the last four days, passing up his weekend at the beach. Blake spoke with him last night, late. Tippet was hacking away, the lawyer said. The British were coming through on their promise. Blake was furious. Goddamn it, Richard, he had said, if you don't have it now, when the hell will you? Matt, we'll have it.

But at 7:30, as he reviews charts and sips dishwater coffee with his junior agent, Blake is worried. This is a one-shot deal, a double-or-nothing, winner-take-all meeting wherein Blake has to convince Donnelly, and the Internal Security division of Justice, that there are grounds, re Starfield—grounds which Blake, Halpern supporting, shall set forth—to officially and irrevocably commit the Bureau and its vast resources, together with the mighty imperium of the United States government.

He and Halpern have spent many hours in preparation, and will go in with a small truckload of material. They each have a portion of the presentation, have worked out their strategy; they have been rehearsing separately, and together, for a week, throwing questions at each other. Halpern's portion is crucial. To make their case, to get the agents, to get the backup, the helicopter, maybe even a spotter plane, the budget lines, they have to show operational capability on Starfield's part. Despite the lawyer's elegant presentation of the fallacy of demonstrability, they have to give the working model. All they had, to date, was a lot of clever conjecture and tantalizing bits and pieces rolling off a dot-matrix printer. They needed more, and that was what Halpern was supposed to be bringing in from Washington this morning.

Spanakos looks at his watch. The younger agent has on a new suit, Blake his best gray plaid. They both wear red ties. They study their flowchart. They will be using an overhead projector for a little variation.

"We have to give them something to look at," Blake had told Spanakos. "And let's use colors."

At 7:45, Blake leaves the table and makes phone calls.

The attorney's not at home, nor at his office. Blake tries Naval Security in Washington, but can't punch through the secretarial flak, and after being put on hold twice, gives up.

When he returns to the table, Spanakos is packing.

Blake shakes his head. "Probably in transit," he says.

Spanakos says nothing, but is worried. They leave.

●

In addition to Blake and Spanakos in Donnelly's conference room at precisely 8:00, are three other men. Murphy is at the head of the table. He's finishing a bagel half, coffee on the side. On his left is Walsh, Halpern's chief at Eastern. He and Blake exchange pleasantries. To Murphy's right is John Guthrie, the ethics man from Justice. He's shuttled in this morning from Washington, and mentions that air traffic delays cost him half an hour. He and Blake shake hands; Spanakos is introduced. On the table next to Murphy is a small brown box speaker. The audio input is a little mesh-covered ball protruding from its top. Black wires connect the speaker to a phone at Murphy's side.

Blake and Spanakos sit. Good, the overhead projector is in the corner, as is the easel.

"We're missing our young lawyer," says Blake. Murphy nods, looks at his watch. There will be fifteen minutes grace. The men talk. Murphy asks Blake about his daughter's wedding. On the table, in front of Blake, is the analysis—the comparisons and matchups and coordinates, all the names and places and dates and bits and pieces of Starfield and Ellis that have been computer matched with NIS data bases, and then run through the fine mesh of a computer's brain for additional linkage. It's all in an oversized loose-leaf binder, about five inches thick. Across the top of the binder are the words ToP SeCReT. Vowels in Navy classification are always lower case to distinguish them from Army's, which are upper, and the Air Force's, mixed. There are three small squares of color: red, blue, red. The blue is circled in white. In front of the other men is the abridged edition of the analysis; it's a hundred pages long, and is basically a set of conclusions, with only a small portion of the supporting data.

Murphy has checked his watch again, and raises his eyebrows at Blake, who nods. They can't wait any longer. Donnelly, out in Denver, is going to speak at 10:00, and even though there's a couple of hours difference, he needs time to prepare.

"Gentlemen. Shall we begin?"

Silence while Murphy punches buttons on his phone. Spanakos is nervous, squirms a bit. Out of the speaker there comes the sound of ringing, and then Donnelly's voice saying hello.

"Tom, how are you out there?"

"Just fine, George, just fine." His voice comes through quite accurately, though more high-pitched than usual, and Murphy adjusts the bass.

Donnelly's voice, properly masculine, asks how everyone is, and the men respond, directing their replies to the brown speaker. It's impossible not to raise one's voice. Donnelly recognizes Guthrie's, asks him a personal question about his wife, and Guthrie answers that her mother is doing much better, thank you.

"Tom," says Murphy, "we're missing a few people, but I know you're pressed for time this morning, so we're going to start anyway."

"Sure, let's go, George."

"How's the reception, Tom?"

"Just fine."

Blake stands, welcomes everyone informally, tells them why they are here, and what they will be hearing. He notes, as he talks, that Guthrie has taken out a small tape recorder. Blake finishes his introduction quickly, asks Spanakos to continue. Spanakos stands, walks around to the other side of the table, near the overhead projector and the easel, opens his binder, and begins.

Blake and Spanakos's portion of the presentation is designed to prove one thing: probable cause. The material is overwhelming, in a prima facie sort of way, and Blake and his junior agent will take turns on it. It will be like an invasion.

Spanakos, activating the overhead, begins the softening-up process with a bombardment of general conclusions, i.e., that they have evidence that a certain man is about to commit certain acts in a certain place and at a certain time, and that such acts constitute a crime as defined by the various statutes and laws of the United States of America, as put forth in Addendum I.

They can hear the pages turning through the brown speaker.

As Spanakos goes on, Blake goes over his index cards. They're numbered and colored and full of arrows and cues indicating graphs and diagrams. He looks at his watch. Where is Halpern? Maybe he should have asked his daughter—

But Blake is unable to pursue his thoughts because Spanakos is yielding the floor to him. He is on his feet delivering now a more specific, tactical fire. Spanakos is at his side, handing out materials: flow charts, brief bios of the principle players, organizational schematics of the Mossad, and Arrita, the Italian secret service. Some of this, perhaps a great deal, is not pertinent, but Blake knows the value of overkill. Nothing convinces the bureaucracy as much as paper, especially when it has footnotes.

Blake is rolling. He's worked on this for days, has taped himself, reviewed the tapes, has honed his presentation to a fine and precise edge, yet not too precise, for he wants to leave room for spontaneity. His fluidity, recall, and precision are intimidating. He gives a chronology of events over the last four months, names, dates, places. He throws out technical material in mouthfuls that fill the air with a relentless barrage of facts and figures and correlations. This, too, is overkill, and leaves them all exhausted. You can see it on Murphy's face, on Walsh's. But he keeps going, firing away for another few minutes. When he sits, there is a long breathing silence.

Which is broken at last by Donnelly's voice from the speaker.

"Thank you, Matt. Thank you. That was quite convincing."

"Thank you, Tom."

"And Ed . . . ?"

"Sir."

"I appreciate it."

"Thank you."

Another silence.

"Hmmm." The man from Justice, Guthrie, has good throat action. Blake takes the floor for Q & A.

No one wants to speak first.

"Interesting, as far as it goes," Guthrie says, at last.

Everyone shifts. Guthrie is top dog here; Walsh, backing Halpern, was supposed to have brought Washington along. Internal Security can kill a case, and often has.

The speaker comes to life. "We're lacking a handle on this, I think."

Murphy says, "Ed."

Spanakos has raised his pencil a few inches off the table, a silent bidder for attention.

"Their communications are still presenting a problem. Until we tap into their network—"

"Assuming there is a network." This from Internal Security.

"Matt," says Murphy.

Blake directs the table's attention to exhibit number three, one file in a stack of perhaps twenty. The files are there for effect, for intimidation. Donnelly is only peripherally interested in operational details, but the more on display the happier he will be.

While they leaf through the file, Blake speaks. "There are two schools of thought here. One is that the Ellis operation was an amateur production, and therefore the seeming confusion that attended it was merely a manifestation of this lack of professionalism. The other school, to which I personally ascribe based upon our best intelligence," here giving the barest of downward glances to the loose-leaf binder, "perceives the operation to be precisely the opposite. We believe that the lack of professionalism is merely in *appearance only,* and was part of its operational cover."

Guthrie leans across the table. "I've been hearing a lot of talk regarding cover and I can't help but wondering if this, if I may be candid, is the wrong tack. I have a background, may I say, in intelligence, and it's been my experience that cover only goes so far. Operational methodology is not an end in itself. It's merely a means, Mr. Blake. And I can't help but notice that this is often something a great many intelligence people lose sight of. They get caught up, shall I say, in the tautology of the process."

Blake, who can dish it out when he has to, replies that he, too, does not wish to get bogged down in what is, really, a teleological argument.

Frowns around the table, pursed lips. The silence is thoughtful.

"Now look." Guthrie is getting impatient; he knows he's being stonewalled. "What we want to see before we go off half-cocked and start signing all kinds of warrants for you guys, is just how the hell according to you they are going to do this."

Okay, thinks Blake, as he and Spanakos make eye contact, we're back to goddamn square one. So much for the presentation, and the efforts of Walsh, who's not looking at anyone.

The son of a bitch is bailing out, thinks Blake. And where the hell is the goddamn lawyer?

"John has a point." Murphy is a judicious syncophant.

Donnelly is silent, letting them fight it out.

"Thanks, George," says Guthrie. "They're going to have to take him through the security perimeter. Right?"

Silence.

Guthrie continues. "He's going to be walked out, driven someplace, during a transfer, am I correct?"

Blake responds. Ellis's attorneys have formally requested that Ellis be placed in a lower-security facility, and have made a motion in court to this effect.

Murphy interjects. They want the spy moved closer to his wife, are arguing on the basis of cruel and inhuman punishment.

And Navy, Blake continues, contrary to the inclinations of the Department of Justice, has, until now, opposed the transfer. But as part of their strategy vis-à-vis Starfield, they are willing to consider it.

This is not quite an answer to Guthrie's question, but Blake hopes it will move them into a different area.

It does not. Guthrie persists. "And from what I've read here, this man Deere, Hirsh, is most likely to be in charge of transport, is that correct?"

"That is correct," answers Spanakos.

"Damn it, Matt." The speakerphone conveys Donnelly's irritation. "This isn't a raid on the PLO. You're talking American citizens here."

They can't get off this point. Blake's inward groan is, he is certain, shared by Spanakos.

"Even if it's a rogue operation?" Murphy likes to take turns on both sides.

This is kicked around until Blake says: "We have no way of knowing just how rogue this thing is. If at all."

Silence.

Spanakos, grabbing at straws, puts forth Halpern's pet theory: an inside job.

"That, and a combination of the usual sloppiness." Blake speaks to Guthrie. "With all respect. We do know what security is like."

The porosity factor.

Blake tries to get something going. "Ed, I like what you're saying. They don't have to come in with Uzis and they don't have to suborn the entire service."

"A little here and a little there," counterpoints Spanakos.

"And they're feeding us just enough to keep us going, is that it?"

This from Murphy, which Guthrie jumps on. "So you think they're playing us off against ourselves, eh?"

Donnelly, murmuring from the box, is very interested.

"There is a difference of opinion on that, John," says Murphy, who surprises Blake by his support. "That wasn't intentional on their part. We had some very good hunching and excellent spadework on the part of the Bureau here."

"Kind of lucked out, is that it?"

"Pure luck." Blake's quiet sarcasm draws Guthrie's stare.

There is a long, awkward silence.

Blake is about to break it, but before he can speak there is the bell of the coffee wagon.

It's an opportunity for quick and intense parlay, and the men separate. Guthrie and Walsh go out in the hall; Murphy stays to talk with Donnelly's disembodied voice; Blake goes into another room to make phone calls; Spanakos opts for coffee.

Blake has no luck; Halpern's nowhere to be found nor has he left any messages. When he comes out into the hall, Murphy stops him. Donnelly wants to know what the hell is going on. Blake is not sure himself. With this meeting, Donnelly has come out into the open, and within a few days all hell is going to break loose with Justice and State. Walsh is going to catch a certain amount of hell from Mullady, and will pass it on to Halpern. Everyone will be running scared, protecting themselves by facing in all directions. And Donnelly will at last be forced to take a position, something no bureaucrat in his right mind will ever do.

Murphy reminds Blake that he had foretold of difficulties, and now sees the fruits about to sowed. Blake, his mind elsewhere, comments that espionage cases bring out the institutional conflicts, don't they, George?

Spanakos appears with coffee and turnovers.

Murphy goes off to find the wagon.

Blake, drinking in the hall, tries to compute the variables. Implicit in Murphy's statement is the threat of withdrawing whatever support Donnelly may have already promised to Eastern District regarding Starfield, in their own, secret negotiations. Because, make no mistake about it, Donnelly and Mullady have been negotiating. As has Navy and State. And Justice. The CIA, suspects Blake, is probably going it alone.

And implicit, too, in Murphy's wary regard of Blake, is his downright amazement that Blake has gone this far out on a very long limb without it being cut off.

This has to give Murphy most heavy pause. He has to wonder just how much, and from where, Blake's hidden support is coming. Is Blake himself more powerful than either Murphy or Donnelly are aware? What other forces are synergizing with Blake? Not only with Blake, but with Halpern, who clearly has a great deal of protection. Too many countervailing forces are at play, too many secret items on hidden agendas.

Spanakos goes off to make more phone calls.

And Blake, drinking his coffee and nibbling on his turnover, which is, as always, too sweet, Blake has to wonder too. Mostly about Donnelly, and almost as much about Halpern. Is Donnelly negotiating one of his famous end runs around Murphy? Is Donnelly in secret cahoots with the Racker, and, if not, then with whom? And what is the real agenda here? Who is served—bureaucratically, professionally—by bashing the Israelis? Long-term and short. For instance, why is Walsh rolling over and playing dead? A little bit of noise off on the side, just for appearances, but meek as a mewling kitten.

Murphy's back. They ran out of turnovers.

Spanakos approaches. "Matt. He's on his way. Traffic on the Grand Central," Spanakos explains. He left a message for Blake at the switchboard. He's coming in with Navy.

Murphy looks at his watch.

"Ten minutes, Matt."

●

The lawyer makes it with a minute to spare. In tow is a lieutenant commander, collar high and tight. Halpern apologizes. A jackknifed trailer truck; all traffic was stopped. Halpern had got out of the cab and, using the uniform of the naval officer, had commandeered a vehicle going in the opposite direction, and had worked their way back into Manhattan by a crazy route impossible to describe. He is unshaven and rumpled, but he's ready. The officer is carrying two boxes.

From the door, Murphy is signaling. Donnelly wants to proceed.

"We've got it, Matt," the attorney says, giving him a thumbs-up sign as they go into the conference room.

●

First Halpern takes the floor. He has diagrams, which he sets up on a portable easel. Punctuating his remarks with a long pointer, he gives a brief overview of espionage law and precedents, first in general, then specifically, as it relates to Starfield.

He's working a jury, thinks Blake, one of his superiors. Watching the young, handsome lawyer with a measuring eye, he does not know how to take him. Blake is still amazed at the ease with which his daughter deals with all of this, how normal their relationship is. As for Halpern, the young man has been, during this last week of close contact during which they thrashed out the presentation, professional in the extreme. Between them there is not exactly an empathy, not quite an affection— they have not spoken at all about the break-in.

The speaker box comes alive with a question from Donnelly that requires Blake's input, and he brings himself back.

Spanakos has to help him. It's a question about Hirsh, and Blake says that yes, it would be possible to work with Immigration, thus avoiding State and their constant carping about delicate diplomatic relations. Blake gets up to speed quickly. Immigration has its own rules and need not be too scrupulous regarding constitutional prohibitions; also, the media finds immigration boring, and so you don't run into PR problems.

"Thank you, Matt."

Halpern finishes, the lieutenant commander stands.

The officer is good. He is good in the way that Tippet, too young and doe-eyed, the way the Racker, hard and razor sharp, cannot be. He has no charts, no diagrams, no scale models. He has only his voice, carrying no discernible regional coloring, emphatic, modulated, unstoppable. He speaks without notes. The essence of his presentation is that they, Navy, in tandem with British intelligence, have succeeded in breaking the cover of a group of Israeli operatives who have been, to the best of their knowledge, sporadically active over a period of approximately fifteen years. Their operations are, for the most part, nonmilitary; the group itself is only loosely affiliated with the Mossad, which enhances, one sees, their deniability.

Indeed, one sees that.

The officer sits. Halpern stands, and there is some business about unpacking the boxes, setting up equipment. He and the lieutenant commander have brought a slide projector, and they spend some time getting it at the correct angle, finding a spot on the wall without cracks. Donnelly, clearly impatient, takes a bathroom break, and they hear him loud and clear. Everyone waits. It is understood that the lawyer has brought what they want and they are expectant. Halpern takes longer than he needs, fiddles too much with the slide carousel. At last he's ready. Spanakos douses the lights.

BRITAIN ORDERS ISRAELI DIPLOMAT TO LEAVE

The masthead reads, *The Spectator. Monday, 31 October 1977*
In the dark silence, disturbed only by the fan of the projector, they read.

> In a terse release that British intelligence officials admitted concealed a not inconsiderable anger, the Foreign Office ordered the immediate expulsion of an embassy attaché discovered to be closely linked with an American citizen who is thought to have engineered the escape of a criminal from a Brussels prison last month. The American, whose identity remains unknown, was said to have been in the employ of the Mossad. The escape has generated much embarrassment for a number of European intelligence services.
>
> British officials, angered to learn of the attaché's connection to the escape, said they were able to verify the Mossad connection. They said they were especially concerned that the American had used British passports in the operation, which have been traced, according to reliable sources, to the London embassy. The Israeli ambassador, Baruch Aviva, was summoned to Whitehall to listen to remonstrances of the British Permanant Under Secretary, Sir Peter Rosbain.

Another slide.
Murphy begins reading in a low voice into the mike.

> The expulsion of the Israeli was said to be very unusual, considering that Britain and Israel have had relatively harmonious dealings in recent years. British officials, speaking off the record, emphasized that the accepted norms of behaviour mandated that host nations be informed of special operations that in any way impinge upon or infract that nation's laws. There was much speculation that the British pique was prompted by their dire need to have the Belgian government squarely on their side in the upcoming negotiations involving British entry into the Common Market. The expulsion order was nonetheless seen as an extremely strong reaction by Downing Street, meant to express the government's displea-

sure at the cloak and dagger adventures of foreign operatives on British soil.

There are more slides, headlines from Belgian newspapers. The lead paragraphs are read by the naval officer in fluent French, then translated. Halpern has asked Spanakos to hand out materials. The gist of all this is that the Belgians had caught one of their citizens stealing classified documents relating to a jet fighter that Belgium and France were developing together. They had formed a consortium; Italy was involved too. The prime market for this jet fighter was, as one might expect, the Middle East, particularly Syria and Iraq. The Belgium citizen was Jewish. The country of receipt of these purloined plans was Israel.

Pictures of the prisoner are shown. Donnelly is irritated; all this is nonverbal and he doesn't know what's happening; Murphy tries to keep him informed, sounds like a broadcaster giving a play-by-play of a baseball game.

And now, alongside the photographs, which seem to be of an ordinary urban street scene, there appears a column of data printouts. Halpern has done an excellent job. Because what they are seeing, Blake realizes, is the same photograph every time: it is of a man entering a house on a busy street in Brussels. You can see the foreign license plates on the cars. Alongside the photograph is a data column. Halpern, controlling the switch on the projector, holds the first image, the distance shot. The man is shown head to foot. He is dressed in a dark suit, carries a briefcase. The data is barely legible. Then he goes to the next slide, which is an enlargement of the first, the text growing with it. He lingers just a little more over this, and more over the next; there are six images in his series, and each is held for an increasing interval.

It's very well done, a very simple, elegant bit of drama. The image is focusing on the square of the man's face. It keeps getting bigger and bigger, grainier and grainier. Murphy's play-by-play increases the tension; the man is genuinely excited. And the text of the data column reveals itself to be a box ad from a newspaper, which in the final frame, juxtaposed with the full-dotted image of a man, like a painting by Seurat, can at last be read.

> *Little Boy Blue.*
> *You owe me five farthings,*
> *Say the bells of St. Martins.*

And the image of the man, though he wears no beard, no hat, and though his head is turned away so that one sees only a quarter of his face, and though the grain of the emulsion is great, and time has taken its toll, is that of Dr. Phillip Starfield.

•

The projector is shut off. The lights come on.

"Gentlemen," says Halpern.

The officer is giving out a file, wherein all shall be revealed.

Triumph gleams in the lawyer's tired eyes.

"Gentlemen. We have, in our Dr. Starfield, a genuine world-class operative."

"Excellent," comes Donnelly's voice from the speaker.

•

It's almost anticlimactic, for now, Donnelly, in a hurry to do his own prep work, wants to get this down to basic case elements and how they pertain to manpower requirements.

The officer speaks to this point. He runs down the order of battle of what they think will be Starfield's team. Composition, rankings, specialties.

There is much talk on this point. The officer reveals, as much as he can without compromising Navy's insane regard for security, their own order of battle for Operation Nova. They cite the Ellis case. By the time they arrested the man they had over a hundred and fifty agents, analysts, support, and communications people; they tailed his ass up and down the East Coast, followed him to Europe three times, once to England; had called in their few remaining chips with the Israelis, got a little from the Italians. The Swiss were cautiously cooperative.

And what they need for Nova is more. Navy, Spanakos joining in, pours it on. Manpower, equipment, communications. Murphy takes notes, Donnelly commenting. They want transportation, maybe a helicopter. Murphy shakes his head; choppers are almost impossible to get. They want a special communications hookup routed through NSA, just in case the Mossad gets funny ideas. Murphy takes more notes, frowning.

"What about this Starfield?" Internal Security asks. Clearly, this is the problem.

Blake nods at Spanakos.

"Starfield," he says, "is an unusual man. He moves fast. We catch him at an airport occasionally, or on the road, but otherwise we don't see him." The agent clears his throat, opens a file. "He delivered a paper at the University of Chicago, then went into conference with their engineering faculty." He reads on, going through an itinerary that takes them on an extended tour of the lands of academia. University of Berkeley, Cold Spring Harbor—"that's a center for genetic research"—Florida Tech, a final touchdown in New York.

"He's got a goddamn inviable shield around him," says Murphy.

"And so you think," says Guthrie, "this is the way to catch him?" The man remains dubious.

Halpern holds up a hand. "I really have to say," he says, "that we're approaching this incorrectly. This is a much different situation than Ellis. And it's hard to say exactly where the problem lies."

It's apparent Halpern has more to say, and they all wait.

"And it's not by accident," he continues.

An alarm goes off in Blake's brain. Everything is going as well as he can expect, and the last thing he wants is the prosecutor going off into the azure of abstraction, but that's exactly what's about to happen.

"Not by accident," Halpern repeats, pauses significantly, clears his throat and launches himself. "I'm into the man." He has, he says, a special connection with Starfield, and he's psyched him out, tapped into his energy. In short, he's achieved a cathexis.

Murphy purses his lips.

"They're trying to confuse us," Halpern says.

For his money, Blake offers, they're doing one hell of a job.

Everyone laughs.

"But don't you see, Matt? Matt!" The lawyer has a look of anguish on his long, handsome face. No one is taking him seriously. "We're mired in this formless muck of data. It's like primal slime! And the man's a geneticist, Matt."

Blake doesn't want to be Halpern's foil, and gives the slightest of nods, hoping, wishing that the lawyer will shut up. He will not.

"And think of his name."

They do.

"Starfield. A nebula, a vast field of stars swirling and pulsing with magnificent energy."

No one has anything to say.

The lawyer's eyes are bright; he's exhausted, thinks Blake.

And suddenly the attorney is out in the wild blue yonder, flying high with talk about how Starfield is a physical biologist—that's in Addendum IIIa—and given to metaphorical constructs. Halpern's thought about this, and he sees what the problem is, and it's confusing, yes, and almost impossible to put into words, but here he is doing it. Some of it is confused in a poetic sort of way, intensely felt, richly metaphoric; the young attorney's passion is profound and overwhelming. He's like a sun, full of bursting fire, or a comet, rushing on with talk of astrophysical phenomena, Einstein, energy conversions. He throws out an allusion to Heisenberg, which Blake catches, and another to Fermi, which Blake does not. Spanakos has leaned back in his seat, staring. Murphy has his hand over his mouth, eyes in small slits. Guthrie gives nothing away, but Blake suspects the man is amazed. Walsh's writing hand is poised just above his yellow pad. From the speaker box comes an intense silence.

"Strands of life," Halpern is saying, trying to calm himself. "Starfield deals with bits of life."

Walsh is looking at Blake, his eyebrows raised.

Halpern has more.

"And that's what Starfield's operations are like. I read about them. That's how his universe is formed. All these elemental bits and pieces coming together into a critical mass until the thing explodes into being. *Bang!*" The sharp clap of his hands startles everyone. He's good, grudges Blake; goddamn overly dramatic, even a bit ridiculous, but good.

"Well," says Guthrie.

Blake is losing patience, and just to make it clear to anyone looking at him that he's disassociating himself from this young lunatic, he shakes his head and looks at his file.

There is a knock on the door.

A man comes into the room; he bends toward the officer's ear.

Without a word the lieutenant commander rises and leaves.

Halpern clears his throat. Everyone turns to him. They're interested in spite of themselves.

"You know about matter and antimatter. It's in the newspapers all the time."

"Quacks," says Murphy.

No one corrects him.

Blake knows. "Matter consuming itself in a reunion of opposites."

Something like that.

"Right. And then once Ellis is free, Starfield and his support team will disappear." Halpern snaps his fingers. "A black hole. They'll vanish."

Blake actually sees the hairs on the back of the lawyer's hands rise; there is color in his cheeks. After, in the postmortem, Halpern predicts, analysis will attempt an understanding of the operation by tracing the trajectories of the outrushing embers—the escape routes of Deere and his assistants, of Starfield and Ellis—much like astrophysicists search for the core of the big bang by extrapolating backward from the fleeing stars. Who was there and when exactly did Ellis break; the names of the agents present, what did they see, where is Deere and his damn blue van and his curly haired handsome assistant? But it will be too late.

The standard protestations will be made through diplomatic channels. The Israelis will deny everything, with hurt anger. Liaisons will confer and exchange memoranda and a joint Senate and House committee on intelligence, ad hoc, will take testimony at which the Bureau will be called upon to take, on orders of those political bastards, a heavy hit.

Unless, he says. "Unless, George, Glen, John, we get what we need. Agents. Vehicles. We want that helicopter. We need the manpower!"

At this instant the door opens and the lieutenant commander takes his seat, silently.

"Gentlemen," says Murphy.

The speaker box is silent; has Donnelly hung up?

"Okay, Richard." This from Murphy. "Convert this into operational needs."

Halpern is ready. "It's obviously not a one-man operation. They need their support people. We know who they are." He lapses again into a poetical turn of phrase using the terminology of physics: critical mass, explosion, ground zero. They have to be there when the fireball goes up, ready with their own support, their own transportation, certainly a helicopter, communications, everything, right there at the center to catch Ellis as he shoots forth from the exploding mass. Halpern speaks with a potent conviction, carrying them along on his torrent: it will be like being at the core of a sunburst, he tells them, like a birth, yes, like a birth. Slow down, kid, thinks Blake.

A silent collective sigh goes round the table.

Halpern sits, spent. He's calmer, but Blake, knowing him as well as his own children, sees it still in his eyes. There's a sweaty sheen on his face, much like a postcoital flush.

But he's done it. We'll get the goddamn chopper.

●

The lieutenant commander takes Blake aside.

The captain has called.

The lieutenant commander will be returning immediately to Washington, and suggests Blake accompany him.

Spanakos has joined them.

The officer imparts his news without inflection, surprise, or pleasure. "The Girlfriend has been located."

She returned, foolhardy young woman, and the Racker has trapped her in Montreal.

# PART III

# CHAPTER 35

**S**ir."

It's 1015 hours in Navy's command post just outside of Washington, and Tippet's cuffs are turned up, once; he's in battle mode. It's a small room, phone banks, consoles, maps. Two other officers are working the phones. The Racker is nowhere to be seen.

The Girlfriend, who the hell is the Girlfriend? was Blake's response when the officer spoke, and then he remembered: Ellis's courier—the girlfriend of the attaché.

Blake, Spanakos at his side, takes stock; this is a full-blown operation. Navy's been holding out.

"When did she get in, Lieutenant?"

"Sir. Three days ago." Tippet briefs them. "Tel Aviv–Athens, sir. We were able to backtrack her to Amsterdam. She's been cleaning herself. She used an American passport that belongs to an exchange student from Chicago. Lori Miller."

That's their technique, sir. They pitch the tourists, especially the Jewish ones: give us your passport while you are here, we have good uses for it, and we will return it undamaged when you leave, except for a page or two, which you will never notice missing.

Tippet explains how they lucked out. This American student, Lori, spent a few unscheduled days in Athens before showing up in Israel—wanted to keep it a secret because she was with a guy, and in some way managed to keep it off her passport, not difficult, considering the lax security—and didn't mention it to the Israeli briefers when she gave them her passport. Or else, knowing, they decided to use it anyway.

Lori Miller is blond, short, with big breasts. The Girlfriend is dark, tall. And flat-chested. They doctored the passport, but the Athens customs man, one of the many free-lancers who likes to pick up extra change here and there, remembered the cute American girl without the bra. One of those things that happens, sir, out of a thousand faces you remember one—it's not the face he remembered, quips Blake to Tippet's unsmiling earnestness—and the customs man passed it along to one of our people who had just happened to stop by on his monthly collection route. Luck, sir.

"She'll switch again," says Blake, "when she crosses over." He has a strong sense of someone behind him.

"We expect that, sir."

She's not yet on American soil, so Blake has no jurisdiction. She's in Montreal, having come in on one of the standard routes many of the Middle East services use to infiltrate agents. She'll make contact, hold over a few days, then come into the States.

"What's her work name?"

The presence is growing stronger.

"We don't know, sir."

"Where's she staying?"

"The Montreal Hilton, sir."

"Who's on her?"

"We have a team, sir. The Crimps are supporting."

But not for long, thinks Blake. The Royal Canadian Mounted Police do not take kindly to American agents cavorting on their streets, usurping their prerogatives. Blake turns.

"Captain."

"Matthew."

The Racker is taller by half a head, officerial in the extreme and smug as a bastard.

"Jack, what the goddamn hell?"

He means all this: the Girlfriend out there, the command center, the Racker's agents on the wrong side of the border, the Mounties running interference. Which means Navy went through the State Department, which is precisely, goddamn it, what he and Halpern have been trying to avoid. The way it should have been done was for the captain to interface with Blake who would have worked with the Bureau's Buffalo field office and brought in his own team—and he, Blake, would have conducted the liaison with the Crimps.

"Matthew, my apologies. We moved expeditiously."

You goddamn certainly did, thinks Blake, but before he can reply an officer joins them, another lieutenant who explains, sir, what's been going on, sir. It's been three days since she roosted. Roosted? The last day, she's been restless, showing signs of wanting to fly south. It's that season. The lieutenant is one of Ryan's boys, cut from the same tight, iron cloth, young, adoringly respectful. Certain signs of a nervous bird; the lieutenant recites. A visit to the Italian consulate. A quick in and out at a restaurant known to be frequented by operatives of a certain nationality. They assume she visited a drop site in the ladies room. Earlier, she had spent time in Reykjavik, where the Mounties are almost certain she made contact with an agent in the gift shop.

Blake presses for details.

"An exchange of handbags at the scrimshaw counter, sir."

Very standard: the two women position themselves side by side, both identical bags on the counter. They dance around each other, exchange signals. A quick rotation is executed as they look over the merchandise, the bags are switched. Lori's passport is taken back to Israel, the Girl-friend has her new identity.

And we are always, thinks Blake, two steps behind. But closing. "Any photographs, Jack?"

The Racker nods, the other lieutenant produces them. Slender, dark-haired woman. Two images in close-up, the third in quarter face, turn-ing away. Blake frowns; Navy's been holding out. The Racker has Tippet pull other images from the Ellis material. Full face of the woman standing under a cherry tree in heavy blossom, smiling. A tall pretty woman.

"Her bio, sir."

Blake and Spanakos stand close and read. Age, thirty-four. Born France, childhood there, parents Israeli diplomatic corps, studied in the United States. Fluent French, Hebrew, English, and Italian. Brief em-ployment by the United Nations World Health Organization. Assumed Mossad, but bio not current by three years. It's obvious to Blake; every-thing stops three, four years ago. CIA is playing games. Harrow, that closemouthed bastard. More photographs. Her carrying an attaché case, the one Ellis presumably used for document transport. In the back-ground are bushes and a fountain. They had a drop site in Central Park and a location out on Long Island, near Ellis's house. The Girlfriend. She was a friend of the military attaché's son, or was it his wife, or was she having an affair with the attaché himself? No, that's too messy; they wouldn't allow it.

Or maybe they encouraged it.

There's more. The other lieutenant hands over a data sheet. The captain points out a few interesting correlations in travel times, cross-flights. Phone calls. Telephone intercepts about a meeting in New York, the usual spook talk about picking up a package, the order coming through, customer needing special attention, fragile shipment. Very standard conversation, transparent as glass, God knows it fools no one. And maybe it's not meant to.

Definite signs, sir, our bird is prepping for flight. She's going through the motions of an ordinary tourist, but it's a dry-cleaning run if ever Navy saw one. Tickets on Air Canada, then cancellation. Rented a car, drove it around Montreal for half a day, stopped a dozen times at historic sites. There is the sense of the watchers that she was looking for surveillance, testing, watching the shadows.

"She visited a synagogue, sir."

Blake reads that.

"In the morning," observes Spanakos.

Blake is aware; Halpern has cued him in. For the observant, prayers three times a day, two less than the Muslims.

"What's her cognizance?" Blake asks.

The Navy team is certain she hasn't spotted them.

Blake isn't, but lets it pass.

Sir. Other signs of an itchy operative. No matter how professional, they all get a case of nerves. Kind of revs them up. She checked out of the Hilton, checked into a motel. The Crimps haven't been able to tap her line yet—this motel has a number of oddities, one of them being that their telephone trunk line passes under a conduit that has limited access due to a construction quirk when it was built. It's been giving the Mounties headaches for years. Wouldn't you know she picked that particular motel. She's got her car gassed and ready to go. This morning she packed her trunk, drove into the city, played another hide-and-seek. In and out of stores, back exits, ladies' room, three stops in telephone booths. Goes into a restaurant, sits, asks for a menu, gets a cup of coffee, and before you know it, while the Racker's men are sitting there assuming they're going to get to finally eat lunch, she's up and out.

So they figure that unless she's one hell of a hyperactive young lady, she's definitely trying to get clear.

"She's not working alone," says Blake.

The Racker attends.

"Jack, she has a spotter working with her. At least one, probably two.

Maybe even a cameraman.'' Blake knows what she's doing: making the opposition work harder, and incidentally picking up some of their own material—photos, work habits—for their files on Navy. The Racker, a theoretician, is deficient in street craft, and is appreciative.

But now the little room is starting to hop. Tippet has on a headset and he's in front of a console, his hands on the keyboard. The phones are lighting up. The other lieutenant's grabbing the receivers. Tippet swivels in his chair and turns toward his captain.

"Jaybird's flying, sir.''

"Jaybird?''

"That's our code name, sir, for the Girlfriend.''

"Could you use the speaker system, Lieutenant, so we can hear what the hell is going on.''

At a nod from the captain, Tippet flips a switch. The room is now full of cross-cutting voices overlaid with static.

Seems that Jaybird has been flying around the city, and the Navy surveillance team has followed her into the Herriot Emporium, one of Montreal's biggest, plushiest department stores. Tippet turns away and speaks into his bullet-shaped mouthpiece. Racker, on the red phone, is standing near the console listening.

The room is full of scratchy static and crackling men's voices. While Tippet works the keyboard, logging in the calls of the watchers, the other lieutenant describes the setup: they worked a deal with the Crimps so that Navy's people are tied in through a Canadian MRU—mobile radio unit—whose signals are being fed through an NSA satellite hookup to this Washington command post. They have three teams of two men each; the van is operated by a Crimp technician.

Blake and Spanakos give each other looks. These Navy bastards have been pulling a fast one.

Sounds are coming out of the speakers, a chorus of words and static.

"Ionospheric aberrations, sir,'' says Tippet.

"Contact lost, sir.''

"Lost?''

"Sir.''

Blake allows his silence to demonstrate his irritation. The Racker has been tracking this woman for close to a month, has, for the last three days, followed her well-formed ass through the streets of Montreal, has finally chased her into this department store, cornering her—and now, goddamn it, has just lost her.

"Let me have that, Lieutenant.'' He holds out his hand. The junior officer hesitates, even though an older, more senior man is giving him an order. Tippet's eyes flick toward his captain. He takes off his headset and gives it to Blake.

"Okay, who's out there? Check in, please."

Blake's is a strange voice.

"Come on guys, check in."

After a moment the men, in chorus, reply.

*One, here.*

*Two team.*

*Three, yo.*

Blake wants names.

Again, a silence, more hostile; who the fuck is this man?

Then the chorus again: John, Mike, Steve, a second John, a Tom, and a Ken.

Blake gets Spanakos's attention, makes a writing motion with his finger. The agent takes a clipboard from the table and moves to Blake's side.

"Sir, the Canadians have an A-DAC."

Area Data Access Center—a graphic-display data base with all the city's building's floor plans: they began as fire-code information banks and then were fed into the Mounties' bases.

"Good. Get in, Lieutenant."

Tippet's already working the keys, coding himself in.

Over the speakers and into Blake's earphones come the sound of the teams talking to each other through the communications matrix. Too much static. One voice, a nasal, high-pitched voice from the Two team is going to be a problem.

"We're in, sir."

"Good boy," says the captain, and for the briefest of moments lays a rewarding hand upon Tippet's shoulder.

Blake leans over Tippet. The screen shows a linear outline of a building. Entrances in green, fire exits in red, underground passages in crosshatch. Tippet brings up the interior schematic showing escalators and elevators, blue and yellow respectively. This is wonderful, something the Bureau needs.

"Okay. Look, guys, I don't like numbers, so I'm going to rename you by color. Red, Blue, and Yellow. Red one, Two blue, Three yellow. Do you hear me?"

There is a long silence.

Spanakos has written the colors in big, block letters, made columns.

Blake repeats the designations.

The high-pitched voice comes on: *"Who the hell are you, Mister?"*

"I'm federal agent Matthew Blake, New York office, and I'm going to direct you guys for a few minutes so that if we come out looking like assholes you can all blame me."

A few chuckles.

"I want a position call. Sound off. Come on. I want Red A, Red B. Pick your letters. A or B. Come on guys, where is everyone?"

He's put some authority in his voice, some pleading. They call in.

"Okay," says Blake. He's looking at Tippet's screen, nods at Spanakos, whose pen starts moving as soon as Blake speaks. "Red and Blue, you're both on Carlton Place. You've got two exits there. I want Red covering both, west and east. You know what the target wore in?"

A number of voices start speaking at once. Blake slows them down. Spanakos uses a separate sheet of paper. Brown coat. Light tan shoes. Handbag on the left, blue, over the shoulder. Carrying a white bag with a red rose on it. There's disagreement on her hat, whether she had one, and Blake decides to go hatless. For easy reference, Spanakos puts the paper with the description on the table, next to the computer screen.

Blake gives him a thumbs-up.

"Guys, watch the shoes." She went in dressed one way, and Blake knows she's not going to come out the same. Shoes are the last thing changed. Coats and hats and decorative paraphernalia are easy—you buy them fast. But not shoes.

"Blue. I want you on Conners Street, there's an exit there, and Yellow, also on Conners, I see a freight receiving bay. I want someone there. Anyone inside?"

A voice comes in.

"Speak up," requests Blake.

*"Third floor."* The voice is surreptitious. Blake imagines a man in a suit pretending to be on shoplifting patrol, talking carefully into his walkie-talkie.

"What's the story?"

A hissing whisper.

"Speak up, Blue."

*"We lost her."*

"I know you lost her. Where are you?"

*"Women's sportswear. Winter stuff."*

"Yeah, they always show it early." A few more chuckles. He looks at Spanakos's clipboard, checks their positions. "Okay, guys. Everyone in position and holding."

Affirmatives come in over the static.

The Racker is watching Blake; Tippet is on the console. Spanakos, holding his clipboard, will be the score keeper.

Okay, thinks Blake, we wait, as we always do.

*"We've got her!"*

"Who's talking here?"

*"Two A—Blue A, Blue A—"*

"Where are you, Blue A?"

*"Third floor, she's going into a fitting room."*

"Blue, who's with you? Blue, come in Blue. Blue!" Stay calm, Blake tells himself, cool and calm.

*"No white bag, repeat, no white bag."*

"What else, Blue? What does she have?"

*"Visual contact terminated."*

"Okay. Thanks. Hold, Blue." Blake has to decide whether to pull the other teams inside or hold them at their posts. He doesn't know how good they are, has his doubts, but will work them to his higher standard.

There's a lot of static on the line, and his ear is beginning to feel it.

"Yellow," says Blake.

*"Here."*

"I want Yellow on the third floor, sportswear."

*"Juniors?"*

"Yes, move it, please."

Over the static, the voices are barely audible.

Spanakos speaks. "Matt, they need a woman."

The Racker is silent. Tippet has his eyes on the screen. Spanakos has his pen poised. Blake listens, watching the lieutenant's fingers waiting on the keyboard.

*"She's out, she's out!"*

"Blue, great. Direction?"

*"She's out!"*

"I hear you, Blue. What's her direction?"

*"Come in control, come in control."*

"Control's on-line." Blake hears the teams talking to each other. He repeats: "Control is on-line."

Something's happened in the radio van.

*"Escalator up, escalator up, this is Red, does anyone read me, Red, escalator up."*

"Yellow, come in Yellow."

*"Fourth floor, higher-priced gowns, fourth floor. Request assistance."*

"We're dead on reception," says Spanakos.

A whining hum begins, then leaps in decibels. Blake whips off his headset, wincing. A mad jumble of voices, static, a lot of cursing, *fuck the van*, static.

*"Interference."* A different voice. It's the man in the van, calm, professional. *"Police interference."*

Blake can only shake his head. They're operating on a frequency too close to what the police use, a goddamn, standard foul-up. He holds the earpiece away from his ear, with his other hand positions the mouthpiece. Through the speakers come the sounds of traffic and a lot of clanking and banging, more voices, then a high-pitched short shriek. Everyone winces. Now Muzak fills the control room. The van man, trying to call up his assigned frequency, has picked up instead the store's audio.

*—to call attention of our shoppers to the special today in domestics, imported table linens in a fine selection of lovely winter colors—*

Another loud hum, then silence. Blake's calm voice asks for Red, then Blue, then Yellow. He waits, then calls again calmly, clearly, as per the manual which states that, in field situations, there is no substitute for the calm soothing voice of the supervisor speaking to his/her agents.

*"Yellow here."*

"Yellow. Where's here?"

Blake bends over the computer screen; Spanakos is standing by with his clipboard tilted up into Blake's face, ready to write in Yellow's location.

"Repeat, Yellow: location please."

*"Fourth floor."*

"Any contact with target?"

*"Negative."*

*"Blue A reporting."*

*"Red here."*

"Blue and Red, give locations."

*"Down escalator, second floor."*

*"Conners, east exit."*

How the hell did they get there?

"Any contact with target?"

Negatives all around.

"Okay." He keeps his voice even. "Keep looking. No white bag. She's in fitting. Just watch for the shoes."

*"Yellow here, Yellow here."*

"Yes, Yellow."

*"Request permission to enter store."*

Blake studies Tippet's screen, split into four windows showing the floors and the outer perimeter of Herriot's. Yellow wants to get inside. The temptation is always to break the perimeter, to jump in and join the hunt. But the value of a picket is precisely in its strict maintenance of position. Break the cordon and you don't stand a chance.

"Permission denied. Hold, please, Yellow."

More static masks the response.

"Van," says Blake, and gets an immediate acknowledgment. "How's your frequency control?"

*"We're fine."* It's a flat Canadian twang.

"Good. Blue, you there?"

Silence, then a lot of traffic noise, horns.

"Blue, come in Blue."

Nothing.

"Yellow team—"

*"Yo."*

"A or B?"

A long pause as the man tries to remember. *"A."* Unconvincing.

"What's your location."

*"Fourth floor. Swimwear."*

Spanakos shakes his head and grimaces. They were supposed to be on picket duty, outside, on Conners.

"And B?"

*"Mike's in outerwear."*

Blake sighs, Spanakos notes B's location.

"Any visual contact with target?"

*"Negative."*

"Red team, A and B, come in please."

Nothing.

"Red, come in."

Nothing. Blake leans toward Spanakos, who tilts the clipboard toward him. Blake grimaces, shakes his head.

"Okay. Blue and Yellow, hold your position. Even if you see the target, hold."

Yellow A's acknowledgment is lost in a squall of static.

"Okay. To all teams. Everyone hold. I want check-ins in two minute intervals, in sequence. Is that clear?"

Their voices are shot through with static. Blake shakes his head and lowers his headset, gives it to Spanakos. "Keep them honest, Ed."

"Captain. A word."

The Racker follows Blake into a corner.

"Matthew."

"I don't like this, Jack." The Racker is standing tall, his face has the smooth, tight-pored look of a man who uses a powder. Blake inventories his objections: poor electronics, no central direction, everything. No woman.

But there's a lot of activity on the speaker.

"Blue's back, Matt."

"Good." Blake speaks over his shoulder. "Keep them where they are." He speaks to the captain. "I'm going to feel more comfortable when she crosses over. Are you assuming she's operational at this point?"

"We have made no assumptions to that effect."

You're a real communicative SOB, thinks Blake as the speaker erupts with squawks and static.

"They've got her, Matt!"

Blake takes the headset.

"Slow down, guys. Who's got her?"

*"Yellow team."*

*"Target's on the escalator down."*

"Who's in front?"

*"Yellow A—no, B, B in front."*

"Where's A?"

Nothing.

"Give us a description, B."

*"Height, five five, hair brown, red-blue suit, plaid, white bag, white scarf."*

"Bag? what kind of bag?"

*"Shopping bag."* Static.

Blake is beginning to recognize the voice signatures. Blue's is very deep, has more than a touch of Canadian flatness. "I'm looking here at the floor plan and she's heading down, you say?"

*"Affirmative."*

Blake is at Tippet's side and he indicates with a rolling motion of his index finger that he is to scroll the screen.

"Third floor, please, Lieutenant."

Tippet brings up the floor plan.

"Guys," says Blake. "Everyone on alert. Yellow B."

*"Yo."*

"Where are you?"

*"Behind target."*

"Good. On the second-floor landing I want Yellow B dropping off to the right—you'll be going into lingerie—and I want Blue, A or B, whoever is closest, to follow her down. There's a ladies' room on the second floor near sleepwear and she might head for it. If she does you take her there, then leave when Red B shows. Is that clear?"

Two voices give affirmatives, though Blake doesn't know who they are. Spanakos is having trouble with his chart. He starts a new page.

"Yellow B, what's happening?"

*"Target's in belts and scarves."*

"What floor?"

*"Mezzanine."*

"Is that first or second?"

*"It's kind of a balcony."*

Tippet doesn't have to be told; he's got it on the screen already. Good. No exits but one, down an escalator and out onto the bottom floor near the information booth. Blake relays this information over the line, hoping the teams get it. It's hit or miss with this radio link.

"Teams. Yellow A get in there behind B. Blue, I want you—I'm looking at the ground floor—to give me position markers as target passes you, is that clear?"

*"Affirmative."*

Over the speakerphone Blue's voice comes in. At the booth, moving toward jewelry, costume, perfumes now, turning left—

"Describe the target, Blue."

*"White bag, plaid suit."*

"Where are you Yellow B?"

*"Right here."*

Where the hell is that?

"Are you on target?"

Affirmative.

Spanakos doesn't like it. These guys are amateurs.

Red's voice, the high one, comes in. *"Cosmetics, Lanvin, moving into Dior, at counter of Dior."*

On the screen, Tippet's put a tracer on the woman, a bright string of dots that follows Jaybird's meandering path through the aisles. Blake likes that and puts his fist with a thumb up in front of the screen, jabbing the air.

*"Target's moving. To the left, through the elevator bank."*

"Blue team, Blue team—bird is flying to you—Blue team . . . come in Blue . . . goddamn it! Van, come in van!"

*"Van here."*

"I've lost contact."

*"The audio is fine."*

"Blue team, come in, Blue team."

Static.

"Guys, fucking wake up!"

Over the squawkers comes something that sounds like *eat my shorts, buddy.*

Tippet's trace is going to the Conner Street exit.

Blake is talking very fast, very pointed. He loves this, being the intense calm in the middle of the storm. He's moving the men into a picket, one team outside, splitting up another to sandwich the revolving doors—no chance of foul-up here. Spanakos has caught up on his clipboard. Blake can visualize the scene: the men dodging the shoppers, sidestepping, twisting and turning through the display racks with their wrist radios held high.

Suddenly there is a new sound, the sound of bells.

"What the hell?!"

"Store alarm," says Spanakos.

And then the speakerphone erupts with voices.

*"Target here, target here!"*

Everyone's shouting. The van puts them through.

*"Tan shoes, tan shoes!"*

*"She's out!"*

Blake is shouting over the cacophony. "Yellow, Yellow! give color of target's shoes! Blue, come in Blue—Blue!"

Tippet's trace is going berserk.

*"She's out! Out on Carlton."*

*"Backup, backup!"*

Blake hates to tell them, but there is no goddamn backup, they're all in the goddamn store.

*"She's a shoplifter! Security's got her."*

Blue comes in: *"Red shoes, she's got red shoes."*

A shoplifter?

Everyone is yelling. Spanakos stops writing. She's out; she's been caught; they're running through the cosmetics department like crazy men. Blake can only wonder what they look like. He knows. They look like assholes.

Blake shakes his head. He takes the headset off. The voices are dying down.

High-pitched Red comes on. He was outside chasing the target.

Jaybird got away in a taxi.

Blake holds the headset to his ear, his mouth.

"Did you get the license of the cab?"

"*Negative.*"

"Okay. Thanks, Red."

He can figure it out, though only in part. Jaybird managed to switch identities. She either had someone working with her, maybe even called a backup in during the chase, or, and this shows what a professional she was, she might have spotted a lookalike in the store—not too difficult if you've been trained—and worked herself to that. She bought or stole the right items, changed in the dressing room, improvised a reverse double then and there. Then she got the Navy boys to tail the decoy. A class act.

But he shares some of the blame. The goddamn shoes. It's his own fault. She was carrying a pair in her bag, and switched.

They should have had a woman.

●

"I'd feel more comfortable, Jack, with our people up there."

"You're going to find us very sensitive on this, Matthew."

"I understand, Captain."

"We would prefer to keep her, then pass her when she crosses over."

"Jack, that's not going to work."

They are off in a corner and the Racker, keeping a hard silence, does not dispute this. Blake is emphatic. The cardinal rule of close tailing is continuity. It's happened too many times, just too goddamn many, Captain, that the target slips between the cracks during the changing of the guard.

"I want to get in," says Blake, "and get my people on her."

The Racker keeps his silence. Navy has operational control. Protocol dictates that the service making first contact calls the shots. But the Naval Investigative Service was not chartered for this type of operation. They need the Bureau's manpower, their field and communications capability.

Spanakos and the other lieutenant have joined them.

"We can mix-team the target," suggests Spanakos.

This provokes some silent thought on everyone's part. Mix-team. Spanakos is suggesting that each team of watchers be composed of Navy and Bureau people. It's not the best of arrangements. The services have different styles, their work patterns don't mesh. Simple things, such as when and where to eat, become sources of friction. Meal allowances are higher in Navy, plus the NIS officers think themselves gourmets, whereas Bureau agents try to save a little money and grab a sandwich in the car. It's just a different culture. Spanakos's idea is left to die of neglect.

"The sooner we get in, Jack, the better. I can have a couple of teams in there tomorrow."

The captain hesitates. Once the Bureau comes in, he loses control, for another of the protocols is that the agency contributing the most resources takes charge, and Blake, now that Donnelly and Guthrie are on board, has the capacity to swamp Navy with street agents and technical backup.

"Matthew. I appreciate your offer of assistance. At this point, however, we would prefer to keep the operation tight."

Blake, in turn, appreciates the captain's position. Indeed, he does—face must be saved, power retained. But Blake, too, has a professional standing to maintain.

"Until she crosses over," says Blake, "Jaybird is yours. Once she comes in, we're prepared to commit. I think we can work pretty well together on this, Jack."

Still, the Racker is reluctant. Dual commands, like mixed teams, never work. Again, as always, it's a question of turf: each agency protects its interests, goes after its own glory, has its unique political considerations. And after what happened with Ellis, Navy is wary; but they need the Bureau's resources.

Blake repeats: "We're ready to commit on this, Jack."

The Racker has already received word about today's meeting, and signifies his acceptance with a nod. As Spanakos and the lieutenant take notes, Blake and the captain work out a preliminary line of communication. They will assign agents and officers of approximately comparable rank and seniority so that for the time being all will perceive themselves to be equals. If the truth be known, neither party quite trusts the other; but Blake believes that their mutual wariness will, in effect, cancel itself out and produce a working relationship.

Also, Blake wants representation in Montreal.

"Observer status, Jack."

After a moment, the Racker agrees. Blake's performance on the chase was impressive.

"Ed."

Spanakos is willing; he spent six months upstate and knows the terrain and most of the supervisors in the Buffalo field office. And he can use the overtime.

Finally, Blake, speaking with professional dispassion, engages the

captain on methodology. Case parametrics, they are called. The captain
is keen on this kind of discussion and he and Blake have a good
exchange. Jaybird's got to have backup, some kind of support. Blake
insists on this, Spanakos seconding; it's inconceivable that she does
not.

"You just don't use singletons on a job like this."

Anything can happen, and often does: delays, missed connections,
illness or accident, a callback or abort arrangement. There has to be a
support team.

Unless, of course, thinks Blake to himself, there isn't.

Spanakos raises another point. From the little they know about Jaybird, and from what he has just seen—this merry Montreal chase—it's
too much of a game. Blake agrees. The Racker is thoughtful. Too much
standard fun, says Spanakos, spook play, and here Blake throws in his
more considerable field experience, pointing out how this play is precisely what a genuine, high-class operation doesn't have.

The lieutenant says, "She's fairly good, we believe. Middle-level
Mossad."

Which means about seven years experience.

"You might recall, sir, she exfiltrated herself through Montreal after
Ellis. She's got her own routes. They're less centralized, you know."

Fine, but Blake's convinced she's got a lot of hidden support.

Assuming she's not alone, and putting aside the question of who is
riding shotgun for her, what Blake wants to see is communications.

"Damn it, Jack. That's one thing they're going to establish right off
the bat regardless of their level. Communications. And I want to know
how the hell they're talking to each other."

"Sir."

Tippet has left his console.

"On communications, sir."

The Racker turns to his lieutenant. "Yes?"

"I think we've hit into their contact."

Blake and Spanakos again exchange looks.

"NSA finally came through, sir, with their telemetric intercepts. It
took some time, because no one knew what to look for, but they got a
few lucky hits on the computer. We've been able to cross-reference the
data with CIA contact reports."

They have a name. All it took was a little luck and a lot of preparation.

You can see it in the young lieutenant's eyes, the cold fire still
burning bright.

"Sir, we believe their communications go through an American contact."

First, Tippet gives background. It's an old field code that has come up
four times in the last three years. That is, four that Tippet can document. He hasn't been able to access anything further back. You catch
only a fraction of the action, so that they can assume that the operative
is more active than this meager record indicates.

"Sir, the data, though circumstantial, is compelling."

Blake and Spanakos wait.

"We believe it's an agent named Anserman."

# CHAPTER 36

T hey won't leave her alone.

Everywhere she turns, they are there. At best she can determine, they are using two teams, one for day, the other for night. And they finally began to use a woman, but only during the day.

This is the first time this has happened. Normally, she would simply have sat quietly in Montreal for three or four days, touring the city, making her contacts, arranging travel. Then she would cross over at any one of a dozen places, and continue south to her rendezvous. It has never been a problem.

Something happened in Europe. She had a premonition in Athens, nothing to put her finger on, just her response to the reaction of a young customs agent. He had looked at her, wanted to smile, then did not. It was a mere thought, not even that, and by takeoff the feeling had disappeared.

Now, as she sits in her motel room, planning an escape from the man and the woman who have been following her since eight this morning, the thought returns. Her controller, the man with the smile, would tell her it was nerves. An occupational hazard, work-related paranoia. But she trusts herself; her instincts have never betrayed her. There was something in the young customs agent's eyes.

But what was it?

Well, they will have to do better on the passports. They take them from anyone. It would be such an easy thing, she thinks now, for someone to track a passport, just as a game, select a passport at random, see where it turns up.

Of course, they have planted a passport!

This Lori Miller, this American college student, must have been an unwitting agent.

The thought is terrifying. She stands. The terror is like another person standing beside her. She must escape. She has procedures, can use them at her discretion. She must get clear. The impulse to act, to run, is irresistible but, instead, she stands very still and forces the terror away, actually pushes the presence toward the door, forces it outside the motel room and into the corridor.

There, it is gone.

She sits again, forces herself to breathe deeply. It has never happened before. Their passport people are too good, would never allow it to happen. It was a lucky break for the Americans. Something in Athens, with that young, grinning customs agent. She will speak to the cover desk when she returns, next month, and they will have to tighten up their procedures.

But she must leave very soon, within the next two days.

She sits, very calm now, and waits for her signal.

# CHAPTER 37

An operation like this, multiple suspects each doing his or her own thing, is very problematical, and Blake needs a couple of dozen agents just for primary surveillance, triple that in backup.

He's got to set up his interfaces with Internal Security in Washington. What Donnelly and Justice fear, above all else, is compromising the case in the postarrest confusion. You don't want evidence thrown out under the exclusionary rule because that is very, very embarrassing. Bureau agents, therefore, won't arrest a goddamn mosquito without first checking in with Justice.

That means Blake's got to arrange radio hookups with Washington, where the lawyers in Internal Security will walk the line agents through the actual arrest. It's complicated, and the agents will also need a thorough briefing from the U.S. attorney's office.

The timing of the arrest will be all-important. You want to catch the perp on the cusp of the crime, perhaps a fraction after, never before. There has already been much discussion as to what shall constitute the irrevocable act; there will be much more.

Lawyers will be picking through the case like monkeys looking for lice, and within a few hours of the arrests, certainly by the morning after, all hell will break loose.

The trick will be to hold Starfield in seclusion as long as possible, work him to the limit. Everyone will want a piece of the man. Navy will insist upon first interrogative rights, but the CIA will be screaming counterintelligence, waving its charter in everyone's face. State will face both ways, as will the House and Senate.

That's okay; the Bureau's role, and Blake's, will be over by then.

But he's got to be there when it happens.

This is his big test, and he's got to get all his forces in synergy. He wants Donnelly throwing his weight behind him, running interference against Navy, opening a path with Justice. He wants Halpern working with Mullady so that they can secure jurisdiction and hold it against the challenge he knows Ricciardi, and maybe even Newcombe, already making angry noises in Washington, will mount.

Murphy has given him assurances on Mullady. The casual criticisms Blake has heard describe Eastern District's U.S. attorney, pejoratively, as predictable, though Blake fails to see that quality as deserving of censure, or its opposite deserving of praise. Predictability, when carried to its poetic extreme, is, arguably, an asset. He has seen Mullady in action, and what you saw is what you got. Good, thinks Blake, no surprises there.

As for the field, a full press court is what the Racker wants, according to Spanakos, who's up in the naval command center in Buffalo waiting for the Girlfriend to do something. Blake has already double-teamed Deere and his boys, waiting while this goddamn assassin installs a new set of french doors in the Greenspans' brownstone in Brooklyn.

●

"What kind of name is Anserman?"

Blake asks this of Halpern as they sit in the lawyer's office. Spanakos is hooked up to the speakerphone on a conference call.

Navy threw the name in their laps.

"Anserman." With his deep voice, Halpern gives it a rich resonance.

Before getting to the obvious, they kick around the possibilities.

Using the Buffalo field office computer facilities, Spanakos has ripped through four or five dozen telephone directories for the northeast, and come up with five listings. It's not a common name. Blake will check them out; you never know when the obvious proves itself.

"Thanks, Ed."

"Dryden's time," offers Halpern.

Blake agrees.

His voice scratchy in the speaker box, Spanakos suggests it might be a notional.

It might. Blake explains. A notional is an agent who doesn't exist except in contact reports, in the air traffic, an agent created for the confusion of it, for play, to get the opposition chasing a chimera, wasting their resources.

A presence conjured out of the air.

They talk to this point, then Blake gets to what he has been thinking all the time, but has saved for last.

"Who do you go to when you have questions?"

Spanakos and Halpern ponder this.

"When you're an agent in the field," Blake hints, "who do you go to?"

Spanakos, playing along, replies, "Your case manager."

"Right. Your controller. You ask him a question, and he gives you, what?"

"An answer," says the box.

Halpern is nodding.

"So let's just put in that unseen *w*."

The silence approves Blake's suggestion.

"The Answerman," says Halpern, finally, his voice even more deep, satisfied.

Spanakos repeats it.

Yes, thinks Blake. The Answerman. The one who knows.

# CHAPTER 38

It is that time of year when Maxwell Harrow feels the coming shadows stretching cold, dark fingers toward him, when the drafts press in, making their way through the window in his tiny office, chilling his thin, dry skin. Sweaters don't help, nor does the little electric heater he has under his desk. The cold fills his bones, makes him shiver. He drinks copious amounts of tea, turns up the fan on the heater, and wraps his legs in blankets.

And he reads his beloved Shakespeare. A few soliloquies, parts of sonnets, one in particular—that time of year when late the song birds sang, the bare, ruined choirs; some such words. Often, he turns to Shakespeare not for solace, but for operational suggestions. For plot. Even as a teenager, when all the other students were moaning about *Julius Caesar* or *Romeo and Juliet,* he loved the plays. Ruthless, bloody, passionate action. And the beautiful way the evil was arranged, full of purpose, full of rushing conviction, surprise and daring, full of blood. And what different kinds of blood there were!

Compare *Macbeth,* for instance, with *Julius Caesar.* When the thane of Cawdor killed, the blood spurted hot and thick and sticky. It could not be washed off; like evil, the stain remained upon one's hand, one's heart, forever. Unlike the blood of Caesar, a clean, flowing fountain of life, wherein Brutus bade the conspirators dip their hands in purification.

Yes, Shakespeare instructed in the ways of death, of power and intrigue, showed his characters in all their open, raw brutality. Murders everywhere, duplicity, cunning, betrayal, and all so glorious, so shimmering with beauty.

Harrow pours himself more tea. He uses the very creamer that the special agent used. Blake was his name. And his assistant, that Greek fellow. He was pleased to have accommodated them.

But now the cold is beginning, and he must be careful. He is no longer the hot-blooded thane, full of youth and ambition, nor the overwrought Hamlet, setting angels to dance on the head of a pin. He is more Lear, wind-wracked, dying, howling defiance into the void.

And the nights are longer now. He must be careful. For he has seen a certain shadow in the failing light, a man, unknown, stalking his poor, frail self.

What was it that old king had said, in his final moments of fury? That, too, was instructive. Lear had raged against the night, his enemies, shouting out to the wind his dark, evil words.

*Then kill, kill, kill, kill, kill, kill!*

# CHAPTER 39

———————————●———————————

**L**et's go over his day."

Blake is making a presentation to a group of agents. Despite Murphy's muscle, he's had to go from squad to squad, begging. No one likes spy cases. Campbell helped him with a few phone calls. Ridiculous, he thinks.

"Morning prayers, evening prayers," Blake tells them.

"What is he, a Muslim? Don't tell me he wants a prayer mat?"

No, a shawl; Blake makes a motion of putting a shroud over his head.

"So what Navy's doing is giving him the shawl for his prayers, then they take it away as soon as he's finished. Security."

No one's taking any chances.

"Now. Reading material," continues Blake. "Prayer books, newspapers, magazines." There is a list and the agents refer to it. Ellis's lawyer negotiated reading rights; they're still working out a deal with Newcombe on writing materials—how many sheets of paper per day, pen or pencil, etc. Of such little things are arguments of great moment made.

"So he's got a rabbi coming in," says one of the agents.

"Yes. Every Saturday."

They talk about religion and life. It's all on tape, but since conversations with clergy are constitutionally privileged, access is denied. The rabbi is an Army chaplain. Ellis wanted a conservative or orthodox one, Navy has only reform.

Letters are censored, of course; both ways.

All his movements are on tape. Twenty-four hours a day.

"They use an infrared camera at night," says an agent.

It's called a perpetual record, and once begun continues forever, because no one wants the responsibility of giving the order to discontinue. Every day some low-level functionary loads the camera and recorder, every evening someone else unloads.

And before long, no one pays it any attention. It's like having nothing, worse than nothing because it engenders a false sense of omniscience.

Blake wants his group of agents to go through the log of Ellis's reading material, pull out the newspapers and magazines and books and catalogs, and start an analysis.

"I want everything reviewed. Larry, you'll coordinate. I want to see if we can pick their communications out of it. They're talking to him, and we want to find out how. Pay attention to the box ads, the crossword puzzles."

The agent makes a note.

Another agent asks, "What about his wife?"

What about her?

"She under watch?"

Blake shakes his head. Again, part of Newcombe's deal. The spy's wife is not surveilled.

They are all silent. Blake knows what they're thinking. Fuck the deal, surveil the shit out of her. That's what Hoover would have done, but today, you can't. Blake is emphatic on this; he doesn't want to be on the receiving end of a rights-violation indictment. They'd have to refinance again, just for the legal fees.

"She's pregnant," says an agent, referring to the file.

"She is," confirms Blake. And adds, just so they all know, "She's dying."

●

"A trap. They're baiting a trap, Matt," Spanakos tells him from Buffalo.

The Racker wants to make it easy for Starfield, is going to make him an offer he can't refuse, and at the same time score a couple of points for Navy. He's been pushing for a transfer of Ellis into Navy custody; Ellis's lawyers have been fighting it, successfully, backed as they are by the CIA. A couple of senators are jumping into the act. There's even been talk, just a leak, of a pardon, a trial balloon from left-behind

Kissingerites within the administration. Fine; Navy is now ready to compromise. The Racker is willing to negotiate a transfer, start a pow-wow over logistics, all the bullshit, drop a few hints to Ellis. Let's take pity on the man, let him spend the last days with his wife.

"Starfield. Deere and the Girlfriend. The Racker wants them all," says Spanakos.

So, a trap, baited with one live spy.

Murphy, in on the conference call, expresses Donnelly's misgivings.

"Matt, look, if we can see the trap, so can the other guy. And you don't walk into an obvious trap."

"No, you don't," agrees Halpern. He's on-line, too, out in his Quogue house, catching the last rays of summer.

"The world is full of obvious traps." Blake's tone is wry. Money traps. Sticky honey traps. "And that doesn't stop anyone."

Murphy chuckles. "Hell, Matt, if people thought like you we'd be out of jobs."

Meaning, wonders Blake, what?

After Murphy hangs up, Spanakos says, "They're not dumb. They know it's a trap."

"They'll walk into it anyway," suggests the attorney.

"On the assumption," puts in Blake, "they have a trap of their own."

A silence. A trap of their own?

"We," replies Spanakos, "are just going to have a better trap."

Halpern is silent.

Blake hopes, prays, that they do.

●

In every operation, there is always the nagging, secret fear that you've missed something. That you've read the opposition incorrectly. That you've gone off on a tangent, such as riding one of the young lawyer's outrushing hypotheses, and that you will soon find yourself in a very cold, dark, and lonely place. Blake is beginning to worry that the Bureau might be outclassed. Halpern's outpouring of metaphysics, the talk about creation and atomic explosions, has left him with a vague disquietude. He doesn't buy into it completely, but his associations have been loosened by the young prosecutor's poetry and he sees himself and his fellow agents as robots caught up in a game of blindman's buff. There's this thing, too, about Newton versus Einstein—one of the world's dichotomies with which Blake has long been teasing himself—about linear versus circular motion.

I am a windup toy, he tells himself, a mass-produced Bureau windup toy that can only go in a straight line, trying to catch someone—Starfield, in this case—running in circles.

That's us in the FBI, an army of dumb goddamn machines.

He doesn't like it.

He's mired in Halpern's formless muck—what did he call it? the data slime—and he's getting a genuine, very much of this world, headache.

●

Spanakos doesn't like it either. He's calling in twice a day, with instructions to catch Blake anytime, anywhere, and the junior agent's reading of the situation is that Navy is stalling.

Of the captain, Spanakos says, "The son of a bitch is using us."

Blake agrees. The Racker needs Blake's street people, the walkers and watchers. He wants them under Navy control. And the helicopter. Murphy says Donnelly has already signed for a chopper. The Racker wants to be in it when it swoops down for the kill. "He hasn't flown for years, Matt. He thinks he's napalming the Vietcong, for Christ's sake."

"Don't let it get to you, Ed."

But it already has. Spanakos is sick and tired of Navy's tight-ass discipline, their secrecy, the Racker's theories. Their military fantasies. He's been listening to the officers.

"Matt, Christ, they're all ex-pilots."

Blake knows the type. They stand in corners moving their hands in complicated patterns, talking about bogey clouds and dogfights.

"What the hell, Matt, is a solo opposing half-Cuban eight?"

Blake hasn't the slightest idea. Some kind of an aerial maneuver?

That's the sort of crap Spanakos's been listening to.

They want operational control, the agent says. And the Racker is going to get it by controlling field communications. They're not giving Spanakos access to their radio codes so that he has to go to Tippet, hat in hand, to find out what the hell is going on.

"Hey." Spanakos is venting. "No fucking way, José."

Before they sign off, Blake brings his agent down a little, but only a little. He wants him angry and alert, and ready to fight.

From Halpern, Blake has learned of the captain's legal strategy. Navy will insist, at first, that Starfield is not, per se, an espionage arrest. Rather, it's a simple, straightforward criminal conspiracy, with possible foreign agent registration overtones. On that basis they will argue that the various guidelines pertinent to spy cases simply do not apply. Of course, no one will take that seriously, but Navy is hoping to gain some maneuvering room. They will need to marshal the various congressional, administrative, and journalistic forces to fend off the massive attack they know will come from a certain quarter. Navy will stall, then hit the opposition hard with a solid barrage of leaks and revelations. With a little extra time, and a handful of Mossad operatives in chains, they will triumph.

But Blake is wary. There's too obvious a game being played.

The Racker is pulling a Starfield. He's feeding me just enough, through Tippet and Halpern, to keep me coming back. The bastard is working his own little counterexplosion, that just might blow up in all our faces. Navy wants our help, the Bureau's means, but to what ends? Blake had talked to Campbell on this point some time ago, and the Irishman's reaction was unsympathetic. Matt, he had said, you're going intellectual on us. This was Campbell's cautionary against introducing too much complexity.

"Just cover your ass, Matty."

And stick with the facts.

And, surely, Tippet had many facts. He gave them to Halpern, who threw them about like pearls before the Bureau swine. Facts—evidentiary things that eager young men such as Halpern have dug up, and scrubbed and polished, and arranged in proper order, bright and shining objects holding the happy glimmer of truth.

But to Blake, even though he values them highly, facts are dirty things, defining dirt in its essential purity of meaning. Platonic dirt, if you will. Dirt being that which is not pertinent. Nor is order, thinks Blake, referring back to the confusions of this case, nor is order that simple.

But Blake likes the turn of his thoughts. Dirt. It's a good working definition—dirt is that which does not belong. Thus, dirt becomes anything you cannot use. Love, food, sex—if you don't want it, it has no value. And that was the difficulty he had with Ellis, with Harrow. All the beautiful and valuable things he might offer were dirt.

And that's what we're getting from Starfield. From the Mossad. They're throwing dirt at us, only we think we're getting precious jewels.

# CHAPTER 40

**M**att, are you wearing your gun again?"

His wife is at the bottom of the living-room steps, his shoulder harness in hand. He's at the top, about to wash up for supper. She holds it like an item of dirty underwear, which, in a way, it is.

Blake apologizes. He's violated a long-standing agreement. Coming into the house with many things on his mind, he had hung it over one of the ladderback chairs in the dining room. Really, he is sorry. He comes down the steps and takes the contraption from his wife's hand, but is at a momentary loss where to put it.

"It's new, isn't it?"

He switched last year, he tells her, so it's not so new. She's never seen it, which shows how unimportant the gun really is to him.

"New rules, honey." He's wrapping the straps around the holster. "Weber wants to make his presence felt."

Weber is the new assistant director at the New York office.

Blake works exasperation into his voice as he opens the basement door. "We're going by the book for a while."

That will cover his target practice sessions, should that issue arise.

Downstairs, he puts the Sig on top of his attaché case, then returns upstairs to the dining room where his daughter is bent over the coffee table, impatiently going through two piles of magazines. His wife is at the table, shows him the invitation responses. The guest list is typed.

Acceptances are circled in green, declines have crosses next to them, in red. Maureen is muttering.

"The Shapiros aren't coming?"

Shapiro is an attorney with Southern District, deputy chief, criminal. He and Blake had worked a series of frauds a couple of years ago. Blake and his wife had gone to the Shapiro boy's bar mitzvah six months ago. There are a few other X marks, the Silversteins and the Chaykins. Maureen has stomped off to the den, where Blake can see her searching the bookshelves.

"It's a holiday weekend," Blake says. "Columbus Day. A lot of people are away."

They chose the date just because it was a long weekend, the theory being that traveling for their out-of-town guests might be easier. And because—Blake knows this because he had overheard the telephone talk between his wife and Margaret—because of the dictates of Maggie's menstrual cycle. No matter that she and Jerry were living together, they wanted to have a proper honeymoon.

"It's a Jewish holiday."

His wife looks up at him.

"Yom Kippur," says Blake, pointing to the calendar. The holiday is clearly marked in small print. They just didn't pay it any attention.

Maureen is back in the dining room, her hands on her hips, frowning.

"Has anyone seen my Camus?"

"No, Maureen, we haven't."

"Mom, I'm asking Dad."

"You haven't finished your paper?"

"Dad, I'm working on it."

"When's it due?"

"Thursday."

"When do you have your final?"

"Thursday."

His wife speaks. "She's been looking for the book for the last two days." Which means she hasn't worked on the paper for the last two weeks. "I suggested," says his wife, "that she buy another one—"

"Mom, I made a lot of notes in the margins."

"If you'd pay more attention to your things this wouldn't happen."

"Yes, Mother." Maureen stomps off to the kitchen, where she can be heard flinging magazines aside.

"I'm going to change," says Blake.

●

In the kitchen, Maureen's papers are all over the table. Two books are open, one facedown, the other weighted open by the heavy, silver carving fork. There is a scattering of dark Oreo crumbs on the plasticized tablecloth. His wife is in the dining room, Maureen has disappeared into her own room.

From the brown paper bag he takes out the Camus and aligns it just so, next to the facedown book. Then, for effect, for balance, for the psychic-esthetic point of it, he places her pen across the cover, bisecting the circle that frames the man's face.

Then he goes down to his basement office.

●

In bed later, Blake and his wife talk about the guest list. "It's a disappointment," he says, referring to the pattern of declinations. He reaches over and pats her thigh through the covers. Most of them were work-related invitations. Though he considers their social circle rather wide and eclectic, they are friendly with only one or two non-Christian couples. It sounds funny to hear it in his thoughts: non-Christian. We associate mostly with fellow gentiles, and are not intimate with those of the Jewish faith. No one he knows, of any denomination, is truly practicing, though the Jews on their autumnal holidays, and the Hasids, always, do stand out in an archaic relief. There was a vague unease to those days, a heavier, darker mystery to them. Many of the prosecutors and the lawyers and the judges stayed out, so that court business came to a standstill; for those few days the sidewalks of downtown Manhattan became suddenly passable, the coffee shops half empty, traffic tolerable.

He arranges himself under the sheets. His wife sighs, puts down her book across her thighs. Given their almost thirty years of connubial association, he believes this to be a signal, and his hand, lingering still upon her leg where he had given her a consoling squeeze, is in perfect position for a gambit. He presses, calculating the squeeze to a delicate caress in place.

Without having to look, he knows he has read the signal correctly. He watches the sheet rise in a traveling wave as beneath it his wife's hand reaches his thigh.

There. With the ball of her thumb she is making him erect.

His hand maintains its pressure, moving up, stopping. When was the last time—about a week ago? Friday morning? No, that was the time before last. The last time—well, whenever.

He now strokes her upper leg, from her knee up, fingers following the curve under the sheet.

She is moving the book to her night table.

He has his hand under her breast when they freeze; Maureen is on the steps.

"We have to be quiet," his wife whispers.

"We always are," he replies.

Maureen passes in the hallway, her footfalls, thinks Blake, more thoughtful than usual. His wife is using her thumb again. Blake smooths his hand up to her breast, palms her nipple, feels it erupt. He's on his side, his erection firm in his wife's hand. He moves his mouth to where the nipple is pushing against her thin summer gown and carefully, wetly, covers it with his lips. Maureen's door closes. They experience a minor confusion as Blake begins a rollover mount just as his wife turns her backside to him. She takes his hand and places it on her belly, right above her pudenda.

"A little rubbing first," she says.

# CHAPTER 41

F or an old man, thinks Campbell, Harrow gets around.

Tonight, for instance, Campbell is following the old codger from his office in midtown to another building on the west side, from which, after half an hour, Harrow emerges and hails a cab with his upraised cane and heads south.

Campbell, in his company car, takes off after. It is an easy tail, Seventh Avenue all the way until they get below Fourteenth. There the traffic suddenly thickens. It is the usual Village congestion compounded by the closing of Bleecker Street for the annual Feast of Saint Anthony.

At one point, Campbell inches his vehicle alongside Harrow's cab. He looks into the rear compartment. The old man sits there, gazing straight ahead. The handle of his cane is visible just above the window line. They are separated by not more than three feet and two panes of glass. The old man's face is wrinkled, his mouth slack; there seems to be a tremor to his head. Just as Harrow turns to the right the cab pulls away and Campbell, letting it distance itself by three car lengths, follows it as Seventh Avenue becomes Varick.

They cross Canal, slowing at the turnoff for the Holland Tunnel, head south into the Financial District, just below Bureau headquarters. Campbell knows the streets well, and the timing of the lights, and is able to give the old man an extra half block. As Harrow continues straight, Campbell turns east toward Broadway, then south again, adds a few more quick turns, first on Exchange Place, then on William, going the wrong way, crosses the next street, and is able to spot the cab sitting, its lights doused, on Wall.

Passing without pause, Campbell overshoots, turns on Hanover Street, and pulls in.

It is almost ten o'clock. There will be some back-office activity through the night as the paperworkers clean up the day's trading, but for the most part the streets are deserted, the buildings shut.

Campbell gets out of the car, walks to the corner.

The cab's left wheels are on the sidewalk.

Campbell passes, walking with purpose.

The driver sits behind the wheel, his light on, reading the newspaper.

Campbell reaches the corner and ducks into a doorway.

He makes a notation in his watch book, time and place, then returns to his car.

He will call his wife, soon; then stay on the hunt.

Unless the old man's broker keeps some very odd hours, Harrow is making one of his diabolical connections.

# CHAPTER 42

———————•———————

**J**ust before Blake left for the day, Spanakos called in. Jaybird was snug in her nest, the Navy hawks keeping her in sight. The Buffalo field office was on alert but the Racker, playing cute, hadn't called in the Bureau. Spanakos wanted to make some noise, and Blake concurred. But only noise, Ed; we don't want to activate our people too soon. They agreed to talk later that evening.

Now, cutting in and out of the traffic, Blake conducts a review of his case.

From Murphy, he has heard that the Mounties, who always get their man, except when they don't, were showing increasing nervousness about the joint operation. They're going along with Operation Nova as a gesture of goodwill, but anything suggesting a tie-in to the CIA gives them the political jitters. It's making Blake nervous too. Too much potential for internal sabotage, especially from the Department of State, which would leak the operation in order to blow it. Which is, Blake knows, one of the options Donnelly is keeping open.

And Blake, of sufficient deviousness, is prepared to exercise it himself: when you get too far out on a limb the only recourse is to take down the entire tree. He has to slow for the merge at the Grand Central Parkway; goddamn drivers, you'd think a license required an IQ of at least 90, but they can never get the alternate feed right.

He's conferred with the SAC—the special agent in charge—in the Buffalo FO, and Blake's gut reading of the field situation, contrary to the

SAC's evaluation, is not encouraging. In spite of Navy's certainty, in spite of Halpern's facile presentations about reality and paradox and fallacy, in spite of Spanakos's cautious enthusiasm, he remains skeptical.

After a while a proper case, a good case, has a definite inevitability. By now there should have developed an unassailable line to Starfield's actions, allowing Blake to set up his own counteraction. It's quite dramatic—but he's got to do some fancy pedal work around this woman in a white Volvo, who can't make up her mind about moving into his lane—a quick toot of his horn convinces her not to. Quite dramatic, he was thinking. Especially the last phase, just before the arrest, when the teams are in place and the target is doing exactly what he should be doing, and you are responding precisely, accordingly, and the helicopter is hovering, ready to swoop down. Then it's like the last act of a Greek tragedy: you've made your bed and now you are going to lie in it, forever.

He has yet to sense this with Starfield. Either the man and his team, assuming there is a team, don't have a plan, a line, or else they are doing something quite extraordinary. In all his years in Banking and Fraud he's never seen anything quite like it. But that is a trap, he tells himself, of the sort to which Halpern has sensitized him. Praises to the boy, if only for that. By Bureau definition, those things that you do not know of, do not exist. The AUSA had argued this with Campbell some time ago. The older agent had insisted that he had never come across a conspiracy which the Bureau couldn't break. There's always at least one conspirator who cracks. Violence, sex, money, ego, there's always a way to apply pressure—this is one of the Bureau's maxims. The uncrackable conspiracy does not exist. To which the lawyer had agreed, pointing out that the Irishman's argument fulfills its own premise—he had used a Latin term—since the only conspiracies you do crack are those you know about. What about, he asked with a smile, those you know nothing of?

And Campbell had riposted with a magnificent glare.

Driving the choking lanes of the Long Island Expressway, this preys upon Blake, the intimation of things unknowable. He reminds himself that these are mere speculations, teasers of the sort that he must avoid. He reminds himself, too, that the rules are different in spy cases. As he well knows. This isn't reality, this is counterintelligence. It's a netherworld peopled with men like Harrow, theorists with bloody knives. Starfield learned his craft from them, through his uncle, who worked under the name of Fielding. Little Boy Blue, come blow your horn.

As Blake must do now, warning off that same woman in the white Volvo.

And there are additional aggravations. He doesn't care for the code names.

Operation Nova. Too obvious. The Racker, like the overqualified naval officer he is, goes in for classical, Latinate nomenclature. Dr. Starfield is Pegasus—winged horse, from Phillip, which is Greek for "lover of horses," though in his own mind Blake thinks of the man as Solarus, whose sound, he thinks, meshes better with its sense.

Blake has been assigned Polaris, in recognition, one assumes, of what the captain regards as his steadfast nature.

Halpern is Icarus, the boy who flew too near the sun and melted the wax that held the feathers to his arms. The lawyer didn't like it, but the captain already had all the names approved by the code-assignment division of NSA. Tippet is Hermes. Messenger of the gods; it fits.

For himself, the Racker took Orion. The hunter, he of the strung bow.

And other assorted names of stars and constellations with ancient mythological connotations.

Blake was piqued; it's a very controlling maneuver, giving out names.

Traffic has slowed again: the left lane closes in five hundred feet. He taps his brakes, then hits them hard. He experiences a moment of profound, intense disquietude.

And Maureen. Well, her paper is almost done, her course is over. In two weeks she will be leaving for Oberlin, where she will be out of harm's way. He has yet to confront her publicly with his knowledge; how can she not know? Her braggadocio does not fool him and, he surmises, is not meant to. Her ironies, her sarcasms, the quiet, almost shy, aggressiveness she displays toward men, all bespeak a sensibility very much in opposition to itself.

It's all this, and more. The higher mortgage, the increased taxes, the goddamn assessment. And it's annual appraisal time, too. Has Blake missed, met, or exceeded job objectives? What is his promotability quotient? And now he's got to work around this idiot who's allowed his pickup truck to break down in the middle lane. Hood up, radiator steaming, looks like a water pump. And no one even offers to push the poor slob to the shoulder.

Halpern's to blame. That horny, young, eager bastard. The attorney sought me out and begged and cajoled and maneuvered until I agreed to take on Starfield. Bored with general crimes, tired of working with accountants poring over ledgers, I got involved with crisp military types, intellectual officers. Led me on with clever talk. No substance, all spun theory, a fine web of conjecture. For country, for fame; for promotion. Donnelly is eager too, angling for a Presidential Rank Award—two Bureau administrators in Washington got five thousand dollars each for Ellis. But there's no line yet to Starfield, no apparent plan. There's still a piece missing. That's what's making Blake anxious. The lack of something timely and specific, something he can put on a piece of paper and send up in triplicate.

Passing the stalled vehicle—it's the poor slob's radiator—Blake accelerates into the open road. He wants confirmation, wants to see a known and unique association of men and women engaged in a sequence of directed, purposeful, and related acts in furtherance of a specific goal, to be achieved within a definite period of time. The manual's definition of an operation.

Failing that, he wants an indication that this isn't a trap into which he and the Bureau are meant to fall, that Halpern and Tippet and the captain are not the devil's helpers, and that this is not all one sadistic joke engineered by some godforsaken bastard like Harrow, of which they shall all become the butt.

Enough. These counterintelligence cases induce confusion. Mature beyond his years, Halpern argued wisely. They're doing it on purpose. Blake accelerates past a step van trying to get into his private left lane. I will play my strong suits, to wit: intelligence, good humor, perseverance, respect for facts and details, and an appreciation for the metaphors of existence. I shall take the middle ground, hold it against either side, tread lightly and come out safely through the thicket of doubt and mishap.

But Lord—he smiles at the supplication he is about to offer—dear Lord of Spies who gave safe passage through the land of Goshen to Joshua and Caleb—dear Lord, give thy poor servant Matthew a sign, and remove Thou his misgivings.

But the only sign Blake sees warns CONSTRUCTION AHEAD, which, together with another stalled vehicle in the right lane, removes any doubts he might have had that the universe was benignly indifferent to the fate of drivers on the Long Island Expressway. He arrives home very late, and hungry.

In the kitchen, he finds Maureen sitting very quietly. She's putting the finishing touches on her paper. *The Stranger* is open, upside down.

He stands at the sink, facing his daughter's back, her tousled mane of red, sun-shot hair.

"Good," she says in response to his question as to how it's going.

He goes around the table and faces her. Under her eyes her skin is peeling with a flaky translucence, and the hectic red on her cheek gives her a feral, quite exotic look.

"What are you writing?"

She doesn't want to talk, but Blake presses, as is his right. She'd rather be in the arms of a young man than in this dreariness of books, stood over by a father who's fretting over her happiness and safety. He wants to talk to her about life and love before, like Margaret, she leaves forever.

He repeats the question.

"The usual, Dad. Existentialism and how it relates to its time. You know, World War Two."

"Yes, good."

"Yeah. Things like the indifference of the universe—"

"Ah!"

"—contrasted with the cruelty of men to each other."

Very good, he thinks.

"The bare existence of things," she goes on, reading now from a piece of paper. "Horrible, mysterious, and fascinating."

"Excellent."

There's more: "The world was sick with horrors, at war with itself, and in the grip of a harsh theology of sin and retribution." She looks up at her father.

Yes, all these things.

"There are no simple answers," he says.

Maureen writes.

"France during the war, right. The Vichy government and the Nazi sympathizers." These are important points, and he wants to be certain she will include them. "The confusion of loyalties, Maureen. The complexity of morality. It's never simple."

"Yes, Dad."

"So you think you have a handle on it?"

"Yeah, Dad, I have a handle on it."

"Good." He wants to talk about other things, though he has no specific topic in mind; something that will start them off on a long conversation, even an argument. Maybe something about the lawyer, about growing up. Something with emotion.

She beats him to the draw.

"Dad," she begins.

He waits.

"Dad, are you and Mom having money problems?"

"Well, no. I'd say concerns, but not problems."

"I was wondering, maybe I should take a leave of absence for the semester, or get a job."

"Oh no. Honey." He gives her a smile. "As you can imagine, this is just a difficult period."

"I could be a waitress in the dining hall."

He smiles again, assures her that they have enough for what they need, repeats that this is just a difficult period.

"Well, don't worry, Dad. I'm not going to get married for a long time."

His wife is coming in at the door.

Maureen's look, he tells himself as he goes to help her with the groceries, reminds him of a child; the world is a hard place.

It reminds him, again, of the eyes of Tippet.

# CHAPTER 43

─────────●─────────

**A**nd now, as the field manual exhorts, Blake waits.

Everything shall happen, many of their own accord.

The guest list is complete, and the rehearsal and its dinner are scheduled for that Friday of the wedding weekend; Jerry's parents are coming in two days earlier, for a little socializing. Maureen has done well in summer school and has left for Oberlin, thus putting a natural end to her involvement with Halpern.

Blake has decided to rent, rather than buy, a tuxedo.

He must wait, too, for a transfer and upgrade. A lot of things are on hold, asserts Murphy.

Blake understands. The entire world is on hold. He knows Starfield is waiting, too. As are Deere, and Jaybird. And the Racker, Orion, hovers in the sky, also waiting.

Halpern, too, is waiting, for a change. Blake knows he's been interviewing. Rumor has it he's landed a job at Cohen Winks Kessler and Stone, one of the premier firms.

Returning by train to Eastmere, in the ruddy evenings of early autumn, Blake has come to see that all things achieve a consummation of sorts. The Bureau thrives, his daughters mate, life is full of blind purpose. The cold nip at twilight puts an end to the mosquitoes and flies, so that the bug lights no longer buzz in the night. The patchy spots in the lawn need seeding, and he must get the oil changed in the station wagon. All things in their season, fertilizer and antifreeze. It's been an educational summer. An existential interlude, a season of expectation. One must define these terms, though at this time in his life, this curious, middle age of time, it seems all the definitions are up for grabs.

●

They sit at the kitchen table. Blake wants a review, and he puts his wife through a Q & A.

"When is Maureen coming home?"

"Friday afternoon."

"Is she flying or getting a ride?"

"Standby, Matt."

"The last thing we need is to have to go dashing out to the airport in Friday traffic."

"Matt, she'll get home on her own."

She will; she's a big girl. He's on edge.

"Jerry's parents," he asks.

"Thursday night."

"What time?"

"Seven twenty-five. We pick them up at the airport, bring them home for a drink. We have a conversation. We drive them to their hotel in Garden City. Traffic is light."

His wife is being amusing.

Now, Friday: the rehearsal at six, in the hall. Figure about an hour. Then dinner at the hotel. Seven-thirty to nine. Jerry's arranged it.

On Saturday, a lot happens.

"Tell me."

There are many items. Fittings for the gowns, tuxedos, Jerry's parents for lunch. The caterer will need a final count. In the afternoon Maureen throws the shower. Bachelor party for the groom Saturday night.

"Bachelor party?"

"The men are going bowling."

"Okay," says Blake.

Now, Sunday.

His wife reads the agenda. Late brunch of cold chicken and champagne for members of the wedding, keeping them fueled for the ceremony and into the afternoon reception. Dressing and makeup. Hair. The photographers. Flowers. The bathrooms are going to be on strict rotation and Blake is down for the early morning, shower and shave, at seven.

"Just a second. I'm going to have to shave in the afternoon then."
On her list his wife marks a little asterisk.

He has an agenda of his own. He will have to go down to Washington, Newcombe's territory, if just to show the New York colors. For as sure as Blake is sitting here listening to his wife inventory the ten dishes in the hot smorgasbord, he knows that if he's not on site, in Washington, he is going to lose the case. Spanakos and his other agents don't have the rank to withstand the onslaught from the Baltimore and Washington field offices, especially with the high-powered management in headquarters.

He knows his opposition there: Robert Glynn, that overweight agent with whom he teamed on the mock arrest for the assessment. Word had just come down the other week that Glynn had been promoted to special agent in charge of the Baltimore FO. Blake was stunned. The man was not higher-management material. Someone in his corner had pushed like the goddamn devil. Would that Donnelly would do the same. Well, New York was tougher. In addition to Glynn, Newcombe will be protecting his Ellis prerogatives, and will try to absorb Starfield into the prior case.

He doesn't trust Navy; the Racker will sleep with anyone.

Moreover, he's not confident of Halpern's ability to hold jurisdiction. Walsh and Mullady, at Eastern, are going to have to pull some very long-distance strings. Donnelly will have to fight, which he won't do unless he's cornered, which is what Blake, in his intense, devious manner, has been trying to arrange all this time. He briefly tends to his wife, who is talking about the caterer. They have to give him a check for five thousand dollars this weekend.

And when it happens, when Navy has laid the trap and the Ellis bait is taken, Blake will have to move fast. There's no substitute for being there. The paperwork will be crucial. Affidavits have to be signed, warrants obtained and executed. He has to be in on the radio hookup. Starfield will move fast; it's going to be a play-by-play operation in which every second will count.

His wife is talking about the processional, but he doesn't hear. He has to get his people in on the actual arrest, do some cuffing, begin the interrogation; in short, muscle the opposition. Newcombe's going to charge in like a bull. Glynn, all 250 pounds of him, will throw his weight around. It's the wrong time. If the case breaks on that weekend, he doesn't know what he'll do. Correction, he does: he's going to be at his daughter's wedding on Sunday. The other events, the rehearsal, the dinner, the goddamn bowling, and the cold chicken brunch, those can be worked around. But for the nuptials themselves, there are no substitutions allowed.

●

So, on his case outline sheet, what does he have?

He has one identified pro, Albert Deere, Hirsh, Zvi, whatever he wants to be called, who's putting up Sheetrock in Brooklyn.

He has Deere's helpers, the best young musclemen money can buy.

And the Girlfriend, Jaybird, a Mossad regular, courier and forger.

And assorted backup and technical teams, transport people, radio players, spotters.

And an unknown voice, their communications nexus, this Anserman.

And finally, he has Starfield. A half-mad physical biologist, an existential wreck of a Jew preparing to pluck his Daniel from the fiery furnace of Navy's wrath.

*Little Boy Blue, come blow your horn.*

Starfield's call signal, heard once before, in Brussels.

The ancient ram's horn that sounded over the mountains, calling the fierce Hebrew tribes to battle.

# CHAPTER 44

A case will always break, according to Bureau wisdom, at the moment calculated to cause the most inconvenience for the greatest number of agents; for Blake, about to embark upon the most important, dramatic, and expensive weekend of his family's life to date, the onset of the crisis in Operation Nova begins at the worst possible time.

It is Thursday afternoon, a chilly, cloudy day. He's in a Bureau car, has just passed the Elmhurst tanks with only a slight delay, when his beeper squawks out. It's 5:07 exactly. Ordinarily, he'd be at his desk at 26 Federal Plaza, but he's left early to get a jump on the traffic so he can get home, wash up, and rush out with his wife to the airport for Jerry's parents.

It looks like clear sailing ahead, so he decides to ignore the piping of the little box. At Exit 32 the beeper goes off again, and for a few moments he debates the possibility of pulling off the road and finding a phone, but decides not to. Traffic is thickening, but moving; in ten minutes he will be home.

Where his wife greets him at the door and hands him a note.

For a moment he is confused. She's written an Irish name, O'Ryan. Shit, thinks Blake.

Blake looks at his watch with a gesture that means he has to go downstairs. "Half an hour," he tells her.

●

On the phone, there is some delay over the password. Blake thought it was *stingray,* but that was yesterday's.

The officer waits.

Blake wracks his brain. Spanakos had told it to him this morning. "Nimrod."

Correct.

He adds, "Polaris calling for Orion."

He waits. The Racker being unavailable, another officer finally comes on. He speaks in code. Naval ornithologists in Washington have been watching an interesting specimen, the black-crested, eastern jaybird. Blake writes down the particulars—time, location, description—in his case log.

He wishes to speak to Spanakos—what's his code designation? That's right, Ajax—but is told he is in the field.

Blake hangs up.

Halpern must be alerted. The case may be breaking. He wants Spanakos's input. He has to remember everyone's code names. He works the phone; Halpern's not in. The switchboard has no idea where he is. The season has long been over at Quogue. He might have got the word and be in transit, he might not.

Upstairs, his wife traverses the living room in slip and bra. Blake asks her where their younger daughter might be. His wife doesn't know. She's due in this afternoon, isn't she? She is. Has she called from the airport or given any indication of her whereabouts? She has not.

He returns to the basement, where his phone is ringing.

It's the Racker.

"Matthew, the stag is running," he informs Blake without preamble. There is a hard, cold timbre in his voice.

Deere has left from a location in Brooklyn with two vans; the two assistants in one, Deere solo in the other. His blue, the other gray.

The captain will not give out operational particulars. The phones are not secure. Blake understands.

He does tell him, however, that Jaybird has been on the wing for three days.

"Three days! Damnit, Jack! Why the hell wasn't I told?"

The captain ignores this. She was last seen entering a Georgetown residence, occupant under the name Alice Moore. NCFO. No current file on.

"They would pick this weekend, wouldn't they?"

"Indeed, they would, Matthew." There is no pity in him, no sympathy of any kind, nothing in his voice that Blake can identify as human.

They hang up.

Blake tries Halpern again, at home, but gets his machine.

He's briefly paralyzed. He's got to orient himself, yet can't. He's got too many things on his mind, everything peripheral; he's paying the price of the generalist, of being too complete a human being. Jerry's parents will be landing in half an hour, the traffic is going to be hell. He should be in Washington, supporting Spanakos against those Navy types.

The Racker was calling code Blue Three, the signal for operational standby, and that means everyone—Blake, Spanakos, every agent, Navy and Bureau, Justice, all the legal people—comes on-line.

"The balloon's up, Matthew," the Racker had said. Another D-day for Navy, guts and glory.

His wife thumps hard on the kitchen floor. He hates that peremptory summons, and she knows it. He shouts up that he needs a minute.

Campbell; he's got to get to Campbell, from whom he has not heard the last three weeks, except for one quick telephone report: tailing Harrow.

The stag is running.

He sees Deere in his blue van, pulls photographs from his file. The round-shouldered carpenter-killer is driving down the New Jersey Turnpike to Washington. Navy has a small spotter plane, a van, and two cars for the tail. The vehicles will trade back and forth, a standard technique, the plane cruising high in the two o'clock position, to the rear, out of sight of the driver.

Donnelly has to be alerted.

Again, his wife stomps on the floor.

"A minute!"

Shifting his imagination from Deere to the Girlfriend, Blake sees her somewhere in Georgetown, sitting on a sofa in a friend's house. Jaybird. Her file. A dark, intense woman, a Mossad operative. She sits at a terminal in her friend's house, tied into a radio network that links her with Deere, with Starfield.

With the Answerman.

He assumes Navy has already tapped the Georgetown house. He should call Spanakos and double-check. What wavelength is Navy using for their own communications? Spanakos will wangle it out of them.

"Matt!"

"Coming!" he shouts through the floorboards, but does not move.

Try as he might, he cannot conjure Starfield. Does the man actually exist? In a fit of dislocation, he takes himself back to that afternoon in the Mitzvah Mobile, the soft, greasy leather being wound about his naked arm, the prayer shawl like a shroud—

"Matt."

His wife has opened the basement door and stands at the top of the stairs. Her voice is as cold as the Racker's. "We have to go."

He is tense and laconic, concentrating on the traffic and making a supreme effort to call forth from his well-stocked inventory the persona of the relaxed and cheerful host. They make better time than he thinks possible, and pull up to La Guardia's arrivals ramp only five minutes late.

"Where's Piedmont?"

"In the middle."

He leans forward with both hands on the wheel. There's a two-lane squeeze just ahead. Goddamn taxis think they own the airport. Giving no quarter, he places himself in the middle of a dispute with a long limbo and a big yellow cab. They play a three-horn game of dare-me, then Blake shoots forward, brakes hard, and cuts off the limo.

"There they are! There!"

He doesn't see them but takes her word for it, fights his way to the curb. He still doesn't see them.

"There, Matt—there!"

The tall man with the madras blazer, the equally tall woman in the mauvish traveling suit. They search the sea of vehicles, poor lost souls.

They spot his wife. Smiles and waves.

Blake pulls over, steps out. Everyone shakes hands. Blake kisses Jerry's mother on her cool, midwestern cheek. Herbert kisses Blake's wife. The air smells ghastly and the traffic is crazy and the roar overhead is deafening. Good flight? They have to shout. Fine, just fine! While the men load the luggage the women get in the rear. When they get home he mixes drinks and once everyone seems safely settled and Blake has contributed ten minutes of good-humored and very intense chitchat, he makes his excuses and slips downstairs.

He's on the phone for an hour and a half, calling his people, briefing them, getting the latest from Spanakos.

He can't reach Campbell. He'll call him later at home.

Halpern is not to be found.

When he comes up the house is empty. He assumes his wife has taken Jerry's parents to their hotel, and eventually finds a note to that effect on the kitchen table. Blake goes outside and stands on the edge of the grass and looks up into the cooling autumn sky. He finds the dippers, very dim, lines up the stars. Polaris is twinkling away.

Their kitchen phone is ringing.

It's Spanakos, on schedule.

They're waiting for the Girlfriend to do something.

The other van, the gray one that left an hour before Deere?

Yeah?

"They followed it over the Delaware Memorial Bridge, took it into Alexandria, and then lost it on the Beltway. Assholes, Matt."

Blake can only shake his head into the phone.

"They expect to pick it up when they make contact with the Stag. No radio from either van."

Spanakos is getting the fever, Blake can tell. He himself is closer to getting an operational feel, but it's not strong enough, not yet. Navy is ready: Ellis is going to be moved. The Racker has made all appropriate arrangements. Spankos wants the damn thing to happen; he's going on vacation on Sunday, to Block Island, so he's hoping it'll be over by Saturday night.

Blake cautions Spanakos on diversionary tactics; they've gone over this with Navy.

As per his operation in Brussels, Starfield will feint in some way, set up a diversion.

You will think it is the real thing, but it will not be.

"Ed, Starfield is going to move very fast."

They review the Bureau's contingency coverage.

Spanakos is prepared.

"Has Halpern checked in?" Blake should use the code names, but has forgotten the lawyer's.

"Not yet."

He looks at his desk clock. It's a few minutes after nine. He has time to make the last Washington shuttle. "Ed, I'm coming down."

●

As for Maureen, he hasn't told his wife, but he called Oberlin yesterday to tell his daughter that she might as well take a regularly scheduled flight, forget standby, it's not that much cheaper.

Her roommate told him she had left the day before.

The roommate, wondering if she had given something away, became nervous.

Blake wished her a pleasant weekend.

He is keeping this tidbit to himself, as well as the printout of the telephone activity on the lawyer's home line. It's called a pen register, and one of his fellow agents in the New York office was kind enough to obtain it. Just a professional favor between friends. Interesting, the pattern of calls between Oberlin, Ohio, and Remsen Street, Brooklyn.

# CHAPTER 45

―――――――●―――――――

**H**oused in one of Navy's elegant properties, the Racker's command center is a twilight zone of muted light and cold damp air. A row of phones rests on a long table, one of them the captain's own red line to a distant, unspecified location. Tippet is on his computer taking the call sheets and feeding them into the machine's memory. For the permanent record, thinks Blake. For the training tapes they will show to their officers and agents.

Spanakos, relieved to see him, gives a status report. They found the second van. It's parked in a motel lot outside Alexandria, a Marriott. They've got the Stag's assistants under watch, code names Castor and Pollux, wouldn't you know it, room 1411.

As for Deere, he's across the river, holed up in what Navy believes to be an Israeli safe house, its owner a vice president of Agritech, a company that produces, reads Spanakos from his clipboard, *root-vectored, slow-release particles of mircronutrients.* Fucking fertilizer, Matt. They do a lot of business with the Israelis.

Spanakos tells him how the captain, who has now arrived and is talking with Tippet, had flown the Piper on the last leg of the Stag's run. Also, they've got Wright from Internal Security on standby. Warrants are being processed for arrest, for searches of the vans, for the Georgetown safe house.

"Jaybird?" asks Blake.

"She's down, Matt."

Meaning, preparing to come up.

There's a feel to everything now, a definite feel of impending action. Spanakos has it, Blake is beginning to get it. The captain is standing hard-jawed and erect, his red phone pressed to his face.

"Jack," says Blake when the officer joins them.

"Matthew."

Blake and the Racker face off. The captain is in battle mode. He's got his people out there, his communications van, this radio-tight command center, his own red phone, a fax that's rolling away in the corner. The chopper is fueled and ready to go.

"We don't want to be blindsided on this. Has anything come in on Starfield?"

Tippet, appearing at their side, replies in the negative.

"Answerman?"

"Nothing, sir."

"No codes, no intercepts? Nothing coming out of their vans, their embassy?"

"No, sir."

A quick glance to Spanakos, who confirms with the slightest of nods.

"Jack, we have to watch for their diversion."

"Matthew. We are prepared for all eventualities."

At this hour, the captain irritates the hell out of Blake. He's so damn quick to jump into an argument over metaphysics and theory, but when it comes to simple, human communication, he closes like a goddamn sphincter.

"And the Girlfriend's secured?"

Tippet is perplexed.

"Jaybird, Lieutenant."

Tippet repeats what Spanakos has already told him.

"Thank you, Robert," says Blake.

The Racker and his officer go off to the side.

As Spanakos talks, Blake watches the blinking lights, the fax spewing forth.

Jaybird's gone down, nesting for the night. At dawn she'll take wing and that's when the Racker, a patient hawk, will be in his chopper circling the sun, looking for his prey, ready to pounce.

"And nothing on Answerman," repeats Blake.

Spanakos shakes his head.

"Well, Ed," says Blake. "We wait."

●

It is now four in the morning, the phones quiet, the fax dead. It is the hour when nothing is supposed to happen. Saturday they transfer Ellis. The window of opportunity when Starfield will make his move. It's an obvious trap, and he will walk into it. Navy is counting on it.

The indefatigable naval officers remain at their posts. It's too late to call Campbell's home; he should try Halpern again, wake Icarus, the impetuous son.

Blake and Spanakos move into a corner, and Spanakos presents the roster of their people, the teams and their stations, tells him who they have in Justice on their side. The Bureau's Division 5, the espionage unit, has been alerted. They went crazy, Matt. Blake knows; they were frozen out. Donnelly is on-line, Murphy's ready. Damn Halpern.

Before Blake leaves, he gives Spanakos a few last words of encouragement. The Navy officers are standing off to the side, very intent and still, and Blake lowers his voice.

"It's a tow-truck operation, Ed. The first one on the scene gets the prize."

Spanakos nods, swallows.

"Murphy's good, Ed. He'll back you. You just have to push him."

Spanakos would feel more comfortable with Halpern here. As would Blake. They need his physical hysteria. They need him to beat off the other attorneys, who are waiting to tear into Starfield's gut.

And Justice is getting some heat from within. The word is out. You can't hide an operation of this magnitude. Already the Israelis, and the British, are asking questions. All hell is going to break loose, and if Blake is not there to contain it Spanakos has to. That's Blake's speciality, containing hell.

He can see that his junior agent is worried. He's good, but he has no juice down here.

Blake's advice is very simple. "You've got to be there when it happens, Ed. They're going to scream at you. But you get the cuffs on the son of a bitch and throw away the key."

Spanakos smiles nervously. Blake is not kidding.

"Ed, you cuff everyone in sight."

Spanakos grins. Blake turns him away and lowers his voice even more.

"I'll be down again as soon as I can, Ed. It's just that I've got my daughter's wedding this weekend."

●

The first shuttle is at 6:00 A.M., and before he leaves he gives the command center a final look. Tippet is taking calls on his headset. At this hour the teams report every thirty minutes. Nothing new anywhere. The Racker has returned, waiting with his officers. There is nothing subtle about him, just a hard-faced warrior waiting for the Lion of God to spring, to take the bait of Ellis.

Blake and Spanakos have worked out a set of signals. Spanakos has instructions to call in to any one of a group of numbers at the first sign of movement.

He has much more to say, but doesn't want to overload his agent with a surfeit of advice.

He decides on a single admonition. "Watch out for the diversion."

# CHAPTER 46

———————●———————

Friday afternoon, Blake arrives home to no greeting. The house is full of bathing women. Loud music comes from two sources. He puts his briefcase in the closet, takes off his jacket and holster. At the top of the stairs his wife appears in her satin-striped robe. No words are wasted on idle inquiry.

"Matt, you can use your shower downstairs."

What time are they leaving for rehearsal?

As soon as he is ready. Margaret is already there.

When did Maureen get in?

His wife has already walked away.

●

There's no hot water left. It's a deserving penance. As is his dirty, cramped, mildewy stall and the dismissive, angry silence of his wife as he stands, wrapped in his towel, in their bedroom.

"I'm sorry," he tells her. "A case might be breaking."

"Cases have been breaking for the last twenty years, Matt."

She has laid out his navy blazer, light gray slacks, the shirt with the blue pinstripes and this festive yellow tie. He does not argue. He wants a drink, and tastes vividly the bite of liquor on his tongue. He dresses quickly and goes to Maureen's door.

His daughter knows his tap, and bids him enter.

It's been only a few weeks since she left for school, but the distance between them now is light-years.

"You've been hiding for two days."

She has been brushing her hair, and stops in mid-gesture. With her silence, her look, she makes him a stranger, a cold and angry man.

"And do not think," he says, "that I do not know where you have been."

Her silence, so unlike her, provokes; he has many admonitions on his tongue, anger to pour forth, understanding to offer, but from the open door his wife cuts in with a hard, peremptory order.

"Let's go. Everyone's there."

"I wanted a quick drink."

This is ignored.

He also wants to reach Campbell; he must speak with Halpern. He'll do it at the restaurant.

●

Margaret is so different, he thinks as they hug in the church. She partakes of little of the family gene pool. She is very easy on herself, and will have few wrinkles, none of those character lines that are the outer sign of inner wrestlings. He hugs her warmly. Pops, she calls him. Blake shakes hands with Jerry, with his father, Herb, with Jerry's younger brother. Maureen stands back, demure in her blue satin gown with the ribbon of gold along the high neck. Off to the side, impatient, are the master of ceremonies and his young woman assistant.

They begin, the MC in a light comedic mode. A tape deck throws out appropriate music. He moves the principles efficiently into position. The ushers and bridesmaids—with a lot of bantering humor from the MC—are arranged. They want to get Herb into the processional and the MC works on this but can't come up with anything simple. They decide to have him walk a couple of steps behind the ushers. The ushers take to the carpet, followed by Herb, then the bridesmaids. Maureen goes alone, her mouth holding its nervous seriousness; she hates to be on display.

Then Blake and his older daughter are on the carpet, her arm through his, and, though it is only a rehearsal, he is gripped by an intense turmoil. What a cliché, he thinks: I once held this woman, so small, in my arms. Another lifetime ago.

The MC cuts in with a joke about fathers, a silly line about paying the bills. He shows Blake how he wants him to disengage from Margaret, how he is to stand, here, and move away so as not to upstage the groom.

At the MC's command they about-face and walk off in the recessional. Then they do it again, with all the ushers and bridesmaids, and finish with a partial run-through from the point where they are pronounced man and wife.

While the others work out who will drive with whom to the restaurant, Chez Napoleon, Blake and his wife present a check to the MC in the privacy of his side office, the balance to be paid at the conclusion of the reception. Hard come, thinks Blake, easy go.

●

At Chez Napoleon, champagne is poured. Jerry offers a toast and carries it off rather smartly. Responding, Blake rises: he, too, is much pleased and, speaking for his wife as well as himself, something he does not get a chance to do as often as he likes, living as he does with his women— laughter all around—looks forward to Sunday when he shall have the distinct pleasure of formally acknowledging Jerry as his son-in-law.

Blake keeps up his end of the various conversations. For half an hour, he has not thought of what is happening in Washington. His *boeuf* is a stew of carrots, peas, and potatoes mixed in with chunks of meat, swimming in a dark gelatinous sauce. Pungent wine vapors rise into his face. The chicken his wife has ordered has a similar sauce, slightly lighter in color.

"Mr. Blake?"

A waiter is leaning over, handing him a message.

Blake stares at the folded piece of paper: *Profit down.* What the hell does that mean? Of all the code signals he and Spanakos have worked out, this isn't one of them. He looks around for the waiter.

"Did you take the phone call?"

"No, sir. The maitre'd."

"Excuse me."

Blake finds the man at the front door. He assures Blake he transcribed the message as it was given.

Blake wants to interrogate him, but a party of six has just come in and the maitre'd has to sweet-talk them into a forty-minute wait. He returns to his table, tense, thoughtful. Field communications follow simple rules: all signals shall be short, unambiguous, previously agreed upon, and understandable to all parties. And now, this. The goddamn profit is down. He sips his wine. Everyone is having a good time.

The waiter is behind him again. Telephone for Mr. Blake.

The phone is on the service end of the bar, and Blake turns away from the bartender, states his name. The voice that comes through is unintelligible. Whoever is speaking is using a scrambler and it's garbling the transmission on the wrong end. The voice speaks louder; it's Spanakos.

"Ed, shut the thing off."

The noise over the line sounds like food frying, *zzzzzst, zzzzzst,* mixed in with the breaking of china.

"Ed." He speaks very clearly. "Turn off the scrambler, Ed."

He hears Spanakos shouting that he's trying, but the sound of plates being smashed continues. Now someone else has broken in. It sounds like Halpern. He and Spanakos are talking at once. *Ellis,* Blake hears.

*Some fucking diversion,* Halpern is saying, practically screaming. *A fucking diversion, Blake.*

"What the hell, Ed?"

Spanakos is cursing, but it is directed at Halpern.

"Ed, I can't hear you! Ed!"

There is a sudden, very strong hum, followed by a crystal silence, and when Spanakos comes on again his voice has lost the garble.

"Matt, we need you down here. Do us a favor and get your fucking ass down here."

The line goes dead.

Within ten seconds the phone rings, and Blake lifts it before the bartender.

Spanakos comes in loud and clear. His voice is shaking.

They don't know how it happened. And Deere, everyone else, Starfield, the Girlfriend—forget the code names—

"Matt, we're running around here like fucking crazy. Justice is going bananas."

Halpern breaks in again, cursing, unintelligible.

"Matt, get down here."

"Ed, what happened?"

"Ellis, Matt."

Blake hears the anguish, the disbelief in the agent's voice.

"Starfield killed Ellis."

●

Blake hears nothing for a long while.

"Ed, are you there?"

"I'm here, Matt. I'm goddamn fucking here."

"I'll be down as soon as I can. Ed—"

There is a click, and Blake stares into a phone as dead and cold as the spy.

●

The bathroom is small, one stall. Mirror to the side. A window of wired glass, a long crack in the upper left corner. A white porcelain basin upon which Blake rests his hands. On the radiator is a stack of brown paper towels. He takes one of them and rubs it across his forehead. He looks in the mirror and, not liking what he sees, looks away.

Ellis is dead.

He can picture the scene: bedlam.

He closes his eyes, puts a hand to his head, and pinches the bridge of his nose between thumb and forefinger. He's had defeats, lost cases, had men slip through his fingers, has compromised and backed off, obeyed his masters, spoken in moderation and with humor. He's always played the game according to the rules, at times coming out ahead. And there's always another case.

Now this.

Ellis dead: the bait rejected.

He feels a rage growing, born of frustration and foolishness and stupidity. All his labor, the countless hours sweating over the printouts, the consultations, the conferences. The untold sums of political capital. His professional judgment. He looks again in the mirror and the sight of this man staring stupidly at himself is too much to bear and he shakes his head again, slowly, and feels—amazing—tears! They are bitter in his heart! He feels his mouth tremble, catches a glimpse of himself in the mirror.

In rage he cries out and with all his strength slams his open hand into the side of the stall. The noise is terrific, the stall shakes on its mounts. He does it again, harder, uttering another cry.

Goddamn them, goddamn them!

He quiets himself. They can hear him in the restaurant. He sees Ellis in the cell, the quiet man for whom he had nothing. Starfield offered him what he wanted. Mine enemies surround me, yet shall I be lifted upon the wings of eagles. The tears threaten to break from his eyes. The work they put into this, the work! The sons of bitches. Starfield killed him. But how, how in God's name did he do it?

He has to go back to the table and talk and smile. Control yourself. Your daughter is out there with her husband-to-be. Go out to them and smile. He has to go to Washington. Heads are going to roll. His career— goddamn them. He almost laughs, thinking of his hopes for a promotion. He wishes he were someplace he could rage and weep. Throw water on your face, wipe your eyes, go out and finish your *boeuf.*

●

"Matt."

They've been married thirty years, and he can't carry it off.

Is he all right, his wife wants to know. Her sister is staring at him.

He tells her he has to go to Washington, but not why; that he will do later.

Thirty years; grant me this.

His voice is flat, and when he tries to move his lips into what he has planned as a smile he feels them pull in a funny way. He'll be back, he assures her, tomorrow.

At home he calls a car service. He needs half an hour. He changes clothes, packs his briefcase. He is thinking all the time, those fuckers, those goddamn fuckers, thinking how they cheated them all of their victories, robbed them of glory and profit. Poor Tippet, eh? And the Racker. Fuck the Racker, and goddamn Halpern to hell. And himself. He doesn't need his gun, but he takes it anyway. In ten minutes a car pulls up and honks twice from the curb. Blake strides out, once more girded for battle.

●

Spanakos meets him at National Airport. It's a few minutes after one. The bright lights and noise and activity momentarily revive him. In the car, Spanakos gives him the sparse details. Ellis is dead. Suicide, definitely. No theories yet. Toxicology will report in the morning.

Is it on video?

Spanakos assumes it is.

●

The command center, their first stop, is a tired room smelling of defeat. The bright lights add a note of false cheer. Tippet's computer is on but its screen has gone blank. The fax is down. An officer he hasn't met before briefs Blake. They had a full field alert out on the Stag and the Girlfriend, tracking them as they went through what looked like a standard run to shake surveillance, U-turns, cutbacks, all the typical tricks. They hadn't got a fix on Starfield; he had boarded in Florida for New York but then deplaned in Atlanta. Then the captain got the call. They wanted him at the prison. An hour later he called back. They wanted him at the prison. An hour later he called back.

"An hour," says Blake. "That's a hell of a long interval."

The officer agrees.

"Who did you pick up?"

The officer has a hard time with this question.

Blake repeats it.

You have to understand. They went into shock here. By the time they got their heads back on it was too late.

"Gone, Matt," Spanakos says, "they are all fucking gone."

●

Back in the car, Blake's mind refuses to function; whenever a thought approaches he loses it in a blank, white, mental opalescence. Like death, he imagines, like what is happening right now to Ellis's brain, the pale, fuzzy phosphorescence of death.

It's probably on the surveillance video, he says.

Unless, replies Spanakos.

Unless they got to the security people, too.

"So everyone cleared out?"

"Everyone, Matt, yeah."

Blake shakes his head and throws out a sound of disbelief. Spanakos drives very slowly, not eager to get to the prison. They pass through the deserted streets like in a ghost car. Months of his career and now they have one dead man, a martyr to the cause, whatever the hell that cause is. What's the prize? Starfield, the Israelis, get the man's spirit; we get the consolation prize, the corpse.

Deere and the Girlfriend would have been real trophies, known operatives engaged in unlawful, clandestine activities upon American soil, sweet, juicy plums for Navy. For the Jew bashers. For them all. Wonderful to add to the inventory, might have got a lot in return. A big bag of goodies for the CIA and the Bureau, and proof, at long last, of Mossad operations in the United States.

The car is very quiet and Spanakos drives slowly. Blake turns his thoughts to damage control. Blame shall accrue to Navy. They had operational control, thank God, and possession of Ellis. They can't get out from under that, Blake will make sure of it. What he has to do, and do it well and quickly, is work the phones and the angles, extricate himself and salvage Spanakos's career. He'll try to contain it to a letter of censure. Murphy is going to be the pivot; the man is capable of going either way. Donnelly will be watching from the sidelines as Blake maneuvers in yet another test of management skills, known as running for cover.

Well, you win some and you lose some, and tomorrow is another day, and they are already in it.

But how the hell did they get away with it? He asks this out loud.

Jesus fucking Christ, says Spanakos, shouting. Navy had the man in custody. Their plan, the Racker's brainstorm, was to create the illusion of greater access to Ellis. They did a great job, a really great job. Easier access. They accessed him all right, straight to the Mossad and out of this world.

Blake is calculating how much time they will have before the story breaks—and break it will, with a vengeance—and figures they have a day, if they're lucky. At this moment agreement is being reached on the fall guy, and one thing he knows, he's not going to take the hit, though he sees how it can be arranged that he does: he was the Bureau's point man. But Navy has to take most of the heat. That's fair. The Racker is an officer, one of those stoic intellectuals who, when so ordered, will drink the hemlock.

"Ed. You were there when the news came in. What happened?"

Spanakos tells him again. The phone call, the Racker leaving, looking like Pearl Harbor had just been hit again. Then, the disbelief. The Navy people just about crapped in their naval-issue trousers.

Blake hopes to hell Ryan at least called for a passport watch, a picket on the airports, threw up a few roadblocks.

But on second thought, what's the point? Gresham's law again. Don't throw good money after bad. They're already out, and we are not going to catch them. The Girlfriend will do the forgery. The vans will vanish. And Deere will show up somewhere else, years from now, on another brownstone renovation.

"What do they accomplish by killing him?"

Spanakos has stopped at a light. "Who do you mean, Matt, by they?"

It's a good question, and Blake after a long pause admits he doesn't know. "Is that why Starfield came in—with Deere and the Girlfriend, to kill Ellis?"

Because Starfield killed him. Suicide or not, it was a killing. Gave him the means. Here, take this pill, if indeed a pill is what he took, for us, for yourself. For your people.

"Matt," says Spanakos, "I don't know."

Blake lapses into silence. He marvels at the limitations they put upon themselves. We thought in terms of them freeing Ellis, taking him out physically. And I knew it was impossible. Halpern, a false prophet, convinced me otherwise.

They continue to wait at the light. It's either exceedingly long or broken.

"Go through it, Ed."

Spanakos obediently violates the law.

●

In the prison compound cars are parked at every angle. Floods illuminate the grass and gravel in overlapping circles of harsh light. There is
a limousine with State Department plates and a couple of big, dark
Buicks belonging to the higher GS's. Everything else is low-level, government-issue plates. Spanakos pulls in at forty-five degrees against the
chain-link fence. Deferring, he waits for Blake. Inside, sides are being
chosen, blame allotted.

Spanakos's hand is on the car door, fidgeting.

"Okay," says Blake with a sigh, and opens his door.

●

The limo belongs to a man in a dark cotton turtleneck and gray pants,
an under secretary of state from the appropriate region. Wright, from
Justice, is there, nodding to Blake as he comes in. The woman with
him, whom he's never met, but who is somehow pertinent to the
situation, has a name that's been in the news. The captain is very tired
in the eyes but hanging tough, if his square shoulders mean anything.
With his boyish, amazed look Tippet stays close. There are a bunch of
naval agents in street mufti, their clean-shaven cheeks and precise
carriage obvious signatures. Blake nods to the four Bureau men with
their walkie-talkies hanging from their belts and their guns on full
display. Halpern is off to the side. Matt, he says. Blake nods curtly. He
slowly looks at the assembled players. He comes in fresh from the
outside, bringing the damp night air with him, an accusing, slender,
dapper man. His hands are on his hips and he is standing as tall as he
can. The captain's look is unflinching. Fuck you, too, Racker.

"Gentlemen." Blake lets a smile out, takes it back. "I hear you've
had an interesting night."

Before anyone responds, a door to the side opens and a Navy ensign
comes in with a portable phone. He brings it to the turtleneck. The
ensign whispers in his ear. The man raises the phone.

"Yes, Senator."

In the listening silence, what strikes Blake is how conspicuously
absent is any identifiable representative of the CIA.

●

It's a long, standard postmortem with very few answers: what we did
wrong, what they did right; what we have to do to improve and why we
didn't do it before. Wright's voice is strident. Spanakos takes the floor

and gives them as much hell as a junior agent can. Blake has a temporary option of silence, which he exercises. The Racker, to his credit, takes the hits from Wright as Tippet, watching his captain with innocent and uncomprehending eyes, stands close.

At one point, and Blake isn't sure how it happened, Tippet and Halpern come to blows. It happens without warning, without argument, though Blake does hear the word *Jew*, registering it a few moments after it is spoken. He thinks someone has dropped a phone or tipped over a coffee mug. The two of them are against the table grunting, a tangle of arms as Tippet tries to get off a punch. They're quickly separated and Blake can see, as the young lieutenant is taken out, a crimson blotch in the corner of his mouth. Pale, Halpern shakes his head, looks once at Blake, and moves off into a neutral corner. In a minute, looking ill, he leaves for the bathroom. The captain does not react, except that the two knots of muscle beneath his sideburns become a little more prominent.

Murphy shows up at four in the morning, confused and testy. Donnelly is pissing blue, per se, he tells Blake. Very soon the dreaded auditors from SOG will arrive, sniffing for prey.

"Some fucking diversion," says one of the men from the Baltimore field unit. "That was the main event."

"They took him out," says Wright, whose neck is on the block. "Only feet first."

Blake recalls the prophetic words: over someone's dead body. Ellis's in this instance.

Murphy wants to know what was salvaged.

In the confusion of the spy's death, the field teams lost contact with their targets. The assumption is that they are already out of the perimeter. Alerts have been sent out.

Water through a sieve, Murphy says.

It's very simple, and everyone knows it. We have met the enemy and have been made fools of. It is galling in the extreme that a handful of foreign operatives—semiretired at that, and some kids wet behind the ears—have done this to the combined security forces of the United States.

It shows the power of smallness, doesn't it?

They talk about decentralization, another standard discussion: large and expensive and centralized, versus small and efficient and autonomous. Other standard topics are introduced: communication lapses between staff and field, always the perennial bugaboo; sharing of data between services, which no one but the politicians ever really wants, though both the Bureau and Navy—the captain speaking to this point—agree that if those sons of secret bitches at Langley would for once give them the sort of cooperation they have always promised this would not have happened. But more of that later, when they write the reports.

They talk into the morning. The light changes from pale gray to a happy yellow. People drift in and out. More coffee is brought in, and more doughnuts, which remain uneaten. Everyone is overtired and beginning to loosen their associations. Jokes are made about their own ineptitude. Two agents get into a food fight. The light shows them all unshaven. Sweat stains darken. It was going to be so glorious, wasn't it? Freeze—the famous cry in the night—FBI! You're under arrest, you son of a treasonous bitch.

This isn't the worst of it. Wait until the Senate Select and the House Standing committees get a hold of it; wait until the administration and the attorney general and Justice and State get into the act; wait until the Israelis put forth their statements of ignorance and disavowal and surprise; wait until the leaks start and the sides are chosen and the recriminations and accusations begin. Wait, too, for the transfers and demotions.

Blake can hardly wait.

●

A little after nine Blake makes the obligatory visit to the scene. Halpern has already been there. Murphy decides to go with Blake. Wright at first hesitates until Blake, sensing the man's apprehensions, makes it known that the body has been removed.

The security is overly elaborate. Like locking the barn doors after the cows are milked, says Murphy. No one even smiles.

They stand in the cell where Blake had visited Ellis just a short time ago. The prisoner's belongings consist of a stack of books and a few magazines. *The New York Times* is on the bed, separated into sections. A piece of glass has been placed over a part of the paper where a corner of the page has been torn off, the tear outlined in red crayon. A prayer shawl is on the floor. It was covering his head when they found him.

The men stand in the tiny square of floor space and look around. A silent fascination holds them. They have been cautioned not to touch anything. Photographs are available. Chalk lines on the floor show the position of the body.

There is nothing to be learned here, for Blake, except that perhaps, if one were to spend one's life upon this bed, in this room, death was not that much of a forfeiture.

But there is always something to be learned, and the forensic team will pick his cell apart, much as they rampaged through his house, looking for the least little thing. His reading material will be gone over with a fine-tooth comb, especially the newspapers, to see if he was given a signal of some sort that triggered his suicide.

Because suicide it was. It's on the tape, they were told as they entered. He ate the newsprint, that corner under glass. It had been impregnated with a cyanide compound.

Blake looks down at the prayer shawl. He had been sitting on the bed, a balding man. Wright and Murphy say nothing. Blake is glad beyond measure he shall never have to make a choice similar to Ellis's. He assumes a choice had been made. One has to put oneself in the proper frame of mind, has to contemplate the eternals.

"I'm ready," says Wright, and they leave.

●

The Saturday noon shuttle is not crowded; Blake boards with Halpern. They have little to say; soon they shall be addressing each other from different parts of the courtroom. They will be much more comfortable with each other once the young lawyer chooses his side. Thinks Blake, in an exhausted and not entirely humorless frame of mind, he, or someone very much like him, might easily have been my next son-in-law.

Which brings him back, with astonishing abruptness, to the fact that Margaret is getting married tomorrow. He is not up to it. He needs gallons of coffee and a few days of sleep. He wants his mind cleared of everything. It's the most pleasant state he can envision: nothingness, just a white blank, like a snowstorm.

●

To the guilty, every little thing informs against them, and the house to which Blake returns echoes in its empty rooms his wife's merciless displeasure.

There is a note pushpinned crookedly to the basement door. *Gone to caterers.*

There is disarray in the kitchen. And the plastic travel bag containing his tux lies on their unmade bed, thrown by an angry hand.

After changing, he goes downstairs and takes the dregs of the morning coffee. He reads his message pad near the phone.

*You have had many calls.*

It is past five, 1700 hours as the Racker flies.

He does penance by cleaning the kitchen. His tiredness is a boon, and he feels, as he goes about loading the dishwasher and wiping off the counters, a slow and pleasant lassitude descending upon him like a heavenly peace. Yet he feels sinful. He has not done his share for this wedding, less for the weekend.

He needs a father confessor. Donnelly; the man has a streak of the cleric. He shall confess to Father Donnelly for his failure to recognize his own limitations and adjust accordingly. For his failure to focus properly on the priorities, squandering in profligate manner the Bureau's resources on the unprofitable, and for his failure to expect the unexpected, as the training videos exhort. For his failure to suppress or, failing to suppress, to ignore the impulses of compassion, enthusiasms, and ambiguities of feeling that have from time to time deterred him from his appointed task of apprehending the criminal. And for his failure, too, to seize the moment, to press onward, giving neither himself nor his enemies quarter or pity.

He is not thinking straight. Like that strange man in Camus's story, he is beside himself with exhaustion, and susceptible to confusion. He goes downstairs and clears the papers off his frayed couch and sets his machine for the third ring. He adjusts the pillows. The last time he slept on it was ten years ago. He can cite the very night and the case, and he remembers now with pleasure, as an animal retains a distant sensory trace, the nubbiness of the upholstery, its wonderful scraggly texture and the faintly mildewish odor of cool dust.

●

Some time later, having found him nowhere else, his wife comes down to peek in. To her gentle question, he is able to murmur a greeting. But he has no recollection of this, nor of her reply.

# CHAPTER 47

In the gray, palpable light of morning the man has been watching the harbor. The statue is but a dark form in the mist; the wind has filled the air with a clotted opacity. Through this dull, slow dawn he has watched the tugboats ply the waters, and the ferries shuttle back and forth across the night. A thick, chill wind makes his eyes tear, and he takes a handkerchief from his pocket and touches the cloth lightly to his eyes. He will be home soon, home to the hot, bright sun, where the very air is burnished by the clean, dry wind.

He stands immobile, watching. The light is stronger now, the wind catching the ocean mist. On the incoming ferry the yellow lamps are already failing. He looks up and down the seawall and sees only a single figure, supine upon a bench, with clothing so ragged and begrimed no human quantity could possibly inhabit it. The figure was there when he arrived an hour ago and has not stirred.

Now the figures on the ferry deck have assumed individual characteristics. The ferry slows for its turn. Spray flies across the lower deck, the flag whips at right angles to the vessel's motion. He thinks he can see in the ferry's bay the outline of a van, though its color, dark, is not precise. The ferry churns into its slip. Then, as the morning clouds break, the sun is suddenly free. On the lower deck, the first vehicle is the blue van.

He turns from the water and hurries past the homeless figures lying fetal on the grass, a dull sheen of night dew upon them. The ferry has docked and the vehicles will be offloading. He crosses State Street, knowing that the man he is about to meet will be furious.

# CHAPTER 48

B lake wakes in the early evening.
His temperature, having fallen slightly during his nap, has made him
curl, as much as the narrow couch allowed, into an instinctively fetal
position. His rise out of sleep has been gradual, with the sounds of the
house impressing upon him, first as elements of vague dreams, then
more persistently, so that when at last he opens his eyes he is perfectly,
absolutely conscious. Except for the faintest trace of light around the
door at the top of the steps, the basement is in total darkness. There is
a faint vibration through the wall behind the couch that, after a few
moments, he recognizes as music. He hears the hum of water in a cold
water pipe that traverses the ceiling. It is chilly and raining; he can
smell it in the dank basement air. Without moving his head, he reads
the desk clock. It is a few minutes after seven.

Blake lies very still. Around him are presences.
Ellis, the poor little man in the cell, hovers in the dark.
And Starfield.
Ellis, not the main event at all.
On the contrary, the diversion.
Ellis, the secondary target. But hit first.
Ellis, then, not the prize.
What does Starfield want?
They thought he wanted Ellis; but why kill him?
Did Ellis ask for death? Kill me, please, or give me the means to kill

myself. Send me a newspaper whose corner has been been impregnated with a water-soluble cyanide compound so that if I tear the little piece of paper off and chew it I will die.

Very dimly he hears his wife calling to Maureen, does not hear the reply.

Was Starfield tasked by others, or did he come in on his own? This they have never, to his satisfaction, determined.

Blake turns again on the narrow sofa, pulls the blanket up to his chest. He laments once more the paucity of their intelligence. Everything stops four years ago.

The cold water pipe is now silent, though the rain continues. He hears the loud clop-clop of heels over his head, a far away staccato.

Lying there in the dark, possessing a clarity and crispness of mind, a singularity of vision he has not had for days, for weeks, he mentally reviews the chronology.

Starfield is asked to exfiltrate Ellis, but gets the word too late. He comes in anyway, and reactivates his contacts, among them one old, arid gentleman hiding in the past. Through a series of jumps and skips he joins forces with Deere, who brings in his own people, a couple of young musclemen. He gets the Girlfriend from another source. He picks up a little support here, more help there. A necromancer, Starfield raises an old ghost in the form of Anserman—the Answerman—thus providing the communications link. Other contacts throw him operational hints now and then. Okay, he's patched a little network together and, though none of the participants are quite sure what he's after, succeeds in breathing his ragtag team into operational life. Everyone is used to compartmentation so they're content with limited knowledge. They're well-disciplined, Mossad people, and old-time Irgun free-lancers, and they give him what he wants: communications, security, surveillance. And muscle.

They target Ellis. But for what?

If all they wanted was to feed the man a couple of milligrams of poison, why the big operation, all the noise, the static?

Go back, he tells himself.

Assume that, originally, Starfield did plan to take Ellis out, as Halpern and Navy insisted, but then, reading the opposition, saw that it could not be done.

I like that, Blake says out loud.

This is, at last, the line he has been looking for. It fits in with his original assessment of the operation as impossible, and confirms his doubts, retrospectively, while affirming his professional acumen.

But Deere—can the Stag do it?

Perhaps.

Continue: the mission is impossible, and Starfield, being a scientist, a supreme realist, does not attempt it. He has a fallback: if you can't free Ellis physically, present him with an alternative.

Thus Starfield gives him, as he lies in prison, the blessing of freedom, or at least its semblance: choice. Their mission, thus, is to provide Ellis with the means of effecting that choice.

Excellent. The line is starting to assume a shape.

Is Starfield authorized? Does it stop there? How high up the chain of command is he? Does the Stag have an operational voice in this, or is he there, with his young musclemen, for firepower? For slapping around young United States attorneys? Or for intimidating agents of the FBI?

The rough upholstery is no longer a pleasure and he scratches at himself. His mouth is stale; he is cold. His eyes have finally adapted to the dark, and he is able to make out raindrops on the high window. He hears, very faintly, the drum of rain upon the metal barbecue he never remembers to take in.

He has lost the line. He sits up and puts the blanket to the side and starts again.

Mounting an operation to take Ellis out, they lead the Bureau and Navy on a merry chase. They succeed, if one can call death success. Do they have a secondary target? From what Blake has learned about their modi operandi, the Mossad doesn't work that way. Starfield's team isn't an ongoing network, more an ad hoc grouping. Special assignment, in and out and run like hell.

Nerves now on edge, muscles crying for movement, Blake stands.

Go back to Starfield. A mad scientist.

Mad with what?

With the madness of his people, mad with the centuries of injustice and murderous hate that has been visited upon them. And, his wife.

That Dutch national. Think, now, of the terror of that unspeakable void she wanders in, sitting numb and half dead somewhere in the ancient sun-filled hills, staring out at the blue sky and parched sands, a soul lost in the realms of an eternal sorrow.

Holding this in abeyance, Blake tells himself to leap. But into what?

Starfield killed Ellis.

He hears his wife and daughter directly above him, their words murmurous and indistinct.

That was the diversion.

The spy's dying wife remains.

And now the dark is suddenly alive with a rushing wind, and a bright flash of golden light bursts over his head. His daughter calls from the top of the basement steps to rouse him from his sleep.

Starfield killed Ellis.

He says something, unthinking, that makes her close the door and go away.

And unto the woman a child shall be born.

The door opens again and his wife calls to him; he does not hear her the first time because the loud rush of his revelation drowns out all else.

The child!

His wife calls again.

Starfield wants the child.

"Matt?"

Ellis's unborn child! Starfield has convinced the woman, in some half-mad way, to give up her baby.

"Matt!"

And unless Blake hunts the man down, Starfield will escape with the infant, carrying it across the skies, across time, to his own dying wife.

●

From the blue van, the fair, smiling man steps out into the street, looks north, then toward the water. Nothing. He gets back in and waits.

Down the street in the dark red car sit his two assistants, Natan and Danny.

They have barely made it in time.

Another ten minutes. The streets are deserted. Deere lights a cigarette. He likes the choice of rendezvous, the reflective facades giving him sight lines along three angles. In the red car the inside light comes on once, is doused, comes on again, and again disappears.

*Tov*, Deere says to himself. Good.

A figure emerges from the left, from the darkness of Exchange Place, almost invisible against the black wall of the building. Deere tracks the shadow's progress as it approaches the van. He carries the newspaper in his right hand, transferring it to the left as he comes up from behind.

The door opens and the man gets in.

# CHAPTER 49

O nce the epidural block is administered all sensation ceases; she feels nothing, neither the pressure of the surgeon's hand, nor the scalpel as it cuts through the epidermal layers and into the envelope of the womb. She is aware, however, of everyone around her, the two doctors and the nurses, the anesthesiologist who tells her to call him Curtis, and the man whose surgical mask covers his face, his beard peeking out in dark curls and whose eyes she remembers even through the haze of medication.

The curtain in front of her is blue, and that is what she sees for the most part. There is quiet, urgent purpose all around her. She is surprised at how quickly the procedure goes, because after what seems to her a very few minutes the doctor says, *Ah, here she is,* and Curtis moves the curtain and she sees the infant raised above, just for a few moments.

The bearded man watches with intense calm. He stands by her and says nothing until the very moment when the child comes out dripping, not really bloody at all, but dusky purple with a whitish claylike oversheen. Then he says, simply, *yes.*

You have a girl, they tell her.

They put the infant on a table alongside her and she watches what they do. They suction fluid from the infant's nose, its mouth, again moving very quickly, a race against death. "Cry," one of the nurses says. *Cry.* And as the child's lungs gather air, take all this life into itself and spread it through its tiny body, the purple gives way to a coursing pink flush. The blush of life, the nurses call it.

Then the infant is given to her to hold forever. She cradles the infant while they stitch, which takes a long time, but she feels nothing.

When the doctors are done she is brought to another room. The man goes with her, still in his mask and gown, and sits at her side. Special arrangements had been made for private care. All this day, she believes it is Wednesday, the man never leaves her. During the night she drifts into sleep, and back into wakefulness, the child always there, never crying, its slate-blue eyes always open.

She is very beautiful, he tells her.

You must, she says, keep her safe from harm. You must promise that.

She will be kept from harm, he promises. Always, and forever, he promises, and beyond this world.

# CHAPTER 50

H e sits as his desk, intent and fe-
verish, charting the events. At long last, the line is unassailable.

He shall assume the child was born on the day before Ellis died,
perhaps two. They made a basic, unforgivable mistake in not tracking
the dying wife. They weren't allowed to; that was Newcombe's deal, the
woman to be left alone, but it was a bad bargain. And he will bring up
with the psych people the matter of Starfield's profile. Looking at the
file now, it leaps from the page.

Once his child is born Ellis is informed in some way—reading material, a newspaper ad, a code word that he picks up on the little radio his
lawyer insisted he be allowed to have—all this, again, part of Newcombe's deal. Thus he learns that his wife has given birth, and then,
because he is himself part of Starfield's operation, perhaps even unknowingly, he does what he has to do.

Blake needs to get a fix on the child. He shall canvass the hospitals.
How many births are there in the city on a given day? A dozen? A
hundred? He doesn't know. A couple of hundred? What hospital is she
in? Has she left? She is suffering from lupus, so she most likely had a
caesarian, so she must stay in the hospital at least a week. A caesarian,
so the birth is scheduled more or less as required. Starfield has given
himself the option of choosing the moment. That explains the timing:
Columbus Day, a Jewish holiday, Blake's daughter's wedding. A good
weekend for an operation, and not by accident.

What he needs is dozens of agents to hit the streets canvassing, to work the phones, activate the communication network, needs people to bring in the data and talk it through. He needs help, vast amounts of help. But the teams are disbanded, the agents sent home to recover; it's a long holiday weekend.

And not by goddamn accident.

All Blake has is himself, and a day or two. If that.

He has already called Spanakos at home and got his wife, who said that Ed had taken the kids out to McDonald's. She was packing for their vacation. Ah yes, Block Island; they leave tomorrow. She will give Ed the message.

Halpern is unavailable; his machine, malfunctioning, produces only a high-pitched whine.

He's called Campbell's office, to no response, and the Irishman's wife has no idea where he is, probably out drinking.

Upstairs, the house is full of activity. His wife has called down to him, asking if he will go bowling with Jerry and the best man and a few of the ushers. He has already forgotten his reply.

Now, he puts his blue pencil down and puts his head in his hands. He must think this out.

First, Starfield makes the baby disappear. They work false identities, manipulate birth time, switch people on paper, and the child does not exist but for a brief interval.

Then Starfield takes possession of the child. It is his, now.

And what does he do with it?

Maureen's music is distracting.

What happens to the child?

He gives it to a woman.

Who?

The Girlfriend.

A warmth suffuses Blake.

The baby is with the Girlfriend, or will soon be. She will not know until the very last moment, nor will Deere, for they, like Blake himself, are being played by Starfield.

He has pulled a fast one on everyone. Taking out an infant is not the sort of operation the Mossad is chartered for. The more he examines this the more confident he is of the truth of this premise: they have all been, Deere and the Girlfriend as well as himself, caught by surprise. With great audacity Starfield is improvising, forcing events, mastering them by dint of superior will and enduring purpose. His team is reluctant, but their training prevails. They shall do his bidding.

And then, with the child in possession, they run.

They will travel as a family, the Girlfriend as mother cover, Starfield as the father.

They will patch an escape route. No time for elaborate procedures, dry cleaning and layovers, they will flee, dispersing in all directions.

I need more time, thinks Blake. More time, more people.

He's supposed to go bowling in a few minutes.

The phone rings. It's Spanakos.

Blake explains the situation; the junior agent listens without comment.

"I need some backup, Ed."

"Matt," says Spanakos.

"Yeah, Ed, I know. It's short notice."

"Matt. I'm going on vacation tomorrow."

Blake doesn't have the heart to pull rank. He understands. He tells him to have a good time.

●

His wife calls down. Is he going bowling or not?

He shouts up something that indicates he probably will, and that Jerry and his brother should go on, and he'll join them at the alley.

Back to his chronology.

Assuming Blake's ordering of events is correct, Starfield's options are, for the first time, not unlimited.

The constraints of time and place at last apply.

The child was born by caesarian either Wednesday or Thursday. He knows that because the newspaper that Ellis used to kill himself was dated yesterday, Friday, which meant that he was informed of his child's birth the day before, most likely. Three days, minimum, are needed before they can risk a flight, three days to be certain that the newborn child is healthy and strong. They have to move fast, but Starfield won't risk traveling with an infant any younger, and even that is pushing it.

And they can't wait any longer. It's either today or tomorrow.

He studies the calendar.

Most likely today.

Tonight.

Now.

The phone rings again. Blake knows it's his wife, calling to demand he go bowling.

But no, it's Halpern. He's just arrived home, and has checked his machine. It has this recurring problem, you see, so he's not sure who's left a message on the tape.

He thinks it's definitely Campbell. The man's words are garbled, and he sounds drunk. Or something else.

Like something else what, Richard.

"Like he's been beaten up."

# CHAPTER 51

———————●———————

P*ashoot,''* says Dr. Starfield. Simple.
"It is very *pashoot.''*

Deere nods and lights a cigarette. Earlier, when he had come into his van, Deere's tight-lipped anger had spewed forth in bursts of English-Hebrew recrimination. Is this the kind of operation he was asked to assist in? To risk so much? He was barely able to get out. And now he does not know which routes are closed. He must know the routes! And the girl—where is the girl? Dr. Starfield had listened, responding with a minimum of words, letting Deere spend his fury into an unprotesting silence.

Deere had come into this expecting to bring out a man. He needed to know only those details that applied to his part of the operation, give or take a little in front. His part, the actual run, getting Ellis to Canada, had long been worked out. It was complicated; he had set up a team with an assortment of regulars and free-lancers—and with this Anserman, a man he has never worked with but of whom he has heard much. Deere uses the Hebrew word for goose—*avahtza*. The Gooseman, as in Mother Goose, as in nursery rhymes; *anser* is Latin for goose.

Deere trusts Starfield, but this Anserman he is not sure of. He is only a voice, a very old voice with a touch of evil. Deere worked with everyone because he had to, but he trusted only some. He knows of no betrayals. Even if they want to, your own kind, they do not betray. He has no doubt that this man beside him, sitting and listening with an impossible composure, has not betrayed him. The doctor has a different operational agenda, that is all. But he, Deere, has himself and his team to exfiltrate. The girl. All in all, about sixteen men and women. They also have a dead man, not a live package, and his team is confused. They are waiting for the signal to run. He wants it from this man. He does not want this to be another Ellis.

His anger partially vented, he smokes his cigarette. He opens the window a crack. The engine is running. Dr. Starfield now debriefs him. Deere tells him what he knows. He was covered by two sets of watchers. They monitored Navy's signals. They were not bad, the Navy people, but it was not difficult evading the surveillance. The Americans are always impatient. Deere smiles his lopsided smile. The tall lawyer, he says, has been too busy *shtupping* the agent's daughter.

As for the girl, he has no doubt about her ability to slip through their net, but he wants to hear from her.

Deere lights another cigarette. The boys down the street are dark shadows in their car. From where will the danger come? Deere asks himself. From the blue-and-gold captain? From the little gray man? From this voice, this Anserman? Or perhaps from one of their own?

"We are taking out another package."

Deere watches the doctor's face, his lips move, and the eyes, looking for signs, for he believes that there is, in the way a man speaks, something of what is hidden in the heart.

"It is a live package." For emphasis, for the power of the ancient tongue, Starfield repeats it in Hebrew, *cha-bee-la shell chaim*: a package of life.

"I will need you one last time."

About Deere's mouth comes that interesting movement that so many mistake for a smile.

"Fishel, you wait for the last possible minute."

"I do."

The mistaken smile remains. "Are we using our *ema avahtza?*" Mother Goose.

"No."

Deere does not reply immediately. He is watching the street, scanning the mirrors, checking the car in back.

"What do you need?"

"It is very *pashoot*, Ephraim."

Simple, this man has said and, as he speaks, Deere thinks how all his training, and therefore his life, has been about simple things. They give you a photograph, show you slides or movies, tell you about the target's habits and preferences, the simple acts of the man or woman. Then you ride a train or a car, an airplane, and when the time comes you present documents which are stamped by another doing his or her simple thing, and you are passed through. There is a great deal of waiting. Someone comes and gives you a signal, such as asking for directions to the nearest library, and you reply that all libraries are closed at this hour, but you know of a bookstore that is open—simple words meaning more complicated things. You take a pistol and you load it and you carry it to another place—very *pashoot*—and when the time comes, and everyone is in their proper place, you raise the pistol and pull the trigger and pull it again, and again, sometimes a third pull, though if you have done well two is enough.

As this Dr. Starfield says, *pashoot*.

And then a man, sometimes a woman, who has by a series of his or her own simple acts come to this juncture where Deere lies in wait in a car, or in a restaurant, a bank, anyplace, falls.

And then you run. That, too, is simple. You run from place to place. You have papers, documents, different this time. You wait in one place, you go to another. It is all very similar to the carpentry work he loves, one thing following the other until the end, obvious, simple, and worthwhile, is achieved. You measure and cut and position and pick up a hammer and strike a nail. You do it again. And before you know it you have finished a room, or killed a man, all very *pashoot*. I was born to do these simple things. I am a simple man.

Dr. Starfield is finishing.

"We want to do this within forty-eight hours. The operation over by Sunday night. The package is small and fragile and requires expeditious delivery."

"And where is this package now?"

"Being prepared for shipment."

Deere's smile returns. Good. He understands. He is to cover the doctor's exit. He will not be leaving with the package or the courier. For that part of the operation the doctor has made other arrangements. And this is to happen sometime during the next forty-eight hours. He will be informed. The usual codes. He is Hector Protector. It translates awkwardly into Hebrew.

"Do you have a *ma-ta-ra*?"

A target.

Starfield hesitates, then reaches into his jacket and takes out from his breast pocket a white envelope, of the size that might hold an invitation reply card, or a card of condolence. Deere takes it and puts it on the console between the two front seats.

They are silent for a few moments more; Deere's ceaselessly moving eyes continue their check of the mirrors, the street in front of them. The gray morning is now in full light, though the streets remain empty.

Dr. Starfield's hand is on the latch and they look at each other one last time. Deere's right hand goes out, not to shake the other man's but to put it lightly on his shoulder.

*Shalom.*

Deere watches in the mirror as Starfield turns the corner, and is able to track him because of the curious angle of the green building. He watches the image waver, diminish, a chimera of a man disappearing into the plate glass.

Behind him the little red car is waiting.

He takes up the envelope and pulls out the photograph.

Ah. The slender gray man.

●

"Richard, play it back to me over the phone."

"Just a sec, let me set it up."

Blake hears clicks and clacks.

"I'm looking for it on the tape. Hold on."

Blake holds.

"Okay, here we go."

Straining, what he hears is gibberish and cacophony, a few words. He can't make anything out. But it is Campbell's voice. Not exactly shouting, but urgent. And in pain. Halpern comes on.

"Matt, that's it."

"There's too much background."

"I think he was calling from an outside phone. There's a lot of traffic noise."

"Let's do it again. Get it close to the phone, Richard, and turn down the volume."

That's better, but not good enough. He can make out the Irishman's tone, which is clearly one of duress. An accident, as Halpern thinks? Or something else? A couple of words are clear, the rest is drowned out by screeching of some sort in the background, a truck's air brakes or a siren. Halpern is waiting on the other end. If he had the time he would take the tape into the lab and they would clean it up, slow it down, transcribe it. But he doesn't have the time.

Halpern speaks. "I can make out a few words, Matt. One of them is *eight hundred.*"

"Is that what the hell that is?"

Halpern plays it back and forth a few times.

"Yeah, eight hundred." But that might just be the power of suggestion.

"And this, Matt."

. . . *eff kay* . . .

He plays it again. . . . *eff kay* . . .

"What the hell does that mean?"

"My machine is broken, Matt. All my messages are chopped up."

And not by accident, Blake thinks. Not at all. "Richard, look, I'm working on something now."

"Congratulations on your daughter's marriage."

"Thanks. Could you give me a couple of hours?"

A long pause, then the lawyer says, "Sure."

"Stick by your phone. We might have another chance," Blake tells him, "on Starfield."

# CHAPTER 52

_____

He tells her what she must do.

Live now, in this eternal moment, and the child shall be yours for all time.

You must live it all now, he explains, compress the years that your child shall live into these few days. Some will call it madness, but it is not.

And he fashions a pathway into the future for the dying woman. By the evening of the first day, when the anesthetic has worn off, the little baby is a schoolgirl of seven. See her as she shall be, he says, comely, dark of hair like your husband.

Live, he urges; no matter how brief, it is your life. His eyes never leave hers. Do not be fooled by time, he implores; it does not exist for you. You will neither lose nor gain by living longer. See how your child has grown. Gaze upon her beauty, the lithe loveliness of her figure and the grace of her smile. She shall marry, too, and have children. For do we not see how one grows old in an instant, how we look back upon the stretch of years as if they were but a moment? So live now, these last remaining hours, and the child shall be yours for all time!

●

It is now three days since the birth, and the child is to be taken from her. And there comes another woman, also with a mask, and she stands near the man, and it is time to give the child up to her, and to this man.

And the child is taken from her arms, as it had been taken from her womb, and is put into the arms of the other woman, a soft bundle of pale, white flannel, an infant child she cannot yet part with.

"I want something of her, something to have with me," the woman cries at the last moment.

"Cut her hair," the man says.

And they take a curl of the infant's thick hair and the man puts it in a paper and folds it into the woman's hand.

"I want this with me when I am buried," the woman says.

It shall be.

"I want her with me."

That, too, shall be.

"And my husband. He, too!"

But they have gone, with the child, all gone, forever.

●

And now everything shall be done at the last possible moment.

There is safety in cutting it close, in reducing the window of potential interference to the smallest possible opening so that even that slender and deliberate and intelligent man cannot slip through.

He knows the courier will not like it. This is not her usual package. But the discipline of her training shall prevail over her initial reluctance. In addition, she will find it impossible to refuse an infant. Once it is in her arms she will protect the tiny, helpless child.

It is all unplanned, and there are dangers in that, but he has seen how operations often succeed out of this very spontaneity, the confusion and uncertainty providing an energizing impulse. He must catch everyone, including his own people, off their guard. My evil associate, that old man, must be kept ignorant, as much as possible, though he knows, he fears, too much already.

I shall strike, strike hard and with precision.

For insurance, I have Deere, the mere threat of whom shall give the slender gray man most heavy pause, enough to give us that extra modicum of time, a mere few seconds, should we need it.

My Ariel, our Lion of God, a card to be flipped off the deck into the face of the little man, a fierce and wild card.

●

Blake cannot concentrate. He keeps asking himself, what is today, what is today, what is today? He tells himself it is Saturday. And he knows he should also be trying to figure out what *eight hundred* means, and also *eff* and *kay*.

But what is today?

It is Saturday.

And what has happened to Campbell?

Eight hundred could be a time, but then Campbell would have said that. The word *hundred* is clear. It could mean 0800 hours, military time, but Blake discounts that, Campbell hated that kind of talk.

It is connected with *eff kay*.

And what is today?

*eff kay eff kay eff kay*

He returns to Starfield.

What mode of transportation will they employ?

Blake doesn't know.

Try again.

Air.

And then it comes to him.

Why doesn't he just put a *jay* in front of the two letters?

It is Saturday.

*Jay Eff Kay.*

And on the third phone call he's done.

He stares down at what he's written.

So obvious. How did Campbell find out? And what price is the ex-agent paying for it?

He has it on paper, now. He will call Halpern. He doesn't want to go in alone.

It is Saturday.

And TWA Flight 800 for Tel Aviv is leaving JFK in an hour.

Blake believes, knows for a certainty, that Starfield and the child will be on that plane.

And he is going to be there.

# CHAPTER 53

Speed is always the best weapon, especially against the Americans, and she wants to run as fast and as far as she can. She is in a motel near the airport, packed, awaiting the signal. Her impatience makes her sit very still in the club chair.

Her specialty is exfiltration, the procurement and provision of all materials necessary for escape. In this capacity she carries passport blanks, glues, scalpels, a camera and portable darkroom, inks and stamps. She knows how to work the long-distance lines with assorted credit cards, moving the calls through certain untraceable numbers set up for precisely that purpose by the Mossad. She knows the code names and recognition signals of men and women who can be called upon for assistance, for transportation, for an hour or a day's hiding; she has the means to provide a switch in cover, ways to hide a package or to receive one on a relay run. On occasion she runs interference for other agents, becoming a cutout, emptying a drop and sometimes carrying a package herself, but at this point in her career she is well beyond that.

And yet always, always she is frightened. It is to be expected, even valued, for a field worker without fear is dangerous to herself and her colleagues. She has been trained to appreciate her fear, to use it.

And now she wishes most urgently to leave. A single word on the phone will trigger her flight. She sits absolutely still, watching the phone, urging it to ring.

When the call finally comes the single word is not forthcoming. He speaks longer than he should. She is dismayed. The phone call is only to give her that all-important word, the French verb meaning "to go." If the word is not to be given, the call is not to be made. This is part of their operational security. No unnecessary contact. After replacing the phone, she sits, not moving a muscle. Her suitcase is packed, her materials are ready for disposal. They will be picked up by another woman whom she has never met but whose voice over the phone reminds her of an aunt who lives in Quebec. That is how she identifies her contacts, by the associations they conjure up. Deere is one of her uncles; Natan a cousin. And the other man, the bearded man with the sorrowful eyes, he is like other men she has met, men who have come out of the camps.

And there is that other voice. The old voice, to whom she is a Child of Different Days. She does not like that voice.

As the minutes go by she becomes ever more still, if that is possible. She had not expected to be in hiding this long. It is only a question of time before they lock the exit points. She has her favorite escape route, her best, the Montreal run, but they will be waiting for her this time. They almost caught her, but she was too fast for them. Yes, against the Americans, you keep moving.

When the knock comes she is startled. She is certain it is not anyone who wishes her well. This isn't the way it has been arranged. The knock sounds again. Holding a small Mace canister a little bigger than an oversize lipstick, she moves softly to the door. This will not work, she thinks. Yes, she says to the door. A voice responds in Hebrew.

"It is I, Rachel's father."

And she replies, "Laban himself?"

"Yes," the voice says.

She recognizes the voice: it is the man who is like those from the camps.

Once he is inside, she is able to relax a little. He has one blank passport for himself, one that he has gotten from elsewhere, his own source. She will make the other for herself. He needs her help, he tells her, with his appearance.

She is already opening her suitcase, laying out materials, when another woman comes in silently through the door. The girl at first thinks this woman is carrying a bundle of clothing, but then she realizes what it is and puts her camera down.

It is an infant.

The man asks, does she know how to care for a newborn? "Give her the baby."

She takes the swaddled child, pushes aside the white flannel receiving blanket.

"And you shall be," the man orders, "her mother."

●

When they are finished, she no longer recognizes him.

She cut as much beard as she could, then he lathered, and shaved with disposable razors. He shaved twice, very carefully so as not to leave nicks and scratches. The blades dulled quickly, and when he was finished a dozen or so razors lay blunted in the sink. He toweled his face dry, wiping off the smudges of shaving cream that clung under his chin and to the lobes of his ears.

"I am too white." He spoke to himself, staring into the mirror.

They did other things. His thick, dark glasses were discarded. His eyes, of a pale hazel, became, with the insertion of tinted contacts, a precise blue. His hair was dyed a dull blond. Using cotton swabs, his eyebrows were lightened. And the hair on his wrists, too, was bleached a lighter shade.

She studies his face. His skin is indeed very pale, and irritated from the unaccustomed razor, but there are no obvious cuts, and no blood. In an hour, his complexion will smooth itself out. His hair has come out well. His new clothes are a good fit. A dark blue business suit of close cut, elegant yet subdued. His tie, very fine, around a shirt collar with a precise flair.

"So," he says. He looks to the courier. The other woman will stay behind and dispose of everything. "We are ready."

# CHAPTER 54

———————◆———————

**D**ad."

Maureen watches in alarm as her father slips one arm through his shoulder holster, twists and lifts, then slips in the other. He has been on the phone, upstairs and down, in short bursts of not more than a minute each. He has been going from room to room, collecting odd bits of papers and pieces of things—handcuffs, a camera, a whistle—and stuffing them into his pockets, his attaché case. He will take the wagon, he says to Maureen.

"Dad."

"Tell your mother," he begins, when the door opens and his wife and her sister enter. They have been buying more champagne for the pre-nuptial brunch.

The women stare at him in amazement, at his shoulder harness, the briefcase at his feet.

He does not pay them any mind as he holds his black Sigsauer and presses the lever on the grip that releases the clip. Foolish me, no bullets! He goes to the kitchen and opens the corner cabinet and reaches into the old white soup tureen that was a wedding gift so many years ago, and which they have never used, and takes from it the small, heavy cardboard box. From the doorway his wife watches. I'm going to the airport, he tells her. Trembling, his fingers press the cartridges into the slot against the retaining plate. Maureen's head is behind her mother's shoulder. His wife's sister is watching from the living room. He glances up at them, has nothing to say except to apologize and to assure his wife he will be back in time for the wedding.

He slaps the clip into the grip of the pistol and, after a moment's thought, during which he debates whether to pour a handful of bullets into his pocket, decides he has enough. The Sigsauer, he reminds himself as he always does, has no safety, so he carefully pulls the slide back to be certain there is no round in the chamber and, satisfied, pushes the gun up into the holster that is dangling under his left armpit, and secures the thumb catch.

"Matt!"

"I'm sorry," he says again, puts on his jacket, and is gone.

# CHAPTER 55

Thee rain is moderate, with more heavy, intermittent squalls expected, and road conditions are hazardous; he is on the exit ramp that is a tight, rising curve to the left, going much too fast. He holds the old station wagon to the turn, the steering wheel shaking. He taps the brake once, gauges the traffic with a quick twist of his head—he's clear except for a fast approaching set of headlights in the middle lane—and he's out, running clean at fifty miles per hour bumper to bumper with cabs and limousines.

The car in front tosses up a thick misty spray. Visibility is poor. He presses higher in the seat, hunches over the steering wheel. The markers flash by, numbers, letters, colors. He's driving too fast. An idiot on the right is drifting into his lane and he honks him off. Too much water on the road, too much spray on the windshield. He turns the wipers to high and they slap furiously from side to side, more distracting than the rain.

He keeps running through his mind his order of battle and the deposition of his forces, his agents, their deployment and assignments, and then must remind himself that he has none, that he is alone, that his despair is genuine, his fear real, because for the first time in his career, in his life, he has only himself.

The road splits, and he takes the left fork, riding close to the shoulder. But the drainage is poor, and the old wagon throws up a high sheet of water into the oncoming vehicles. He brakes, aquaplanes, and for a sickening moment he is gliding into the median barrier, the wheel in his hand loose. But the heavy wagon holds the road, and he is able to slow. Ahead is the TWA terminal. He turns out on a ramp and pulls up in front of the upscooped clamshell of a building. A cop is running out of the night at him: this is a no-parking, no-standing zone. Blake flashes his ID. He leaps over a puddle and keeps on going through the doors that slide open and bring him, safe and barely wet, inside.

And there he stands, goddamned alone.

He is in a vast hall. He takes his bearings. On either side are helix stairways whose spirals open at the top and flow into balconies. They curl up and away, then double back across his line of vision. Directly ahead is a rise of steps leading to a mezzanine, ramps running off on either side. To his sharp right is a long, wide corridor of check-in stations, clusters of service people gathered here and there along the counters, talking among themselves. The layout is a field man's nightmare, full of hiding places and observation posts.

He must deploy his forces, confer with his squad leaders, activate the communications.

He is alone.

He whirls as the figure approaches swiftly from the side.

''Matt.''

It's Spanakos.

He's got a sheepish look on his dark face. He'd called Blake's home, spoken with his wife. He decided to come, he explains; he can use the overtime.

''Ed.'' Blake almost weeps with relief.

Arriving ten minutes earlier, Spanakos has already done some prep work. From the terminal manager, he's got the poop sheet for Terminal A. Concerned about their exposure, Blake moves Spanakos to the side under one of the staircases. Two of this evening's flights have not yet departed. Flight 900 to Lisbon, boarding now, and Flight 800. They should have boarded by now, but the plane is equipment delayed. The poop sheet gives the code destinations. Flight 800 has a stopover in Rome, then hops the Mediterranean to Tel Aviv. They have the passenger breakdown: 16 First Class, 27 Ambassador, 462 Coach.

Big flight, remarks Blake. Is there a printout on the passengers?

Not available yet; they'll have it in about fifteen minutes.

''Gate Thirty-two,'' says Spanakos. He nods to the left, where up the steps and across the mezzanine are the departure gates, and where a guard in blue stands with a walkie-talkie.

"They're in the holding area," Spanakos tells him, "waiting to board."

"Any customs people around?"

Spanakos had made a few phone calls, and customs is overloaded at the arrival building; they can't spare any of their people. Besides, he's a junior agent; they just about told him to go to hell.

"Okay," says Blake. The space is strangely confusing, full of weird contours, and the light seems to be caught in the higher reaches—Spanakos is looking at him, waiting.

The agent is dressed to cover: chino pants, sport coat with an open shirt, an in-flight bag with a long, broad shoulder strap, the very image of an experienced, casual traveler. He stands patiently, a little taller, much younger, waiting for his supervisor to tell him what to do.

Blake's thoughts are supercompressed. He's played out the options on the drive to the airport, the best and worse case scenarios, and has found nothing in between. Starfield has come this far; he has found a child for his wife, having killed the father and convinced the mother to give the baby to him, and he's taking out the child tonight, on this flight, and if I catch the man, Blake tells himself, he will not get out of jail alive. Nor dead, for that matter. The Racker will see to that.

An abyss opens beneath Blake, the reverse of this huge, vaulting canopy of light. Spanakos waits for an order, a word, a suggestion.

Shall I, Blake thinks, shall I open this pit into whose unsustaining emptiness I and Dr. Starfield shall tumble, as into the darkness of a black night? The man wants that child. More than wants, for to use that word is to imply a consciousness that is subject to rational thought and change of mind, and that is not how Dr. Starfield behaves. Blake's read his profile, his biography; he has faced him, looked into his eyes, knows the soft, dark curl of his beard, felt the power of his being. He works not by committee, nor by consensus, nor by computer models. And he brooks no frustration, abides by no powers, not even that power exercised by two special agents of the mighty United States government packing all the might and firepower of one new Sigsauer and a .38 special. Having brought events to this pass, will he go down without a struggle? Will he go down at all? What horrible and violent scenario has he prepared for me? Is the Stag here?

"Matt."

Blake looks at his agent.

"Who do we have, Matt?"

"It's just us, Ed."

Spanakos thinks his boss is giving out one of his low-key, wry comments, and laughs.

But he's serious. He couldn't get anyone else. "It's a vacation weekend."

"Matt." Spanakos is stunned. Like Blake, he's a product of his training. You don't do these things alone. What is this, fucking *High Noon* or something?

Blake takes control. "Ed," he says, "here's what we're going to do." He speaks. Spanakos listens, understands. They work out a couple of visuals they will use for communication. They need props. Spanakos has an old newspaper from his last trip to Block Island—*Around the Block*—a pair of sunglasses, and a yellow tennis ball in his flight bag. Blake takes the newspaper, folds it so that *Block* shows. Together they cross the floor and take the mezzanine steps in a determined, professional manner. On the left is a window wall looking out upon the airport tarmac. Brilliant arc lamps illuminate the loading area. A monstrous widebody for Flight 800 is outside, its rain-pelted skin filling the window. He and Spanakos show the bored guard their ID and he nods them through. They are now at the entrance to the tunnel that will take them to the holding area where Starfield, along with five hundred other beleaguered travelers, waits.

If he is there at all.

Blake doesn't want to come on like a two-man posse, and sends Spanakos first.

"Ed."

Thumbs up; go.

As Spanakos strides up the ramp, he unbuttons his jacket in the classic gesture of the agent approaching his target; he's got the swagger, the free swing of his gun arm. The agent crests the ramp, descends until only his shoulders are visible, then his head, which, bobbing to the right, disappears.

Giving Spanakos time to get into position, Blake waits at the mouth of the tunnel. His adrenaline, which had abated in the car, has started pumping again. His armpits are trickling sweat, his shirt is damp through, and the leather holster is sticking to his ribs.

He checks his watch and steps upon the rich crimson carpet that is like spilled blood against the soft, salmon tint of the walls. The ascent is less steep than it appears, the tunnel is not as long as he'd thought, and, too soon, he is through.

●

The holding pen is a large, circular room, the central area from which the jets take on passengers. Off to the left is a retail complex: a combination candy store and newspaper stand; a liquor store for duty-free shopping; a shop selling souvenirs; a bar. Straight ahead is the main sitting area, banks upon banks of armless plastic seats of different colors, and all of them, all but a dozen rows of orange in the smoking section, occupied by five hundred passengers waiting for Flight 800's equipment problem to be resolved.

Blake stands on the edge of the carpeting and buttons his jacket. The air-conditioning is not up to all this breathing humanity, and the room is warm and overly damp, almost fetid. The lighting is unpleasant. Children are sleeping on their parents' laps, a group of teenagers are bunked on the floor, their green and silver sleeping bags a definite safety violation; they look, by their coloring, to be young Scandinavians. Talk is muted; everyone is tired, tense, wanting to leave. A baby cries and Blake's head turns slowly, casually: it's not the lost, anguished cry of a newborn, but the frustrated protest of a toddler too tired to sleep but whose parents are insisting that it must. The passengers have been shedding their outerwear, and their belongings are overflowing into the aisles. The place looks like the last hour of a goddamn community rummage sale.

Spanakos is on the far side, sitting in the third row of a bank of orange smoking seats. He faces the newsstand. Blake makes cursory contact as he sweeps the room. Be inconspicuous, he tells himself, efface, reduce yourself to an absolute minimum, become invisible.

Catching himself in the plate glass, he is too obvious a man, another specimen of plainclothes cop. With nothing but an old newspaper, yellowing around the edges, that is picking up his hand's moisture and is slowly becoming a wet, pulpy mass, he's conspicuously out of cover. Hide, he tells himself, move in and take a seat next to that nice family with the two boys. Come on, in you go, say excuse me, smile, step over the GI Joe figures on the floor, give the wife a brief smile with closed mouth, no need to be too effusive, nod to the husband. Sit. Cross your legs, open the jacket carefully, let some of the heat out. A quick glance down; the black grip of the Sig, covered.

Effecting the natural curiosity of a people watcher, he looks around. He's on the outer edge of the sitting area, staring across a sea of people toward Spanakos, who is now lounging quite comfortably in the orange smoking section with about two dozen fellow pariahs.

Settling down, he begins. There are techniques of spotting. Look around casually, then at the floor. Bring up in your febrile brain the visual profile of your target. A man, tall, dark, bearded. Recall the details of his physical inventory. Weight, height. No visible scars. And recall what the psychologists refer to as the affect, the intangible sense of the man: his quiet purpose and strength, his will; his madness. Remember what it was like standing next to him in the camera store, a lifetime ago. And remind yourself, too, that with him, not far away, within the sphere of eye contact, shall be a woman, and with that woman shall be an infant.

He looks around for a natural starting point, pretends to yawn, brings on a real one. The seats are grouped in blocks of color and are arranged to form a theater in the round, with a small, open area like a stage in the center. From where he sits, he has a good line on all the groupings, except for two sections of blue on either side, and a bank of reds, behind. They will be covered by Spanakos, who is walking slowly to a garbage receptacle, holding a magazine.

Blake tenses. None of this has been agreed upon.

Spanakos deposits the magazine into the mouth of the container. Then he turns and appears to stretch, rotates his neck a few times in imitation of a weary and cramped man. He is still smoking. He returns to his seat, crosses his legs, and looks around.

That was, thinks Blake, a perfect demonstration of natural cover, unpremeditated, well done. When this is over he will make sure that the agent gets a couple of letters in his file; he's pretty good in the field, and has assumed all the characteristics of a bored, restless traveler.

Unlike myself.

As if, he thinks, I fool anyone.

As if I look anything but what I am: a fed on a stakeout.

As if Starfield, assuming he is here, does not have support.

As if, assuming that support, that it is not the most professional set of cold killing bastards he, with Harrow's help, could put his hands on.

As if he and Spanakos, the two gentleman-cop types, government goons who inexplicably show up after everyone's been sitting around for an hour waiting for the technical difficulties to be cleared up, two men who waltz in one after the other and take seats opposite and begin elaborate eye games, so unconvincingly casual and seemingly purpose-less, as if we were not made the moment we came in, true and ignorant fools, waiting for Starfield to strike.

As if the young man that Blake is now aware of, that young, curly headed boy sitting off to the side with the newspaper folded on his lap in a meticulous arrangement, is not in perfect position to watch the access ramp from which Blake and Spanakos have just entered. And he has direct eye contact with another man, who Blake has suddenly become aware of on his right, and who, though reading a magazine so that its cover clearly shows its name and date, is not engaged in anything remotely resembling reading, having just permitted his gaze to dwell on Blake for a lingering, caressing moment.

His sweat is a torrent, his holster is sticking to his shirt. He looks down; he should have worn a darker jacket. He forces himself to begin his search. He works his first quadrant, the bank of seats directly in front of him. Slowly, casually, he goes over the faces. Men and women, children, teenagers. He looks, discards, moves on. Some of them look back at him, others don't know he's looking, most are too tired to care.

He's on to his second quadrant. A promising prospect here, a man and woman who just might come in under profile, but who, upon further inspection, are eliminated. The woman is too short, the man has the wrong style of beard.

He passes quickly over a woman in a green dress sitting with a man, both blond.

He's got about four quadrants to go before he will have to reposition. Casting a glance at the smoking section, he can see Spanakos working the seats. The agent is lighting a cigarette. Blake's eyes are feeling the strain of this light; it's poorly designed for anyone who has to be under it for more than fifteen minutes. He closes his eyes, presses them with the meaty base of his hands.

When he opens them again he is aware immediately of a subtle shift in the section he's just scanned.

Where's the woman in green?

There, on her way to the ladies' room.

Is there anything about her he should pay attention to?

She turns the corner before he makes up his mind.

There is the blond man, her companion, semireclining in his seat.

Now, what about those two men, the one with the magazine and the other with the precisely folded newspaper? Where has the newspaper gone? They have left his field of vision. He resists the temptation to turn around. The temptation grows stronger, becomes an urge, grows even more, but still he resists.

When he looks up, Spanakos is calling for a meeting.

The agent has stood and is looking around. Now he scratches his head on the right. A conference call. The next sequence determines where. If he touches his face, it's the water fountain. If he takes out his sunglasses they go to the duty-free shop. His hand in his pants pocket, and it's the men's room.

●

Though a man is in one of the stalls, none of the six urinals are occupied, so that is where they stand side by side and, in the best Bureau tradition of living their cover, manage to pee.

"Large crowd," says Blake for the sake of the stall. "These late flights are always full."

"Especially Saturday night."

"Yeah, last flight out."

The man in the stall comes out, no one they are concerned about. He washes, dries on a couple of paper towels, leaves.

"Anything out there, Ed?"

They stand at the long bank of basins, ready to begin a washing sequence should anyone come in.

Spanakos shakes his head.

"The woman in green," offers Blake.

Spanakos had looked at her.

Anything from your angle? A long pause. Not that Spanakos could see.

"Ed, you hesitate."

Spanakos shakes his head. He's tired, is still recovering from Friday, and is here only as a favor to this older, supervising agent whom he suspects no longer has the power to do him any good. And because he wants the overtime.

Blake asks if Spanakos made anyone: the two young men, one with a newspaper, the other with a magazine.

On this Spanakos has nothing to offer; the smoking section is a little lower down and the sight lines precluded observation of that particular quadrant.

Blake wants Spanakos to get the passenger manifest. He wants to see names. Very often the cover name is close to the real. Operatives don't like to confuse themselves with too radical an alteration. He's to look for anything with a star or field in it, or any of its variations. The participle form, for instance, such as Fielding, or Starling. Spanakos nods. Think, too, in terms of a foreign language. Stella, for instance. Or the Latin, *astra*, which is similar to the Greek, *astro*. He gets the idea.

Second, he wants Spanakos to use the paging system, calling Dr. Starfield, just to see what happens.

The door opens and a man comes in with his son, the family Blake was sitting next to. The boy goes into a stall, the father waits outside.

Spanakos leaves. Blake finds a stall where he airs out his torso, lifting his jacket, flapping it to push out the body heat. His holster is sticky, the gun heavy. Blake washes, goes dripping to the wall, hits the blower button with his elbow, and rotates his hands in the hot air. He hits it again, leaves in the middle of the cycle.

He doesn't return to his original seat but instead goes around to the boarding gate and takes a stance off to the side of the service counter. Doubts assail him, thick and fast. Campbell's message, so fragmentary; Halpern's utter lack of enthusiasm. He had called the attorney back, practically begging his help, but Halpern was driving out to be with his parents; Yom Kippur, Matt.

He picks out the blond man, doesn't see the woman in green. He has to factor in the infant. Where is it? Hidden, until the last minute. With whom? How are they doing this? His eye is drawn to the man with the elegant suit and blond hair. No glasses. I keep thinking about him. Why? And the woman? Where has she disappeared to?

There is an electronic crackle in the air and immediately, momentarily, all movement stops, conversations cease. Flight 800 will commence boarding in ten minutes. First Class passengers and those with little children will be allowed to board first. Please have your boarding passes ready. There is an immense stirring, like that of a herd rising from a bovine torpor, and the passengers stand and stretch and wake their children and gather their belongings, and slowly mill toward the gates.

●

The blond man in the blue suit is rising. Blake, by instinct, takes a step forward, then turns toward him.

In his peripheral vision, he notes how a circular movement about him has begun. The blond man, slowly gathering himself, has let other passengers surround him. And now one of the two young men, the one who had the magazine, is moving clockwise around Blake. He's caught in a press of passengers and remains stationary. Yet he is able, keeping his head turned to the left, to ascertain yet another motion in back of him. All this is distinct and separate from all the other movements and millings and sittings and shufflings of these five hundred impatient souls.

Blake, carried by the little knot of passengers he has allowed himself to become part of, closes the distance between himself and the blond man. He senses the young man at his back, senses the other man, who he cannot see but knows is there because he has been caught on the invisible line that connects the two of them, senses a wheeling motion as they turn with him, neither coming closer nor drawing away.

Nothing to be alarmed about.

But now the blond man has turned and is coming toward him, walking against the passenger flow. Blake tenses. The man is closing. Blake extricates himself from his grouping and steps into the aisle, where the man must pass.

Blake has to move aside.

What did he say?

*Pardon me.*

The man's back presents itself.

Passengers are flowing around him. He looks around, pretending to search for someone as he looks toward the duty-free shop, checks his watch, then gets out of the aisle by cutting through a bank of blue seats and takes up position where, by a slight turn of his body, he can spot the bathroom accessway.

Suddenly, the heat is insufferable. Sit, he tells himself. He looks around nonchalantly. He then looks directly ahead, and starts. On a facing seat is the dark young man with the newspaper. Curly hair, dark, handsome. Casually dressed. He tries to match the face with the photographs of Deere's assistants, can't be certain. Without pretense, for now none is needed, Blake studies him for tell-tale signs, bulges, weapons, anything. The newspaper lies across his lap. The boy's hands rest open, lightly, just above his knees. Springing position. His hand shaking, Blake goes to his inside breast pocket, allowing just a brief glimpse of the black grip of the Sigsauer. Their eyes meet. He knows the type: quick, strong, Mossad muscleman. The boy's eyes go elsewhere, over Blake's left shoulder, hold, then slowly look away. The newspaper remains across his legs. His hands are open, very slightly curled, fingertips just above the knees. Okay, you sons of goddamn bitches. He resists the irresistible urge to turn, resists until he feels his neck screaming to be released from its unnatural lock, resists even when he knows the man in back is standing, moving again, taking up position.

When he looks again, the newspaper has changed positions, and is now pointing directly at him, a spotter's arrow.

The air suddenly comes alive with a voice directing passengers in seats 1 through 35 to make their way to the boarding gate. Passengers in seats 36 through 70 are requested at this time to proceed to the rear gate. Already, however, a milling throng has accumulated at both gates, the passengers moving as one vast, dumb herd toward the exits.

The young, curly haired man is gone. Blake stands and turns. He cannot spot the person the young man was signaling to. Without a doubt, someone was there.

Where is the woman in green?

●

In the men's room, the mirror shows how complete is his transformation. He had thought he was home free, but then the little man came, the gray agent with the other man, the one with the mustache and the flight bag.

How did he manage to track them? Are they uncovered? How many others did he bring? Whatever, the man from the FBI has found him. But the agent was frightened, his fear a flaring prominence around him as they passed in the aisle.

They will be boarding soon. The woman has gone to change. They have time; they will board neither the very first nor the last. There is a proper moment for this.

In the mirror, checking his appearance, his hand goes to his neck, still raw from the unaccustomed razor, but covered with light makeup. He shall be glad when it is over and he is safe at last, never to go forth again. He shall bring the infant to his home, a gift from the poor spy and his dying wife. Alas, their time was wrong for them.

He must leave the washroom. The two agents have concocted a plan. The one with the mustache has gone off to do something, some stupid trick such as page him on the loudspeaker, a typical ruse, while the little man remains behind. He knows these men. They hunt in packs; alone, they cannot act. And the agent must be reduced even further, to a futile paralysis. The little man will wait for the one definitive, revelatory move on our part that will be his *primum mobile,* his prime mover— and we will not give it to him. The increments shall be so precise, so slight, that there shall never be enough to achieve the critical mass impelling him toward the irrevocable act. I shall have to be careful. The little man must not be allowed to act. For then I shall have to respond, and the consequences—and there shall be consequences—will be terrible.

He turns from the mirror. This night he is Simon Acker, a work name he has used only once, years ago, a name that even Anserman does not know. Simon, in Hebrew spoken *see-mone,* meaning star, *Acker,* the German for field. They will not know. Their other helper, the tall lawyer, with his knowledge of language and his academic background, might have worked it out, but he is not with them, as they had planned.

He has a sudden urge to call a meeting with his support, but decides against it. He is sure they have spotted the two agents. The woman has to be calmed. He halts himself in mid-thought. It shall be done. Concentrate your will. You shall deliver unto your half-dead wife this infant taken from the hands of Moloch, the fire god of old who demands sacrifice upon cruel sacrifice; unto thy wife shall the child be delivered, she who sits in perpetual mourning for her dead. And it shall be done through death's dark door if need be, over the bodies of such men as that gray-haired agent with the semiautomatic beneath his jacket.

And later there shall be time. He thinks of that poor woman, the spy's wife. He had told her death is nothing, that one lives forever, but he knows that is not so.

They are boarding. He must go out and face the little man.

●

The blond man has been in the men's room a long time, and when he comes out Blake picks him up immediately. Shortly after, the announcement for Dr. Phillip Starfield is read once, then again after a brief interval. Blake, watching, notes no response. A good many of the passengers have boarded, but the lines are still thick and confused. Children are tired and cranky, the adults more so, everyone queueing up, pushing silently.

Blake maneuvers through the crowd to the gate where they must pass, showing their tickets. The blond man has taken his place in line.

Blake cannot be sure.

He will concentrate on the woman instead.

And where is she, this woman in green?

There is no woman in green.

Unless she has boarded already, and he has missed her.

But they were sitting together, the blond man in the blue suit and the woman in green, an obvious couple. Now Blake tells himself to ignore color; whatever she wears she will be in front of the blond man. She will have the infant with her. That is the given. Starfield will not get on the plane unless she and the infant get on first, even if it's only a step ahead. He needs a visual confirmation.

Blake watches the blond man approach, holding his boarding pass.

There is no woman, no infant.

The blond man is not paying him any attention. He simply waits on line, eyes ahead, impassive.

Blake stands, watching, no pretense now. His jacket is open and his hands are on his hips, showing the slightest bit of his Sigsauer, the black handle with the little flaring catch that releases the clip.

Again, over the crackling air, comes the request that Dr. Starfield go to the ticket counter, Dr. Starfield to the ticket counter, please.

The blond man does not react.

The passengers are crowding, pressing on the gate, impatient, two hundred yet to go, and they are of all kinds and colors and configurations of families and sizes and ethnic origin, and Blake is ready to give up. He can't do it by himself. He cannot find the woman. And there is the tall, blond man with blue eyes, a dark suit of dapper cut. Just an attractive man holding a light calfskin briefcase. What is there about this gentleman that draws Blake's eye? The man is contrary to everything he knows about Starfield. Asymptotic reality, small differences; Starfield will be a quiet, contained man, bearded, affecting a scholarly air. The woman will be of the same age as his wife, and she will carry a tiny infant. Or perhaps the infant will have been passed along to someone else. But the infant will not be out of Starfield's sight. A tiny, three-day-old child. How do you disguise such a thing? You don't. You travel as you are, a man and a woman and a baby. Perhaps they will do it in opposite fashion, large differences rather than small. He is going around in circles.

Blake stands, legs apart, hands on his hips, his gun showing more blatantly. Time has stopped. He wants to suspend the world. He wants a clear sign. He wants to confront a man, any man, the right man, with his drawn gun, to announce, identify, and control, to cuff him and have Spanakos running up behind, supporting. But he sees nothing. Blake stares at the blond man, abreast now, and he is almost embarrassed that he is doing this; is the man just another passenger? His behavior is unforgivable.

But there's the woman! No longer in green, but in blue, a simple blue dress, a bag slung over her shoulder—where the hell is Spanakos?

Is that a wig?

Yes, and a child. A little bundle wrapped in white.

Blake holds his breath. The woman is walking slowly, not even looking his way. The blond man has fallen back, is looking through his briefcase for something, opening a space for the woman. She slips in front with a little dip of the bundle. The blond man closes his briefcase. She looks straight ahead.

It is the Girlfriend. She hasn't had time to dye her eyebrows. Is he certain? No, he is not. The blond man has closed the space and is now directly behind the woman. They are maybe ten, twelve feet from Blake, surrounded by shuffling, silent passengers. They have their boarding passes in hand.

The announcement asking Dr. Starfield to make his way to the ticket counter is repeated to no effect.

The woman turns, lifting her head, and speaks. Though Blake can see her lips move, he cannot, even at this close distance, hear her. Nor can the blond man in blue, for he pays her no attention.

The woman repeats what she said, touching the arm of the blond man, who bends, inclining his head, and lowers his ear to her mouth.

And this is Blake's sign.

●

On the little man's left—Starfield has moved him there—is Natan. Good. To his right, where he should be, is Deere's other man, a step behind the agent, positioned on his gun side, ready to leap. Something has given them away, for the little man is stepping purposefully into the crowd. That announcement over the public address system was standard, and he did not pay it any mind. The girl, however, was flustered, and reacted. Has she given them away?

Through the crowd the little gray man is pushing. For a few seconds, enough time for Natan to get closer, he will be delayed by a woman with a heavy carry-on who will bump him, as she is doing now, and then turn against him with her suitcase, hitting him lightly in the side. Natan is closing. The other man is moving too, cutting in ahead of them. Something has happened. Natan is almost in position, his hands are ready.

He will use force, and that will destroy everything.

As required, Natan looks to him for the go-ahead.

The child must be brought out.

Starfield shakes his head.

Natan, confused for a moment, still closing, veers off to the right, lightly brushing Blake. The other man falls back.

Blake is coming on.

Act, Starfield commands himself.

But before he can, another man does.

●

A long arm reaches for Blake.

"Matt."

It's Halpern.

Out of nowhere the lawyer has appeared. His hand is on Blake's shoulder. They have caused a minor jam in the line.

"Matt."

"Goddamn it, Richard, what the hell."

The lawyer's hair is dark and dripping, his jacket sopping.

"Matt." Blake, thrown off balance, allows himself to be pulled out of line.

"Campbell's dead," the lawyer says.

"What?"

"Matt. Campbell. They called me. He's dead."

The passengers are shuffling past them, boarding. Halpern is pulling him away and Blake, uncomprehending, allows himself to be led.

Halpern takes them both around a corner.

"Campbell," says the lawyer.

Blake hears what the lawyer is telling him, and if he had more time, he would react. He's going to, later, but there are too many questions, too many implications, just too much for him to deal with now.

"Richard," he says. "Starfield's here."

"Let him go."

Blake isn't sure he heard it.

"Let him go."

"Richard."

"Goddamn it, Matt, let the poor bastard go!"

Blake looks up at him in disbelief.

"Just let him go, Matt!"

Amazed, disbelieving, Blake almost laughs. In similar fashion to the news of Campbell, Blake understands in a flash the implications, the meaning of the young lawyer's words. They got to him, too. Starfield's suborned half the goddamn government. And with this, too, will Blake deal, but later. Halpern no longer exists. Blake turns.

The hand of the lawyer is on his upper arm.

Blake shakes it off, walks. The hand returns.

Blake turns to face the lawyer.

"The man," begins Halpern. He stops, his head shaking. "We don't have a case, Matt."

"What?"

"I said, we don't have a case."

Blake can only stare at him.

"Matt, Matt, Starfield's a sick man. He didn't kill Campbell. Someone else did. We don't have a case. Let him go, Matt."

"We don't have a case? We don't have a case? You're telling me we don't have a goddamn case? Are you goddamn crazy?"

"Matt. It's entrapment. Navy screwed it up. I was talking with Wright—the Racker's pulling a fast one—entrapment, Matt."

"You're goddamn out of your fucking mind."

"As a United States attorney, for the Eastern District, I expressly forbid you to arrest him."

Again, Blake understands perfectly, absolutely perfectly, but he doesn't have the time.

He turns, walking briskly. He has to get back. Halpern has his hand again on his shoulder. Blake shrugs it off. The lawyer, catching up, stands in front of him.

Blake says nothing, goes around him, pushing him away.

Halpern is back, his hand on Blake's jacket.

"Fuck it, Matt. You're not going to arrest him."

Blake shoves at him. Halpern throws his hand away. He's reaching for Blake's gun. What the hell! He's trying to get Blake's gun! They are cursing and pushing at each other. He's crazy, thinks Blake, he's gone goddamn crazy. But he understands, too, though he will deal with it later, because now Halpern is shoving him back toward the wall, trying to reach in and get to Blake's holster. Goddamn it! Halpern swings, the punch hits Blake in the chest, very light. The lawyer hits out again, catches Blake on the upper arm. Nothing serious. And Blake swings hard, wanting to hurt the young lawyer, wanting at last to make him feel the might of this little, middle-aged man with the daughter he's been fucking, hits him somewhere in the lower chest.

The blow is short and sharp and powerful, and Halpern backs off and slowly doubles up. He leans carefully against the wall, clutching his sides. Then he gasps. Blake watches him. The lawyer groans, his chest heaves, and fluid comes out of his mouth.

Blake looks at him for a moment and then turns, walking quickly, to find Starfield.

●

The appearance of the lawyer is a surprise to the blond man. Very strange. Even stranger was their long disappearance, then the reemergence of the agent, very pale. All these are unknown quantities, the most dangerous. There are choices. He could abort, both of them fleeing, he and the woman, with the child. There can be no second attempt, for he knows what evil waits in hiding. An old man's evil. He knows, too, the power of a special agent of the FBI. The little man, if he acted, could hold the flight. A phone call will do it. The man must not be allowed that phone call. He must be drawn away. There is time, just enough time. The woman, with the infant child, has already boarded. His people are with her. If he can prevent the little man from exercising his powers, they will be safe.

●

When Blake returns, there are fifty or so passengers still waiting. The woman is not among them, nor is the blond man. Ah, but there he is, the tall blond man in the blue suit, heading toward the exit ramp, back to the terminal.

Blake, with sharp, cold clarity, computes everything with great rapidity. The woman has boarded. Starfield has not. If he prioritizes the plane, he gets the woman and the baby—and there are problems with that, many problems, both legal and political. If he targets Starfield, he gets his man. The case is made. Promotion, blessings from Donnelly, bonus money, everything. And he still has time to hold the plane. On the runway, even in the air; a phone call to Justice will do it.

●

The blond man is very still now. He stands quietly near the entrance to the tunnel that will take him back to the terminal, and out into the rainy night, from there to freedom. He can see the agent swallow, reach inside his jacket, then bring his hand back out, empty. Hold him to you, draw him in, capture this little man. Starfield breaks off eye contact, turns, walks. Then he pauses for a moment, turning again to see if the man is following. He is. Starfield walks, without looking back, into the tunnel. He walks with purpose, daring the little man to follow, and when he turns, once again, indeed, connected to him by that invisible thread of will he has been spinning for the entire summer, perhaps for years before, for a lifetime, Blake is close behind.

For this is their moment, together.

●

The blond man is walking briskly toward the tunnel where the security guards are no longer standing, and Blake, once and forever, has made his choice. He is decoying me, thinks Blake, like a bird leading a predator, he leads me from his young, but I follow, knowing, picking up my pace, for I choose, of my own free will, to be drawn by the blond man's will. I shall reach in and put my hand on my gun for assurance. And I have my cuffs in my lower-right jacket pocket so that when necessary I can switch the gun to my left hand and use my right to cuff the suspect in that hard, swift, down-slapping motion I have practiced but never used in my twenty years. And rights, I will not forget to read him his rights, being certain that I have the Miranda card in my breast pocket.

Then the blond man turns in the middle of the tunnel, turns and looks at Blake. They are twenty feet apart. Blake stops, like a hunter immobilized with a momentary fear of his prey. For an eternity they look at each other, and then with a sudden bounding leap, the blond man in the blue suit disappears into the tunnel, running.

●

Outside in the slashing rain, Blake, with a gun in his hand, is running hard. Starfield runs before him, and already has dashed across the roadway to enter, running still, the floodlit parking lot. Blake bursts out into the road. Cars screech to a halt, horns blaring. Running, he enters the lot. Starfield is a bounding silhouette among the cars, his blond hair catching the light.

Blake is standing as he has been trained, legs apart and knees flexed. Both hands grip the handle of the Sigsauer, the right punching forward, the left pulling back. He has introduced a cartridge into the chamber, doing this on the run, pulling back the slide, not thinking. Ahead, the tall shadow runs through the black, driving rain. Blake waits a moment. The figure runs into the night.

He aims.

The trigger of its own catches, the report is loud, cracking, and there is a spit of flame. The recoiling kick has a sharp quality against his palm. The running man has jumped upward with sudden levitation, his legs wheeling in the air. For a moment he is suspended in the rain, then, in a wild tumble against a black car, falls from the light and disappears from Blake's sight.

Blake's entire being exults in a pure and wild joy. Then he is running to where the man has fallen. His gun is in his left hand and his right is reaching for his cuffs. It was a lucky, dumb, blind, amazing shot, never to happen again as long as he shall live. He runs, keeping his eye on the place where the man fell. It was there, against the black car glistening in the rain. There will be blood, perhaps death. Blake runs, his gun up and cuffs ready, going in to take Starfield prisoner.

●

could hold the flight. A phone call will do it. The man must not be allowed that phone call. He must be drawn away. There is time, just enough time. The woman, with the infant child, has already boarded. His people are with her. If he can prevent the little man from exercising his powers, they will be safe.

●

When Blake returns, there are fifty or so passengers still waiting. The woman is not among them, nor is the blond man. Ah, but there he is, the tall blond man in the blue suit, heading toward the exit ramp, back to the terminal.

Blake, with sharp, cold clarity, computes everything with great rapidity. The woman has boarded. Starfield has not. If he prioritizes the plane, he gets the woman and the baby—and there are problems with that, many problems, both legal and political. If he targets Starfield, he gets his man. The case is made. Promotion, blessings from Donnelly, bonus money, everything. And he still has time to hold the plane. On the runway, even in the air; a phone call to Justice will do it.

●

The blond man is very still now. He stands quietly near the entrance to the tunnel that will take him back to the terminal, and out into the rainy night, from there to freedom. He can see the agent swallow, reach inside his jacket, then bring his hand back out, empty. Hold him to you, draw him in, capture this little man. Starfield breaks off eye contact, turns, walks. Then he pauses for a moment, turning again to see if the man is following. He is. Starfield walks, without looking back, into the tunnel. He walks with purpose, daring the little man to follow, and when he turns, once again, indeed, connected to him by that invisible thread of will he has been spinning for the entire summer, perhaps for years before, for a lifetime, Blake is close behind.

For this is their moment, together.

●

The blond man is walking briskly toward the tunnel where the security guards are no longer standing, and Blake, once and forever, has made his choice. He is decoying me, thinks Blake, like a bird leading a predator, he leads me from his young, but I follow, knowing, picking up my pace, for I choose, of my own free will, to be drawn by the blond man's will. I shall reach in and put my hand on my gun for assurance. And I have my cuffs in my lower-right jacket pocket so that when necessary I can switch the gun to my left hand and use my right to cuff the suspect in that hard, swift, down-slapping motion I have practiced but never used in my twenty years. And rights, I will not forget to read him his rights, being certain that I have the Miranda card in my breast pocket.

Then the blond man turns in the middle of the tunnel, turns and looks at Blake. They are twenty feet apart. Blake stops, like a hunter immobilized with a momentary fear of his prey. For an eternity they look at each other, and then with a sudden bounding leap, the blond man in the blue suit disappears into the tunnel, running.

●

Outside in the slashing rain, Blake, with a gun in his hand, is running hard. Starfield runs before him, and already has dashed across the roadway to enter, running still, the floodlit parking lot. Blake bursts out into the road. Cars screech to a halt, horns blaring. Running, he enters the lot. Starfield is a bounding silhouette among the cars, his blond hair catching the light.

Blake is standing as he has been trained, legs apart and knees flexed. Both hands grip the handle of the Sigsauer, the right punching forward, the left pulling back. He has introduced a cartridge into the chamber, doing this on the run, pulling back the slide, not thinking. Ahead, the tall shadow runs through the black, driving rain. Blake waits a moment. The figure runs into the night.

He aims.

The trigger of its own catches, the report is loud, cracking, and there is a spit of flame. The recoiling kick has a sharp quality against his palm. The running man has jumped upward with sudden levitation, his legs wheeling in the air. For a moment he is suspended in the rain, then, in a wild tumble against a black car, falls from the light and disappears from Blake's sight.

Blake's entire being exults in a pure and wild joy. Then he is running to where the man has fallen. His gun is in his left hand and his right is reaching for his cuffs. It was a lucky, dumb, blind, amazing shot, never to happen again as long as he shall live. He runs, keeping his eye on the place where the man fell. It was there, against the black car glistening in the rain. There will be blood, perhaps death. Blake runs, his gun up and cuffs ready, going in to take Starfield prisoner.

●

Who knew the little man would shoot!

He had wanted him out of the terminal, away from the woman and the child, where he could be dealt with in another way, and then he had fired!

He has never been shot before and now thinks, this is what it is to be shot. A hard, hammerlike impact, more a blow than a penetration. He had been about to cut sharply to the left, and then the shot rang out. It had hit solid bone and with a tremendous vectoring force had knocked him off balance. And now the agent is coming after him.

He lies for a few moments on the hard, wet asphalt, his cheek against the cold grit.

Between the cars, he sees the little man running, glint of bright metal in his hand. Very little blood, nothing wet or warm except on his knee, shattered bone and pain, but bearable.

Push up to hands and knees. Pain, dizziness; run, now, twisted, crouching, through the parked cars.

The agent is looking around.

Stand, he commands himself. Quickly, into the roadway—flag that taxi.

●

Blake stands where Starfield fell.

There is no man. He cannot believe this. He fell against this black car.

Is this blood? He cannot tell in the rain, whether or not it is black water on the asphalt.

It was a hit, a definite hit, enough to knock Starfield off balance, enough to give him that crazy jerk as his legs flew out from under him.

Blake stands, his gun in his right hand, cuffs in his left. The rain is heavy now and his hair is dripping. Movement off to the side catches his eye. About thirty yards away a man on the edge of the road has stopped a taxi, a tall blond man favoring his right shoulder as he lurches into the roadway, limping, and twists to open the door with his left hand.

Blake shouts, but his voice does not carry. He bellows. He thinks of firing his Sigsauer into the air, but that would serve no purpose.

The cab is moving. Blake breaks into a furious run. The parking lot is almost empty, and he runs on a direct intercepting path toward the moving taxi. The rain is very cold, and his feet drive up water as he pounds through the puddles. The taxi stops for a light. There are about half a dozen cabs in the road, all yellow, and his is second from the front, in the middle lane. Running, he keeps his eye on it. A chain-link fence is suddenly there and he slogs along its length hoping for an opening. He is breathless now, his chest killing him. The light changes, and his cab pulls away, taillights receding rectangles of red.

He comes to an exhausted, panting halt. Hardly able to stand, he watches the yellow cab speeding over a rise toward the exit ramp, and then, with a little swerve, more like a twitch, veers off and continues straight.

He stands wet and panting. His gun is still in his hand. Get back to the terminal, he tells himself. Starfield is doubling back. He will board at the last moment, join the woman and the infant waiting for him on the plane.

●

The taxi has braked hard, fishtailing slightly, coming to a halt in the middle of the road; anything for a fare. He manages to get the door open with his left hand, falls in. The pain is a wave carrying him to a terrible shore. Yet it is nothing he cannot dominate, and he shakes the dizziness off. To Manhattan, he says to the driver, and the car, already moving, picks up speed. He turns, searching the night. The little man is running through the lot, cutting through the parked cars toward him on a fast diagonal, dodging, running. The rain, heavy, will slow him. He has got the upper hand of the pain, localized and contained it. A burning sensation remains, however, very intense. The skin on his leg is abraded, his ankle swollen. The taxi stops for a light, and the little man closes in, but then they speed away. The fates have decreed it. They accelerate, the running man falling back, gone.

Just before the turnoff onto the parkway that would take them to Manhattan, Starfield leans forward and speaks through the Plexiglas partition.

"Go back," he orders. The driver grunts. "I left luggage at the TWA terminal. I'm sorry. Go back, please."

●

Blake now moves in a panting trot, and is able to see through the driving rain, standing beneath the concrete wings of the terminal, Spanakos against the light. The agent peers out toward the parking lot. A cab has just pulled up and the blond man is slowly, crookedly, getting out. Spanakos is searching the night. He is looking for a man with a beard, if he is looking at all. Blake has slowed to a heavy, wet walk. He should shout, but he is too far away, and doesn't have the breath.

Somewhere along the fence he has dropped his cuffs, their loss recorded as a fragmentary flash upon his thoughts.

He has stopped altogether. His shoes are full of water and his clothes are soaked and heavy with the cold, drenching rain. His lungs seem to be on fire, and high in his throat is a dry, burning sensation. Contrary to all training, he still holds his pistol—and he knows there is a round in the chamber.

He has time to get back and abort the flight. He will use his powers and hold the plane on the runway, seal the exists, put a cordon around the airport. He has powers, once he gets inside. He will command the customs people and airport security, take Starfield and the Girlfriend off in cuffs. Assume custody of the infant. He must return to the terminal. He begins a semblance of a run but cannot do it for more than a few strides, and slows immediately to a slogging walk.

He can still see Spanakos, who has turned now and is looking into the brightness of the terminal. Starfield has disappeared. Blake picks up his pace to a faster walk. He will hold the flight, has powers to bring it back even after takeoff. A single call to Wright at Justice will suffice. And if not Wright, then someone else—there's always someone there—they can execute a verbal warrant, he's read about them.

Thinking this, keeping his eye on the bright lights of the terminal, Blake is not aware of the approaching van, its headlights doused. Finally, crossing through a circle of light, a moving shadow reveals its presence. He turns. The van is pulling up. Blake increases his stride. The van follows. He breaks into a run. Now the van is alongside, its wheels kicking up spray. Blake veers sharply and runs toward a break in the fence.

There are footsteps behind him. His pursuer is light on his feet, very fast, and Blake has just enough time to turn around, lift his Sigsauer, and catch the briefest flash of a dark, handsome face before his pistol arm is grabbed. He is a toy mannequin being manipulated by an expert, and he is spun around, his arm pulled straight, twisted up, then struck, very hard and sharp, just above the wrist. His fingers ring with shock, fly open, and his gun is no longer in his hand. That same arm is then twisted back and around to the breaking point. Another man is there, and Blake has a momentary vision of a fair-skinned man with freckles, but that is a mere projection of his unconscious mind. And all this has happened so quickly he has not had time to panic.

But now, in the black, cold rain, tired and drenched and not able to breathe, he flies into a rage, a roaring, cursing, desperate silent rage against these two men who are trying to pull him into Deere's blue van.

His training for unarmed combat is a joke, but he has the adrenaline surge of the truly terrified, and with a sudden burst of strength he wrenches free, ducks down, bobbing and weaving, and scrambles away like a wild, frightened animal. A quick, strong hand catches him, drags him back. He fights the only way he can, without shame, without plan, clawing and hitting and kicking and cursing. At one point he knows he's hit something hard, a bone on a face perhaps, because there is a sharp grunt off to the side. He swings again, and hits only air.

It seems to go on for hours, but in reality lasts only a scant minute until Blake's hair is grabbed from behind. An arm goes under his chin and lifts him off his feet far enough to cause him to lose purchase. Then a blow is delivered to his solar plexus, but is slightly off and does not do its trick. The choke hold is increased, followed by a quick wrench and squeeze, unbelievably cold and hard and unforgiving, and he knows, in the few moments of consciousness left to him, that this force is superior and irresistible, and will be applied in whatever manner necessary to subdue him.

Through the driving rain he sees a distant light, and in it stands Spanakos beneath the winglike marquee of the terminal. And another man. It is young Halpern, talking with the agent. Both peer out into the wet night. The light is far away, so peaceful, a bright safe land. God, oh God, he is being dragged a short distance. Already the light is fading. His breath will not come, his hands paw the air. Don't kill me, he wants to tell them. He'll plead, beg them, grant them immunities, pardons— he has powers, still. The van door is being opened. Another hard twist, more pressure. He grunts with pain and hears a gurgling in his throat. Another blow. He doesn't want to die. His last thought is of Maureen, and then, as they close the van doors, all the light is gone.

# CHAPTER 56

For most of the flight, Mr. Simon Acker sits unmoving in his seat, scarcely seeming to breathe. The wound is more serious than he'd thought, and the one time he leaves his seat he does so in order to administer, in the privacy of the tiny bathroom, a painkiller into his right arm, which wears off an hour before they touch down in Rome. His eyes closed, skin pale, his face is a study in deliberate closure.

Two seats down, over the wing, sits a young woman with an infant, the baby wrapped in a soft white blanket so that only its mouth and nose and eyes show. The woman is not breast-feeding, and has a number of bottles of formula ready, of which, by the time Flight 800 touches down at Leonardo da Vinci at about three-thirty on a beautiful Roman afternoon, all but one has been emptied. Though she has been ticketed through to Tel Aviv, the woman and child deplane, as does Mr. Acker.

Anyone looking closely, and no one is, would wonder at the blond gentleman's stagger, his deathly pale skin. And wonder, too, what pain it is that plays such a delicate tremolo upon his thin face. He and the woman are met at customs by an older couple, who lead them to a car which is last seen on the Via Appia Nuova, speeding toward Rome.

# CHAPTER 57

**N**ow, in the light, Blake stands before his god, or more precisely, God's representative on earth. The music has ceased and the assembled guests at his back are silent. Slightly to his left is Maureen, very pretty, very poised. On his right, the best man shifts his weight from foot to foot. On either side of the minister are Margaret, veiled, and the groom, exceedingly clean-shaven and looking younger than his years. The minister speaks of the sacrament of marriage, asking that those gathered here this day, having come from near and far, be the happy witnesses thereof.

•

Blake had returned at ten this morning, receiving little, if any, sympathy. Or attention, for that matter, except for a brief, angry encounter with his wife. She was not interested in hearing of his adventures. His household was in a ferment, his wife and daughters rushing about, his sister-in-law casting him admonishing glances. He had missed the cold chicken and champagne. The photographers would be here at any moment. He understood. Life goes on. The events of the last twelve hours were not important, not today. He had done his best. The wedding will soon be over, the toasting and the feasting, and tomorrow he will be back at his desk. Spanakos will be on vacation. There are no reports to file, no time cards to fill out. This was strictly a Bureau special, dead and buried, stricken from the ledger. Halpern, too, will not take it any further.

The minister is speaking, pauses for a moment, now intones the Old Testament selection. There are three readings, three selections: Old and New Testaments, something from the Gospels.

*Your people shall be my people.*

It is from the Book of Ruth.

*Your god shall be my god.*

●

They weren't going to kill him. He understood that very soon. There were two of them, very professional, and they told him in accented English that he was to stay with them until a suitable interval had passed. Also, that he would please refrain from any hostile attempts against them during that interval. One of the voices was older, and almost gentle, amused. Though he did not favor them with a reply, it was understood he was acquiescing.

They kept him bound and gagged until eight that morning, allowing Starfield a few extra hours on the European end. He was blindfolded and never got to see their faces, though once he raised his head, leaning back, in the hope of seeing something under the bottom of the black cloth, and was able to make out white shirts, and a tuft of curly gray-white hair beneath a chin.

He was soaked through, and the cold draft of the air-conditioning—he knew they were in a hotel room by many and various signs—increased his discomfort. Time passed slowly, allowing him to work through a succession of moods: rage, disbelief, shame and humiliation, rage again, then various combinations of the above.

The disbelief was the first to vanish. This was real. The gag and the blindfold, the hobbles on his feet, the ties around his wrists. His various body parts felt the effect of coarse handling. Real, too, were the men guarding him. He knew one of them was Deere, the other the young man whose photograph had shown him to be quite handsome. It would make quite a training video.

He had been caught, was now bound, and there was no power on earth that might free him. But they weren't going to kill him. He perceived their basic lack of interest in doing him violence. No unnecessary bloodshed. He wasn't the sort of man they would kill. He really hadn't done anyone any harm. It was his job, after all; he was a chance participant, an essentially insignificant man. Perhaps Halpern, unknowingly, had helped.

At one point, the man with the older voice suggested Blake might lie down and sleep and he did—managing surprisingly well, considering how he was tied. Events had been taken out of his hands. He subjected himself to a few moments of intense fantasy in which he saw himself breaking his bonds, a Superman, overcoming his captors and dashing out to a phone where, alerting Murphy, the Bureau then intercepted Starfield in Europe, or Israel, wherever, rolling up their complete network while the captain, Racker Ryan, danced in a fury of envy. But the fit passed and, at last, knowing perfect peace for three hours, the peace of complete surrender, he dozed.

He knew it was morning when he woke, because the darkness behind his blindfold held a different quality, almost an odor of hope, a seepage of heavenly promise. Then he realized he was not bound. *Good morning.* No one answered. *Anyone home?* He was alone. He untied the blindfold. As he suspected, he was in a motel room. He was free to go. His clothing was still damp, he was chilled to the bone.

Outside, he discovered how close he was to the airport. Again, the thought occurred to him that he might sound an alarm, alert the New York field office—they might be able to catch Deere. But it was Sunday morning, the trails were cold, he was exhausted and had to get home for his daughter's wedding, and it just didn't seem to be in accord with what had to be done. He had all his personal belongings, his Sigsauer, too; minus the clip, however. Curious people. His car had been towed by airport security, and he had to go through some paperwork to get it back, but was gratified at how much respect his Bureau badge commanded, even with the New York City police.

●

And now Blake stands in the center of this little universe of sacramental participants, close to them, yet alone. Directly in front are the minister, and the bride and groom; Maureen and Jerry's brother, on the flank; to the rear, on either side, are the bridesmaids and ushers. Herb has decided not to include himself, and sits behind, on the right, with the other members of the groom's family.

We shall meet again, he knows. He feels Starfield as a steady wind blowing from the dark future, as it shall blow toward him all the days of his life. In another time and another place we shall meet. But now he is here, before God's anointed, and he shall drink and be merry and rejoice with his family and guests.

He is very tired, but shall see the evening through. The wake for Campbell takes place tomorrow, and with the other Bureau agents Blake shall speak good of the man. They'll give him the watch, posthumously. Tell me another. He will also do a postmortem with Murphy, close out the file.

Now he must attend to what is happening before his very eyes, and he pushes aside the clamorous images that press upon him, pushes them aside until later. Afternoon light illumines the carpet at his feet, a soft wash of red. He wants no profound thoughts, no mystical imaginings intruding upon the moment. He is extraordinarily calm, his body washed through with the fierce outpourings of hormones and fluids of the last three days, cleansed by purgatives. As Margaret gives her response Maureen turns, serious and demure, wanting to know if he is all right. He cannot smile, but he assures her with his eyes he is. The minister is speaking the words of the sacrament, but what comes to Blake are other words, perhaps from the Bible, he doesn't know.

*What a pleasant thing it is for the eyes to behold the sun.*

Nothing profound, Blake thinks; a mere reminder of the blessings of light, and how good it is to be alive.

# ABOUT THE AUTHOR

MARK LINDER was born and raised in Brooklyn, New York. He received a master's degree in English literature from the City University of New York and also attended NYU Law School. This is his second novel. His first, *There Came a Proud Beggar*, was published in 1986. He is now at work on a sequel to *Little Boy Blue*, tentatively titled *Five, Six, Pick Up Sticks*.

# ABOUT THE TYPE

This book was set in Meridien, a classic roman typeface designed in 1957 by the Swiss-born Adrian Frutiger for the French typefoundry Deberny et Peignot. Frutiger also designed the famous and much-used typeface Univers.